BEAUS AND ARROWS

Rashida T. Williams

Beaus and Arrows
Red Adept Publishing, LLC
104 Bugenfield Court
Garner, NC 27529
http://RedAdeptPublishing.com/

For my husband

CHAPTER 1

The pleasant aroma of freshly ground coffee did little to stifle Emory's irritation as he waited in the seemingly motionless line. He masked his impatience by immersing himself in a book. He didn't really enjoy reading *Les Misérables*, but it gave him an excuse not to communicate with the other patrons. A few minutes later, he purchased his usual, a medium coffee with two shots of espresso.

The cashier whisked loose strands of inky violet hair away from her face. "Anything else?"

"No, thank you."

She returned his credit card without looking at him. Her thin lips were painted with matte ruby lipstick, and her dark mascara contrasted with her sandy complexion. Emory often wondered why humans poked tiny holes through the skin above their eyelids, but he refrained from staring. It was a shame such a pretty girl made a point of not smiling at customers.

The coffee warmed Emory's fingertips even through the thick paper cup. He retreated to the quiet corner near the windows where he spent most of his mornings, watching. He had come to the coffee shop every day for the past five years, but no one there remembered him. Although it didn't necessarily have to be that way, that was how he liked it. He found it fascinating that humans were unaware of his true nature. But if he paraded around town dressed in a skimpy white tunic with wings strapped to his back, he would have half a mind to check himself into an asylum. Vycrin despised being referred to as Cupid. As a species, they were far more advanced than that fat mythological creature.

Emory's assigned jurisdiction was a small, insignificant city on the east coast of the United States within the realm of Earth. One of the advantages of working in Washington, DC, was the abundance of free entertainment. People were always dashing from place to place, looking terribly busy but not actually accomplishing much of anything. The activity mirrored his occupation. But unlike others of his kind, he preferred a light caseload, and he was certain it was going to be an easy night because his favorite client, Blair, was fewer than thirty feet away.

Blair plowed through the glass front doors, the straps of her purse slithering down her arm as she rummaged through it. Short people fascinated Emory, and Blair was one of those pocket-sized human beings. Without her four-inch snakeskin heels, she stood about eye level with most ten-year-old boys. Fortunately, she did not possess the body of a ten-year-old boy. A fitted white blazer cinched her waist, accentuating her hourglass frame, and dark-wash jeans enhanced her curves. A thin layer of powder dusted her deep reddish-brown skin. Emory wondered who she was trying to impress.

Blair had straightened her naturally curly hair, and her thick jet-black locks fell just below her shoulders, hiding the Bluetooth device jammed in her ear. "Good morning, Greg!"

A large gentleman in line turned, looked down, and scowled at her. Blair smiled and winked at the stranger. Emory tuned in to the radio waves traveling to Blair's device to hear both sides of the conversation.

A hoarse voice responded over the phone. "Hey, Blair."

"Are you still sleeping?" she asked.

"Not anymore." He sounded irritated.

A tube of lipstick appeared in her slender fingers. She pulled out the long black cylinder and cranked it twice, her dark-brown eyes inspecting the remaining waxy solid. "Remind me to buy more lipstick," she mumbled before dabbing some on her full lips. She reached back into her handbag. "I was thinking about you this morning."

"Is that right?" Greg's tone held little enthusiasm.

"That's right. And guess what today is?"

Emory rolled his eyes. That explained the makeup.

"Happy anniversary!" Blair shouted, startling several nearby customers.

On the other end of the line came the sound of the phone hitting a wood floor, followed by a thump, the shattering of some glass, and heavy breathing. "Blair..." Greg's patience was clearly waning.

"I'm sorry. Did I startle you? You're so accident-prone." She held up her wallet. "Found it! Get some rest, honey. We have a busy evening planned."

She ended the call and tossed her earpiece into the abyss of her purse. At the front of the line, she placed an order for a medium black coffee and was on her way out before most of the other customers could articulate their choices of elaborate caffeinated confections.

Emory consumed the last of his now lukewarm coffee, never once taking his focus away from Blair. He stared at her until she was out of his field of vision. The slight bounce in her stride could not be attributed to the brisk fall weather. *What a lovesick fool.*

Emory found Blair's devotion to Greg nauseating. One year had passed since Emory had established their union, and there wasn't even a hint of excitement in their relationship to warrant his attention. Blair had been a reliable source of entertainment for five years, falling in and out of love faster than he could ready his bow. He had taken her on as a single client with the intent of finding her a match, and while he should have been satisfied that she and Greg were on a trajectory toward "wedded bliss," he couldn't help but feel that she would become nothing more than a sad statistic, married with two kids and a dog and living in the suburbs. *What a waste.*

Emory crumpled the empty cup in one hand and tossed it into a nearby trash bin on his way to the exit. Blair's energetic sparkle had almost spoiled his day. He peered back across the coffee shop at the cashier, who still had a sullen look plastered on her face. He smiled. At least he wasn't the only one.

On the way to his black-and-chrome Honda Shadow motorcycle, he zipped his leather jacket to ward off the cool breeze. Sitting, he caught his reflection in the mirror. A scruffy layer of dark stubble covered his face. He sighed. He'd have to shave before dinner. Blair's boyfriend insisted on taking her to the most expensive restaurants just so he could complain about portion-to-cost ratios.

Emory ran his fingers through his thick wavy hair then slipped on his helmet and snapped the tinted visor down over his eyes. He quickly maneuvered through irritating blocks of traffic. He was going to be late for class.

• • ❧ • •

EMORY ENJOYED FEW THINGS in life more than wreaking havoc in the lives of unsuspecting college students. Most young people had enough difficulty just trying to manage their studies, but the real drama began when a relationship was thrown into the mix. Emory did it all in the name of love, of course. He stayed in the Enarine realm, a place beyond human perception, watching people move at a languid pace that was out of phase with his reality. It was like watching a movie in slow motion—not that he watched many movies, as they were a complete waste of time.

He sat in the very back of the classroom and scanned the unsuspecting pupils. Each human emitted a distinct aura, exposing the condition of his or her heart. Yellow auras bored him—individuals open to new relationships required only a single arrow to ignite the flames of desire. Green auras were overzealous—victims of recent breakups tried hard not to repeat the mistakes of their failed relationships and often overcompensated by smothering their new partners with love and affection, thus starting the vicious cycle over again.

Gray auras were reserved for healers, since humans suffering from a traumatic loss or the death of a loved one required special care and attention. Blue auras were Emory's favorite—fickle hearts were easy to manipulate, and someone bouncing from lover to lover made for dramatic viewing. Their unstable relationships were destined for failure. He avoided auras with a metallic sheen—sexual frustration wasn't fun for anyone involved. The results were too unpredictable.

Emory twirled a silver arrow between his fingers. Four rows in front of him, a miserable-looking individual named Amir stared at a blank sheet of paper. The young man's pen was propped in his hand, but he had yet to scribble any notes. His downhearted expression was far from hidden, and his pigmentation lacked its usual glow, causing his golden-brown skin to appear dull. He clearly hadn't slept in days.

Emory shook his head and suppressed the smirk creeping into the corners of his mouth. It had been two weeks since he'd pierced the young man's heart, and the thin aura surrounding Amir's body still burned bright red. He was in love.

Across the large lecture hall sat the source of the young man's agony—a shapely young redhead with frizzy hair and rosy cheeks. Her aura was white, indicating that she had never been in love. Her pen dashed across her notebook in wild, uneven strokes as she tried to keep up with the professor. Every so often, she looked up long enough to prevent her thick glasses from slipping off her face.

Emory delighted in how blind she was to the man who was besotted with her. Amir's blind infatuation was destined to lead him down a path of pain and sorrow... unless there was someone with the power to intervene, someone with the ability to make her notice him.

Emory nodded, accepting his call to duty. Matchmakers were permitted to choose their clients, and most spent months observing potential couples to ensure a happy and successful union. Emory felt fourteen days was long enough. It was time to add the two clients to his roster.

As the professor wrapped up the class, Emory tore himself from the pathetic swooning of the young man long enough to strap his custom leather quiver to his back. He eyed the tall fellow, imagining with amusement what an odd pair he and the girl would make—Amir's lanky build contrasting with her short, curvaceous figure. The young man sported the latest trends in men's fashion, his keen sense of style offset by his disheveled hair and five o'clock shadow. By contrast, the young woman's wardrobe looked as though it had been gathered from vintage clothing stores and local consignment shops. Emory hoped their personalities would clash as much as their styles.

Bow clenched in his left hand, Emory headed for the exit the girl had taken. Amir stumbled in his haste to catch up with the object of his affections. The young woman stood in the crowded hallway, squinting at a cluttered message board. Amir ran toward her, paused, opened his mouth, and closed it again. She mumbled to herself as though sorting out her thoughts.

Emory supposed her brain was as scattered as her hair. She was perfect for disrupting the routine of the meticulous and structured man who loomed behind her if poor Amir could ever work up enough nerve to talk to her. Emory stopped several yards away from the pair. Humans veered around him without even realizing it, completely oblivious to his presence. He quite enjoyed being in his own private bubble.

Amir finally spoke up. "Excuse me. I... um..."

The girl continued her search, unaware of her nervous admirer. Emory drew an arrow from his quiver and blew on the sharp silver tip, removing any microscopic dust that might have accumulated. He nocked the arrow to the bowstring, then he raised his left arm and drew back on the string in one swift motion. The taut bowstring creaked and whined as he pulled it farther back toward his jaw. He aimed the tip of the arrow at the young man's heart.

Emory released the bowstring. The arrow slammed into Amir's heart, pulsed bright red, then disappeared. The student squared his shoulders and raised his head. The girl finished at the information board and turned on her heel to leave.

Amir moved into her path. "Hello. Joey, right?"

She looked up, startled. "Yeah. And you are...?"

"My name's Amir. We've had four classes together this year."

Joey pushed some of her thick hair behind her ear. "We have?"

"You might not have noticed me. I sit in the back, and you tend to sit in the front corner seat near the door."

"It helps me concentrate when I'm in the front." She giggled. "Otherwise, my mind wanders."

At Joey's nervous laugh, Amir smiled.

Wandering minds. That's one thing they have in common. Emory drew another arrow.

"I'm sure you're busy with your classes." Amir did not take his eyes from her. "But I was wondering if you'd like to hang out sometime."

"When?" There was a hint of surprise in her voice.

"Tonight."

Joey curled a finger around the bottom of her floral blouse. "Well, I usually study on Friday nights." She peered into his sincere eyes.

Emory released an arrow. The missile penetrated the young woman's chest then disappeared.

Amir shifted to avoid her gaze. "I understand if you're too busy."

"Hey." Joey grabbed his arm. "I can always study on Saturday."

"You're serious?" Amir's voice was an octave too high, and he cleared his throat.

"Yeah, let's hang out."

Emory lowered the bow, quite pleased with himself. As the giddy couple planned their first evening together, a sly grin swept across Emory's face. *Let the games begin.*

Still out of phase with the humans, Emory maneuvered around clusters of vibrant auras and hurried out of the college. He rushed down the broad steps with his bow in hand, paying little attention to the black clouds looming overhead. Mounds of leaves parted from his path as he entered an empty courtyard. A sudden chill pricked his body, and his skin tingled.

"Emory Reginald Odin the Second."

Heat crawled up his neck. He turned to face his cousin. Argus was tall and wore a dark trench coat and sunglasses. His black hair was slicked back, exposing the sharp angles of his face. His skin was ashen, as though he spent far too many hours behind a desk.

Emory sensed the smugness behind those hidden eyes, and he fought the look of disdain creeping into his own face. "Argus."

His cousin sauntered over with a crooked smile. The sticky sound of him chomping gum irritated Emory to no end. Argus reached inside his coat and pulled out a cream-colored envelope.

Emory slung his longbow over his shoulder and snatched the missive out of his cousin's hand. "What's this?"

"You're being audited. Additional details will be provided in the coming weeks. At this time, we require organizational material detailing artillery expenditures as well as individual status reports of all current clients."

Emory scanned the official memo, and his throat tightened. "I haven't broken any rules. This must be some sort of mistake."

"No mistake." Argus's tone was indifferent. "Your entrance conference will be held on the first day of the vernal equinox."

"But—"

"See you soon." Argus walked away and crossed back into the Earth realm.

Emory reread the letter. His head was spinning. He'd never imagined he would come under review. The whole reason he maintained a minimal caseload was to prevent such a thing from ever happening. With one false step, one wrong move, he would be banished from the Earth realm—the only home he'd ever known—forever.

CHAPTER 2

Emory sat alone at the bar, struggling to read the short menu in the dim lighting. The ornate chandeliers dangling overhead did little to illuminate the space in front of him. He wondered why the posh establishment didn't want patrons to see what they were putting into their mouths. Deciding to stick to drinking, he shoved the menu aside.

Emory tapped the narrow stem of his martini glass and stared at the clear liquid as it rippled. He enjoyed the taste of liquor, but his Vycrin body chemistry prevented the rapid absorption of alcohol. Therefore, he drank indiscriminately, often allowing the bartenders to pick what brand of swill to serve him.

Petros arrived and hefted his bulk onto the stool beside Emory. His thick mustache was streaked with strands of gray, and his snug brown suit looked as though it had been trapped in a time warp from the 1970s. The large man was winded, his face an alarming shade of red. He raised a hand to the female bartender and said, "I'll have whatever the boy's having." He jerked a thumb in Emory's direction.

Emory straightened the jacket of his dark Armani suit. "Sorry for the short notice, Petros."

Petros pulled a pink paisley handkerchief out of his pocket and dabbed his brow. "Your message sounded urgent."

The bartender poured a dirty martini and dropped three olives into the glass. She slid the cocktail toward Petros.

"Leave us the container, doll," Petros said, gesturing at the olives.

"I'm sorry, I can't just—"

Petros slid two hundred-dollar bills across the bar.

She tucked the money into her pocket, poured the entire plastic container of olives into a bowl, and placed it between Emory and Petros. With a smile, she said, "Let me know if you two need anything else."

Petros raised his glass to her before turning his attention back to Emory. "What's this all about?"

Emory gulped down his entire martini and motioned for another one. "I'm being audited."

"I know." Petros plunked two more olives into his glass. "I petitioned to be on your committee."

"Why didn't you warn me?"

"You know that's not how this works, boy." Petros took a sip of his cocktail. "It has to go through the proper channels."

Emory shook his head. "They're going to massacre me."

"Nonsense. This is just a routine evaluation."

"Routine..." Emory picked up a fork and stabbed at the olives. As the bartender put his new drink in front of him, he shoved three olives into his mouth. "They want to punish me for what *he* did."

"This isn't about your old man." Petros moved the bowl closer to himself and ate several more olives. "However, the board won't tolerate any of your usual antics."

"What antics? I just—"

Petros gave him a stern look. "No shenanigans. Matchmaking is a job, not a sport. You need to take this seriously and be extremely careful with all of your clients."

Emory sighed. "I should be able to avoid any breakups."

"It's not just about liabilities. They'll be evaluating the validity of your matches as well. A good match isn't ranked by its entertainment value. A solid relationship should result in emotional growth. Did you secure the engagement between Samuel and Isabel?"

"No."

The older man frowned. "What happened?"

"Last month, Samuel moved across the country to be with a woman he met online." Emory swallowed hard. "And Isabel eloped with his best friend." He shook his head. "That one wasn't my fault."

Petros yanked his tight suit jacket down over his stomach. "Part of your job is to identify issues in a relationship and prevent them from escalating, not to sit on your hands and watch the madness unfold!"

Emory started on his fourth martini. At that moment, he wished the cocktails had the same effect on him as they did on humans.

"What's the status of your open cases?" Petros asked.

"I established a new relationship between two college students."

"That's a good start."

"I have Laith and Karina."

Petros grunted.

"I know. They're no help." Emory drank half of his martini. "And I have Blair." He pointed across the restaurant at a couple enjoying their evening together. "She's a perfect client. Consistent, dependable, and—"

"I don't care how easily you can make her fall in love. The board needs to see that you can successfully close your cases. Why haven't you sealed an engagement for the girl?"

Emory shrugged. "She can't seem to keep a man interested."

"For goodness' sake." Petros swallowed the rest of his drink.

"It's not totally my fault."

Petros slammed his empty glass down on the bar. "You're her matchmaker, Emory."

"In my defense, she's been with this guy for a year. But she's difficult to get to kn—"

"Handle it." Petros got to his feet and tossed some bills on the bar. "Tonight."

Emory downed his drink as his supervisor stormed out of the restaurant. He couldn't quite picture Blair as a bride, but he could already hear Greg complaining about wedding preparations and the exorbitant price of flowers. Hopefully, they would have a brief engagement.

He paid his tab, crossed into the Enarine realm, and headed over to his client. Greg held Blair's hands in his, and Emory swore he was shaking. The waiter had cleared their dessert plates, and only a single candle remained on the small round table. He looked like he was having trouble meeting her eyes. The anticipation was almost unbearable, but she sat very still.

"Blair..."

It was the sixth time he'd said her name. Emory sighed heavily and drew a silver arrow from his quiver.

"Yes, Greg?"

"This is very hard for me to say."

"That's okay. Take your time."

"We've been together for a year now, and these past few weeks have given me a lot of time to think about you and me. You're everything I could have asked for in a woman. You're sweet, you're a great cook, and you rarely complain."

Her eyes fluttered as she fought back tears. Emory twirled the arrow between his fingers.

"Which is why..."

"Yes?"

"I don't think we should continue to see each other."

The arrow flipped out of Emory's hand, and he fumbled to retrieve it.

Blair blinked and smiled nervously. "What?"

"You've been wonderful to me, and I'm going to miss that, but things aren't working between us." He let go of her hands. "I just don't see any reason to prolong the inevitable."

A waiter walked by, and Blair snapped her fingers at him. "Can I get two gin martinis, please? Hendricks."

"Yes, miss."

"Dirty," she added through a toothy smile.

As the waiter strode off, Greg said, "I'm sure this comes as quite a shock."

Blair gaped at him. "Why would you think that?"

"I know how special you wanted this day to be, but it's better that you know the truth before one of us gets hurt."

"You're absolutely right."

Emory couldn't believe what he was hearing. He knew Greg was unhappy—but he was *always* unhappy, even when he wasn't with Blair.

The waiter returned with the drinks. "I'm sorry, but we're out of olives."

Blair waved him off and downed one of the martinis in three hearty gulps.

Greg whispered to the waiter, "Could we have the check, please?"

The waiter was one step ahead. He plucked the bill from his pocket and placed it in front of Greg. After a second glance at Blair, he hurried away.

"You were saying?" She was halfway through the second drink.

Greg shook his head. "It's just that I'm not in love with you anymore."

She wiped her mouth with the back of her hand. "And when did you realize that?"

He gave a little shrug and looked away. "About an hour after our first date."

"That's about right," Emory muttered. Greg had one of the weakest auras he'd ever seen.

Blair choked on the remainder of the drink. Greg jumped to his feet and patted her back with a heavy hand, but she pushed him away.

After a short coughing fit, she asked, "And you decide to mention that now?" She tried to clear her throat again. "After an entire year?"

"I thought it would get better." He settled back in his seat. "But it didn't."

"What you're saying is, you're breaking up with me."

"Yes."

She smiled. "And all of this could have been avoided if you had been honest with me in the first place and said you weren't interested."

He twisted his cloth napkin. "Pretty much."

"But you've enjoyed how wonderful I've been to you."

"Yes, very much so."

She glanced around the elegant dining room. Guests were immersed in their own private conversations, and only Emory was listening with rapt attention. "And this elaborate dinner was to soften the blow?"

Greg nodded.

Blair's wide smile was alarming. "All this time, I thought we were getting serious, but really, you had no interest in marrying me."

"Exactly." He let out a sigh of relief. "I'm glad you're taking this so well. I was worried you would throw a horrible fit and cause a scene, but you seem to be handling this like a real trooper."

Blair closed her eyes. At least one positive thing had come out of the evening—she'd gotten a free dinner. Emory shook his head. It wasn't much, but at least the relationship hadn't been a total waste.

"Now that all the nasty business is settled," Greg said, "I think it's wise we split the check."

She opened her eyes again. "Excuse me?"

"Since we're not dating anymore, I think it's only fair to split tonight's bill, so there are no hard feelings."

Emory's jaw dropped. He was certain Blair was going to reach across the table and strangle Greg with his checkered tie. She was visibly shaking, but she maintained her composure. Her voice was deeper than normal. "What's the total?"

Greg examined the check. "Two hundred sixty-seven dollars. Since I didn't order those last two drinks, you can pay one fifty. I'll cover the rest plus the whole tip."

Blair stared at Greg as though seeing him clearly for the first time. Deep down, Emory had always known the man didn't truly love her, but he'd assumed their mediocre relationship would evolve into a mediocre marriage. That was how things usually worked out.

"Blair?" Greg tore her from her trance. "The money?"

"I have to use the ladies' room." She picked up her small clutch and rose to her feet. "I'll be right back."

"You shouldn't have downed those drinks so fast." Greg flipped through his cash, not meeting her eyes. "You have a bladder the size of a pea."

Blair stared beyond him. "You know me too well."

As she hurried past the bar and headed to the coat check at the front of the restaurant, Emory, alarmed by the sudden turn of events, staggered a few paces behind in the Enarine realm. He glanced back at the table. Greg was picking lint off his suit jacket while he waited for his ex-girlfriend to return.

"Bad form," Emory said. "Bad form, indeed."

He clutched his bow and grabbed an arrow from the quiver strapped to his back. His most prized possession was about to be reclaimed. A breakup would sully his report, but he was fortunate that Blair was his best client. She had countless hours of misery, bitterness, and pain ahead of her, but she would get over it. She always did. His arrows would help her find another hapless entity to dote on, thus cutting the grieving period in half. All he had to do was ensure she was in a steady, progressive relationship by the time he met with the audit committee.

Emory raised his bow and aimed at her heart. The arrow flew through the air, letting out a melodious whistle as it sailed toward its target. He closed his eyes and relished the familiar sound.

The arrow clanked as though hitting a solid object. Emory's eyes shot open in time to see it plunge to the polished wood floor. His jaw dropped. A gloved concierge opened the door for Blair as Emory rushed over, reloading his bow.

The second arrow neared the woman's heart and rebounded off an invisible barrier. He fired a third time. The arrow never reached its target. Heat crept into his face. He pulled out a fourth arrow, but his hands shook, and he had trouble steadying his bow.

Emory took a moment to calm his nerves. Holding his breath, he released the string. The silver arrow bounced back and dropped to the sidewalk.

Emory gaped at Blair in horror. He had never seen an impenetrable heart. Light drops of rain started falling, and she increased her pace. Emory charged after her. She jogged three blocks, turned a corner, continued down a quiet street, and stopped. Other pedestrians sought shelter inside coffee shops and under store awnings, but she closed her eyes and leaned her back against the brick building, allowing the rain to soak her clothes.

Emory examined her delicate face from a few yards away. Her aura was completely gone. The familiar scarlet haze was... gone. He couldn't read her.

He fired another arrow in a desperate attempt to regain control of her heart. The small missile tumbled to the ground, bent and broken. He clutched his bow. He had to fix her heart, and he knew of only one way. It was a desperate act, but he couldn't have such a disaster on his record when he was about to be audited.

He moved closer to her and phased into the Earth realm. "Blair?"

Blair jumped back and swiped at her face.

He raised his hands. "I didn't mean to startle you."

She held her wet coat closed with one hand and tightened her grip on her purse with the other.

Emory shifted uncomfortably. "I saw you at the restaurant."

She straightened. "The gentleman I was with will pay."

"I don't work there." He stepped closer and peered into her dark-brown eyes. "You should be in a crumpled heap by now. Why aren't you crying yet?"

"About what? My hair? I know. I just spent a fortune getting it done. Waste of money."

"I mean about Greg."

Her mouth opened, but no sound came out. He waited for her to be overcome with emotion and dissolve into a state of madness, but she just stared at him with her mouth agape. There wasn't a tear in her eyes. *Strange. Not her usual reaction.*

"Well, Blair, you just set a new record for getting over an ex-lover."

Emory was no expert on female emotions and how to talk to distraught women, but he was fairly certain that had not been the correct thing to say. His client took off running, and he found himself in hot pursuit of the frazzled woman. The pattering of her frantic steps echoed down the street.

"I'm sorry. I didn't mean to scare you!" he shouted as he ran after her. "Let me explain!"

The heel of her shoe caught in a metal grate in the sidewalk, and she stumbled forward, twisting her ankle and yelping loudly. Her silk clutch flew out of her hands as she fell to the concrete. Emory caught up to her as she struggled to pull her heel out of the grate.

"Stay away from me!" She yanked at the stubborn stiletto. The heel snapped under the pressure and fell into the sewer.

Emory knelt and plucked her purse out of a shallow puddle. He held it out to her.

She eyed him suspiciously before snatching it from his hand. "How do you know my name?"

"I know a lot of things about you."

"Who are you?"

Emory hesitated. He needed to get closer to her to accurately assess the condition of her heart and mitigate the damage. If necessary, he could summon a retrieval agent to wipe her memory. *If necessary.* "I'm... well, I'm Vycrin."

"Vy... what?"

Reluctantly, he responded with the one name she would understand. "Cupid."

She sat there, her face blank. Emory imagined such a revelation would be a difficult thing for a human to grasp. He tensed, prepared for any reaction she might have.

Blair suddenly let out a shrill laugh that pierced his eardrums. She slumped over, cackling so hard she gasped for breath.

Emory sighed and stepped over to the street to hail a taxi. A cab swerved across two lanes and screeched to a stop next to them. He turned back to find Blair still hunched over and giggling. He figured it was better for her to be amused than frightened.

"Get up," Emory said. "I'm taking you home."

"Forget it." She curled her legs under her body. "I'm not going anywhere with you."

Emory crouched next to her. "You can either go back to the restaurant and ride home with your cheapskate ex-boyfriend, or you can let me take you home."

She glared at him. "I don't need either of you."

"I happen to know that you never carry more than five dollars when you go on a date. And when you do offer to pay, you use that maxed-out credit card and pretend to be shocked when it's declined."

Her eyes narrowed. "How could you know that?"

He ignored her question. "Is it going to be me or him?"

Blair unzipped her small purse, grabbed a wad of bills, and threw them at Emory. The thin green papers hit him in the chest then twisted away in the wind, floating into the street.

"I had six," she snapped.

Emory extended his hand. Blair hesitated. Without thinking, he dilated his pupils and captured her gaze. She stared at him, entranced. He watched with relief as the uneasiness disappeared from her face. She reached out and clasped his hand. Her skin felt like ice, which confirmed his worst fear—her heart was broken.

He helped her to her feet. Through her frozen touch, he tried to sense her deepest emotions. She was wary but not afraid. He led her to the taxi and opened the door. After she crawled into the back seat and scooted over, he settled next to her. She sat completely still, transfixed by his presence.

Emory blinked hard. "The driver needs your address, Blair."

She shook off her mild disorientation. "Yes, of course." She reeled off her address to the driver.

As the taxi pulled away from the curb, Emory ensured that the front straps of his leather backpack were fastened before placing it next to his feet. Trances were harmless but effective. Vycrin were sworn to protect the emotional and physical well-being of humans, and Blair was safer with him than with anyone else. He certainly wasn't going to leave her in the middle of the street with no way of getting home. That would look bad on his report.

"What's in the backpack?" she asked.

Emory placed a finger on his lips. "Shh..." He cut his eyes toward the driver, who kept glancing into the rearview mirror, obviously eavesdropping.

Blair wrapped her wet coat around her body. After a few minutes of silence, the driver seemed to lose interest and returned his full attention to the road.

She moved closer to Emory. "Who are you really?" she whispered.

"I told you who I am."

"How is that possible?" Blair put a hand on his knee and squeezed as if checking to make sure he was solid. "Cupid isn't real."

Emory grabbed her cold hand and placed it back in her lap, trying to mask his acute ticklishness. "I'm as real as you are."

She peered at him intently. He stared straight ahead, uncomfortable with her close proximity.

"Where are your wings?"

"A common misconception, I assure you."

Blair settled back in her seat. "You're not Cupid."

He winced. "Technically, I'm Vycrin."

"You look human to me."

"We all look human."

She patted his arm. "Sure."

"Why would I lie to you?"

"I have no idea, but you blew your credibility with the Greek-god thing." She glanced out the window. "It's a creative pickup line, though."

Emory bristled. "My intentions are nothing of the sort."

"You don't have to get defensive," she said with a chuckle.

"I'm not. I'm trying to have an honest conversation with you."

"Cupid isn't real. He's a figment of someone's overactive imagination."

Emory folded his arms over his chest, irritated by her simple-minded view. "Your inability to imagine the reality of things you've only known from stories is your problem, not mine."

"I may be a little gullible, but I'm certainly not stupid."

"Why would I make up such a ridiculous story?"

"I assume you're a pathological liar. You didn't even flinch when you told me your name."

"I told you who I was. I never told you my name."

She sighed. "Fine, what's your name?"

"Emory."

Blair frowned. "Not very godlike, is it?"

"I'm only half... *god*." He loosened his tie. "My mother was human."

"Oh!" She giggled. "Well, *that* makes much more sense."

Reasoning with the obstinate creature was proving far more difficult than he'd imagined. "How could I possibly know so much about you if I wasn't telling the truth?"

She flicked chunks of mud and dirt off her ruined purse. "You could be a stalker."

Emory leaned his head back and closed his eyes. "Why don't you believe me?"

"For starters, you're not very convincing." Blair rifled through her purse and pulled out her keys as the taxi approached her building. "You have no wings, no bow, and no arrows, and you're not wearing any pink."

Emory scowled. "I loathe pink."

"See what I mean?"

He sighed. Audit or no audit, Petros was going to be furious about her broken heart. Emory could hear him already: *Fix it, boy!*

Emory knew from his brief studies that a broken heart would require much more than arrows. In the past, Blair had entered each new relationship completely open and unguarded. The repeated trauma of having her heart trampled and crushed meant the damage could only be repaired from the inside out, requiring the client's direct involvement. Therefore, he'd have little chance of mending her heart if she wasn't convinced of who he was and what he could do.

The taxi came to a stop in front of her apartment building. A light mist permeated the air. Emory paid the driver and climbed out onto the sidewalk.

Blair slid out behind him and placed a hand on his arm. "Thank you," she said sincerely. "I normally don't accept rides from men who have chased me through the city at night, but you seem more delusional than dangerous."

She headed toward the building and climbed the steps on the tips of her toes, her uneven heels never touching the stairs.

"Blair, what would make you believe me?"

Her keys made a light clanking sound as she turned to face him. "Persistent, aren't you?" She didn't seem alarmed by his continued presence, which gave Emory some hope. "Maybe I'd believe you if you showed me some of your special powers." She grinned.

Emory snapped his fingers. "I can give you a demonstration. My current caseload is fairly light, so I can easily schedule a match. And I have the perfect candidate. She works at the coffee shop on the corner. Meet me there tomorrow morning at ten."

"Just don't forget your arrows." Blair snickered and opened the door of her building. "Thanks again, Emory."

He crossed into the Enarine realm. Blair turned, and the wind blew light drops of rain into her face. Bright orange streetlights lit the broad sidewalk. She scanned the boulevard, her gaze moving blithely over the spot where he stood watching her.

She frowned then laughed. "A figment of someone's overactive imagination," she said into the air. "Cupid isn't real."

CHAPTER 3

The caffeine wasn't working. Emory was on his fifth cup of coffee, which would have rendered most Vycrin comatose, yet he couldn't keep his knee from bouncing. Blair was late. Very late. Emory absentmindedly turned a page in his book while keeping a close eye out for her. He fought the urge to go to her apartment and remind her about their appointment. Frightening the female when she was already so guarded would only make it harder to break down her walls. He needed to be patient because Blair had absolutely no problem with cutting people out of her life if they broke her trust. He'd seen it before. Once a relationship was over, she would purge every single item that reminded her of that person—clothes, jewelry, gifts—and return her life to a blank slate, as if the relationship had never happened. She'd even tossed a string of pearls out of her apartment window before realizing how much she could have made by selling them. Watching his client dig through muddy snow in mismatched pajamas and a tattered bathrobe had been a particularly low point in Emory's career.

Blair clutched a glossy red shoebox as she bypassed a group of slow pedestrians. Emory leapt out of his chair and banged on the window before she could slip away. She jumped back and tore off her dark sunglasses. He wasn't quite sure what to make of her wide-eyed stare, but he gestured to the empty seat at his table. She spun around and pressed her back against the window. Emory ground his teeth. The last thing he wanted to do was chase her down again. Perhaps she responded better to subtlety. He lightly tapped the glass, and when she turned around, he gave her a friendly wave.

Moments later, Blair entered the busy coffee shop and settled in the seat across from him. She zipped her hoodie up a little higher over her vintage Star Wars T-shirt and reached up to brush back stray ringlets that had escaped her headband on the windy trek.

He looked at his watch. "You're late."

Blair placed the shoebox under her chair. "There was traffic."

"Your apartment is less than four blocks from here." He sipped the last of his drink. "And you don't own a car." He eyed her up and down. "You look absolutely dreadful."

She glared at him. "You'd better be glad I even bothered to put on pants this morning."

He glanced under the table, took note of her jeans, and nodded. "Coffee?"

"Black."

While Emory got in line for their drinks, Blair waited at their table and grabbed her phone from her purse. He pretended to be pre-occupied with the menu as he heightened his senses and honed in on the radio waves emitted from her phone. All other sounds faded into the background as he listened in on her conversation.

"Blair!" Her sister had her on speakerphone. "We were just about to order. Where are you?"

"Hey, Malena. I'm not going to make brunch today."

Plates and silverware clanked in the background. "He broke up with you."

Emory heard her two friends gasp. He was quite familiar with Preya and Savannah from all the times Blair had dragged her new boyfriends along to meet them. They were tough critics.

"Not on their anniversary!" Preya said.

"What an insensitive..." Savannah didn't complete her sentence.

Blair seemed to ignore all of it. "So I'll have to catch up with you ladies another time."

"Are you okay?" Malena asked. "Do you want us to come by later?"

"No, I was headed to the store to return some shoes, but I stopped for coffee."

"She's out of the house?" Preya asked.

"Are you sure you should be wandering the streets in your condition?" Savannah asked.

Blair sighed. "I'm sober, Savannah."

They started murmuring amongst themselves.

"Trust me, I'm fine. I haven't even cried about it."

After a long silence, Malena said, "So, Greg broke up with you last night, and you feel...?"

Blair reached across the table and picked up Emory's book. "Nothing."

Emory's stomach dropped. He'd secretly hoped she felt something—resentment, sorrow, anger—*anything* to indicate that the damage to her heart wasn't as bad as he feared.

"We never liked him anyway," Preya said.

Savannah added, "You are way too good for him!"

"I can always count on you ladies to take the correct side," Blair said with a smile. "So anyway, I'm having coffee with the man who took me home last night."

"Did she say she went home with a new man last night?" Preya asked.

Savannah sighed. "I knew she wasn't all right."

"Who are you talking about?" Malena demanded.

"There was this guy who saw me at the restaurant last night," Blair said. "He felt bad for me, so he took me home."

"He knows where you live?" Preya asked.

Savannah spoke up. "Is he hot?"

Emory's skin prickled, and he stared straight ahead, wishing the line would move faster.

"Dark hair, high cheekbones, square jawline. Kind of rigid. He looks like he could use a good ruffling," Blair replied.

He briefly caught her eye then looked away when she winked at him.

"He's got a great body," she said in a lower voice. "It's shameful when a man can pull off a fitted sweater better than I can, but I'm not complaining. It's wrong to complain about things like that."

The ladies broke into laughter, and Emory fumbled with his wallet to avoid glancing in her direction.

"He's probably one of those guys who eats anything he wants and never gains a pound," she continued. "I'm pretty sure his designer jeans wouldn't even clear my hips."

Emory frowned. He was fairly certain she would be able to fit into his jeans. On the other hand, if he tried to get into her skinny jeans—*that* would be a snug fit. He shook his head at the very notion and broke the connection. He couldn't afford distractions. Whatever Blair thought of him was irrelevant. He was there for one reason only—to salvage his floundering career.

By the time Emory ordered her drink and returned to the table, Blair was off the phone and flipping through his book. He placed the steaming cup of coffee in front of her and sat down.

Blair took a sip and raised her eyebrows. "I asked for it black."

"You don't like it extra sweet?"

She shrugged. "Why is your book in French?"

"What difference does it make?"

"Naturally, you speak French." She slid the book back to him. "The language of love."

He tugged at his sweater. "Vycrin have the ability to speak all languages. Love has nothing to do with it."

"Right." Blair's smile was hidden behind her cup. "I noticed you forgot your bow and arrows again."

"No, I didn't. They're just not visible in this realm."

"You were serious about giving me a demonstration?"

Emory motioned toward the cashier. "Do you see that sad-looking creature taking orders?"

Blair looked over at the young woman. "What about her?"

"The next suitable gentleman who enters this building will fall madly in love with her."

She smothered a giggle. "Is that right?"

He nodded. "These particular encounters follow a very basic pattern, but you need to pay attention because everything is going to happen very quickly."

Blair put down her cup. "Okay, break it down."

"Guy meets girl. Guy falls for girl. Guy nervously asks girl out. Girl hesitates. Guy convinces girl to give him a chance. First unofficial official date."

Blair looked like she was struggling to keep a straight face. "I'm ready when you are." She twisted in her chair to get a better view of the front door.

A tall man with dark-brown skin entered, staring down at his phone. His curly black hair was cut into a polished fade, and a trimmed mustache and goatee offset his youthful appearance. He looked similar in age to the cashier. Emory phased out of the Earth realm to catch a glimpse of the man's aura and was delighted to find him surrounded by a shimmering yellow light. That meant the man was unattached and open to pursuing a new relationship. Only one person was in line, and the man got behind her. He started typing something on his phone and didn't notice when the line moved.

The cashier cleared her throat. "Can I help you?"

Emory jumped up, grabbed his bow from across his chest, and plucked a silver arrow from the quiver dangling behind his chair.

The man raised his head, and Emory shot him in the heart. He smiled at the cashier. "I'd like... um..."

She sighed. "Yes?"

He placed his phone in the messenger bag strapped across his chest and stared up at the menu. "A regular coffee with cream and sugar, please."

Emory materialized back into the Earth realm before Blair turned around.

"Anything else?" the woman asked.

"Yes." He drummed his fingers on the counter. "I mean, yes and no."

She rolled her eyes and tapped his order into the register.

Blair glanced at Emory, who gestured for her to keep watching. Everything was going exactly according to plan.

"Do you work late?" the man asked.

The cashier met his eyes. "What?"

"I mean, I usually work late. But not today, obviously, because it's Saturday." He let out a laugh and handed her cash.

The young man's nervous energy was almost painful, but Emory remained still. One arrow would suffice.

The cashier shoved his money into the register and started preparing his coffee.

He watched her put the lid on his cup. "What I meant was—"

She slammed his drink on the counter. "What?"

"Can I buy you lunch?"

The woman blinked. "What?"

He leaned against the counter. "If you have a short break, I'd like to buy you lunch."

One of her coworkers moved closer to listen, and Blair was equally enthralled with the conversation. Humans were so easily amused.

"Sorry," the young woman replied. "I only have a half-hour break."

"I'll make it quick, then," he said. "I know a great hot dog stand in the park down the street."

Emory sat back in his chair, feeling smug. Blair wouldn't be able to dispute his abilities after such a display.

The cashier bit her lower lip and looked at her coworker. When the other woman nodded, the cashier said, "My shift is over in about five minutes."

"Great! I'm Darion, by the way."

"Hana," she said, tucking her hair behind her ear.

He gave her a warm smile. "I'll just wait over there." He strode to a table by the wall and sat down.

Emory turned to Blair with a triumphant grin. "Now do you believe me?"

Blair sipped her coffee. "Nothing really happened."

"You didn't just see how they connected?"

"You didn't even move. All I saw was some guy asking a girl to lunch. That doesn't prove anything."

"But... but he wouldn't have asked her if I hadn't shot him in the heart!"

"With what? Your invisible arrows?" Blair swirled her coffee around in her cup. "I expected more from you, Emory."

Darion and Hana slipped out of the coffee shop together, and he shoved his book into his backpack. He'd just increased his client list to six by adding Darion to his roster, and she still wasn't convinced. Managing seven clients would be difficult, but it would be better to secure them as a couple than to try to justify another solo client to the audit committee. Blair was already enough of a handful. "Fine. We'll try this again."

"Actually, I have some things to do today." She finished her drink and picked up her shoebox. "Thanks for the coffee and the uneventful afternoon."

She stacked their empty cups and tossed them into the garbage on her way out of the shop. Emory scooped up his backpack and followed her out. The cool air was refreshing after the two hours he'd spent drinking copious hot beverages.

"What other things do you need to do today?" he called after her.

"First, I have to return these shoes."

Emory snatched the box from her hands and peeked inside to find the ruined shoes from the night before. "I doubt the store will give you a full refund." He shoved the shoebox into a trash bin near a light post.

"Hey! I just bought those."

"I'll buy you a new pair. Right now, we have business to take care of." He grabbed her arm and started pulling her across the busy street.

"You're insane!" She half-heartedly tried to wiggle out of his grasp, but he wouldn't let go. "This had better be interesting. I could be at brunch right now."

They entered the park as Darion and Hana were ordering lunch from a hot dog vendor.

As Emory strolled past them, he pulled out his oval locket from beneath his sweater, opened it, and retrieved his love token. He held it out to Blair. "Put this in your pocket."

She eyed the small coin warily. "Why?"

"Just do it. I'll explain later."

She grabbed the copper token from his fingers and shoved it into the back pocket of her jeans.

"You're not going to like how this feels," Emory said as he phased out of the Earth realm.

A familiar tingling sensation spread under Emory's skin, but he was so used to the feeling of pins and needles creeping through every inch of his body he barely registered the pain. Blair, on the other hand, let out an agonized cry. For a human, crossing realms was ex-cruciating—at least, that was what he'd been told. He'd never actually done it with one of their kind. Blair stood paralyzed. Emory wrapped his arm around her waist and forced her to walk. After a few steps, the painful stinging would fade, leaving her entire body numb. Light-headedness would follow.

Emory relaxed his grip and gazed up at the clear blue sky. Leaves broke free from swaying tree branches and danced in the wind. The loud honking of angry drivers was muted, speeding cars had slowed to a crawl, and bands of pedestrians looked as though they were suspended in place. Off in the distance, he caught sight of the couple from the coffee shop, their lingering pace out of phase with his and Blair's. Blair reached out to touch a withered leaf floating in front of her face, and it shifted just out of her reach as though repelled by a magnetic force. She recoiled and stepped back.

"Watch this," Emory said.

His bow and quiver materialized in place of his leather backpack, and he pulled out an arrow. He aimed his bow at Hana, wielding the weapon with practiced ease. Blair shrieked just as he released the arrow. The silver missile sailed through the air, emitting a melodious hum as it approached its target. Blair lunged forward as if to warn the unsuspecting victim.

Emory held her back. "Keep watching!"

The arrow slammed into the girl's chest. The cashier stood motionless, seemingly unaware of the sharp object protruding from her body. The arrow pulsed bright red then vanished. Blair's mouth dropped open.

Hana let out a nervous laugh. "Thanks."

"I mean it," Darion said. "You have the cutest smile I've ever seen."

A small grin swept across her face. "That's very sweet of you to say."

Though the words were slow and muffled, the conversation was perfectly clear, as if Emory and Blair were standing right in front of them in real time.

"I'm dizzy," Blair muttered.

"Your senses are absorbing both worlds simultaneously. The disorientation will pass."

She turned to stare at Emory. "You just shot that woman in the heart."

"Yes, I did."

Blair spun back to the couple. They were deep in conversation as they sauntered away with the distinct haze of love in their eyes, a look that Emory was all too familiar with.

"You're Cupid." Her forehead wrinkled as though she had difficulty believing the words even as she spoke them.

"I am."

"Cupid... is real."

"As I've mentioned before, we don't refer to ourselves by our mythical misidentification. We're not a single entity. Our species is tasked with spreading love throughout the universe. But yes, we are real."

"Are you the cause of all my heartaches and failed relationships?"

He ran his fingers over the remaining arrows in his quiver. "Only the ones in the last five years." He shrugged. "But I like to think of my job as more of an entertaining pastime than an actual profession."

Blair shoved her hands into the pockets of her hoodie. "You made me fall in love for fun?"

Watching her cry over her failed relationships wasn't fun. Watching her strained interactions with Greg hadn't been fun. But watching her fall completely and hopelessly head over heels in love—that was fun. Few humans possessed that level of passion. "Most of the time, yes."

"If everything you've told me is true, then I don't have poor taste in men. You do."

"Touché."

She narrowed her eyes. "How many times have you shot me?"

"This year?"

Blair slapped him hard across the face.

Emory shook off the sudden blow and tried to maintain his composure despite the heat rising up the back of his neck. Allowing himself to feed off her anger would only create a barrier between them and make it harder to sense her emotions. He had to suppress his negative feelings. "I understand you're upset, but—"

She spun and started walking away.

"Blair!"

She broke into a jog.

"Please, let me explain!"

She increased her pace.

Their appointment was spiraling out of control. He drew an arrow and aimed at her heart. "I didn't want to have to show you this, but you need to see it. Please. Stop."

Blair turned around and gasped, clutching her purse to her chest. "You wouldn't dare!"

He released the bowstring. With a scream, she dove to the ground. The arrow ricocheted off her heart and landed in the grass a foot away from her.

Emory walked over and stood next to her. "I realize this is a lot to take in. Why don't we sit down so I can explain everything?" He offered his hand.

She scooted away then got up without his help.

"I promise I won't try to shoot you again," he said. *This afternoon, at least.*

Turning away, she headed down a bush-lined path toward some metal park benches. He carefully examined her. She was small, but if she resisted in any way... for her own safety, he would have to catch her off guard.

Emory sprinted up behind her. "Don't tense up!"

Before she could turn around, he slammed his open palms into her back. The explosive force knocked the breath from her lungs and threw her off her feet. He cringed. For a split second, they shared a horrible connection of pain and fear. He felt what she felt. Blair careened into the bushes and landed on her side with a loud thud.

Emory knelt beside her, trembling. He'd never experienced the physical or emotional effects of pushing a human back into the Earth realm. Nothing could have prepared him for the shock. He drew back into himself. She didn't need to know how much it had frightened him.

He kept his deep voice steady. "That wasn't so bad, was it?"

Terror gripped him when Blair's eyes rolled back in her head.

"I told you not to tense up!" Emory grabbed her shoulders and started shaking her. "Breathe!"

Blair's eyes fluttered open, and she gasped for air. She coughed, and Emory patted her on the back.

"Get your hands off me!" She attempted to push him away, but she was too weak to engage in anything resembling a fight.

Emory hauled her out of the hedging. He grabbed her purse from the sidewalk and guided her to a bench. The buses and cars on the street had returned to normal speed, and pedestrians were once again moving at a regular pace.

"I'm sorry if I hurt you," Emory said. "Blunt physical trauma creates just enough force to push you back into your realm."

"Realm?" she asked, plopping down on a park bench.

"The Earth realm." Emory sat next to her. "I told you that I'm only half human. My mother was human, and my father is Vycrin. The Vycrin species has the ability to travel through dimensional space and cross worlds."

"It still looked like we were on Earth."

"That was the realm of Enarine, the closest parallel dimension to Earth. Similar natural laws govern the two universes, but they function under different time frequencies. That allows us to move at a faster rate than the human eye can see."

Blair grabbed his backpack from his arm and tore it open. His ragged copy of *Les Misérables* and a set of keys lay inside. "What happened to the bow and arrows?"

Emory tugged his bag free of her grip. "Objects with strong mystical properties can't be seen in this realm, but they materialize into their true forms in Enarine." He reached behind her and slid his hand into the back pocket of her tight jeans. *Way too tight.*

She squealed. "Hey!"

He held up the small copper coin. "Objects that retain their true form in both worlds can be used to open a gateway between space and time."

Blair adjusted her hoodie over the back of her pants. "What is that?"

"It's a love token. Every Vycrin receives one at birth." Emory put the precious coin back in his silver locket. "Humans have used them for centuries to cross realms with us... *gods*. Unfortunately, it only works one way, which is why I had to push you back here."

Blair steadied herself on the edge of the bench. "If you've been following me around for five years, why haven't I noticed you before?"

"You have, many times. But you always forgot. Yesterday was the first time I ever touched you."

He took her hand and brushed his fingers across her frozen palm. "It's called *resonance*. The tactile connection unlocked the subconscious part of your mind that's prevented you from remembering me after our encounters."

"That's impossible. I'm certain I'd remember someone like you."

He let go of her cold fingers and rubbed his hands together to warm them up. "You mean someone who sits in the same corner of the coffee shop every morning and watches you order a medium black coffee, knowing you prefer it with sugar but you're too impatient to wait?"

"I..." Her forehead wrinkled. "Well..."

"Now that we've made physical contact, you won't forget me," he said. "To all other humans, I'm there but not really there. I exist on a plane above human perception. I can interact with others, but once I'm out of sight—"

"You're out of mind."

"Something like that."

"Why did you approach me last night?"

He looked away from her. "Because I accidentally broke your heart."

Blair let out a cynical chuckle. "No, you didn't. My ex-boyfriend did." Her smile faded. "Actually, he didn't either. I'm not even sad we broke up."

"That's because there's a barrier surrounding your heart. It's preventing you from feeling any sort of romantic attachment or sentiment. That barrier that was created as a result of my arrows."

"What's that supposed to mean?"

"It means you can no longer fall in love." Emory stared at her intently, waiting to see her reaction.

Blair shrugged. "So what?"

Emory reached into his coat pocket, pulled out the letter from the audit committee, and held it out to her. She opened it and unfolded the single piece of paper tucked inside.

Dear Emory Reginald Odin II,

We are currently reviewing and evaluating procurement policies and guidelines to ensure compliance with district regulations. As you know, we are committed to providing exceptional protection and cus-

tomer service to our clients while remaining within the legal bounds of our contract. This protection involves safeguarding both the physical and emotional well-being of Homo sapiens. Therefore, it is imperative that all employees behave in an ethical manner as outlined in section 3Y-MTH of your guidebook. The responsible use of power is our first priority.

At present, we are conducting audits to identify unions made within the last twenty-four synodic months, and we are following up on all open or unresolved cases. To facilitate this request, we require a detailed list of resources and materials used in this process. We would appreciate receiving the following information from you in preparation for your entrance conference:

inventory (arrows, bows, quivers, etcetera)

equity (proposals, engagements, marriages, etcetera)

liabilities (fights, breakups, broken hearts, etcetera)

Any misuse of power will receive punishment of the utmost severity, including—but not limited to—loss of license, jurisdictional termination, artillery repossession, and banishment.

Thank you, in advance, for your prompt attention to this request.

Sincerely,

The Powers That Be

Blair handed back the letter. "Okay, so you're getting audited. What do you want me to do about it?"

"I've never told another human who I really am."

"I'm honored," she said sarcastically.

He grabbed her arm. "And I've never broken anyone's heart before." She clearly didn't understand the seriousness of their situation. She would be numb, unable to form any sort of deep emotional connection—and he would be exiled. "I must resolve your case as soon as possible."

"How?"

"I'm certain I can find you a suitable mate who will mend your broken heart. You just have to be open to it."

She pulled her arm away. "You've been at it for five years and haven't been very successful."

"Please?" Emory took her hand and held it to his heart. "I swear I'll take it seriously this time. A broken heart on my record could destroy my future."

Blair's dark eyes met his. He didn't know humans were capable of peering so deeply into another's soul. "Fine. But I don't want just anyone. I want the perfect man."

He nearly choked. "But there's no such thing as a perfect man."

"I said *the* perfect man, meaning perfect for *me*."

Emory jumped up and started pacing in front of the bench, muttering to himself. She couldn't possibly be serious. He was her matchmaker, yes, but he was not a miracle worker. He didn't even know where to begin. Blair curled her legs onto the bench and rested her arm against the back of the metal seat.

After a couple of minutes, he stopped and sat back down. "I feel like you're trustworthy, but you have to promise not to tell anyone what I've told you today." Emory lowered his voice—there was always a chance that someone was watching. "If my superiors determine that you pose any sort of threat or think you might spread knowledge of who we are and what we do, they will send someone to wipe all traces of me from your memory."

"Like that *Star Trek* episode when the *Enterprise* is scanned by that alien ship and the crew loses their memories?" she asked shrilly.

Emory shook his head. "I'm sorry, but I didn't understand half of the words you just spewed out. I'm telling you this as a warning because I don't want you to be flagged as a security risk. Promise me you won't tell anyone the truth about who I am or what I do."

Her expression turned serious. "I promise."

"Also, I can't put the lives of my other clients on hold while we sort out your situation." He put his backpack over his shoulder. "We'll have to search for your perfect man during my assignments."

She smiled. "Is that a yes? You'll find me the perfect man?"

Emory looked her up and down. "I guess we'll have to get you a helmet."

CHAPTER 4

Emory shifted into neutral and brought his bike to a stop behind a silver Chevrolet Camaro. As he waited for the light to turn green, he tilted his head. "Are you comfortable?"

Blair leaned back slightly. "Yes."

Earlier that day, he'd bought her a pair of goggles and a shiny black road helmet. The intricate silver wings decorating the sides of her helmet weren't Emory's taste, but he had allowed her to pick out the accessories she liked. She wrapped her arms around his waist as he balanced their body weight on the bike.

Emory tightened his hand on the throttle. The bitter cold emanating from her body enveloped him despite the layers of clothing separating their skin. Even his backpack couldn't provide enough of a barrier between them. She had no idea how uncomfortable her closeness made him. He shifted to the side, thinking a slight change in position might fend off the chill caused by her broken heart. She eased her grip, but the adjustment did nothing to stop the cold from seeping through her skin.

The light changed, and the Camaro thundered down the avenue. Emory trailed behind at a distance. There was no need to alert the couple that they were being followed.

"Who's in the car?" Blair asked over the rushing wind.

"My problem children, Laith and Karina."

"How long have they been together?"

Emory cleared his throat. "Eight years."

"Eight years, and you still can't close the deal?"

"It's complicated." He shifted into fourth gear. "They have some issues to work out."

"What kind of issues?"

"Trust issues, jealousy, anger management, lack of commitment, lack of sex... the list goes on."

"What made you match them up? Did they have a lot in common back then?"

He shrugged. "They looked amazing together."

"That's the dumbest thing I've ever heard. Is that why you set me up with Greg?"

Emory thought back to the uneventful day he'd matched Blair with Greg. "Do you want the truth?"

"Yes."

"It was because I thought you two would make goofy-looking babies."

Blair burst into laughter. "You're a jerk."

"I'm being honest. I never understood what you saw in that man."

"Hmm... I wonder what made me fall in love with him."

"You can't blame it all on me," Emory said. "My arrows plant the seeds of love or enhance love that's already there. No number of arrows can force a person to feel love for someone if it's not truly in their heart."

He followed the Camaro into the parking lot of a crowded billiard hall. The car went left, so Emory went to the right. He found an empty space and came to a stop. He tilted the bike, allowing Blair to slide off. The distance granted him some much-needed relief, and his body temperature began to rise. He was not looking forward to their ride home.

"So even your difficult clients truly love each other?"

"Yes." He waved toward the opposite end of the parking lot, where Karina had just emerged from the passenger side of the silver sports car. "They just don't like each other."

Karina flipped her wavy auburn locks out of her face. The wispy strands floated over her shoulder and cascaded down her back. Her light skin was kissed with a bronze hue, and her makeup was flawless. She wore a short button-down dress with a thin leather belt that accentuated her small waist. The faint clicks of her heels echoed as she walked toward the entrance of the pool hall.

Moments later, her blond counterpart stepped out of the driver's side. Laith's tan was impeccable, and his golden hair perfectly framed his rugged jawline. He carried himself with a confidence that showed he was aware of his looks.

"You weren't kidding," Blair said. "They're both really hot."

"I told you."

Blair gave him a skeptical glance. "How bad could their relationship be?"

Laith caught up with his girlfriend, her strides being limited by the short dress and high heels, and moved ahead of her. When he stopped to wait at the double doors, she slowed her pace. After a few seconds, he lost patience and entered the building without her. The door slammed shut just as she reached the entrance. She stared at the glass barrier as though debating her next course of action. After some time, she straightened her dress and entered.

Emory retrieved his love token and handed it to Blair. "You'll see."

She slipped it into the back pocket of her jeans then hesitated.

"Don't think about the pain." He wrapped his arm around her waist and stepped forward, sweeping her into the Enarine realm. He ignored her high-pitched shriek. In time, she would get used to crossing over.

She sagged against him and slurred, "That is so weird. Everything looks so slow."

Emory hoisted her upright. "I know you're dizzy, but can you walk?"

"I'm fine." She took a step, swayed, then regained her balance. "Perfectly fine."

Emory lifted his bow from across his chest and led the way into the pool hall. The musty room was crowded, but it didn't take him long to trace the pale-orange aura of his client. Karina leaned against the smooth surface of the bar as they wandered up behind her.

"Excuse me." Karina signaled the bartender with a wave.

The bartender spotted her and smiled. "What can I get you?"

"Two Samuel Adams, please." She glanced over at Laith, who was setting up a table in the far corner of the pool hall. He was paying no attention to her.

"Does he always ignore her like that?" Blair asked.

"Only when he's in a foul mood," Emory said. "I just need to make sure they get through the evening without a major fight."

Blair gave him a sly look. "That's your idea of a successful date?"

Emory bit back his irritation. "You're just here as a spectator."

"You have a very sexy accent," the bartender said as he placed the beers on the counter. "Where are you from?"

"Colombia," Karina replied.

"I'm from Chicago. Not as exotic."

She giggled and sat on the barstool. "My country has better weather."

Emory pulled out an arrow. "The fact that she's making herself comfortable at the bar is a bad sign, but it's an easy fix."

Blair's eyes widened. "You're going to make her fall in love with the bartender so Laith will get jealous?"

Emory cocked his head. "I see where you've gotten confused." He handed her the heavy silver arrow. "Those are used exclusively for my clients. Laith is in Karina's heart, and Karina is in Laith's. The love they feel from my arrows will be for each other, not anyone else."

She pointed at his quiver. "What do the other ones do?"

"Those are throwaways." Emory handed her a lighter titanium arrow. "They're for general use to spark attraction or soften a human's heart. The effects usually last for about an hour, but it varies, depending on an individual's aura and emotional state."

"Aura?" Blair handed back the arrows.

"Each human emits a distinct aura that reveals certain things about their nature and temperament."

Her face lit up. "What does mine tell you?"

Emory forced a smile. "That you're complicated."

Blair folded her arms across her chest and flashed him a satisfied grin. "I like that."

"I figured you would." Emory turned back to the scene at the bar.

Karina drank her beer while the bartender stacked glassware.

"So, do you have a boyfriend?" the bartender asked.

"Sometimes," she replied coyly.

Emory ground his teeth. He couldn't leave Karina alone for more than five minutes without her flirting with other men.

The bartender chuckled. "It's like that, huh?"

Karina pointed at Laith, who was testing out pool cues. "That one."

"Not getting along?"

She twisted her hair over her shoulder. "I think I get along better with you."

"Everyone gets along better with me." He leaned closer and lowered his voice. "I'm the one serving the alcohol."

She let out a laugh. Emory shifted his focus to Laith and shot him in the heart. Laith looked up in time to see his girlfriend playfully stroking the bartender's hand. He tossed the cue stick on the table and charged toward the bar.

The bartender's laugh was cut short as Laith came up behind Karina and placed his hand on her lower back. "I thought you were getting us drinks."

"I did." Karina pointed at the two bottles, one of which she had almost emptied.

The bartender moved away and started wiping down the other end of the bar.

"What are you talking to him for?" Laith demanded.

Karina gestured toward the billiard area. "You seemed preoccupied."

"I was setting up our table."

"You left me outside."

Laith dropped a wad of bills on the bar. "I'm sorry. I came in to get a spot because I was afraid it was getting crowded."

Emory and Blair followed the tense couple to their billiard table.

"This is exciting," Blair whispered.

"You don't have to whisper. They can't hear us." Emory looked around to find what she was talking about. "And what's exciting?"

"This. Your job!"

"I guess that's one way of looking at it."

Billiard balls scattered across the felt table as Laith made the first break. "You were the one who said we should go out tonight," he said.

"This isn't what I had in mind," Karina replied.

"What did you have in mind?"

Karina knocked a striped ball into a corner pocket. "Something a little more romantic."

"I thought we were trying to save money."

"What for?"

He blew chalk from the tip of his cue stick. "I don't know. You keep saying we need to save money."

Emory stood between them, twirling an arrow between his fingers. Their thin auras burned bright orange, so despite the tension and discord, they were committed to each other. The relationship was steady but not nearly as stable as he would have liked.

"Not if you don't want to," Karina grumbled as the cue ball ricocheted off two sides and slipped into a corner pocket.

"I think we should be on the same page if we're going to put some money aside." Laith lined up an easy shot. "What were you thinking?"

"Maybe a trip to the Bahamas?" she suggested.

Emory loaded the arrow into his bow. He knew exactly what Karina was trying to say, but it had been months since she'd broached the topic. Emory couldn't afford for them to delay any longer. He shot Karina in the heart.

"And a small destination wedding," Karina added as Laith slid the cue in front of him.

The cue ball slammed forward and bounced off the table. Karina circled the table to retrieve it. She placed it back on the table and pocketed two striped balls with a single shot. She missed the next and backed away for the silent Laith to take his turn.

"What do you think?" she asked.

He stepped toward the table. "I like the Bahamas idea."

"I figured you would."

Laith put the end of his cue stick on the floor and leaned it against the edge of the table. "What do you think about getting a puppy?"

Karina's face lit up as he inched closer to her. "You said you hated animals in the house."

Laith cornered her against the pool table. "Would it make you happy?"

She nodded emphatically, and Laith kissed her lips.

Karina was satisfied—for the moment. Emory knew she would bring up the marriage issue again when she tired of the puppy. He couldn't fathom Laith's aversion to marrying her. It wasn't as though wearing a stupid ring would cause some sort of dramatic shift in the man's life. Humans fixated on the most trivial details.

Blair clapped. "Well done."

Emory shifted uncomfortably. He'd almost forgotten he had an audience. "Do you want to play a game?"

"Okay."

"Let's head to the back. I don't want to be around a lot of people."

"You like to keep a low profile, huh?"

"Sometimes it's necessary." Emory led her to a dimly lit corner of the pool hall. He eyed an abandoned cue stick on a nearby table, but then he got a better idea. He gently took hold of her frozen hand. "Blair, can I show you something?"

She smiled. "What?"

Emory grabbed her shoulders and slammed her back against the exposed brick wall as hard as he could. The sudden blow forced her into the Earth realm and knocked the air out of her lungs. He winced, sharing her pain and shock. Blair stared up at him with wide eyes but didn't make a sound.

Emory kept her pinned against the wall as he leaned forward and brushed his cheek against hers. "Breathe," he whispered.

Blair gasped and began to cough. Emory let out a sigh of relief and attempted to slow his racing heart. He glanced around, but no one seemed to care about a random couple having a private moment in a dark corner of a billiard hall. Vycrin were careful not to draw undue attention to themselves, but even if people happened to catch a momentary glimpse of them appearing out of the Enarine realm, they would forget it a moment later. The human mind rejected anything it couldn't process logically.

"Are you okay?" he asked.

Blair's chest heaved as she leaned against the wall. "There has to be a better way to do that."

He shrugged. "I was going to knock you over the head with a cue stick, but I've never hit a woman before."

"No?" Blair grabbed the collar of his leather jacket and pulled him closer. "You prefer manhandling them instead?"

He frowned. "No, never. Just you."

Blair pushed him away and handed back his love token. "I thought you said you were an advanced species. Your people haven't devised an easier way for humans to cross back over?"

"There is another way." Emory sealed the token in his locket and tucked it under his shirt. "But it won't work on you."

"Why not?"

"If an arrow strikes a human who is in the Enarine realm, it immediately throws them back into this realm. Well, you have a barrier around your heart."

Blair turned serious. "Oh. I forgot."

"I didn't." Emory opened his backpack and retrieved his wallet. "We're here to find you a suitable match."

Emory wasted little time paying for a table in the middle of the room. He planned to set up a "casual" encounter for Blair. She seemed more excited about the game than the prospect of meeting someone, which was completely out of character for her.

She slouched on her cue stick. "Now what should I do? Strike a sexy pose or something?"

"Please don't. I need you to act natural and be yourself. It won't do us any good if a man falls in love with someone you're not."

"I'm going to pretend you didn't just offend me." Without looking at him, she arranged the balls in a worn plastic rack, applied chalk to the tip of her cue stick, and lined up a break shot.

Emory couldn't understand how he'd managed to offend her. He had just been stating a fact. "I'll send someone to join you."

"Preferably someone who doesn't insult me," she said sweetly.

He sighed and crossed into the Enarine realm. He hadn't realized that dealing with a client one-on-one would be so taxing. A spiky-haired man engulfed in a hazy green aura was heading for the bathroom. He would have to pass near Blair's table to get to his destination. Of the half dozen gentlemen in the bar, Spiky was the only one who was unattached. He would suffice. Emory loaded his bow with a titanium arrow.

Blair leaned over her table to make the break. When she pulled back her cue stick, the butt went into Spiky's side as he walked past her.

"Ouch!"

Emory released the arrow into the man's chest, striking his heart.

Blair spun around. "I'm so sorry! Are you okay?"

Spiky's hazel eyes were shining. "I'll take a shot to the gut from a beautiful woman any day. Let me buy you a drink."

She gaped at him. "Just like that?"

"Yeah, what do you drink?"

"Guinness."

"Great!" He placed his beer on the edge of her pool table as though claiming his territory. "Don't go anywhere."

"I won't." Blair glanced around while Spiky chased down a waitress. "Emory? Are you still there?"

Emory ignored her whispering and remained out of phase. Keeping track of three clients at once had proved to be less complicated than he had anticipated. It certainly provided better entertainment value.

Spiky returned and tapped her shoulder. "Looking for someone?"

"I thought I spotted someone I knew." She extended her hand. "I'm Blair, by the way"

He shook her hand. "Jake."

"Do you want to play? I promise I'll try not to maim you this time."

"Sure." Jake laughed and tore his attention away from her long enough to retrieve a cue stick.

Blair took the first shot, and the ivory ball spun into action, scattering the colorful orbs across the billiard table.

Jake gave a nod of approval. "Beautiful *and* talented."

Emory grunted. Apparently, one arrow would be enough to satisfy the young man for the evening. His emerald-green aura exposed his desperation. He had recently gone through a breakup. A rebound relationship wasn't ideal, but it would be good for keeping Blair busy.

Satisfied with his work, Emory placed his bow across his chest. At the rate things were going, he'd be off work in an hour—less than that if Jake was amicable enough to drop Blair off at home. That would spare Emory the uncomfortable ride back.

Emory glanced over at Karina in time to see her flashing a smile at a group of men playing at a neighboring table. She stretched to line up a complicated shot, and her skirt inched up her legs. One of the men nudged his friend then moved toward Karina.

Laith charged over with two pints of beer sloshing in his hands. He set them down and got between Karina and a burly man with unsightly stains on his shirt. "Back off, man."

"She was the one flirting with me!" Burly said.

"I was not—" Karina began.

Laith scowled, and she fell silent. "Just leave us alone," he said.

Burly stepped backward with his hands raised. Laith grabbed Karina's arm and headed for the exit. Emory followed, wishing they would move faster.

"I'm sorry," Karina said.

"You're always sorry," Laith said.

"You should keep your little slut on a tighter leash," Burly called after them. His friends' mocking laughter joined his.

Laith froze.

"Ignore him." Karina clutched his hand and tugged him toward the door. "Let's just go."

Laith jerked his hand away and stormed toward the boisterous group.

"Laith, don't!" Karina cried.

Ignoring her, he dragged the inebriated man off his barstool and punched him in the face. Burly stumbled backward into a small cocktail table, and beer glasses shattered against the concrete floor. Burly overpowered Laith in one swift motion, slamming him against one of the pool tables and knocking the breath out of him. He wrapped his beefy hands around Laith's throat.

"Get off of him!" Karina screamed as Laith gasped, trying to breathe.

Laith clawed at the table. His grasping hand found a pool stick, and he brought it around to smash it over the larger man's head. Burly dropped to his knees, and Laith greedily gulped air.

The bartender picked up the phone. "Break it up, or I'm calling the police!"

Emory was surprised the bartender hadn't already made the call, but he guessed that would be bad for business. Burly's two friends got on either side of him and hauled him to his feet. They headed for the door.

Karina ran to Laith's side. "Are you crazy?" she shouted. "What were you thinking?"

"I couldn't let him say that about you." He reached up and rubbed his neck.

Emory shot Karina in the heart, reinforcing positive emotions about her defender.

Karina helped Laith to his feet and held on to his waist. "You're crazy, but I love you."

Laith wrapped an arm around her. "I love you too."

Emory slung his bow over his shoulder. His work was done for the evening. Blair had a potential suitor, and his clients were still madly in love—*madly* being the operative word. The brawl wouldn't look great on his report, but the outcome was positive nonetheless.

Emory looked over at Jake, who was in the midst of an animated discussion with other players whose games had been interrupted by the violent commotion. Emory decided he didn't care much for Jake. A sensible man would have immediately escorted Blair out of the building, not sat around and relished the excitement.

Emory emerged from the Enarine realm and waved to catch Blair's attention. He pointed at the door, and she nodded. After a last glance at Karina and Laith, who were talking to the bartender, he went outside. A few minutes later, Blair burst through the door and jogged over to him.

"Did you give him your number?" Emory asked.

"I wasn't interested."

He nodded. "Because he lacked good sense?"

"What? No." She fiddled with the strap of her helmet. "I just... didn't feel a connection."

"Blair, it's not going to feel like it did before. There isn't going to be a surge of overwhelming emotion. It's going to be a gradual buildup." Emory held out her goggles. "What did you tell him?"

"I told him I was relocating across the country and couldn't get involved in a serious relationship. He was really nice and wished me the best."

Emory shook his head as he mounted his bike. He needed to find her someone who wouldn't be so easily deterred, someone with a more radiant aura. He decided to focus on individuals who were open to a new relationship *and* emotionally stable. Narrowing the selection to yellow auras would limit his search, but it would likely result in a higher success rate.

"When will the arrows wear off?" Blair asked.

He checked his watch. "Without the expectation of seeing you again, it shouldn't take more than twenty minutes."

"Perfect. Let's get out of here." She climbed onto the seat behind him. "That was a wild night. Have you ever fought anyone over a woman?"

"Absolutely not." His motorcycle roared to life. "No woman is worth the scars."

CHAPTER 5

Emory stood next to Blair in a long line of people awaiting entrance into an exclusive nightclub. It had been a week since the incident at the billiard hall, and he was grateful to be working with his low-maintenance couple from the coffee shop instead of Laith and Karina. It gave him a little more time to focus on Blair's case.

She pulled her faux fur coat tighter around her. "It's October. It shouldn't be this cold already."

"No one told you to wear such a ridiculously short skirt," Emory said. "It doesn't make any sense."

"But that's why I wore boots!"

Emory glanced down at her shapely legs and knee-high suede boots. "I'm sure that twelve-inch gap of bare skin isn't doing you any favors."

Blair moved closer and whispered, "Can't we just skip the line?"

Emory tightened his backpack over his shoulder. "That's considered a misuse of power, and I can't afford an infraction with an audit looming."

She stayed near him in an obvious effort to absorb some of his body heat. He took a step to the right, and she moved, too, ignoring his blatant body language. He shifted to the left.

"I'm cold, Emory!"

"That doesn't mean both of us have to be uncomfortable."

A menacing smile curved her lips. "I make you uncomfortable?"

He ignored her and pretended to be interested in the storefront to their right.

She moved in front of him and wrapped her arms around his waist. "What about now?"

He stiffened, determined not to let her unnerve him. Blair snaked her left leg around his. The feel of her body, despite the iciness, caused his heart to beat faster. She squeezed tighter.

He raised his hands. "Yes, you make me very uncomfortable!"

She chuckled and let go. "You shouldn't let me rile you up so easily."

He took a few steps forward to catch up to the people ahead of them. "You're ridiculous, Blair." He tugged at his leather jacket.

When the well-muscled bouncer at the door waved them forward, he looked Blair up and down then unhooked the red velvet rope that blocked the entrance. She giggled, and the gruff security guard cracked a smile. He stared at her curvy figure as she made her way inside the nightclub.

His smile disappeared when he turned to Emory. "Forty-dollar cover charge."

Emory pulled out his wallet, retrieved two twenties, and handed them to the bouncer.

"What's in the backpack?" the bouncer asked.

Rolling his eyes, Emory took his bag off his shoulder and opened it.

The guard peered in, saw his book, and frowned. "What's with the book?"

"I thought I'd get some light reading done tonight."

The bouncer smirked but let him pass. Irritated, Emory closed his bag and slung it back over his shoulder. Nightclubs were his least favorite date spots. *Who came up with the idea of cramming a bunch of sweaty, sex-crazed humans into a tight space then overloading their senses with blaring music and flashing lights? Madness.*

By the time he found Blair, she was standing at a tall cocktail table with a double shot of whiskey. She waved and draped her furry coat over a barstool. "I'm trying to warm up!" she shouted over the music. She raised her glass. "Do you want some?"

His eyes drifted down the front of her plunging halter top. It looked like a dinner napkin masquerading as a shirt. No wonder she was cold. "No. I never drink after other people."

She swallowed a large gulp. "You don't want my girlie cooties. Is that it?"

"Something like that." Emory scanned the dance floor, searching for Darion and Hana.

"Will you dance with me?" Blair asked.

"Absolutely not."

"Come on!" She slinked closer to him and pinched his side. "You know you want to."

Emory shifted out of her reach. "We don't have all night!"

She laughed and readjusted her top. "I'm sorry. I'll be serious now."

"Get moving."

Blair downed the rest of her drink then danced her way across the main floor, weaving between throngs of partiers. Bright lights flashed in a dizzying array of colors, and the music pulsed, overwhelming Emory's senses. He crossed into the Enarine realm to get away from the noise.

An indigo-blue aura immediately caught his attention. The man's lecherous eyes were fixed on Blair's backside. A fickle heart *and* a pervert. A man who had no intention of committing to a long-term relationship with Blair was a waste of his time.

Emory climbed onto the cocktail table so he could see over the crowd. He loaded his bow with a titanium arrow and shot the pervert in the heart. Without pausing, he reloaded twice to shoot two women standing near the guy.

The first woman stepped in front of the pervert and asked if he wanted a drink. Startled, the man stepped back, and her friend jumped forward, insisting he join them. The man flashed a cocky smile, wrapped an arm around each of their shoulders, and went with them to the bar.

Emory searched for Blair in the crowd and spotted her just as a man engulfed in a cloudy-orange aura approached her from behind and reached for her hips. *Shameful.* The man was already in a committed relationship.

Emory opened fire on an uncoordinated woman to Blair's left. The woman whirled around and caught sight of the would-be adulterer. Mistaking his proximity for interest, she grabbed the man's arm and shimmied against him. Emory fired again. The melodious hum of his arrow drowned out the muffled music from the Earth realm. The man pulled his new interest closer, and the awkward couple moved across the floor.

Emory caught sight of a handsome gentleman surrounded by a bright-yellow aura—unattached and open to a relationship. The man even had halfway-decent control over his limbs. When the guy glanced over at Blair, Emory shot him in the chest. As Yellow Aura moved toward Blair, Emory followed so he could hear the conversation.

Yellow Aura tapped Blair on the shoulder. "You're a good dancer!" he yelled over the loud music.

Blair turned to him and smiled. "Thanks!"

"And you're really pretty!"

"Thanks!"

"Are you with anyone?"

She raised her left hand and wiggled her bare fingers. "I'm single!"

He leaned closer. "Can we continue this shouting match at the bar?"

She smiled and followed him off the dance floor. The music was deafening, but they found a secluded corner away from the blaring speakers.

Satisfied, Emory turned his attention back to Darion and Hana. Emory was scheduled to meet with his supervisor and one of the board members in the morning. It was imperative for Darion and Hana's date to go well to help solidify their bond and secure his client list.

Still in the Enarine realm, Emory made his way up a narrow flight of stairs to the second floor. He spotted Darion and Hana sitting on an armless velvet couch in the VIP section of the club. The loud music that pulsed throughout the rest of the club barely reached the private lounge. Hana's dark-violet hair was swept back into a sleek ponytail, exposing a tattoo on her neck. Her silky blouse was fastened at the back by a zipper that ran the length of the garment, and her black leather pants drew attention to her long, slender legs.

Darion stroked the back of Hana's neck with his finger. "What does your tattoo mean?"

"*Haengbog*. It means 'happiness' in Korean."

"Oh yeah? Are you fluent?"

"Yes." Hana sipped her pomegranate martini. "When I was growing up, it was the only language my parents would speak at home."

Darion seemed impressed. "Did they like the tattoo?"

Hana gave him a faint smile. "They got used to it."

"I think it's beautiful." Darion lightly traced the bold characters. "But why is it in such a hidden spot, where you can't see it?"

Hana shrugged and looked away. "It doesn't mean anything. Just a spur-of-the-moment decision."

He grinned and leaned closer to whisper, "I think I'm dating a rebel."

She let out a soft laugh, almost spilling her drink.

Emory couldn't have asked for a more affable pair. Couples on their second or third dates were usually nervous and tense, but these two were already quite comfortable with each other. He was about to leave and check on Blair's status when a woman entered the lounge and made a beeline for the couple.

"Darion Bishop?" The woman had stuffed herself into a shimmery gold tube dress that was two sizes too small, and her dark make-up had been applied with a heavy hand.

Darion's smile faded as he looked up at her. "Hello, Kaylin."

"How have you been?" Kaylin's shrill voice could be heard throughout the lounge.

"Fine." Darion's expression was blank. "How are you?"

Kaylin wedged herself between them, nudging Hana aside. Emory yanked an arrow from his quiver. *Better to be prepared.*

"I've been great," Kaylin said cheerfully. "How are Tyrone and Dominic doing? I bet they're getting so big."

"My nephews are fine." Darion gestured to Hana. "Kaylin, this is Hana, my date." His tone was emphatic.

Kaylin gave a shallow smile. "So nice to meet you."

A waitress approached and handed Darion a pint of beer. Emory paced in front of them. Kaylin clearly wasn't going to leave of her own accord, but Darion drank in silence. His client obviously had an aversion to confrontation.

Hana leaned forward to look at Darion. "How do you two know each other?"

"Our families have been friends for—"

Kaylin interrupted. "We used to hook up."

Darion closed his eyes and shook his head. He put his beer on the small side table.

Kaylin patted Hana's arm. "Not to worry. He made it clear there would never be anything serious between us. And that was a long time ago. Right, Darion?"

Darion glared at her. Emory glared at Darion. He needed his client to show some assertiveness. His arrows would have a limited effect on Darion if he had unresolved feelings for another woman, and they certainly wouldn't be able to soften Hana's heart if she lost respect for him.

"The last time I saw you..." Kaylin crossed her legs, lightly swiping her foot against Darion's shin. "Was it two months ago or three?"

"Four," Darion replied through clenched teeth.

"I'm so absentminded. You're right. It was June, when we were at your sister's house." She looked Hana up and down. "I see your tastes have changed since then."

Hana drank the rest of her cocktail and rose from the couch. "Excuse me."

Darion jumped up to follow her, but Kaylin grabbed his arm. "Let her go. Let's catch up."

Darion looked toward the door, but Hana was already out of sight. He sank back down on the couch. Emory clenched his bow and stayed behind. Shooting Hana in such a heightened state would only serve to confuse her feelings for Darion. He couldn't risk her mistaking jealousy for love.

Kaylin leaned across Darion, making sure to brush her chest against him, and picked up his beer. She took a sip. "She seemed nice."

"Why do you always do this?" Darion asked. "I don't want to be with you, Kay."

She waved dismissively. "You say that, but you always come back to me."

"I'm serious. There's nothing between us anymore."

"So you admit there *was* something?"

"In the past, I thought we might work well together because our families are close." He sighed. "But it's different now."

She clenched the beer glass tighter. "You'd rather be with her?"

"Yes."

"Why?"

Emory shot him in the heart with a silver arrow. He needed Darion to express his true feelings and remove all hope of reconciliation.

"Because... what I feel with her, I never did with you."

Kaylin tossed the remaining beer in Darion's face and slammed the glass down on the cocktail table. The frothy liquid dripped down his thin goatee and into his lap as Kaylin stormed off.

Darion picked up a napkin and wiped the beer from his face. "And because you're crazy," he muttered as he got up and headed in the direction Hana had gone.

Emory hurried past Darion, moved down the stairs, and found Hana trying to maneuver around the feral dancers on the first floor. Emory did a quick visual sweep of the lower level in search of Blair and her new suitor. He couldn't find her. Without her radiant aura, it was nearly impossible to keep track of her.

Frustrated, Emory materialized in the Earth realm. The bass vibrated through his body, and he pretended to dance in a jerky offbeat way. It was harder than it looked. When Hana crossed his path, he flung his arms out, knocking her small purse out of her hands. Hana scrambled to retrieve it.

Darion got to it first. "Please, don't leave!"

Scowling, she grabbed her purse from him. "You already have someone you can go home with."

"I'm sorry about Kaylin. We ended on bad terms, and there were hurt feelings. But that has nothing to do with you and me."

"I can't have that kind of negative energy in my life. I have enough issues as it is."

Emory crossed back into the Enarine realm and nocked a silver arrow.

Darion moved in front of her. "Hana, I want to be with you and only you."

Her gaze was fixed on the floor. "Why?"

"Because you're not like anyone I've ever met." He tilted her chin up and looked into her eyes. "And I want to get to know everything about you."

Emory let the arrow fly. It slammed into Hana's chest and pulsed bright red with the beating of her heart before disappearing.

"How many ex-girlfriends will I have to contend with?" she asked.

"It's a short list. And I promise I'll be the one contending with them, not you." Darion extended his hand. Hana smiled and took it.

Emory lowered his bow and watched the couple ascend the narrow stairs. He caught sight of Kaylin and shook his head. Her interference had almost cost him an important account. He kept a watchful eye on her until she settled back with her friends. Her deep-red aura morphed into the purple hue of unrequited love.

With Hana and Darion secure, Emory turned his mind back to Blair. Since he couldn't search for her aura, he looked for her new suitor's. He spotted the guy at the bar, talking to another woman. He frowned. His arrows never wore off *that* fast. After twenty minutes, he was certain she wasn't on the dance floor or in the lounge. There was only one place he hadn't checked. He moved through the Enarine realm and came upon a long line of women waiting for the ladies' room.

He entered the small single-occupancy restroom. A dim yellow light flickered overhead, and drops of water plunked into a sink that looked as though it hadn't been cleaned in months. Random DJ flyers and club programs hid the burgundy paint chipping off the grungy walls, and wads of toilet paper littered the cramped space.

Blair sat fully clothed on the toilet seat, watching videos on her phone.

"Get off that disgusting toilet," Emory said.

Blair startled. "Boundaries, Emory!"

He snatched the phone and looked at the screen. "I'm out there trying to find you a suitable mate, and you're in here watching *The X-Files*?"

"I'm already on episode twelve of season five." She stood up and grabbed her phone. "Have you seen it?"

"What happened to the man I sent you?"

"He lost interest." She straightened her short skirt.

"Impossible. A man with an aura that bright should have lasted a solid hour."

She shrugged. "Maybe it was because I showed him a picture of my nieces, and he assumed I had toddlers at home."

"You don't have children. You don't even have a pet." Emory glared at her. "You can barely keep your houseplants alive."

"He doesn't know that."

Emory threw his hands up. "You're impossible to work with."

"To be honest, I thought this was going to be fun, but it's exhausting meeting attractive men day in and day out."

"What is wrong with you? You were never like this before."

"What was I like before?"

He shook his head. "Easy."

Blair's lips pressed together, and he realized "easy" probably wasn't a good thing to call a human female. She yanked her furry coat from the silver hook on the wall.

"I didn't mean it like that!" he said, staying between her and the door.

"I don't care how you meant it."

"I'm sorry." Emory made a mental note to think before speaking in the future. He wasn't used to dealing with his clients in person. "I shouldn't have said that."

"Why are you so surprised I'm not connecting with anyone?" She shoved her arms through her coat sleeves. "You did this to me!"

"I realize I botched your case," he said softly. "But I need you to be open to finding love, or your heart will never mend."

"How am I supposed to do that when I can't feel anything?"

"I have no idea. I've been a matchmaker for almost twelve years, but I've never dealt with a broken heart."

"Well, then, what do the other love gods do in these situations?"

Emory didn't want to think about it. He'd never imagined he would be in such dire straits. "A Vycrin who breaks a human's heart and can't remedy it... gets banished to a foreign realm."

Blair sighed. "We can talk about this later."

He moved out of the way so she could open the door. The angry women waiting in line looked at them in disgust.

"It's not what you think," Emory said as he followed Blair out. "She's not even my girlfriend."

Several of the women gasped, while others flashed them disapproving glances. Blair winked at them and laced her cold fingers with Emory's. She led him down the cramped hallway, away from the irritated mob.

Nothing had gone according to plan. Emory decided that setting up a match for Blair in such an environment was the wrong approach. She needed a more intimate setting, where she could have a genuine conversation and get to know someone at her own pace.

When they exited the noisy club, she asked, "How did it go with your coffee shop couple?"

Emory's hand was starting to go numb, but he didn't let go. He sensed contentment and happiness in her. "They're stable."

"Nice. Since you're off work, do you want to grab dinner?"

He glanced at his watch. "It's almost three in the morning."

"You're right." She linked her arm with his. "Let's hit a diner and get a jump on breakfast."

CHAPTER 6

Emory hated going into the office, but he especially hated going in on a Saturday. It was a reminder that matchmaking was a never-ending job—although, he had to admit, staying out with Blair all night had been an exciting way to start the weekend. He'd completely lost track of time. The only downside was the fact that her report was bleak. In the two weeks Emory had been working with her, Blair had already rejected seven suitors.

When the elevator doors opened onto the twelfth floor, he quickly ran his fingers through his hair and straightened his leather jacket. He hadn't been able to make it home in time to shower and shave, but he thought he was fairly presentable. *Fairly.*

He entered the small waiting room and approached the secretary. "I'm here for my meeting."

"Please have a seat, Emory," the young woman said without looking up from her computer. "They'll be with you shortly."

Emory dropped his backpack and slumped down on the narrow leather couch a few feet away.

The secretary dialed a number on her phone. "He's here," she said in a cryptic tone.

Emory glared at the wispy blonde and reached for one of the magazines lining the glass coffee table. He paused. They were all bridal magazines. He sat back in disgruntled silence.

Petros burst through double glass doors on the opposite end of the room. "You're late," he said gruffly.

"Sorry." Emory got to his feet and followed his supervisor back through the doors and down the hall.

"Remember, this is just a preliminary meeting." Petros fumbled with the buttons on his suit jacket. "There's nothing to be nervous about."

Emory yawned. "I'm not nervous."

Petros opened a door on the right, and they entered a small conference room. At the end of a table stood a statuesque woman in a tailored white pantsuit with a patterned silk scarf draped around her slender neck. Her fair skin had a neutral tone. So did her expression.

"Good of you to join us, Emory." She placed her teacup on the table. "I'm Themis. I will be overseeing your audit and managing the proceedings."

Petros moved to stand beside her. "Have a seat, my boy."

Emory plopped down in the chair across from them. He flinched. The furniture was unreasonably hard.

"As you know," Themis said, "Petros has been assigned to manage your personal assessment. We thought it would be best to meet with you privately in preparation for your entrance conference in March, when we will be evaluating your performance. Today, we would just like to get a general idea of where you stand with your current clients."

Emory reached into his backpack. "I have my documentation."

Petros clapped his hands together. "Excellent!" He gave Themis a nod. "I told you he was ready."

Emory handed Themis a manila folder. She flipped it open, and a thin piece of paper slipped out onto the mahogany table.

"That's it?" she asked.

Emory swore he saw Petros's thick eyebrows touch, and he sat up straighter. "That's everything I've compiled about my clients so far. I will no doubt have more in the coming months."

Themis flashed him a skeptical glance and slipped on a pair of pink reading glasses. She read through his handwritten notes in silence. Emory grabbed a pen from his bag and began twirling it between his fingers under the table.

After several minutes, Themis looked up at him. "Seven clients? Your approved caseload is eight."

Emory shifted slightly. "At the time I secured one of my clients, there were no suitable individuals to match her with."

"You took her as a solo client?"

"Yes." Emory wanted to take off his jacket, but his long-sleeved shirt was sweaty from the club.

"The girl's aura was very strong," Petros chimed in. "Emory was confident he could find her an acceptable partner."

Themis put a star next to Blair's name. "Yet she is still single."

"What?" Petros leaned over to inspect Emory's notes then glowered at Emory across the conference room table. "Explain yourself."

Emory clutched the pen tightly. "She was in a relationship for a year. However, her partner recently terminated their union." For some reason, he felt awkward discussing Blair's personal affairs. He reminded himself that she was just another human—nothing special.

"Why did the gentleman end their relationship?" Themis asked.

Emory blinked. He hadn't given the breakup any thought since the night it had happened. "She wasn't his type."

Themis removed her glasses. "I believe the objective was for you, her matchmaker, to find someone who was *her* type." She turned to Petros. "Am I missing something here?"

Petros shook his head. "No, ma'am."

"Um... what I meant was, Blair could do better."

Themis put her glasses back on and wrote something in the margin. "She certainly could."

Petros cleared his throat. "Emory will make sure that securing a steady match for the young lady is his top priority. In the meantime, he also has six other promising clients."

Themis peered down at the paper. "It says here that Laith and Karina have been together for... eight years?"

"It will be nine in December," Emory added.

"That's not helping your case," Petros muttered.

Themis circled their names. "What seems to be the problem?"

"I believe they're—" Emory put a hand over his mouth and faked a cough to stall for time. "Well, lately, they've been... I mean, there is still love between them."

Themis gave Petros a questioning look.

Petros nodded. "Emory will be working much more closely with them in the coming months."

Emory leaned forward and pointed at his notes. "I've also recently secured two younger clients."

"College students," Themis said flatly. "I suppose that's a start."

"A budding romance." Petros smiled. "And finally, he has a promising new couple that were matched at a coffee shop."

Emory rested his clenched hands on the table. "They've already been on two very successful dates."

Themis flipped the paper over. The other side was blank. "I wouldn't know anything about that because it's not in your client's file."

Emory's cheeks burned. "I—"

"As I said, this is just a preliminary hearing to assess your current status." Themis folded the paper in half and stood. "Thank you, gentlemen." She left the conference room without so much as a glance behind her.

Petros yanked his suit jacket so hard Emory feared the buttons would pop off. "We'll continue this in my office." He got up and led the way out of the room.

One of the advantages of being Vycrin in an office building *full* of Vycrin was the fact that cameras were forbidden, and as a general rule, everyone remained in the Earth realm. Eavesdropping was considered very bad form. For that reason, supervisors spent a great deal of their time shouting at their subordinates in the privacy of the Enarine realm.

In his office, Petros walked behind his desk, but instead of sitting, he started pacing. "A sheet of paper with the names of your clients written on it is not documentation!"

Emory took a seat in one of the two chairs across from the desk. "I wasn't aware my notes were supposed to be that detailed." He put his quiver between his knees, but he resisted the urge to twirl one of his arrows. Petros hated that.

"You're under investigation, and you're running around here like you're footloose and fancy-free. And what are you wearing? You look like you just got out of a club!"

Emory kept his mouth shut. Seven hours ago, he'd been watching Blair dance. Four hours ago, he ate pancakes with her at a diner. Two hours ago, he carried her up three flights of stairs to her apartment because of her poor choices in footwear. One hour ago, he rushed out of her apartment after she'd convinced him to stay and watch an episode of *Stranger Things*. None of that needed to be in her report.

"I'll wear a suit next time," Emory said.

"That's the *least* of your problems!"

There was a loud knock at the door, and Petros phased into the Earth realm. "Come in!"

Still hidden in the Enarine realm, Emory scowled when his cousin entered the room.

"Here are the files you asked for," Argus said, crossing the room to hold them out to Petros.

"Leave them on my desk," Petros said. "I'm in the middle of a meeting."

Argus placed the folders on the corner of the desk. He glanced at the visitor chairs. Though he couldn't possibly see Emory through the thin veil separating the two realms, he flashed a sly smile before exiting the room.

Petros snatched up the folders and crossed back into the Enarine realm to continue his tirade. "And I thought I told you to seal an engagement for that Blair girl!"

Emory's back stiffened. "They were incompatible."

Petros pounded his fist against his desk. "Boy!"

"It was completely my fault. She wouldn't have been happy with him in the long run. I made a mistake."

Petros yanked his pink handkerchief out of his pocket and wiped his brow. "Well, that's the first sensible thing that's come out of your mouth all day. What's your plan?"

"I'm in the process of conducting extensive research on my client to determine who would make a suitable match."

Petros unbuttoned his suit jacket and finally sat down. "She's been your client for five years, and you still don't know her preferences?"

Emory swiped his fingers across the arrows in his quiver. "She's always been very open to new relationships and experiences, but she's never been consistent."

"Fortunately for you, she has an aura as brilliant as the sun. An engagement for her should be a cakewalk."

Nothing with Blair is a cakewalk. "I need to tell you something. Off the record." Emory gripped his quiver and swallowed hard. His usual methods for selecting a suitable partner for Blair had failed. Miserably. He was no closer to finding her the perfect man than the day they'd met up at the coffee shop. His inexperience was going to be his downfall. "I accidentally broke Blair's heart."

All the color drained from Petros's face. "You're certain of this?"

"My arrows don't work on her."

"She just went through a difficult breakup." Petros opened one of the folders and started flipping through the papers. "It's not a common defense mechanism, but your arrows should be able to weaken the barrier after a couple of weeks."

Emory hung his head and whispered, "Her aura is gone."

Petros scribbled across the top of the paper. "That could mean any number of things. So, the girl's not entirely open to a relationship, but—"

"I touched her." Emory raised his head and looked Petros in the eye. "Her skin feels like ice. It's unnatural."

Petros pushed the documents aside. He rose from his chair, walked over to the large corner window, and stared down at the bustling city. Emory had thought the yelling was bad, but the silence was worse. The room felt heavy.

"You bled the love out of her heart," Petros muttered.

"What should I do?"

"We have to contain this." Petros spun around. "What does she know? How much did you tell her?"

"I told her who I am and what I do, but she doesn't understand the magnitude of the situation. And I only told her about my arrows being deflected."

"Good. Don't reveal anything else about her condition." Petros loosened his tie. "If she knows you can sense her deepest emotions just by touching her, she'll always have her guard up, and it will be even harder for you to break down the barrier surrounding her heart."

"I think I can gain her trust."

Petros's expression hardened. "Nothing superficial. It won't hold."

"I don't intend to entrance her." Emory huffed. "I can make a genuine connection with a human."

"Make sure you do. If she trusts you and feels you're doing everything in her best interests, then she'll be more inclined to open her heart to someone new."

Emory sighed. "But the board will eventually find out."

"Of course they will. That's their job. But if we can show that you're on track, that Blair's heart is starting to mend, then you have a fighting chance."

Emory rubbed his eyes, which burned from lack of sleep. "She is so difficult to work with."

"Have you crossed into the Thiyden realm recently?"

Emory's stomach turned. "No. It's been years."

Petros's gaze was distant. "Vycrin who live in worlds without love eventually lose their souls."

Emory stood, picked up his quiver, and headed for the door. "I can handle her."

CHAPTER 7

Emory stifled a yawn. He and Blair had been out late four weekends in a row. He'd never worked so hard in his life, but Petros's words kept echoing in his mind. Despite his renewed determination, Blair seemed more and more disconnected. He needed a better plan and decided it would be best to start working with her alone, without the distractions of his other clients.

Blair's small cubicle isolated her from the normal office commotion, and she spent most of her day alternating between the eight-by-ten-foot space and the break room. He didn't know how she could stand squinting at a bright monitor day after day, analyzing data. His head hurt just watching her. She swayed to the music playing into her headphones and clattered away on her keyboard.

Emory materialized in the swivel chair next to her desk. "We need to talk."

Blair jumped back, and he wondered if all humans were so skittish. She yanked off her headphones and stood to pop her head over the cubicle wall. He was quite adept at making swift departures and wasn't overly concerned with being spotted by her coworkers.

"What are you doing here?" she whispered, sitting back down. "You shouldn't be following me to work."

"Our current strategy isn't working." Emory picked up a Catwoman figurine from the small toys lining her desk.

"What strategy?"

Emory rocked back in the chair, bouncing one knee. "Exactly my point."

"I thought things were going well."

He poked her in the arm with the toy. "You've had twelve promising suitors, and not a single one asked you for a second date."

She sighed. "I didn't have anything in common with them."

He smiled. "That's why I thought we'd try an office romance."

"Are you insane? I work with these people. I don't want to see them outside of the office."

"We'll find someone from a different department. Maybe someone in advertising or sales."

She shook her head. "This is a bad idea."

One of her coworkers approached the cubicle, and Emory dropped the toy, retreating into the Enarine realm.

"Blair?"

She spun around. "Brent, you scared me."

"Who were you talking to?" Brent asked, peeking around the cubicle wall.

The man's blinding-yellow aura turned ultraviolet when his eyes fell upon Blair. Emory jumped up and grabbed his bow from across his chest.

"No one," she said casually. "Sometimes I talk to myself when I'm bored."

"I do the same thing."

Brent sat down in the chair Emory had recently vacated. His round cheeks and conservative cropped haircut gave him a boyish appearance, but his bright-purple aura said so much more about him. Emory gaped. *Unrequited love.* Brent had a hopeless crush on Blair.

Blair smiled politely. "What brings you to the fifth floor?"

He picked up the Catwoman figurine from the floor and put it on her desk. "I just got out of a budget meeting."

"That sounds exciting."

"It's not as exciting as marketing. You look like you're having a blast."

Blair laughed, and Emory couldn't believe his good fortune. He should have *started* the search for her perfect man at her job. They had something in common, and the foundation for a friendship was already solidified through mutual experiences. Upon reflection, the most logical place to seek a mate was the workplace.

Emory drew a titanium arrow from his quiver and shot the lovesick man in the heart. The arrow pulsed fire red then disappeared.

Brent leaned forward to rest an arm on her desk. "Do you want to grab some coffee with me?"

"I think the cafeteria's closed." She glanced at the lower right corner of her screen. "It's already four thirty."

"What about the break room?"

"I still have a report I need to finish before I leave today."

"Stop making excuses!" Emory shouted at her from the Enarine realm, wishing he had telepathic abilities. "Brent was practically handed to us on a platter!"

The familiar glint in the man's eye meant the arrow was already taking effect. He would be difficult to dissuade.

"Fifteen minutes?"

Blair locked her computer. "No more than fifteen." She grabbed her blazer from the back of her chair, slipped it on over her silk blouse, and buttoned it.

Following them down the hall, Emory noticed a slight metallic shimmer in Brent's aura. He blinked, and the anomaly disappeared. He shifted. It was probably his imagination. Things were finally lining up for them, and he couldn't allow paranoia to overtake him. Blair kept a respectable distance from Brent when they passed a coworker, and he wondered if *her* paranoia was taking hold as well. They would both have to get a grip. There was nothing wrong with Brent, and an office romance would survive petty rumors if they formed a solid union. Brent held the break-room door open for her.

A round table with three small metal-and-plastic chairs occupied the cramped space. He found a full container of French roast in a cabinet, and she set up the coffee maker.

"How do you like yours?" he asked, scooping out a hefty tablespoon of coffee grounds.

"Strong."

Emory hovered in the corner of the room. He had another appointment later that evening, but if the *mini date* went according to plan, he would consider adding Brent to his client list. Securing a steady partner for Blair would show the committee how seriously he was taking the audit, and a full roster would prove he could handle his allotted caseload.

"How long have you worked here?" Brent asked.

"Three years."

"I've been here five."

She grabbed a handful of sugar packets. "They just converted our 401(k)s."

Brent perked up. "I think it's a better retirement strategy."

"I wouldn't know. I cashed mine out last year to pay for a new wardrobe."

His jaw dropped, and Emory held his breath.

She grinned. "I'm kidding. It was to pay off the credit card I used to buy the new wardrobe."

Brent stared at her with a concerned look, then he chuckled. "You almost had me," he said, wagging his finger at her.

She smiled, and Emory let out a sigh. There was no need to elaborate on her disastrous personal finances.

Brent filled two foam cups with the fresh brew, set their coffees on the table, and slid out her chair. She took a seat, and he settled into the one across from her. Emory leaned against the counter behind them. They both looked like they were struggling to fill the agonizing silence.

Blair stacked five sugar packets together, tore them open, and dumped them into her cup. Emory was grateful that Brent was smart enough not to comment on her sugar consumption. Blair hated when men felt the need to point out the health risks of her diet. He'd made that mistake at the diner when he tactlessly asked how much syrup she needed for one pancake. The answer was three. Three containers. Then she politely let him know what he could do with the rest of his opinions.

"So, what frivolous things do you spend your money on?" Blair asked.

"I'm a saver."

Blair flashed Brent a devious grin. "Not a single guilty pleasure?"

He twisted his cup around. "Just one. Ham radio."

Blair blinked. "Is that some sort of gourmet station?"

"No, I'm a licensed amateur radio operator," he said with a chuckle. "In fact, I built a Morse code transmitter last weekend for fun."

"You know Morse code?" Blair placed her coffee on the table. "Can you teach me something?"

The fact that he'd piqued her curiosity was a good sign, but Brent was still fidgeting with his cup. Emory slowly removed another arrow.

Brent's voice was shaky. "Like what?"

"My name."

Brent reached across the table and took her hand. He held her index finger and tapped the letters of her name in Morse code. "B. L. A. I. R."

"Impressive."

Emory aimed at Brent's heart. He needed to smother the man's nerves so he would be bold enough to ask Blair out on a real date. The titanium arrow slammed into Brent's chest, fluttered and twitched, then vanished into oblivion. Emory stepped back. He'd never seen such an unusual reaction.

Brent intertwined Blair's fingers with his and continued holding her hand.

She flashed a weak smile, withdrew her hand, and stood. "I'd better get back to work."

She picked up her cup and stuffed it into the overflowing garbage bin. When she turned toward the door, Brent was standing in her path. His violet aura shimmered with a metallic sheen. Emory's mind was racing. He'd never dealt with a human enflamed with passion as a result of his arrows, and he had no idea how to counter the effects. Blair stepped back.

He moved forward, reached out, and stroked her cheek. "We've worked together for three years, and I've never worked up the courage to tell you how pretty you are."

She stepped back again, and her butt hit the counter. "I don't think it's a good idea to—"

Brent suddenly lowered his head and pressed his lips against hers, sliding his hands down her hips. Emory gasped.

Blair shoved Brent. "Get away from me!"

He stumbled backward, looking dazed and horrified. "I'm sorry! I—"

"I told you this was a bad idea!" she yelled into the air at Emory. She charged out of the break room.

Brent staggered forward, but Emory materialized in front of him with his arms across his chest. Brent halted and blinked in surprise. Emory dilated his pupils as he caught Brent's gaze, and he channeled his anger to intensify the entrancement. Brent's eyes were vacant.

Emory kept his voice low. "Don't you ever put your hands on Blair again, do you understand me?"

There was a slight nod.

"Now, go sit in a corner by yourself, and don't move." Emory blinked hard, releasing his power over the man, then crossed back into the Enarine realm.

Brent pulled out a chair and sat staring at the wall blankly. Emory rushed out of the break room and searched for Blair. He found her in the bathroom, hunched over the sink. Her whole body was shaking.

Emory swallowed back his guilt and crossed into the Earth realm. "That was a complete miscalculation on my part."

Blair spun around. "Are you trying to add a sexual harassment suit to your list of liabilities?"

Emory ran his trembling fingers through his hair. "I may have used one too many arrows."

"Obviously!" She turned on the faucet and splashed water on her face. "Do you realize how fast gossip spreads around here? It's hard enough to get them to take any of my ideas seriously. I don't need a bad reputation overshadowing my work."

"I'm sorry." He started pacing. "I thought I'd give him some encouragement since he seemed a little shy."

Blair dried her face with a paper towel. "You always overdo it."

He shook his head. "I knew his aura was a little metallic, but I didn't realize he was *that* horny. I just thought—"

She glowered at him in the mirror.

He raised his hands. "Okay. I'm sorry. I can't let you go back out there until my arrows wear off."

"How long will that take?"

The entrancement was strong enough to hold for two hours, but erring on the side of caution, he replied, "Two hours and nine minutes."

"What?"

He took off his backpack. "I'll use an arrow to jam the lock. No one will be able to get in or out for at least two hours."

She clenched her fists. "I'm under a deadline, Emory! If I don't get my report done tonight, it will throw off the timetable for the entire project."

"You don't have a choice. He's too unpredictable in his current state." He fiddled with his watch. "I'd offer to keep you company, but I can't stay. Amir is taking Joey to a football game tonight." He shook his head. "Mondays." He walked to the door then turned. "Do you want me to bring you a snack?"

Blair hurled a basket of paper towels at him. He darted into the Enarine realm before it reached him. He retrieved a silver arrow from his quiver as he exited the bathroom and examined the simple metal lock. His client was furious with him, and rightly so, but there was nothing else he could do. He clenched the arrow and slammed the sharp tip into the lock. It remained in place, protruding out of the door.

Emory headed down the hall toward the exit. Blair was safe, but the entire incident could have been avoided if he hadn't been so determined to impress the audit committee by increasing his roster. He hadn't just ruined a potential romantic relationship for Blair—he'd destroyed an office friendship. Themis had chastised him for failing to keep Blair's emotional well-being his first priority, and now he was going to leave her locked in a bathroom for the next two hours and eight minutes. Alone.

Emory stopped short. He was her matchmaker—it was his responsibility to protect her. He returned to the ladies' room, removed his bow and quiver, and sat by the door. Amir and Joey would have to wait.

• • ❧ • •

TWO HOURS AND SEVEN minutes later, Emory jumped to his feet when Blair cracked the bathroom door and peeked through the small opening. It was well after six, and almost everyone had gone home. He slung his quiver and bow over his stiff shoulder. She slowly opened the door the rest of the way and headed down the narrow corridor. Emory stayed close behind her in the Enarine realm. When she turned the corner to go back to her office, she almost bumped right into Brent. Sweat beaded up on his forehead, and his wide eyes were glassy.

"Blair, please forgive me." The remorse on his face was palpable. "I have no idea what came over me. It was all so sudden."

She swerved around him and hurried to her desk. Emory followed her through the maze of empty cubicles, not surprised to find Brent trailing them at a distance. The lighting was dim, and the cleaning crews were busy at the other end of the room. Emory took the seat next to Blair's desk. She plopped down in her chair and moved her mouse to wake up her computer as Brent stood just outside her cubicle and stared at her.

"I'm not going to report you or anything," she said without turning around.

"I'm so sorry," Brent whispered.

Emory swallowed hard. Things between them would never go back to normal, and it was his fault.

"That was completely out of character. It's rare that I even talk to women, let alone..." Brent sighed. "Do you think we could start over?"

"Brent, you're interesting, pleasant to be around, and have the cutest smile I've ever seen." She spun around to face him. "Under normal circumstances, just one of those traits would be enough for me, but right now, my situation is complicated."

He nodded. "I understand."

Blair turned back at her computer screen. "The coffee part was nice, though." She started flipping through a legal pad. "I'll see you tomorrow, Brent."

He finally left, and Blair was able to continue working undisturbed. A few minutes later, Emory heard her stomach growl. He got up and crossed into the Earth realm.

"I secured items for you from the vending machine." Emory flipped open his backpack and dumped a bag full of candy and chips onto her desk. "Just to hold you over until the Chinese food gets here."

"What are you still doing here?" she demanded.

"I wanted to apologize for disrupting your workday." He cleared his throat. "And for putting you in a harmful situation."

An icy silence fell between them. Blair tore open a bag of salt-and-vinegar chips and popped one into her mouth. "Sit."

Emory took off his leather jacket and sat in the chair beside her as she unwrapped a Snickers bar. He lined the chips in a neat row along her desk then did the same with the chocolate bars and candy until everything was organized according to size. He had purchased all of her favorite snacks—or so he thought.

"What's with the granola bars?" Blair asked.

"I assumed you liked them. I saw you buy one once."

"No, that was a mistake." Blair took a large bite out of her candy. "I wasn't paying attention, and I accidentally pressed the wrong button."

Emory stacked the nutritional bars and put them in his backpack. "Noted."

"Do you have a Red Bull?"

He reached into his backpack, pulled out a can, and slid it over to her. "I bought you two because I wasn't sure how long we would be here tonight."

"Smart man." Blair chugged the entire thing and tossed the empty container into her trash can. "I thought you had a football game to go to."

"I realized my priorities were out of alignment."

She ripped open a Cheez-It bag and started munching on the small crackers. "You've been sitting here all this time, watching me?"

"*Guarding* you."

"That's even creepier," she teased.

"I'm sorry for what I did to you today." He gently took her cold hand and held it over his heart. "I promise I'll never let anything like that happen to you again."

Blair looked deeply into his eyes, and he dropped his guard. Raw emotions radiated from his heart as he attempted to link with her. Forming such a connection with another Vycrin was effortless—only a touch was required. But with her, his efforts yielded nothing. Just as he was about to draw back, he felt her reaching out for comfort. He clung to her faint emotions and in his heart reaffirmed his determination to keep her safe. A warm feeling spread through his body as they shared a mutual bond of trust. Their connection was strong, and for the first time, he could sense her feelings toward *him*. Blair hadn't needed him to come back. She would have worked through the night alone. But he was there, and that meant something to her.

"I forgive you," she said softly. She pulled her hand away, breaking their link.

Emory suddenly felt dizzy and adrift. He closed his heart and mind, focusing only on what was physically in front of him to regain his bearings. Blair turned back to her computer, and he quickly gathered the plastic candy wrappers.

"So, you're my new guardian?" she said.

"Just until we find you a better replacement. Preferably someone you *don't* work with."

She smiled. "Preferably."

CHAPTER 8

"What exactly are you supposed to be?" Emory asked. "A homeless fairy?"

Blair adjusted her long silk skirt as they walked along a dirt path. The translucent wings strapped to her bodice glistened in the sunlight when she moved. Emory never knew what to expect with her.

"I did the best I could under the circumstances," she said. "You didn't give me very much notice."

"I wasn't aware *you* would be in costume."

"Why? Because I'm Black?" she asked sarcastically.

He frowned. "No. Because I've never been to a renaissance festival. What does your pigmentation have to do with dressing like a woodland creature?"

"Oh, sorry," she said with a chuckle. "People make asinine comments like that to me all the time."

Emory shook his head. "Humans choose the strangest details to fixate on." For some reason, he was unable to take his eyes off her. "How do you make it flare out like that?" He lifted her green skirt to reveal overlapping layers of floral fabric underneath. He grabbed a handful of the cotton material. "Did you destroy your bedsheets?"

Blair yanked her skirt out of his hands. "I had to make do with what I had."

The sweet smell of roasting nuts filled the cool air as knights practiced sparring behind broad fences. A drunken pirate bumped into Emory then shuffled out of the way with a mumbled apology.

"What are you in the mood for today?" he asked.

"Someone quirky."

"That shouldn't be a problem here."

"And turkey legs." Blair made a slight detour off the path.

Emory sighed. Her stomach was an ongoing source of irritation in his life. She counted down to every meal yet insisted on a steady flow of snacks. Then she would complain about the stubborn twelve pounds she was unable to shed. It was phantom weight, in his opinion, but he still had to listen to her grouse.

Medieval-style building facades lined the curving trail, where costumed vendors offered an assortment of cured meats, fresh baked bread bowls, and roasted corn on the cob. Blair found the shortest line for food.

"We don't have time for this," Emory grumbled.

"But I skipped brunch with my girlfriends to work on my costume, and you refused to stop on the way here, so—"

He raised a hand. "Stop whining and hurry up."

"Did you find your clients yet?"

"They're watching the jester's routine."

Blair opened a small gold pouch and paid the vendor. "They get along so well."

"For now," Emory said, distracted. New couples were always nerve-racking due to their unstable nature. One negative exchange or thoughtless gesture could stifle the flame of love and shatter a relationship. He couldn't afford to reduce his client list. Themis had made that clear.

Blair bit into the steaming turkey leg. "Do you want some?"

"With your saliva on it?" He shuddered. "No, thank you."

She rolled her eyes and took another bite. "Will you relax?"

"I can't match you with anyone while you're stuffing food into your mouth like a savage animal."

Blair stood on her toes and took an obscenely large bite in Emory's face. He snatched the hot turkey leg out of her hands and threw it in the trash.

"Emory!" The meat in her mouth muffled her outraged voice.

He handed her a napkin. "Enjoy your pub crawl."

"My what?" Blair wiped her hands.

Without responding, Emory crossed into the Enarine realm. He had to be alert. Her knight was coming. Earlier, while Blair was buying her ticket, he'd been scouting potential suitors. Three patrons behind her stood a man dressed in chainmail. His yellow aura was so bright it almost burned Emory's eyes. When the knight caught sight of Blair, Emory shot him in the heart. Blair had been so preoccupied with her costume that she hadn't noticed the nervous gentleman who was trying to work up the courage to talk to her, but Emory was certain they would make a good match. They already had one hobby in common.

Emory fired another arrow at the potential suitor to shore up his confidence.

The knight finally approached Blair. "Hello. I'm a lonely knight looking for a fairy to join me on a pub crawl."

She swallowed the last of the turkey and smiled. "I'm the fairy for you."

Emory lowered his bow. His arrows would help the knight overlook Blair's flaws for at least the first hour. She needed all the help she could get. He headed to the jester's circle and arrived before the show ended.

Amir and Joey were sitting on one of the long wooden benches set up for the audience. Like Blair, they were clad in strange costumes. Emory perched on the stage to get a clear view of his clients. A man in a colorful jester's suit danced past him, unaware of his presence, the bells on his hat jingling.

Joey's hand was on the bench between them, while Amir's hands were folded in his lap. Emory pitied the young man. He obviously wasn't picking up on Joey's body language. Emory stood up and shot Amir in the heart.

Amir's eyes shifted down. He inched one hand off his lap and laid it on top of hers. Joey curled her fingers around his hand and smiled. Emory sat back down, satisfied. It was going to be an easy day.

The show came to an end, and the crowd broke into enthusiastic applause. Emory followed his clients, who walked hand in hand as they exited the makeshift theater. The hem of Joey's pale-blue dress swept across the dry ground, and a dainty metal belt dangled from her hips. Long bell sleeves fell by her sides, overwhelming her small frame. Amir was dressed in a green hooded shirt, a brown vest, and pants that were entirely too tight. Emory appreciated his gauntlet gloves, which seemed practical for archery practice.

"Did you know court jesters in medieval times were actually highly educated?" Joey asked. "They were allowed to speak openly and even criticize the monarch, and they used humor to help navigate tricky affairs of the state and ease tensions."

"Really?" Amir said. "I didn't know that."

Joey leaned her head against Amir's arm.

Emory hadn't known that about court jesters either. Joey was a repository of random information and obscure facts. Emory decided he would share that interesting tidbit with Blair after her date.

"Bambi!"

Amir and Joey turned around.

"Not today," Emory grumbled. So much for his easy afternoon.

Three gangly young men approached. Their clothes were disheveled, and they reeked of beer.

"Guys! You made it!" Amir greeted the new arrivals with elaborate handshakes for each. He turned to Joey, who looked confused. "These are my friends." He put his arm around her. "I invited them so they could meet you."

Emory approved. His client was showing a willingness to incorporate Joey into his personal life. That was progress.

Amir pointed at the shortest member of the group, a stocky young man who kept both hands in his pockets. "That's Pyro."

Pyro bobbed his head. He clearly wasn't one for talking.

Amir moved his finger to indicate the next guy. "That's Duke."

"Nice to meet you." Duke removed his baseball cap and bowed. His long blond hair flopped over his face.

Amir gestured to his jittery friend, who had a pick sticking out of his perfectly rounded Afro. "And that's Trigger."

Trigger looked from Amir to Joey then back to Amir. "This is the girl?"

Amir beamed. "Yes, this is Joey."

She gave them a weak smile. "What are your real names?"

They exchanged glances, and Duke stepped forward. "I'm sorry, that was a lot to take in at once. I'm Duke, that's Trigger, he's Pyro, and"—Duke wrapped an arm around Amir's neck—"this skinny jackass is Bambi!"

Emory knew that their *real* real names were Fredrick, Jimar, and Carlos. He preferred the nicknames.

Pyro stepped back, eying Amir up and down. "What in the—what are you wearing, man?"

Amir puffed out his chest a little. "I'm Robin Hood."

Trigger laughed. "Nice tights." He turned to Joey. "And who are you supposed to be?"

"It's obvious. She's Maid Marian," Duke said. "Who else would be with Robin Hood?"

"Where did you get those costumes?" Pyro asked.

"I made them," Joey said through clenched teeth.

Emory pulled out an arrow. He could ease some of Joey's tension, but he needed her to associate the positive feelings with Amir's actions. The timing had to be perfect.

"She's got crazy sewing skills," Amir said proudly.

"Nice! That means my girlfriend will love her," Duke said. "The women can get all artsy-craftsy together."

Trigger clapped his hands. "Where are we off to next?"

"We?" Joey squeaked.

Amir brought his hood up over his head. "We're heading to the jousting competition."

"Jousting!" his three friends shouted in unison.

Duke bowed low in front of Joey. "Please lead the way, my lady."

Joey and Amir headed down the path. The guys trailed a few yards behind them, laughing and joking. Emory walked next to them, twirling an arrow.

Amir leaned down. "Well? What do you think?"

"About what?"

"Bambi!" Pyro called out. "What are you two whispering about?"

Joey frowned. "Why do they call you that?"

Amir shrugged. "It's just a nickname."

Duke caught up, maneuvered between them, and wrapped his arms around their shoulders. He was lopsided due to their height difference, but he didn't seem to mind. He grinned at Joey. "Did he tell you the two of us have been friends since elementary school?"

She flinched, most likely because of his beer breath. "No. He's never mentioned you."

Duke laughed. "I'm not surprised. He's a quiet guy." He backed off and rejoined the other two.

The group strolled through the marketplace, pausing occasionally at merchant stalls so Joey could examine the unique handmade jewelry and intricate costumes. The three boys made a collective decision to attend the next festival as pirates. Emory found it fitting. They were already drunk and disorderly. All they needed were eye patches. They might have interrupted a romantic encounter between his clients, but Emory had no intention of manipulating events to force them to leave. Amir's friends were an integral part of his life, and he would need to learn how to balance his relationships with them and with his new girlfriend.

The guys suddenly veered into one of the merchant booths and started rummaging through aisles of women's clothing. Trigger grabbed a purple bodice and tried it on. The other two broke into wild laughter. Joey blushed and pulled Amir back onto the path.

Emory could only take so much. He wondered if Blair was anywhere nearby. She was always a good distraction, even if he could only watch her with a new suitor. He hoped she was having a better time than he was.

Twenty minutes later, Joey was able to rally the loud group to the artisan village, where skilled craftsmen demonstrated glassblowing, candle-making, and blacksmithing techniques. The rustic smell of leather permeated the air. Joey kept silent as the boys darted between vendors, not staying long enough at any one of them to really take in the informative expositions. Emory ground his teeth. They had the collective attention span of a gnat.

After twenty minutes, Joey cleared her throat and tugged on Amir's shirtsleeve. "The jousting?"

"Oh. Yeah." Amir called to his friends, "Guys, we need to take Joey to the jousting place."

She yanked her unwieldy skirt up to her knees and quickly led the way, choosing a route with the fewest distractions. When they reached the clearing, the jousting tournament was already in progress. Long wooden benches were arranged on a hill overlooking the dusty stadium. Amir and his friends rushed to find empty seats while Joey remained below. The guys weaved through the crowds, apologizing to the costumed fairgoers they trampled in their haste.

"Up here, Joey!" Amir called down from the top row.

Joey took her time climbing to the seat. Emory followed her then reclined on the steps as she plopped down next to Amir.

On the field below, two fighters faced each other on horseback. Metal helmets hid their faces, but they wore different colors to represent their respective teams. The one to the left was dressed in blue and yellow, and his opponent waved a purple-and-black flag on his side.

"Are you okay?" Amir asked.

Joey stared down at the jousters. "I'm fine."

"You don't seem fine."

The fighters charged forward with their lances outstretched. The sound of clashing metal filled the air as the fighters collided. Amir's friends cheered. The blue-and-yellow rider skewed to the side, almost falling from his horse. He reached the opposite end of the track and readjusted his stance.

Emory wondered if there would be another show. Jousting seemed like the sort of thing Blair would enjoy, but he didn't see her anywhere in the audience. The jousters lined up again.

"I didn't realize I'd be on display," Joey said.

"You're not on display," Amir replied. "I wanted my friends to meet you."

"It's interesting—you don't seem anything like them."

He frowned. "Really?"

She shrugged.

The blue-and-yellow rider jabbed his opponent in the chest with his lance, and the purple knight tumbled from his horse. He hit the ground with a thud, and the crowd jumped to their feet, applauding wildly. Amir and Joey were the only people who remained seated.

"Did you see that?" Trigger shouted.

Pyro pumped his fist. "That was amazing!"

Duke punched Amir in the arm. "You two aren't even watching."

Joey rose from her seat and clapped. Amir followed suit. Neither said a word. The crowd began filtering out of the stands.

"Where to next?" Trigger asked.

Joey sighed. "I guess we can try some of the games."

The group headed through the festival grounds, the guys searching for booths where they could test their strength and agility. Joey fanned her face with one hand. Emory shot Amir in the heart. He needed his client to be more attentive to Joey's needs.

"Are you feeling all right?" Amir asked.

Her shoulders slumped. "Maybe we should sit down and let them go on ahead of us."

Amir led her to a nearby bench. "Guys," he called out, "Joey isn't feeling well."

The trio jogged over to the bench.

"Did you eat something that made you sick?" Duke asked.

"No, I—"

"I'll get you a bottle of water," Trigger said.

"No, that's not necess—"

Trigger was out of sight before she could finish her sentence.

"You need some shade. I'll find a seat," Pyro declared. He wasted little time securing a picnic table under a shady spot.

Amir led Joey to the table, keeping an arm around her waist. She sat down, and he perched next to her. Trigger returned with a cold bottle of water.

She took it from him with a weak smile. "Thank you." She took a few swallows and seemed to perk up a little. She looked up at Trigger. "How long have you and Amir been friends?"

"Forever! I think like five years. Or it may be four. It could be two."

"We met three years ago playing paintball," Amir clarified. "We used to go every weekend, and one day, we ran into this nut. He was all over the place."

"No one could catch him except Pyro, who's stealthy," Duke said. "When we team up, we're unstoppable."

She turned to Amir. "Why does everyone in the group have a cool nickname except you?"

The others broke into laughter, but Amir didn't flinch. "It's dumb," he replied.

"It's because as soon as he's around a girl he likes, he freezes like a deer in headlights," Duke said with a laugh.

Trigger chuckled. "He can't make a move to save his life."

Emory supposed Joey would still have been just a crush if he hadn't encouraged the young man to take action.

"This time, I did," Amir said. "I asked Joey out, didn't I?"

"And he's been a perfect gentleman," she added.

After a couple of seconds, Duke laughed harder. "He hasn't even kissed you, has he?"

Joey shook her head, her wavy curls tumbling over her face and hiding her eyes.

"Dump the loser!" Trigger said.

Pyro added, "You can do better."

Amir slammed his fist against the wooden table. "Ten dollars says I'll kiss her right now!"

Joey jumped a little then smirked. "Ten says you won't... Bambi."

"Ooh!" his friends said in unison. "Kiss her! Kiss her! Kiss her!" They pounded the table as they chanted.

Amir hesitated. Emory shot him in the heart.

Amir cupped Joey's face in his hands and leaned in for the kiss. His tongue brushed against hers as he devoured her. Emory shot Joey in the back, stabbing her heart and intensifying the longing she already felt for Amir. She melted against her suitor.

Amir pulled back and gazed into Joey's eyes, ignoring his friends' cheering in the background. Joey opened her mouth as if about to speak, but nothing came out. Smiling and flushed, she reached into her bodice and pulled out a ten-dollar bill. He brushed it away and kissed her again.

Duke slid off the picnic bench. "We'll leave you two lovebirds alone."

"Meet us at the fire-juggling act when you're done sucking her face," Pyro said with a smirk.

"But I want to watch!" Trigger jokingly protested.

Duke punched him in the arm, and they both laughed. The loud entourage left the enamored couple alone on the picnic bench.

Amir searched Joey's face. "What do you think of my friends?"

A smile crept across her lips. "I love them."

Emory positioned his bow across his chest, pleased with the turn of events. His youngest clients had proven to be even easier to manage than he'd anticipated. Both exhibited true emotional growth. All that remained was ensuring that Blair was getting along with her knight.

He walked through the festival in search of her. He finally spotted Blair's frayed fairy wings in a secluded area near the rock-climbing wall. There was no sign of her new suitor. Just as he reached her, she staggered into a tree trunk.

Emory frowned and phased into the Earth realm. "Are you drunk?"

Blair gave him a droopy-eyed stare. "I knew you'd find me." She grabbed the lapels of his leather jacket. "You have to get me out of here."

Emory propped her up in his arms. "What's wrong with you?"

She burped. "I just had five beers on an empty stomach."

"But they don't even give people a full serving during those pub crawls."

She swayed. "My knight thought he was being chivalrous by giving me his portions."

"That was *very* chivalrous. Where is the good man now?"

She pointed into the air then covered her mouth. "I'm going to be sick."

"Blair?" someone called.

Emory caught sight of the persistent knight a few yards away. There would be little hope of a second date if the gentleman saw her in such a wretched state. He grabbed Blair by the waist and slipped his love token into her hand. They quickly crossed realms. Her body seized up in pain, but she didn't make a sound. The knight drifted past them in slow motion.

Emory looked down at her. "Are you okay?"

She dropped to her knees and vomited. He decided he'd made the right choice. The vomiting was an instant turnoff.

He stared up at the sky. "Let it all out."

"You're useless." She threw the copper coin at him, and he caught it with one hand.

"I'd offer to summon my healer for you, but Selene can't exactly cure a hangover." He knelt and helped her pull off the cumbersome wings. He rubbed her icy back. "Good girl. You didn't even ruin your costume."

She moaned and crawled across his lap. "I want to go home."

The poor woman looked downright pitiful. Her dark-green dress was spotted with dirt, and her skin glistened with sweat—but not in an attractive way. He massaged her back with gentle strokes, and every now and then, she let out a nauseated groan. After a few minutes, the cold emanating from her body became too much for him to bear, and he clenched his hand in a fist, trying to regain feeling in his fingers.

"You know," Emory said, "you were right in the middle of a very promising date."

She pushed herself up to a sitting position, though she still listed a bit to the side. "I'm not going back out there."

Seeing her drunkenness coupled with the effects of crossing over, he had little doubt that she felt as miserable as she appeared. He almost experienced a twinge of guilt for suggesting she continue the date. *Almost.*

"Look how sad you'll make that man if you just disappear," Emory said.

Blair glanced over at the considerate knight who was still searching for her. "It doesn't matter. It wasn't a good match. We didn't click."

"I'm positive he likes you. My arrows have already worn off."

Blair climbed to her feet. "Well, go shoot a princess for him to fall in love with."

Emory watched the distraught knight walk past them with his head down. He was headed for the exit. "It seems like such a waste."

She sighed. "My entire body hurts, I have a headache, I can't focus—"

"Those are mostly side effects from crossing ov—"

"And I'm hungry!"

Emory fell silent, knowing how bad-tempered she could become when her blood sugar dropped. He should have let her finish the turkey leg. "I'm sorry." Three or four dates would at least look like some sort of progress on his report, but he could barely get her through one. "I'd just hate for you to miss an opportunity to get to know someone who's interested in you."

"I don't care. I'm going home." She tottered down the narrow path toward the exit.

"Shake it off, Blair! You have a date to finish."

"Forget it, you luna—"

He sprinted after her, slammed into her frozen back, and threw her off her feet. They shared a brief connection, and a wave of her nausea came over him. He gagged. Blair clawed at the air, struggling to catch her breath as she crossed realms. She landed in a haystack right behind her unsuspecting suitor.

The knight turned at the sound of her gasping and rushed over to her. "Are you all right, Blair? What happened?"

"I'm okay," she said as he helped her up. "I just tripped and fell."

"When I couldn't find you, I assumed you weren't coming back."

She shook her head. Strands of dried grass protruded from her thick black hair. "Apparently, I'm going to finish this date if it kills me."

Emory fought through his lingering queasiness and readjusted his bow across his chest. They were *both* going to get through the date, no matter how uncomfortable they were.

"Are you hungry?" the knight asked.

Blair yanked some straw out of her hair and glared over her shoulder. "Starving."

Emory was okay with Blair being mad at him. He was used to it. But he would never get used to her body. He rubbed his hands together and blew into them. The frost was too much.

CHAPTER 9

Emory was surprised that the brisk weather did little to deter the throngs of people gathered for the fall car show. Enthusiasts proudly displayed their collections of vintage automobiles, custom trucks, and muscle cars. Even Blair seemed excited about the event as they trailed his clients in the Enarine realm.

A stiff breeze swept up Karina's long hair and tossed it back in her face. She grumbled something about Laith's obsession with motor vehicles. Laith held her hand as he led her through the vehicles, searching up and down each row. The dainty heels of her boots clattered against the pavement as she tried to keep up. Emory feared their relationship was stagnating. They needed to make some sort of forward progress.

Laith stopped in front of a pristine red Corvette Stingray. He turned to Karina. "What do you think?"

She glanced inside the sports car but didn't appear impressed. "It's all right," she said after a prolonged pause.

"All right?" He gestured at the leather interior. "It's perfection."

"The man has incredible taste," Blair said to Emory.

"That's the type of car you would buy?" he asked.

Blair laughed. "Of course not! It's too fancy."

Emory had trouble following her logic. She was the epitome of a contradiction.

"There's no back seat," Karina said. "Where's a baby supposed to go?"

"In the trunk. With your mother." Laith let out a hearty chuckle. When he saw that she was not amused, he immediately sobered.

Karina let go of his hand and circled the vehicle. "It's a bit out of your budget."

"Not if I sell my car and use the money as a down payment."

"I think you have more important things to be saving for. Like a ring."

"Babe, I've bought you at least six rings since we've been together," Laith said dryly. "You're going to run out of fingers soon."

Blair nudged Emory. "I'd take the car over an engagement ring any day."

"That's a lie," he said.

She narrowed her eyes. "Just because you've watched me for years doesn't mean you know everything about me."

"I know more than you think."

Blair climbed onto the trunk of the Corvette and sat with her feet dangling over the end. "Where do my parents live?"

"Virginia Beach. They spend most of their time traveling and don't visit as often as they'd like, but neither do you. Your family overcompensates for the physical distance by sending an insane amount of group text messages so everyone still feels connected."

She grinned. "What's my mother's maiden name?"

"Waymon."

"What's my favorite flower?"

Emory hesitated. Blair got excited every single time she received flowers from one of her suitors. There was no pattern. "You don't have one," he said finally.

"You got one wrong!" Blair exclaimed with delight. She jumped off the car. "You'd better do some more research."

Emory tried not to appear as rattled as he was. He knew her favorite food. He knew her favorite drink. He even knew her favorite outfit, the one with all the frills and lace. Flowers should have been easy.

"I don't understand why you have to rush everything," Laith said.

"I'm not trying to rush you." Karina took his hand again and rubbed his arm. "We already bought the house, and I feel like this is the next step for us."

Emory recalled one of Blair's dates three years back. Her suitor had arranged a romantic picnic in a field, and he'd handpicked wild flowers for her. She had practically swooned. "Daisies."

Blair smirked. "Guess again."

"Maybe it feels like the next step for you," Laith said. "But what you're talking about is a major decision."

Greg had been too cheap to buy Blair anything other than grocery-store flowers, but she'd always proudly displayed them on her desk at work. "Carnations."

"I'm really disappointed in you," Blair said.

Karina said, "I know it's a big decision. It's life changing. I just thought that by now you would know if you wanted to be with me."

Emory knew Blair prided herself on being complicated. No doubt her favorite flower was something obscure. "Marigolds."

"Not even close," Blair replied.

Laith stared into the convertible. "To be honest, I don't know what I want anymore."

Karina's face fell. She sniffed and wiped away a single tear.

Laith sighed. "Don't start, Karina."

"Wait! What just happened?" Emory cried.

"Laith isn't ready to get married, and he's questioning their entire relationship," Blair said. "Pay attention, Emory."

He grabbed his bow from across his chest and yanked a silver arrow out of his quiver.

Karina swiped at another tear. "Eight years, and you still can't figure out if you want to be with me?"

"Do you really want to have this conversation here?" Laith asked. "Can't I enjoy one day doing something I like?"

Karina glared at him. "Enjoy your stupid cars by yourself, then." She turned and strode away.

Laith rushed after her. "Karina, don't go! I'm sorry!"

Emory raised his bow and aimed at Karina's heart. He could stop her, just as he'd done every time they had an argument. *They fight, they run, they make up.* But if he shot either of his clients in their current emotional state, it would only perpetuate the cycle. Emory needed them to be in calm, rational frames of mind to truly work out their differences, or there would be no chance of them moving forward as a couple.

Blair tapped Emory on the shoulder. "Shouldn't you do something?"

"I need you to stop distracting me," Emory said through his teeth. He lowered his bow. "Lilies."

She put her hands on her hips. "I hope you're better at this game with your other lady friends."

He shoved the arrow back into his quiver. "Why do you assume I ever sent flowers to any of my girlfriends?"

"That's not very romantic."

"I'm not about *romance*." Neither were his girlfriends. That was why his relationships worked. For a while. Then they became monotonous.

"Were all your girlfriends love gods too?"

He inhaled sharply. "It's unprofessional for me to discuss my personal affairs with a client."

"You inserted yourself into *my* life, and now I'm not allowed to ask you any questions?"

Emory hated when she was right. "You can ask me five questions."

"Just five?"

"Four."

Blair bit her lower lip. "Are Vycrin allowed to date humans? What were your girlfriends like? Can I play with your bow and arrows? Do you really not know my favorite flower?"

"We can date any species. Love is love. Wayward and unruly. Absolutely not." He paused. "Gardenias?"

She shook her head. "Shameful."

"I guess I'll have to think harder."

"Yep." She stood on her toes and scanned the crowd. "In the meantime, shouldn't you be more concerned about your other clients?"

"Yes." Emory swiped his leg into the back of her knees and threw her off her feet. Blair yelped. Her back hit the hard pavement, and she was knocked back into the Earth realm. Guilt pricked his conscience. He'd been a coward, sparing himself the discomfort of connecting with her. He swore never to do that again. If she was going to continue to accompany him on assignments, the least he could do was figure out how to make crossing over less unpleasant.

Emory switched realms and stood over her. "Are you all right?"

Blair stared up at him, gasping for air. "I didn't enjoy that at all."

"Neither did I." Emory helped her up and brushed gravel off the back of her coat. "I'll slam you onto the hood of a car next time."

She coughed. "Such a gentleman."

"I try." He offered his arm and escorted her through the maze of vehicles to the sleek new sports cars.

Blair let go to circle around a white car with blue lightning stripes down the center of the hood. "Mustangs are my favorite."

Emory didn't think her smile could get any bigger. "Why Mustangs?"

"My first car was a Ford Pinto. It had a rusted-out roof and a twitchy clutch—you know, real character. I feel like my adult car should be a Mustang."

"Is that a prerequisite for your perfect man?"

"That's a good point. Yes, make sure he has a sports car."

"Noted. I've got to do some damage control before Laith and Karina get out of hand." Emory crossed realms and looked around until he spotted a young man sporting a comical graphic T-shirt. His aura was strong, but he seemed little young for Blair. However, the slender man drooling over the same Mustang appeared to be closer in age.

"Send me someone fun," Blair said into the air as she began buttoning her double-breasted jacket. "And I don't know this area of Baltimore very well, so let me know the best places to go for dinner."

Slim glanced over at Blair, and Emory shot him in the heart. He moved closer and stood next to her.

"Hi," Slim said.

"Hello." Blair flashed a smile. "I'm sorry. I thought my friend was there."

The man's shoulders slumped. "Too bad. I thought you were asking me to dinner."

"Well, I can't very well ask you out without knowing your name."

He held out his hand. "Rodney."

"I'm Blair." While shaking his hand, she glanced over his shoulder. "Where are Rodney's friends?"

"Rodney doesn't have any friends," he said flatly.

She looked skeptical. "And why is that?"

"Because Rodney talks in the third person." He cracked a smile and winked.

Blair laughed. "I see."

"Do you want to check out the rat rods together? Or will your friend get mad at me?"

"My friend won't mind at all. He's imaginary."

Emory shot Rodney a second time. The man's yellow aura was faint, and Emory needed Blair occupied for at least an hour so he could handle the situation with Laith and Karina. He left Blair to her new interest and found his troubled couple near the exit to the parking lot.

"I'm sorry, Karina," Laith said. "I didn't mean to upset you." He placed a hand on her shoulder.

Emory prepared to take aim at her heart and waited for the couple to reach a more equitable state, but Karina wouldn't meet Laith's eyes.

"I don't understand why we keep going in circles," she said.

"I don't know." He rubbed the back of his neck. "The whole marriage thing freaks me out."

"So what am I supposed to do?"

"You need to be patient. This isn't easy for me. I told you from the beginning that I wasn't big on marriage."

"Neither was I, but I don't feel that way anymore."

"I realize that, but we can't just push ahead if we're not on the same page, right?"

Emory was tired of excuses. At the very least, Laith needed to reaffirm his commitment to Karina. He shot Laith in the heart.

"One thing I *am* certain of is that I love you."

Karina wrapped her hand around his. "I love you too."

"Please be patient with me." He kissed her cheek.

Emory refrained from shooting another arrow at Laith. Flooding his client with overwhelming emotions would only incite rash behavior. He would just have to wait for Laith to sort out his feelings.

"How about this," Laith said. "After we finish up with the import cars, I'll take you out for sushi?"

"But you hate sushi."

"I know, but you love sushi." He kissed her again. "Fair enough?"

She rested her head on his shoulder but said nothing.

They walked back into the main show area hand in hand, but there was a strange tension between them. Emory dilated his pupils and examined Karina's aura, searching through her with unfiltered eyes. Twisted around her ruby aura was a thin murky black thread—cold, detached apathy. Emory's stomach turned. He'd spent so much time working on Laith that he'd failed to gauge Karina's true feelings for her boyfriend. The dark haze surrounding her said it all. She was falling out of love with him. If timed poorly, his arrows would have an opposite effect on her heart. Love would turn to hate.

"Do they do that often?"

Emory tensed at the sound of his cousin's voice. He suppressed his agitation and lifted his bow over his head. "They're having an off day."

"More like an off decade." Argus adjusted the collar of his trench coat and came up to stand beside Emory.

"What are you doing here?"

"Working," Argus said with a condescending smile.

"They promoted you to field agent?"

Argus popped his gum.

"That's fitting," Emory said. Field agents were known for meddling in the affairs of others—all in the name of research.

"You're my first assignment," Argus said. "I noticed you're working three clients at once."

"You're very perceptive."

"It seems as though your single female has trouble committing to a relationship."

"She's particular."

Argus pulled out a notebook, flipped a few pages, and wrote something in it. "Is her situation manageable?"

"If I can't find some lovesick fool to propose to her in time, I'll marry her myself," Emory said sarcastically. "Problem solved."

"Is that your official strategy?" Argus said with false good humor. "Because I'm trying to compile an accurate report, and I'd hate for your actions to be misinterpreted."

Realizing he was speaking to a superior officer, Emory bit back a cutting remark. "Her situation is manageable. I'm in the process of securing her trust for the sole purpose of establishing a suitable match."

Argus scribbled in his notepad again. "Her circumstance warrants serious attention, but don't neglect your three open cases. You must prove the legitimacy of your matches and provide a detailed status report before your official meeting with the audit committee on March twentieth. Any accounts of solidarity between that quarrelsome couple would be helpful to your testimony."

"I'll try to minimize their arguments."

"Please do."

Blair strolled by, heading for a vintage Ford Model T. She was alone. Emory hoped Argus wouldn't notice, but nothing escaped his prying eyes.

Argus glanced at his watch. "She almost made it thirty minutes that time."

Emory ground his teeth. "She has difficulty maintaining interest in potential mates."

"Her broken heart might have something to do with that."

"She... I..."

Argus raised one eyebrow. "That was just a guess, but thank you for the confirmation." He slipped his notebook back into his coat pocket. "Which reminds me, how's your father?"

Emory clenched his fists. "Ask your mother."

"She hasn't heard from him."

"What makes you think I have? And what difference does it make to you?"

Argus shrugged.

"Are we done here?" Emory asked.

"For now, cousin." Argus dusted off the sleeves of his trench coat and started to walk away. He stopped short and turned around.

"Please send your father my warmest regards. If you see him." Argus gave him a lazy salute and crossed out of Enarine.

Emory's entire body shook with rage as he materialized into the Earth realm. Someone tapped him on the shoulder, and he spun around to see Blair standing there. "What do you want?"

"I'm sorry," Blair said, stepping back. "I was going to ask if you wanted to see the muscle cars."

"No."

"What's wrong?"

"Nothing."

Blair looked at the ground. "I probably shouldn't have told Rodney that I was just getting out of a messy divorce. That's not something to joke about."

"I don't care about him."

She frowned. "Then what are you mad about?"

"None of your business."

She walked over to a small mobile vending cart and ordered two hot chocolates. After paying for the drinks, she went to sit on an empty bench a few yards away. Emory ground his teeth and reluctantly joined her. She handed him one of the Styrofoam cups then took a sip from hers.

After a few minutes, she said, "This could use more sug—"

"My father was banished for doing exactly what I did to you." Emory drank the entire contents of his cup without looking at her. "Except that the damage was permanent."

"You didn't cause me any permanent damage," she said softly. "At least, I don't think so."

Not yet. He stared down at the dying grass beneath his feet. "The audit committee already has your broken heart on record."

"How do you know?"

"My cousin just informed me."

Blair twisted around to look at the crowd.

"He's gone," Emory said. "He only came to gloat about being assigned to my case."

"Isn't that a good thing? He's part of your family, so won't he go easy on you?"

Emory sighed. "His mother was on the disciplinary committee that banished my father to the Thiyden realm, a chaotic world without rules or restrictions. Some Vycrin choose to live there purely to escape the confines of our society, but those who are forced into exile are barred from returning to the Earth realm."

She twisted her cup around in her hands. "Were you and your dad close?"

He couldn't remember the last time he'd spoken openly about his father. "We were, yes."

"You're not able to visit him?"

"No. I promised him I would never go back. It wasn't a good environment for me." He scraped the sides of the cup with his thumbnail. "That's why this audit is so important. And your fickleness isn't helping our situation."

Her eyes widened. "What did I do?"

"You couldn't even stay with Rodney for an hour. That looks bad for both of us."

"I wasn't interested in him."

"He was interested in you."

"Because of you!"

Emory threw his hands up. "You still don't understand how this works?"

"I realize you're frustrated, but it's not as though you've taken this seriously."

"I've sent you countless suitors, and you've rejected all of them."

"That's because you don't put any thought into the type of man I might be interested in. You just shoot the closest single man in my vicinity." She waved her hand around as if to include the entire crowd. "You don't even try."

"How am I supposed to know who's a good match for you?"

"That's your job, Emory!"

He crumpled his empty cup. "I'm not the sort of Vycrin who can read minds."

"How long have you been watching me?"

He sighed. "Five years."

"And what do I like?"

He glared at her. "Fast cars, cheap wine, and attractive men."

"What do I *like*?"

He thought about that for a couple of minutes. "You like people who are kindhearted and considerate. You like men who are strong-willed and decisive but not overbearing." He stared into her dark eyes. "And you want someone deeply loyal to you."

Blair patted him on the knee. "Find him." She took his mangled drink container, got up, and threw their cups in a nearby trash can. She looked back at him. "What should we get for dinner?"

"Anything but sushi."

CHAPTER 10

The bowling alley boomed with music while colorful images flickered across the overhead monitors. Emory was sitting in the Enarine realm, observing his two clients.

When eight pins fell, Darion clapped. "Nice job!"

"Thanks!" Hana joined him on the stiff orange couch.

"I thought you said you were bad at bowling." He nudged her. "You're beating me by ten points!"

"Are you sure you're not just letting me win?"

"No way!" Darion got up and grabbed his ball. "I'm too competitive." He threw the heavy ball down the lane and knocked down nine pins.

Hana applauded. "You're catching up."

"Trying. I can't let a girl beat me."

Emory checked his watch, expecting hours to have passed, but it had only been thirty minutes. Blair was six lanes over with her suitor. He fought the urge to go over there. Darion and Hana's file was so scant that he feared the audit committee would accuse him of neglecting their case. He needed something to pad their report.

A young girl in the next lane reached into the ball return to pick up her purple ball. Darion's bowling ball rolled out of the chute, and the young man grabbed the girl's hand.

"Be careful, sweetie," Darion said. "You almost got hurt."

Startled, she stepped back. Darion picked up the purple ball and handed it to her.

"Thank you," she said, taking the ball with both hands.

Her mother came over and placed her hands on the young girl's shoulders. "I told you not to stick your hands in there!"

"I'm sorry," the girl said.

Darion grabbed his ball. "No worries. Go ahead and take your turn."

After the girl bowled, Darion knocked down his last pin for the spare. He raised his hands and danced back to the couch.

"That was sweet of you," Hana said. "I probably wouldn't have noticed, and her little fingers would have gotten squished. I'm terrible with kids."

"I don't believe you." Darion lifted her chin with his finger. "You're too perfect." He gently kissed her lips.

Emory laid his quiver and bow on the seat and got up to stretch. He raised his arms over his head and wandered over to the ball shoot. He was half-tempted to stick his head inside. Anything for a little excitement. He sauntered down the gutter lane.

"Trust me," Hana said with a chuckle as she lined up with her green bowling ball. "I couldn't even keep a babysitting job as a teenager."

"You just need practice," he said.

She released the ball, and it flew into the gutter.

Darion's eyes widened. "That's the first time that happened tonight. And in the tenth frame too. Sorry, babe."

She shook out her hands and waited for the ball to return. "No amount of practice will compensate for motherly instincts."

Hana's second attempt started to roll too far to the left. The subtle magnetic force of Emory's presence in the Enarine realm repelled the ball and pushed it back into the center of the lane. Nine pins toppled over. Hana squealed and jumped up and down.

After congratulating her, Darion grabbed his ball and positioned himself in front of the lane. "My niece and nephews are going to love you." He bowled a perfect strike, and the monitors lit up to play victory music.

"Nice shot!" She brushed her hair out of her face. "You want me to meet your family?"

"Of course I do." His second throw knocked down nine of the pins, then he picked up the spare to finish the game. "How about some food?"

Hana agreed, and they went to the snack bar to order. Emory decided to slowly count the arrows in his quiver while they ate. That would kill at least two minutes. A low wall separated the tables from the lanes and provided players a place to dine.

When they returned with their food, Darion pulled out a metal chair for Hana. "Dinner is served."

"This is all so fancy." She dipped a fried mozzarella stick in tomato sauce.

"Just wait until you see what I have planned for dessert."

She raised one eyebrow. "There's more?"

He leaned closer and lowered his voice. "Baskin Robbins."

"Someone had better put a stop to your wild spending."

"What can I say?" He shoved a loaded nacho into his mouth. "I like to show ladies a good time."

Hana giggled. "If you keep spoiling me like this, I won't want to go out with any other guys."

He caught her eyes. "How do you say 'good' in Korean?"

She sipped her soda and met his stare. "*Joh-ah*."

"*Joh-ah*," he repeated.

"Is that what you want?"

He shifted slightly and stroked his goatee. Emory jumped out of his seat and shot him with a silver arrow, seizing the opportunity to shore up the young man's confidence and solidify the couple's bond.

Darion reached across the table and grasped her fingers. "How do you say 'I want you to myself'?"

"*Na naul gajigo sipuh.*"

Darion repeated the phrase emphatically.

Emory fired an arrow at Hana.

She smiled. "*Joh-ah.*"

Emory lowered his bow. Their relationship was child's play compared to the ongoing conflicts he'd found himself engaged in with Laith and Karina. The status report for Darion and Hana was going to be neat and tidy.

Feeling his work there was done, he headed down to Blair's lane. He perched on one of the empty chairs as Blair picked up her ball and got ready for her turn. Checking the scoreboard, he saw that they were finishing up the ninth frame.

"Remember," her dark-haired companion said, "take your time and don't—"

She hurled the ball down the lane. The heavy orb veered to the right and rolled into the gutter. "What did you say, Kelvin?"

He shook his head. "Never mind."

She didn't bother glancing up at the scoreboard as she returned to the couch. "Your turn."

Kelvin grabbed his ball from the return. He lined up his shot, took a breath, and threw the ball down the lane. All ten pins collapsed as the heavy ball collided with them.

"You're very good," Blair said in a polite tone.

"You could be too. You just need to follow my instructions."

"Where's the fun in that?" she teased.

Before the date, Emory had encouraged Blair to try to be more open by allowing her true personality to shine through. She was actually behaving for once.

Not appearing the least bit amused, Kelvin bowled again. Three pins remained standing. When he failed to pick up the spare, he mumbled something. Blair gave a forced smile when he plopped down next to her.

He swiped at his forehead. "I think I need something to drink."

"I'll get you something." Blair jumped up. "What did you want? Soda, iced tea, beer?"

"Just water. I don't want anything to interfere with my game."

She strolled over to the snack bar. There were two lines, and Blair chose the longest one. Emory frowned, wondering if she'd done that on purpose. When she reached the front, she ordered a bottle of water and an iced tea. After handing the cashier a ten-dollar bill, she leaned against the counter to wait for her order.

Emory phased into the Earth realm and walked over to stand next to her. "How's your date going?"

"It's going great," she said flatly.

"You're having fun?"

"Yep. How's it going with Darion and Hana?"

"Same as always."

"Boring, huh?"

"It's horrible. If I didn't have you providing me with the bulk of my entertainment, I'd be forced to buy a television."

Blair raised her hand. "I'm not your personal Hulu."

"You're better. You don't cost me anything. How's Kelvin working out for you?" He and Blair looked over at Kelvin, who was practicing his bowling swing without his ball.

After a pause, she replied, "Tonight, I feel like I'm getting to know his true personality."

"He seems a little tense. Do you want me to relax him?"

"No!" She cleared her throat. "I mean, I'd like to get to know him when he's not under the influence."

He shrugged. "Give me a signal if you change your mind."

"What kind of signal?"

"I don't know. Cough twice."

The cashier passed two bottles to Blair and gave her some change. Emory crossed into the Enarine realm as Blair walked back to her lane. He sat across from them and drew a titanium arrow from his quiver, just to be prepared.

"How much do I owe you?" Kelvin asked, pulling out his wallet.

Blair waved him off. "Don't worry about it."

"I insist. How much was it?"

"Fifty dollars," she said, holding out her hand.

He frowned. "I'm serious."

"So am I," she replied with a straight face. "Cough it up."

Emory knew her game. She would take his money then make a game out of giving it back to him. With a scowl, Kelvin opened his water and took a long drink.

"So, are you ready to go?" she asked.

"We paid for two games," Kelvin said.

Blair slumped a little. "Maybe we should see if they can raise the bumpers on my turns."

Emory chuckled.

"Do you take anything seriously?" Kelvin asked.

She stared into the air as though deep in thought. "Global warming." She snapped her fingers. "And science fiction."

"Science fiction? *That's* what you take seriously?"

"Have you ever gotten into an argument with a hardcore Trekkie? You have to know your stuff, or you end up sounding like a fool."

Twirling the arrow between his fingers, Emory barked a laugh. Blair loved teasing people. Kelvin wasn't going to last long if he continued to let her get under his skin, though Emory suspected he would eventually get used to her lighthearted jesting.

Kelvin sighed. "I suppose you believe in the Force as well?"

She gave him a haughty stare. "Two different universes, Kelvin." She opened her tea and took a sip. "Have you been to any good concerts lately?"

"I hate concerts."

Blair chuckled, and iced tea sprayed from her lips, some landing on her date. She swallowed and coughed. "That wasn't the signal," she muttered.

Looking disgusted, Kelvin wiped the liquid from his face with the tail of his shirt. "What signal?"

"Nothing." She twisted the cap onto the tea so tightly the plastic cracked. "I'm sorry about that."

Emory realized there was no salvaging the date. It was a total bust. He slid the titanium arrow back into his quiver.

"I don't understand you," Kelvin said. "We got along so well the first few times we went out."

"Sorry."

"I am too." He pulled off his bowling shoes and started putting on his street ones. "I think I'm going to call it a night." He retrieved his ball and started stuffing it into his customized bag. "Do you want me to call you a taxi?"

"I'm going to play another game," she said. "I'll call my friend to take me home."

Once Kelvin cleared the area, Emory materialized behind Blair. "Well, that didn't go according to plan."

"He said he didn't like concerts. Who doesn't like concerts?"

Emory agreed. He couldn't think of a single concert he didn't enjoy, and not just for the performances—he found it amusing to watch humans go wild over other humans. "You made it two solid weeks."

Her jaw flexed. "I really was trying."

"I wasn't being sarcastic. You were fine. He just wasn't a good match for you." He went over and reset the scoreboard. "So do I start, or do you?"

"It doesn't matter. I'm terrible."

"I know." He entered their names into the system. "You'll make me look even better. Okay, since you don't care, I'll start."

Emory went to the rack and picked up a red ball. Sticking his fingers in the holes, he found it to be a good fit. Positioned behind the line, he drew back his arm the way he'd seen Kelvin do it. When he released the ball, it immediately careened toward the left gutter. He tilted his head to the right, as though trying to will the ball back to the center of the lane. The computer had little trouble tallying his score of naught.

"Hmm. Maybe I should try with my left hand."

"Are you ambidextrous?" Blair asked.

"Absolutely not." When his ball returned, he grabbed it with his left hand. He hurled the ball down the lane, and it knocked over seven pins. With a grin, he returned to his seat. "I think I figured it out. Just have fun and do anything you want."

Walking over to the ball return, Blair let out a cynical chuckle. "That's what I've been doing all night." She tossed her ball down the lane. It spun as it rolled then curved a bit to hit the front pin. All ten fell.

Blair spun and gaped at him. They both screamed at the same time. Emory gave her a high five, and their excited cheers dissolved into uncontrollable laughter.

When they had calmed a bit, Emory had another go. He got six pins but wasn't able to pick up the spare.

After some good-natured trash talk, Blair stepped up to the line and threw the ball. Eight pins went town. She flashed him two thumbs up.

Emory smiled, happy that her evening with Kelvin had failed. The man was an absolute bore, and he wasn't right for Blair on any level. She needed someone who could get beyond the playful exterior she often used to draw attention away from her true emotions. The two of them spent the remaining rounds experimenting with unusual throwing positions and encouraging each other's wild antics.

At the end of their last round, Blair plopped down next to him and started untying her bowling shoes. "That was a good game."

Emory gestured up at the screen as it tallied their final scores. "Should we get a printout?"

"No need." She picked up her cell phone and snapped a picture of the monitor. Next, leaning closer to Emory to get both of them in the frame, she took another shot.

"Did you have fun tonight?" he asked.

Blair kicked off her shoes and winked at him. "Best worst date ever."

CHAPTER 11

"What do you think of these?"

Emory tore his attention away from Joey long enough to catch a glimpse of Blair's feet. She strutted across the tile floor of the small boutique, modeling shiny red stilettos. This was the fourth store they had browsed through that afternoon. Frantic holiday shoppers crowded the expansive mall, creating a flurry of excitement. It was Emory's favorite time of year—humans went completely mad.

He sipped coffee out of a paper cup. "Are they comfortable?"

"They're so sexy."

They were. "Take them off."

Blair sighed and returned the shoes to their box. "You said I could get anything I wanted!"

"I told you I'd replace the shoes I threw out when we first met," Emory said, watching Joey from afar. "But I'm not paying for anything you can't walk in."

Blair braced herself against a long wooden bench and squeezed her feet into six-inch zebra-print heels. "Sometimes the reason to buy shoes is because they're cute," she explained. She stood and walked in front of him.

Emory barely glanced at her. "Are you trading in your career to become a prostitute?"

"No..."

"Then take them off."

She sighed, and the shoes clunked against the floor. "Where's Amir?"

"Late."

"That's not like him." Blair strapped on bright-yellow platforms and got to her feet.

Emory scowled. "I need you to attract men, not repel them."

She held her hand to her heart and slumped onto the bench, her eyes wide with false shock. "You really hurt my feelings that time."

He ignored her feigned sentiments. "Meet me at Neiman Marcus when I'm done working." Emory placed his coffee cup next to her. "You can have the rest."

She unstrapped the pleather shoes. "I only have forty minutes left for my lunch break." Blair looked up, but Emory had already crossed into the Enarine realm. She peered into his abandoned coffee cup, which was empty. She flicked it off the bench and smiled. "Jerk."

Emory smiled back and headed off to work. It didn't take him long to reach his favorite college students. He took a seat next to an ornate water fountain and watched Amir greet his girlfriend with a kiss on the cheek.

"Sorry I'm late," Amir said.

"Where were you?" Joey asked.

He sighed. "My professor insisted on meeting with me this after-noon."

Joey frowned. "Why?"

"She's worried about my grades."

Joey gave him an uneasy glance. "You said you passed all your midterms."

"I did." His voice was partially muffled by the cascading water. "For the most part."

Emory grimaced. Failing marks wouldn't reflect well on him in his audit. A relationship that negatively affected important aspects of a client's life would not lead to the couple having a lasting com-mitment.

"Should we be ditching our afternoon classes to see a double feature if your grades are slipping?" Joey asked.

"They're not slipping," Amir protested. "I'm maintaining a C in the class."

She raised her eyebrows. "You haven't been studying because we've been hanging out too much?"

"No, that has nothing to do with it." He smiled broadly. "I'm just a little behind in my studies, but don't worry. I'll make it up by the time I do my finals."

He wrapped his arm around her shoulder and escorted her to the food court. They opted for twelve-inch subs, chips, cookies, and sodas in preparation for their five-hour movie binge. They settled at one of the few empty tables in the center of the food court.

"How are the costumes coming?" Amir asked.

"I finished yours and Trigger's." Joey took a small bite of her sandwich. "Pyro's is taking me a little longer, but I have plenty of time to get it done before the convention."

Emory decided the comic book convention was definitely a rendezvous Blair should accompany him on. He would just have to make sure he gave her advanced notice. She would want to have a costume in order.

"Did you decide who you want to go as?"

Joey fidgeted with her straw. "Not yet."

"You'd be perfect as Poison Ivy."

Her shoulders dropped. "But will I be the only one dressed as a plant?"

Amir laughed. "It's a character from *Batman*."

"Oh, yes, of course." Joey began to blush. She readjusted her glasses and cleared her throat. "Did you know that urushiol, the oil found in poison ivy, can stay active on just about any surface for up to five years?"

"I didn't know that," Amir said with a smile.

"It's fascinating to research. I was originally going to major in biology."

"Really?" He sounded surprised. "Were your parents mad when you switched your major to English?"

"Of course not. They just want me to be happy." Joey sipped her soda and sat quietly for a long time. "I talked to Mom and Dad yesterday. "They can't wait to meet you."

Amir bit off a large mouthful of his sandwich. "Cool."

"In fact," she continued, "they said you can stay with our family during winter break."

Amir inhaled a piece of his sandwich. The thick chunk of bread lodged in his throat. He pounded his fist against his chest as he struggled for air.

"Are you okay?" Joey exclaimed. "Can you breathe?"

Amir grabbed his throat, his eyes wide with terror.

Panic spread across Joey's face, and she jumped to her feet. "Somebody help!" she screamed.

Alarmed customers rushed over and formed a circle around Amir, but no one stepped in to help.

Emory dove into the Earth realm. "Get out of the way!" He shoved stunned bystanders aside then tore off his backpack, dragged Amir to his feet from behind, and wrapped his arms around the lanky man's waist.

Joey broke into a fit of hysteria. "Help him!"

"Move back!" Emory ordered her.

She stumbled backward with tears streaming down her face. "He can't breathe!"

Emory clenched his fist and pressed both hands against Amir's upper abdomen in a quick upward movement. "Come on!" he shouted. He made a thrusting motion in the direction of Amir's windpipe again and again. "I'm not adding a choking death to my report!"

Suddenly, a solid mass flew out of Amir's mouth, and he coughed violently, slumping to the ground. Joey ran to his side, and the bystanders broke into applause.

"Are you okay?" she cried.

Emory backed away, his heart racing. *Another crisis averted.* Breathless, he scooped up his backpack and made a hasty departure, stepping back into the Enarine realm.

Amir gasped for air. "Who was that?"

"I don't know." Joey grabbed Amir's hand and searched for Emory among the crowd closing in around them. "It all happened so fast." Tears fell from her eyes and landed on his chest.

"Don't cry," he soothed. "I'm okay."

She wrapped her arms around his neck. "You scared me."

Amir breathed heavily, gulping air into his lungs.

"I didn't mean to catch you off guard," Joey whispered, clinging to him. "If you think it's too soon, I understand."

Emory shot Amir in the back. He needed to quell any anxiety the young man felt about meeting Joey's family. The silver arrow penetrated his heart.

Amir held Joey close. "I can't wait to meet your parents."

• • ❧ • •

BLAIR STROLLED THROUGH Neiman Marcus, admiring the formal wear. Emory followed behind her in the Enarine realm. His nerves were still rattled. Blair lingered on a red chiffon gown with an open back, running her fingers over the delicate fabric. She lifted it off the chrome rack and held it over her clothes, viewing it from various angles in a tall mirror.

"Did you find any shoes you like?" Emory asked.

Blair jumped back, startled. "Not yet."

"That's because you're in the wrong department." He snatched the dress out of her hands and returned it to the rack. "Focus, Blair."

She followed him to the shoe department. "You need to lay off the coffee."

"Caffeine has the opposite effect on Vycrin."

"Are you sure? You weren't this wired in the last store."

"It's not because of the coffee," Emory retorted, scanning the shelves of women's shoes. Subtle under-mount lighting cast a soft glow on the attractive displays.

"That sexy fireman is taking me to an Italian restaurant tonight." Blair's fingers brushed a row of shoes. "Are you coming?"

Masking his disappointment, he said, "Not tonight."

She spun around, her face pinched with worry. "Why not?"

"Karina is planning an anniversary dinner for Laith."

She winced in sympathy. "Oh dear."

"Exactly." Emory picked up a pointy-toed pump with red soles. He spied a saleswoman standing nearby and tapped her on the shoulder. "Can I get these in a six and a half?"

"Of course," the woman replied in a cheerful voice. She scurried away.

Blair plucked a delicate open-toed shoe from the shelf and glanced at the price. Her eyes widened, and she placed the shoe back where she'd found it. "We should go back to that last store."

"We didn't find anything there."

"I liked the red pair I tried on," she argued.

At that moment, the pleasant saleswoman returned with the black pumps and offered them to Blair. "Here you are."

"That's okay, ma'am!" Blair said with a forced, nervous smile. "We changed our minds."

Emory took the box from the saleswoman. "Sit down and try them on."

Blair bit her lower lip. "They're not really my style."

He peeked inside. "You own three pairs of shoes that look exactly like them."

"Not *exactly*."

"Just see if they're comfortable. You're always complaining your feet hurt, and I'm tired of carrying you around when we can't find a taxi."

Her eyes narrowed. "That was one time."

"And you nearly broke my back."

The saleswoman stepped to the side.

"Are you saying I'm fat?" Blair demanded.

Emory inhaled and tried not to lose his temper. "Of course not."

"Admit it. That's why you're always trying to get me to order salad."

"We both agreed we would start eating healthier after that food-truck debacle." Emory placed the box on a velvet couch. "Nobody should order every item off a menu. Nobody."

"You let me do it."

"And it cost you dearly."

"So you do think I'm f—"

"Stop deflecting and try them on!" he insisted. Her mind games drove him mad sometimes.

Blair fell silent and plopped down on the narrow sofa, glaring at him. Then she looked away, opened the box, and tried on the shoes.

"Was that so difficult?" Emory said.

Blair didn't respond. She crossed the sales floor, and he tilted his head, inspecting her as she walked. His eyes drifted down her backside.

"They make her butt look good, don't they?" he said just loud enough for the saleswoman to hear.

The woman was taken aback. "They're very flattering on her," she stammered.

"The heels are a good height too."

"I agree."

"She's a full-grown human and she's barely five-one." Emory shook his head. "It's mind-boggling."

The saleswoman hesitated. "Well, three-inch stilettos are a good choice for her."

"I'm not saying it bothers me that she's short. I like that I can pick her up and put her wherever I want." Emory chuckled. "And it's funny to see some of the positions she's able to get into. In park benches, movie theaters, taxis..."

Emory wondered why the saleswoman's cheeks were suddenly turning red. Maybe she was having a hot flash.

Blair walked toward them. "Can I speak to you, please?" She grabbed Emory's arm and pulled him aside.

The saleswoman took her cue and wandered out of earshot.

"Emory," Blair muttered, "we can't get these."

"Why not?"

Blair's tone was exasperated. "These shoes are Louboutin."

This clarified nothing for him. "What's your point?"

Her eyes darted about, and she lowered her voice to a whisper. "They're *very* expensive."

"Are they comfortable?" he whispered back.

"Yes."

"Do you like them?"

"I *love* them."

"Then we're getting them." Emory signaled the saleswoman. "Excuse me, do you have the same shoes in red?"

"Certainly! I'll get them for you." She appeared more than happy to assist such discerning customers, and she hustled away again.

Blair sat down on the couch and returned the stylish heels to their box. "I really don't need to try anything else on. These are perfect."

"You said earlier that you wanted red shoes."

"But—"

Before Blair could raise another objection, the woman returned with the red stilettos. "We have your size, miss."

"Excellent!" Emory clapped his hands. "We'll take both."

The saleswoman's face lit up. "I can check you out at my register." She eagerly stacked the boxes on top of each other. "Unless you want to continue shopping."

Blair's mouth was open, but nothing came out. That was a refreshing change.

"I think we're done shopping for today," Emory said.

They followed the gleeful saleswoman to the checkout counter. Emory grabbed his wallet from the back pocket of his jeans while the saleswoman scanned the boxes.

"Your total comes to $1,431.67," she said cheerfully.

Emory tossed a black credit card on the glass countertop, and the woman snatched it up with her manicured fingernails. Shoes would barely register as a blip on his monthly expense report. Clothes were a necessity.

"That didn't take as long as I thought it would." Emory glanced at his watch. "We'll get you back to work with five minutes to spare."

Blair nodded but said nothing.

The saleswoman placed the merchandise in a large bag. "Would you like your receipt, or do you want it in the bag with your girlfriend's shoes?"

"I'll take the receipt," Emory said.

The woman handed him the thin piece of paper. He folded it and tucked it into his wallet next to his limitless credit card. Blair looked dazed as he handed her the glossy bag.

He turned back to the saleswoman. "And she's not my girlfriend."

CHAPTER 12

Blair leaned back against the couch, settling next to a handsome gentleman with floppy blond hair and deep-blue eyes. Emory sat on an armchair in the Enarine realm, watching them. He was quite pleased with Blair's status report—at week three, Philip couldn't seem to get enough of her. He used any excuse to see her, sneaking in casual dates and late-night rendezvous whenever he was off duty. Blair decided to invite him to her apartment for a quiet evening in, and he was more than amenable. He didn't even seem to mind that she picked the programs they watched on television. She alternated between HGTV and the Food Network, skipping through a batch of commercials.

"Okay, Philip," she said. "Which house do you think they'll pick?"

He ran his fingers through his hair. "Number two."

"I think they'll pick number one. It's the only one with the closet space the wife wanted."

Philip watched her intently, but she seemed oblivious to his attention.

"We chose house number one!" the television blared.

"Ha! I knew it!" she cried. "They couldn't beat that backyard for the kids."

Philip pried the remote from her hands and placed it on the coffee table next to her cell phone. She gazed into his eyes.

"Now that I have your undivided attention..." He leaned closer and kissed her.

Blair hesitated then kissed him back. In one strong motion, he pulled her onto his lap then caressed her neck with his mouth as she straddled him. She helped him peel off his sweater to reveal his perfectly sculpted abs. The strong scent of his cologne filled her apartment, and he clawed at her clothes, tearing off her shirt. He explored her smooth skin with his tongue and ran his hands up her back. His fingers lingered around the hooks of her lacy red bra.

Blair let out a quiet sob.

Philip froze. "What's wrong? Is it too fast?"

She shook her head, unable to speak. Emory cautiously slid a titanium arrow out of his quiver. Something was off. Philip brushed her dark curly hair out of her face and stared worriedly into her tear-filled eyes.

"It's just..." Blair hesitated.

"It's okay," he whispered. "You can tell me anything."

She let out an uncontrolled sob that echoed throughout the room. "My cat just died."

Emory closed his eyes and cracked his neck as tears streamed down Blair's cheeks.

"I-I had no idea," Philip stammered. "How did it happen?"

Blair covered her face. "A car."

Philip rubbed her back while she cried on his shoulder. "What was the little guy's name?"

Blair sniffed. "Mr. Snuggles."

"I'm so sorry," he said softly. "If I had known—"

"It's not your fault," she choked out. "It's just when you started kissing me, I remembered this was his favorite spot." Her tears fell on his shoulder, and he stroked her back as she wept.

After a few minutes, Philip shifted and pulled away. "Maybe I should go."

"You're probably right." She tilted her head back, blinking away more tears. "I think I need to be alone tonight."

Blair crawled off his lap. He wasted little time dressing and gathering his belongings. She walked him to the front door, crossing her arms over her bare stomach.

He opened the door. "I'll call you?"

Blair nodded and turned away as though too emotional to speak. He quickly left the apartment, and she locked the door behind him. Her thin fingers brushed away the tears marring her cheeks as she returned to the living room.

She threw her shirt onto the oversized armchair, grabbed her phone from the coffee table, and plopped down on the couch. "What do you want on your pizza?"

Emory ground his teeth and shoved the arrow back into his quiver. He materialized into the Earth realm and grabbed her silk blouse. "Olives."

He hurled the shirt at her, and it landed on her head, covering her face. Blair brushed the garment out of her way and let it drop to the ground. He fumed in silence while she tapped the small screen of her cell phone, ignoring his agitation.

"Mr. Snuggles?" he demanded. "That was the best you could come up with?"

"Nothing turns a man off faster than a woman crying." Blair didn't look up from her phone. "I couldn't let him leave here all wound up."

"I don't understand why he had to leave in the first place!"

She entered her credit card number into the phone. "Then *you* can sleep with him next time."

Emory slammed his backpack to the floor and stormed into Blair's small galley kitchen. The refrigerator door rattled open in his strong grip, and he pulled out a beer. He pried off the cap. It hissed open and dropped to the laminate countertop. He took a sip and caught a glimpse of a wilting plant on the counter near the sink.

Emory grabbed the plant, adjusted the faucet to a slow, steady trickle, and watered the dried soil.

"Philip was perfect," he muttered, returning the plant to the counter.

"He was nice, wasn't he?" Her tone was indifferent. "A little too nice."

Emory opened the cabinets, searching for something to supplement the beer. "Next time, I'll find you someone a bit more abusive. Maybe someone who beats you?"

"Only if you can justify it on your audit report."

He opened a bag of chips and ate a handful, crunching loudly. "We worked with him for three weeks, and you blew it all on a fictional cat!"

"Snuggles was real." Blair tossed her phone back onto the coffee table. "He got hit by a car when I was ten years old."

"You're missing my point." Emory grabbed a jar of olives from the refrigerator and popped it open.

Blair leaned over the edge of her couch, watching him. "What's your point?"

"I'd like to know why you sabotaged a perfectly good relation—" His eyes shifted to her lacy red bra. "Put your shirt on!"

Blair rolled her eyes and snatched her blouse from the floor. "It didn't seem to bother you when Philip was ripping off my clothes," she mumbled, pulling the garment over her head.

Emory scooped two olives onto a large chip and shoved them in his mouth. "That was business." He would have left Blair and Philip to themselves... eventually.

"You're going to make yourself sick," she said, frowning.

"I'm Vycrin. Nothing in this realm makes me sick." Emory swallowed another salty mouthful. "And stop changing the subject."

Blair stared into the kitchen. "It wasn't going to work with Philip."

"You didn't give him a chance."

"He was too good for me. The perfect hair, the gorgeous eyes. I think you overdid it."

Emory threw his hands in the air, almost spilling olive juice on the floor. "You asked for a sensitive blond firefighter who loved his mom, played guitar in a band, enjoyed cooking, and modeled in his spare time."

"Who would have guessed a guy like that actually existed?" Blair exclaimed. "I would have been happy with just the firefighter part!"

Emory found her stash of Thin Mints in the freezer. "So why weren't you happy with him?" He stacked chips and olives between two chocolate cookies. Shocking cold radiated through the nerves of his teeth as he ate the cookie sandwich.

Blair shook her head, looking forlorn. "I couldn't compete with his abs."

Emory refused to let her get to him. That was just what she wanted. He returned to the living room with what was left of his beer, slumped onto the wide chair, and cranked up the volume on the television, refusing to engage in further conversation. The house hunters on the screen complained about paint colors.

"Do you want to know the truth?" Blair asked.

Emory looked at her and nodded.

"When he touched me... I felt nothing."

Emory sighed. "As I've explained on numerous occasions," he said with forced patience, "you won't be able to fall in love while your heart is broken. You just need to be open to a relationship and let someone who is capable of loving you into your heart. Then it will begin to mend on its own."

"You don't understand. There was no connection between us. I couldn't even fake it."

"Why not?" Emory glared at her. "You fake everything else. Fake children, fake divorces, fake cats."

Blair got to her feet and stood in front of him, blocking the television. "You don't get it, do you?"

Emory had another swig of the bitter liquid and peeked around her curvy figure.

Blair stepped forward and straddled his lap.

"What are you—"

She pressed her lips against his and slipped her soft tongue into his mouth before he could utter another word. Her icy skin stung his face, but he instinctively kissed her back. His heightened senses lured him to her despite the overwhelming chill. She ran her fingers through his hair, drawing him closer. Her touch was emotionless and detached, lacking even the slightest hint of excitement.

After a moment, Blair pulled back and rested her forehead against his. "Could you feel that?" she whispered.

Emory, still reeling from her unexpected gesture, searched her eyes. Deep emptiness permeated her soul. He knew he was responsible for the hollow darkness that had replaced the love she'd once held in her heart. He regretted how recklessly he'd wielded his arrows, never grasping the true pain he was capable of inflicting. Banishment suddenly felt like an appropriate punishment. He didn't break her gaze.

"I couldn't feel anything," he said softly.

"Exactly." Blair took the bottle from his fingers and drank the rest of his beer. "I can't even fake it."

She climbed off his lap and returned to the opposite couch, collapsing across the cushions. Emory stared at the television. He could do better. He would have to do better. It wasn't simply a matter of reversing her condition. He wanted her to feel fulfillment on a deeper level. He needed her to be whole again.

"Which one do you think they'll pick?" Blair asked.

"Number three. It has the best kitchen."

CHAPTER 13

"You're a police box?" Emory squinted to read Blair's choker. "I don't get it."

Blair adjusted her dark-blue wig. "I'm the Tardis."

Her white bodice was covered in black rectangles that mimicked window frames, and her short blue skirt flared into an A-line silhouette. Shiny black boots and a matching belt completed the ensemble.

Emory scanned the crowds of people flooding the hotel lobby for the comic book convention. He jumped back as a man in facial prosthetics passed by. "What was that?"

"A Klingon." Blair appeared unfazed by the peculiar characters surrounding them. "I made a list of movies and shows you and I are going to watch so I don't have to keep explaining these things."

"Absolutely not." Emory clung to the strap of his backpack. "I don't have time for that kind of nonsense."

"Sure you do. Laith and Karina's dates always end early."

He couldn't argue with the facts.

Another creature walked past, this one with pointy ears. Humans had the oddest notions about alien races. He wondered why they assumed no one else in the universe looked like them. He spotted a stocky individual cloaked in black. The ninja perusing the convention schedule had a sword strapped across his back, and only his eyes were visible through his authentic costume.

"Ah!" Emory clapped his hands together. "There's your date now."

Blair reached into his backpack and retrieved her gloves. "Tell me something about him."

"He's a volunteer firefighter, he loves his mother, and he models in his spare time." Emory snapped his fingers. "Wait, I have that backward—he *plays* with models in his spare time. As in toys."

Blair slipped on the long black gloves. "Still bitter about Philip?"

"Which one was Philip?" he asked innocently. It had been two weeks, but he still couldn't let it go. He decided her punishment would be spending the day with a less attractive man. That would teach her.

Blair studied her prospective suitor. "He's got beautiful eyes."

Emory playfully yanked at the back of her shiny belt. "Have fun."

She slapped his hand away. "I intend to."

Emory crossed into the Enarine realm as Blair headed in the direction of the ninja.

Her masked suitor folded up his program and followed the signs to the conference center, where the main events were being held. Suddenly, he slammed into Blair's shoulder. Her badge and program fell to the ground, and he quickly reached down to pick up her effects.

"I'm so sorry!" Blair said with a gasp. "I should have been paying attention."

"Don't worry about it," he replied.

Emory shot the ninja in the heart.

The man locked eyes with Blair. Even through his mask, it was clear he was smiling. "Do you come to these things often?"

"I haven't in a while. But I was excited about some of the events they have lined up."

"Me too! I was just on my way to an independent video-game panel. Do you want to join me?"

Blair gestured for him to lead the way. He offered his arm, all too eager to escort his new acquaintance. The ninja's pale-yellow aura meant he would keep her busy for at least forty minutes—longer if she displayed any interest in him. Blair clung to his arm and whispered something only loud enough for him to hear. Their muffled laughter was agitating.

Emory had no intention of watching Blair flirt with her new beau. The man was nothing more than a filler until he could secure a more stable partner for her. They hadn't spoken about her kiss, but Emory couldn't get it out of his mind. Redoubling his efforts, he'd spent the last week scouting for potential suitors from a pool of government employees. An intelligence analyst seemed like a good fit—a man who could successfully pass a security clearance and who held a steady job shrouded in mystery.

Emory overtook the newly paired couple and exited the lower level of the hotel to find his college students. He moved around clusters of slow-moving superheroes and down a winding covered sidewalk to the adjoining conference center. He arrived at the registration counter and spotted a familiar bright-red haze. He couldn't understand why his clients and their friends were dressed like demented clowns. Blair had failed to mention circus acts. He sighed. It was going to be a strange day.

Emory circled around Joey as she helped Trigger button his long green suit jacket. Black question marks littered the young man's garment, but he didn't seem to mind the chaotic pattern that was sewn onto his suit.

"You outdid yourself, Joe." Trigger tilted his bowler hat to the side with the top of his gold cane. "How do I look?"

"Perfect." Joey appeared to be very satisfied with her work.

"What about me?" Pyro asked. Half of his suit was solid black, and the other half was pinstriped. His dark hair was slicked down on one side, and heavy makeup was smeared across half of his face.

Joey reached into her purse for a tube of dark-purple lipstick. She smeared a little onto his left cheek, covering the last spot on his face that was exposed. "You're all set."

Duke's girlfriend was dressed in a tight red-and-black corset and a short ruffled skirt. Kali's long blond hair was swept into two ponytails, and oddly enough, her wild makeup complemented Duke's. She ran her fingers through his green hair, making sure it was disheveled.

"I love your Poison Ivy costume," she said to Joey. "How long did it take to sew on all the leaves?"

"Just a few days," Joey replied modestly.

Every inch of Joey's strapless dress was covered in artificial leaves. Bright-green stockings and gold heels put the final touches to her botanical outfit. It certainly wasn't Emory's taste, but Amir couldn't take his eyes off of her. He leaned down and whispered, "You look amazing."

She smiled and straightened his bowtie. "Thanks."

Amir was the only member in the group dressed in a sensible manner. His black tuxedo was well tailored and immaculate, and his umbrella doubled as a cane. Emory didn't understand the significance behind Amir's top hat and monocle. He decided he would ask Blair about it later. She was well versed in such matters.

"What does everyone want to do this afternoon?" Joey asked.

Pyro handed out programs. "Trigger and I entered a video-game tournament that's being held in the main ballroom."

"After that, we're going to watch anime in one of the viewing rooms on the second floor," Trigger said.

"Let's all just be sure we meet back here in time for the costume contest," Amir said.

Kali hooked her arm around Joey's. "Let's walk around."

The young women wandered into the massive exhibition, with Emory trailing close behind. Hundreds of booths filled with comic books, themed merchandise, games, and toys greeted them. Tall purple and white curtains sectioned off the vendors, artists, and celebrity guests. Joey glanced over at Amir as he began an intensive search for replica swords with Duke.

Emory was a little surprised to see Amir and Joey split up. It wasn't like them to be apart in a group setting, but they appeared to be content. He placed his bow across his chest and strolled through the crowded venue, away from his clients.

A stack of decorative glass coasters suddenly caught Emory's attention. He materialized into the Earth realm and picked one up. Bold yellow letters were printed above some sort of spaceship.

"I've heard of this," Emory said, surprised.

The bearded seller turned his attention to Emory. "A *Star Trek* fan, huh?"

"No. I have absolutely no interest." Emory pulled out his wallet. "I'll take four."

The man seemed more than happy to take his money, despite Emory's lack of enthusiasm. Emory was certain Blair would like the small gift, and it was practical. He prided himself on only buying her things that served a useful purpose.

Emory felt someone behind him as the vendor wrapped up the merchandise. He cursed under his breath.

"Are you working or shopping?" Argus asked.

The seller handed Emory the coasters, and he quickly stuffed them into his backpack. "Working."

Argus popped his gum and scribbled something in his notebook. "I guess my definition of *work* differs from yours."

"All of my clients are stable. I was simply taking a break."

Argus put his notebook in his leather backpack. "It's funny how a seemingly stable situation can change in an instant."

Emory blinked, and Argus disappeared. Emory rushed into the Enarine realm after him. His heart was racing. Argus ran toward Joey, drew an iron arrow from his quiver, and shot her in the heart without breaking his stride. The arrow pulsed black and disappeared. Argus spun around, and Emory skidded to a stop next to him.

"I had it under control!" Emory shouted.

Argus flashed him a crooked smile as he chewed his gum. "A little doubt should have no effect on a relationship—if it's a solid match."

Emory grabbed his bow from across his chest and hurried over to his client while Argus lingered behind.

"You and Bambi are so cute together," Kali said.

Joey gave her a weary smile. "Thanks." The arrow was already taking effect. "He kind of left me behind, though."

"That's what they do," Kali said with the casual wave of her hand. "It's so nice to finally have another girl around." The ladies stopped in front of an artist who had a whimsical take on comic book characters, and Kali flipped through pages of laminated drawings.

Joey glanced at the intricate artwork. "How long have you and Duke been together?"

"We've known each other since middle school, but we started dating two years ago." Kali's voice turned serious. "It's incredible to think that my soul mate was right in front of my face all those years, and I never realized it."

Joey raised her eyebrows. "When did you realize it?"

Kali closed the artist's leather-bound book. "We both got piss drunk one night and made out," she said with a giggle.

Joey stepped back. "That's it?"

"True love is funny that way, isn't it?"

"I guess." Joey had a distant look in her eyes. "Amir and I don't have a very romantic story about how we met either."

Emory reached for a silver arrow. He paused. His arrow would reinforce Joey's love for Amir, but coupled with the negative feelings stirred up by Argus's arrow, it would forever taint the memory of their first meeting.

"It's all a matter of perspective," Kali said brightly as they moved on to a different vendor. "You got any plans for spring break?"

Joey shrugged. "Amir hasn't mentioned anything."

Kali gasped and grabbed Joey by the arm. "We should backpack through Europe together! Do you want to?"

Joey seemed startled. "Okay—"

"Great!" Kali exclaimed. "I just have to tell my sweetie."

"Wait, are you serious?"

Emory masked his dissatisfaction. It was healthy for his clients to maintain separate interests and goals at this stage in their relationship. The committee would see it at as an emotional stepping-stone, not an obstacle.

Kali dragged Joey through the maze of retailers until she reached Duke, who was haggling down the price for a DVD set. Duke pinched her backside, and she suppressed a snicker. Emory positioned himself in front of his clients as Amir put his arm around Joey. She shifted and readjusted her formfitting dress, the stiff fake leaves crunching under her fingers.

"We have great news," Kali announced. "Me and Joey are backpacking through Europe for spring break!"

"Oh, good! You found someone to go with you." Duke kissed her on the cheek. "You girls will have a blast."

"Just like that?" Amir frowned and let go of Joey. "You made plans without even considering me?"

Emory quickly grabbed a silver arrow. He caught a whiff of his cousin's pungent cologne but didn't bother to turn around.

Joey shifted. "Um, I didn't realize I had to clear my travel plans with you."

He shrugged. "Why would you? I'm just your boyfriend."

Duke and Kali exchanged glances.

"Nothing is official yet," Kali said. "We were just talking—"

"I don't see how it concerns you where I go for spring break," Joey pressed on. "Unless you're planning for me to meet your parents that weekend."

"Well!" Duke said a little too loudly, clapping his hands together. "Kali and I are going to grab something to eat."

"Baby doll, I couldn't possibly eat anything in this tight costume."

"I'll loosen your corset," he muttered, quickly leading her away from the ensuing firestorm.

Argus popped his gum in Emory's ear. "And now we get to the crux of the matter."

Emory stifled the heat that was crawling up his neck. He couldn't afford to add assault charges to his record.

Amir's monocle fell from his eye as he stepped closer to Joey. "I can't believe you just brought that up."

"Obviously, it's not a secret," Joey replied harshly.

He lowered his voice. "I didn't think our issues would be broadcast in front of my friends."

Joey scowled. "We wouldn't have any issues if you just told your parents about me."

"You think it's easy for me to tell my parents I'm seriously dating someone? Not to mention the fact that our families aren't even the same religion—"

She gaped at him. "Neither of us practices!"

"That's not the point!"

Joey backed away. "What *is* the point?"

Amir twisted his umbrella into the floor. "I don't know."

"You don't know what?"

"I don't know anymore," he replied, not meeting her eyes. "I don't know what I think or how I feel."

Joey's voice trembled. "You don't know how you feel about me?"

"No, I think I do—"

"You *think* you do?" Tears began to fall from Joey's eyes. She ran to the ladies' room and was out of sight before Amir could even utter her name.

"Are you just going to stand there?" Argus demanded.

Emory's mind was racing. "Amir's frustrated and angry. If I shoot him now, he'll internalize his emotions and become defensive, which will prevent him from apologizing. I have to deal with him first then deal with Joey."

"So, you actually *do* know how to perform your job." Argus closed his pen in his notepad. "And all these years, I thought you were pretending."

Emory clenched his bow. Just then, Duke and Kali reappeared.

"What happened?" Kali asked.

Amir sighed. "She's in the bathroom, crying."

"Oh, Bambi—"

"Babe." Duke gestured toward the restroom. "If you please."

"Sorry." Kali gave Amir a reassuring hug. "I'll go get her for you." She darted off, leaving Amir and Duke alone.

"What's the deal, man?" Duke said.

"She's being emotional."

"Of course she is." Duke flipped through his new comic book. "She's a woman."

"She just doesn't get it." Amir pounded his umbrella into the floor with each word. "My parents aren't like hers."

"How many times have you been through this?" Duke's tone was serious. "Is it really your parents that are the problem?"

Emory shot Amir in the chest. He needed to reinforce the love that was already in the young man's heart to help him overcome his reservations.

Amir avoided eye contact with Duke. "I hate you."

"I hate you too." Duke patted him on the back a little harder than necessary. "Now, go wait for her to come out."

Amir made his way to the ladies' room, but Emory was already far ahead of him. Argus stayed behind, documenting the encounter. His fastidiousness was maddening. Emory loaded his bow as he entered the restroom and found Kali leaning against the wall near a corner stall.

"Joe, are you okay?" Kali asked. There was a muffled sob from inside the stall. "Do you want to talk about it?"

The door unlatched, and Joey stepped out, dark-green makeup smeared down her cheeks. "He's going to break up with me."

"No, he's not!" Kali hugged Joey. "He's just confused."

Joey sniffed. "About what?"

"Who knows?" Kali said with a shrug. "He's a guy."

Joey nodded as though Kali's answer explained everything. Kali grabbed a handful of paper towels and patted Joey's face dry.

"Amir really likes you." Kali wet a paper towel under the faucet and fixed Joey's makeup. "Usually, he ends a relationship before it gets too serious. Not with you, though."

Emory shot Joey in the back, striking her heart. The shroud of uncertainty slowly faded from her eyes. "Really?"

"And just so you know," Kali continued, "he *never* mentioned bringing a girl home to meet his parents until he started dating you."

"Never?" Her voice was hopeful.

"Ever." Kali unzipped a small makeup pouch and brushed Joey's face with powder. "All done."

Joey examined her reflection in the mirror. "Thank you, Kali."

They exited the bathroom with Emory following them. Amir was pacing by the door. He tugged on his suit jacket when he caught sight of Joey.

"Joey, I need to talk to you." Amir took her aside and led her to a quiet corner of the conference lobby. "I'm sorry I upset you. I didn't mean what I said."

"About what?" Joey asked nervously.

Emory drew a silver arrow.

"About not knowing how I feel about you," Amir said. "I think..."

When he hesitated, Emory shot him and reloaded.

"I think I'm in love with you," Amir said quickly.

"Really?" A silver arrow slammed into Joey's back. She lifted herself onto her toes to whisper in his ear.

He bent down to hear what she wanted to say.

"I think I'm in love with you too."

Amir smiled broadly and kissed her lips. He wrapped his arms around her. "I don't know what to do about everything else right now. But I know I want to be with you."

"It's okay." She smiled up at him. "We'll figure it out."

Emory let out a sigh of relief. He glanced at Argus, who hadn't even looked up from his notepad. Emory roughly straightened his leather jacket.

Pyro and Trigger sauntered up to Amir and Joey with a large bag of popcorn.

"What did we miss?" Trigger asked.

• • ❧ • •

EMORY AND ARGUS STOOD on the second floor of the conference center, away from the crowds.

"Congratulations," Argus said as he scrawled his final notes. "You've proven your ability to create a viable match and successfully resolve conflicts."

Emory leaned his palms against a long railing in an attempt to hide his nerves. His college students required more attention than he had anticipated. Their intense red auras failed to radiate even the slightest hints of orange—they weren't fully committed. He would have to put forth greater effort to make them feel secure in their relationship.

There was a light tug on Emory's backpack. He and Argus turned around to find a young boy with red face paint smeared across his tiny cheeks. For some odd reason, his red-and-blue costume showcased an arachnid. The boy couldn't have been more than five years old. Children were notorious for spotting Vycrin in a crowd. They were drawn to anything out of the ordinary that sparked their curiosity.

"Are you twins?" the boy asked. "My sisters are twins."

Emory ground his teeth, and Argus inhaled sharply.

"No," Emory said. "We're not twins."

"Why do people always ask that?" Argus cried. "We look nothing alike."

"Yes, you do," the child continued. "And you've got the same backpacks. Who are you supposed to be?"

"Vycrin," they said at the same time. Emory and Argus glared at each other.

Emory knelt down to the boy's eye level. He dilated his pupils and captured his gaze. The child stared at him, entranced.

"Go find your parents," Emory said. "And don't talk to strangers—it's not safe. Do you understand?"

The boy had a glassy stare as he nodded. Emory blinked hard, and the youngster wandered away, calling out for his mother.

Emory rose and tried to keep the sarcasm out of his voice. "Is there anything else I can do for you today?"

"No, cousin." Argus sucked in and popped his gum. "That will be all for now."

Argus departed from his company and boarded the escalator to the first floor. Emory relaxed for the first time that afternoon. He didn't want Argus anywhere near Blair when she returned. His cousin wouldn't dare attempt to use an iron arrow on someone whose heart wasn't fully mended, but Emory disliked Argus's presence on principle.

Blair's deep-blue skirt swayed from side to side as she approached. "What's the status?"

"Four arrows to get an 'I think I'm in love with you' out of them." Emory squeezed the wood railing. "It was a difficult afternoon."

"I thought today was supposed to be your easy day."

"Things got a little heated about his parents."

Blair's jaw dropped. "He still hasn't told them about her?"

"Not yet."

"I don't know what he's waiting for."

Emory massaged his stiff neck. "Now Joey's going to Europe for spring break."

"That should give him time to focus on school. His parents will hit the roof if he fails another class."

"Good point." Emory studied her carefully. "What happened to your ninja?"

"His name is Drew, and I told him my friends were leaving early." Blair stared into the crowds. "He asked me to dinner and a movie next week."

"That's a shame," Emory said, glancing at his watch. "At least he'll be over you in the next five minutes. His aura was a little dull anyway."

"I agreed to see him again," she replied flatly.

"Oh." Emory attempted to mask his surprise. "Well... good for you."

Dinner and a movie. Emory decided he didn't like Drew. *Too unoriginal.*

"He seems nice enough." Blair tore off her gloves, stuffed them into his backpack, and went back to people watching.

Emory was grateful she didn't notice the souvenir he'd bought her. There wasn't anything special about the gift, but he wanted to give it to her when they were alone... so *she* would feel special.

Blair spoke up. "Twenty-eight years of comic-book knowledge finally paid off."

"I'm sure your mother would be proud," he said sarcastically.

Blair smiled. "My dad would be. He took me to my first comic convention when I was thirteen." She brushed the long blue strands of hair out of her face. "Thanks for buying me the wig. I'll pay you back as soon as I get my check on Friday."

Emory shrugged. "I already wrote it off."

She chuckled. "As a business expense?"

"Something like that."

Blair leaned against the railing as they watched costumed characters walk by. "Your superiors let you spend money on anything you want?"

"Almost anything. All of our expenses are monitored to ensure that funds aren't being used to harm humans in any way."

Blair flattened out the front of her skirt. "They know everything you buy?"

"Of course."

She peered at him with curious eyes. "That doesn't bother you?"

He frowned. "Why would it?"

"It seems so personal."

Her statement left him puzzled. "What's personal about money?"

Blair shook her head, amused. "No wonder you lack boundaries. Love gods have no sense of privacy."

Emory looked in her eyes. "There are certain things I keep private."

"Oh yeah?" Blair poked him in the arm with her cold finger. "Like what?"

Emory grabbed her hand and pulled her to his side, and she stumbled next to him, startled. "Like the fact that you're my favorite client," he replied easily.

Blair laughed. "That's not a secret. I provide you with the highest entertainment value."

"I like being with you," Emory said in a serious tone. "Not watching you."

"Oh..." Her smile faded, and she cleared her throat. "So that's not going in your report?"

"No." Emory slowly released her frigid hand. "It's none of their business."

CHAPTER 14

"That's too tight," Emory complained as Blair tied the tattered laces of his rented ice skates.

She looked up at him from the frozen ground. "It's supposed to be tight so you don't break your ankles."

He shifted around and scanned the outdoor ice rink. The Sculpture Garden housed impressive works of art, but Emory had no interest in the human artifacts. He had more important things to worry about. There was no sign of Blair's date, despite the sizable crowd.

"Where's Drew? He was supposed to be here twenty minutes ago."

Blair yanked his foot back down and clenched it between her legs. "Hold still."

"He's going to miss out on your torture session."

Blair wove the laces through the tiny holes of his boot. She stared at the skates while she spoke. "He said he'd text me when he got here." She finished tightening the laces and climbed onto the bench next to him.

Emory handed her a caramel latte as a reward. She drank the warm beverage but didn't offer any additional conversation.

"You two seem to get along well even when I'm not around," he mused.

"Yep."

Emory drank the rest of his cappuccino. "I'll admit, I didn't think he was a good match for you at first."

"Why not?" she asked without meeting his eyes.

"I thought he was too quiet and timid for your lively personality. But he's turned out to be a nice complement."

Blair swirled the contents of her drink around in the cup. "It's too bad you weren't with us last week. You missed all the action."

"I *knew* you were keeping something from me."

It wasn't like her to withhold information, and she hadn't mentioned a single detail about her date with Drew. Emory didn't press the issue. Eventually, she would give him an exhaustive account of everything that transpired, like she always did.

"After dinner, he insisted on walking me up to my apartment," she said.

"A gentleman, like you asked for."

"We were saying good night, and I accidentally dropped my keys. When I reached down to pick them up, he leaned in for a kiss and—bam!" Blair clapped her hands together. "I head-butted him in the nose. Blood was gushing everywhere."

Emory gaped at her. "That's a horrible way to end a date!"

"I know." Her tone was flat. "I had to wrap his face with my scarf to stop the bleeding. He took it like a champ, though."

Emory dropped his head, disappointed.

"But look how cute my new scarf is," she said brightly, sweeping the fluffy lime-green pompoms against his cheeks.

"That's great, Blair." He brushed them out of his face. "But how do you feel?"

"About what?"

Emory couldn't think of any reason for her to be unhappy with her courteous suitor. Even *he* was getting used to the man. "Drew."

"Good. Very good." She drank the rest of her latte. "He's a great guy."

Blair picked up their empty paper cups, struggled to steady herself on the skates, and wobbled to the trash bins.

Her phone vibrated on the bench next to Emory. He picked it up and swiped the screen.

I respect your decision, and I won't try to contact you again. Goodbye, Blair.

Emory reread the text message three times. He attempted to scroll up to see what had prompted Drew's response, but Blair had already deleted the entire message thread. He placed the phone facedown on the bench as she approached.

She grabbed hold of his shoulders to stabilize her body weight on the unsteady skates. "I think these things are safer on the ice."

Emory searched her expression. He expected her to speak up, but she didn't say a word. "I agree."

Blair scooped up her phone and shoved it into the pocket of her thick winter jacket. Emory followed behind and waited for a break between skaters before escorting her onto the rink. He guided her through clusters of lumbering couples, careless adolescents, and wild children who had yet to develop a natural sense of fear. Darion and Hana skated past, and Emory swept Blair to his side.

"You're pretty good at this." There was a hint of surprise in Blair's voice.

"I should be," Emory said. "I've been here on countless occasions."

"How's their date going?" Blair asked, catching his watchful eyes.

"No one is bleeding yet."

She smiled.

The intense white lights of the outdoor skating rink were almost blinding. "Why did you lie to me?"

The cheer in her expression faded. "About what?"

"You broke up with Drew."

Blair increased her speed. "I never gave you permission to read my text messages, Emory."

"I'm sorry." He matched her pace and caught up to her. "I shouldn't have done that."

"You don't respect my privacy."

He took her by the arm to slow her down. "I won't do it again."

She slipped out of his grasp and skated on. "And I'll choose whoever I want to be with."

"That's not the issue."

She sped around a corner. "Then what is?"

Emory skated in front of her and spun around, forcing her to stop and face him. "Ever since we met, I've watched you lie to every man who's come into your life."

"I haven't lied to every—"

"Did they mean anything to you?"

"You *know* they didn't," Blair said with barely suppressed irritation.

Clumsy skaters awkwardly maneuvered around them, but he remained motionless. "Are you going to get rid of me just as quickly when we're done?"

She gritted her teeth. "No..."

"So I'm not just one of your disposable partners?"

"Of course not." Blair bore her right toe pick into the ice. "You're my friend."

Emory stared at her with piercing eyes. "Then don't ever lie to me again."

Blair blinked, and Emory left her. From the Enarine realm, he skated around a dawdling family of three and increased his pace. After nearly six months, Blair still didn't trust him completely. He attempted to clear his mind. He needed to focus on work, not his personal relationships.

It didn't take Emory long to spot his clients leaning against the low wall on the far end of the ice rink. Light flakes of snow fell and landed around the two of them. Hana reached up to catch them in the palm of her hands. Each melted snowflake was replaced by another frozen crystal. Darion gazed at her with an enamored look in his eyes. He removed his glove and stroked her cheek.

Emory pulled an arrow from his quiver. It was time for the couple to take their relationship to the next level. They just needed a little prodding. He raised his bow and aimed at Darion's heart. Hana's hair swept across her face as the wind picked up. Darion pushed her silky hair behind her ear and leaned closer. He brushed his lips against hers. Emory released the arrow. It struck the man's heart and pulsed red as it disappeared.

Darion kissed Hana, holding her close.

Emory steadied his bow once more. A silver arrow whistled through the air, striking Hana's heart. She smiled up at Darion.

"I love you," Hana whispered.

"I...um..." Darion stammered, avoiding her yearning eyes. "I..."

Hana's face fell. "Sorry, I shouldn't have said that."

Emory frantically scanned the ice-skating rink, half expecting to find Argus with his bow drawn and a condescending smirk on his face. He couldn't sense his cousin's presence. Argus wasn't there. Emory had misjudged Darion's true feelings.

"No, it's okay," Darion said. "I'm glad you did, it's just that—"

"I don't need an explanation," Hana interjected. "I just wanted you to know how I felt." She skated away before he could reply.

"Hana, wait!"

Hana hurried to the exit, blushing hard, eyes downcast. Darion followed her, trying to catch up. Emory couldn't understand where he'd gone wrong. Darion was clearly in love with Hana—she was in his heart. Reinforcing their love during such an intimate moment should have solidified their bond.

Emory trailed behind as Hana stepped off the ice and found the closest bench. Darion sat next to her on the hard surface and clutched the edge of his seat. She untied the laces of her skates to avoid his stare.

"I'm sorry," Darion said.

"There's no need to apologize." Her tone was indifferent.

"Hana, I'm not very good at this." He cracked his knuckles. "In the past, I've kept my relationships casual so I didn't have to deal with any—I'm just not used to talking about my feelings."

She tore off her gloves. "I understand." Now her tone was bitter.

"Please believe me when I say that I truly do care about you. I just..." He clenched his jaw. "I don't want to say it until I mean it."

Hana folded her fleece gloves in her lap and let out a nervous laugh. "I feel like such an idiot."

Darion tilted her head up with a single finger. "You're not an idiot." He leaned closer and kissed her on the cheek.

Emory fired a single arrow into Hana's heart. If she felt secure in the relationship, it would be easier for her to exhibit a level of patience as Darion worked through his feelings. Even without Darion's profession of love, her cardinal-red aura brightened to pale orange. Commitment.

Emory had been wrong about Darion—and Blair. He could not rely on instincts alone to fully comprehend the motives of humans. Their emotions were far more complex than he'd imagined.

He placed his bow over his shoulder and scanned the ice rink as skaters floated past, out of pace with the Enarine realm. Blair glided across the smooth ice, her head downcast. Emory materialized in the Earth realm and skated up behind her. She barely acknowledged his presence. Their sharp blades scraped into the ice, leaving a choppy, uneven trail in their wake.

"Are you cold?" Emory asked after a while.

She nodded.

"Then let's get out of here," he said. He hated being cold.

Blair led the way off the frozen rink to an empty bench. Emory knelt on the ground and untied her skates.

"I'm sorry," Blair said. "I promise I won't lie to you again. Please forgive me."

He peered into her eyes. "I forgive you."

Emory gently pulled off her skates and sat by her side, untying his own laces. He stacked the two sets of skates next to each other and leaned back. Contemporary music played over the speakers in the background, filling the silence.

Emory sighed. "Did you really head-butt Drew last week?"

"It was a bloodbath." She looked at him, and the two of them broke into laughter. "I was mortified." Blair covered her face with her gloved hands. "I had no idea what to do."

"How did you get the bleeding to stop?"

"I wrapped some ice cubes in my scarf and put it on his nose. I thought I could simultaneously slow the bleeding and absorb the blood that was gushing out of his face."

"You used a dirty, beat-up scarf?" Emory winced. "I take it you've never completed a first-aid course."

"The evening was an absolute disaster," Blair said in a daze. "I was too embarrassed to see him again."

He remained silent, pondering the unfortunate incident. "Well," he said after much thought, "I guess we'll have to get you a first-aid kit."

CHAPTER 15

"Grab her!" Laith yelled to Karina as their gray-and-white pit bull broke free from her leash.

In the Enarine realm, Emory and Blair followed behind Karina as she chased their new puppy through the crowded parking lot of a pet store. From Emory's perspective, the couple looked as though they were running under water.

"I still don't understand how we're going to stop Shelby," Blair said as they overtook the puppy. "I thought you said no one can see us."

"They can't see us," Emory said. "But dogs can sense us."

Emory positioned himself directly in the puppy's path with outstretched arms. The canine bounced to a stop and barked wildly at him.

"We just need to keep her cornered until they catch up," Emory said.

Shelby darted off in the opposite direction. Blair stepped forward, startling the puppy. The excitable pup quickly found a hiding spot under a Toyota Camry. Emory and Blair stood on opposite sides of the car, blocking her in.

"I'm not sure the puppy thing was a good idea," Blair stated.

"It's not ideal, but it shows a level of commitment." Across the parking lot, a gentleman in navy blue scrubs climbed out of his Escalade. His bold-yellow aura caught Emory's attention. He was well over six feet tall—but Blair was never one to complain about height differences. Plus, she would probably get a kick out of wearing his shirts as dresses. "What do you think about dating a nurse?"

Blair stood on her toes and folded her arms against the roof of the car. "Caring, empathetic, stable. What's not to like?"

Karina lowered herself to the ground in front of the car, getting dirt all over her expensive gym attire. "Come on, Shelby," she pleaded, holding out a dog treat.

Laith squatted next to her. "I don't think bribery is working."

She glowered at him. "If you hadn't let her out before I secured her leash, we wouldn't have to chase her around."

"She was barking," he protested.

"She always barks," Karina said. "We're never going to be able to train her if you're always doing one thing and I'm doing another."

Laith reached under the car and grabbed hold of the frisky puppy.

"Don't hurt her!" Karina shrieked as he dragged her across the pavement.

"She's fine." He pulled her onto his lap, and she licked his face. "See?"

Karina brushed the rocks and debris from her running pants. "It's so nice to see you two have such a good bond."

"Don't be jealous," Laith said. "Shelby just loves me unconditionally."

Karina tossed him the leash and walked away.

Laith turned back to their puppy. "Isn't that right, Shelby?"

Emory sighed heavily.

"Well, at least he's happy about the dog," Blair said. Emory knew she was trying to sound optimistic, but her voice was too high.

Laith hooked the leash onto her collar and led her to the entrance of the pet store. Karina yanked a large blue shopping cart free of the chain of carts and followed them inside. The store reeked of dried pet food and plastic. Emory waved his hand to waft away the unpleasant odor.

"You weren't around a lot of animals growing up, huh?" Blair said.

"No." He grabbed his bow from over his shoulder. "And dogs don't particularly like our species. If one suddenly turns fierce or loses control for no apparent reason, there's likely a Vycrin nearby."

Blair smothered a chuckle. "What about cats?"

"Cats couldn't care less about Vycrin. Or about humans, for that matter."

Shelby trotted next to Laith, happy to guard *her* loyal human. While Karina loaded their cart with a bag of dog food, Laith became distracted by a doggy bed. He placed it down in front of Shelby, and she rolled across the plush bedding.

"We have to get her this. She loves it." He added the bed to their cart just as a yellow squeaky toy caught Shelby's attention. "Do you want this?" He picked up the soft round toy.

She jumped and grabbed it in her mouth.

"I swear you spend more on the dog than you do on me," Karina muttered.

Emory drew an arrow from his quiver.

Laith watched Shelby play with the small toy. "You were the one who begged me for a puppy."

"I didn't beg."

He shook his head. "Nothing I do makes you happy."

"Well, it's not like you let me pick the dog I wanted." She slid an elastic band off her wrist and tied her long hair back into a loose bun. "You just came home with some mutt from the shelter."

"Don't listen to her, baby," Laith soothed as he patted Shelby's head.

Blair played with the zipper on her leather jacket. "I know it's none of my business, but why don't you shoot Karina so she feels better about Laith and the puppy?"

Emory didn't make eye contact with her. "I'm no longer focusing my attention on Karina."

Blair grabbed his arm. "Did you—is her heart damaged as well?"

"No, her situation isn't like yours," he said quickly. "Her aura is a little off, and I can't risk making a mistake."

"You wanted a dog, and she needed a good home," Laith said. "You should be proud that I solved two problems in one day."

"Whatever," Karina said under her breath.

Emory shot Laith in the heart.

"And"—Laith took Karina by the hand—"you should also be proud that you are talking to the new vice president of sales and marketing."

Karina's expression softened. "You got the promotion?"

He grinned. "They're going to announce it on Monday."

She jabbed him in the arm. "When were you going to tell me?"

"I was going to surprise you tonight at the hotel."

"He's taking her on a romantic getaway!" Blair jumped up and down, clapping. "Did you know about this? Is that why you were at his job all week?"

"Yes." Emory placed his bow over his chest. "As soon as he found out about his promotion, he started researching home entertainment systems. I had to do a course correction."

Laith pulled out his phone and showed Karina a confirmation email. "We'll be staying downtown at the Ritz Carlton."

"You're always full of surprises." Karina wrapped her arms around his neck and smothered him with light kisses. Suddenly, she stopped and stroked the back of their puppy's head. "Wait, what about Shelby?"

"I booked a spot for Shelby in one of the fanciest canine hotels in the area." He bent down and rubbed behind Shelby's ears. "But I couldn't let our baby leave us without a couple of new toys."

Karina massaged his shoulders. "That's why I love you."

He straightened up and kissed her cheek. "I love you too."

Blair held her hand to her heart and sighed. "You have the best job in the world."

"Hmm..." Emory tried to empty his mind. Crossing over was easier on both of them when he was emotionally numb.

"That wrapped up sooner than I expected." Blair strolled down the aisle away from his clients and headed to the feline department. "We might even make happy hour—"

Emory grabbed her shoulders, spun her around, and shoved her back against a large metal pillar. A sharp burst of pain tore through his limbs as they reentered the Earth realm, and he gasped. Dulling his senses allowed him to absorb some of her shock, but he couldn't completely shield her from the pain. Blair gulped in a breath.

"That's the part of my job I hate most." Emory held her shaking body. "I wish you could come with me on assignments without them ending like this."

Blair's voice trembled. "I think I'm getting used to it."

"I don't want you to get used to it."

"I'm perfectly fine—trust me." Blair freed herself from his grip and stood upright without his help. "See?"

Emory readjusted his backpack. "As long as you're okay."

She nodded but didn't attempt to take a step. "You don't have to worry about me. I know you have to work."

He gave her shoulder a firm squeeze. "I'll find you someone."

"You always do," she said sweetly.

He hurried back down the aisle and crossed into the Enarine realm as he darted around a corner. Ever since Blair broke up with Drew, Emory had been relentless in his search. It had almost become an obsession. In the last week, he'd set her up on six separate dates with six different intelligence analysts. She finally begged him to stop spending so much time at the Pentagon. The analyst thing wasn't working... for either of them.

Emory went in search of the man in blue scrubs. During their Pentagon experiment, he'd gotten out of the habit of setting Blair up with chance encounters, but a couple of successful dates with Blue might be just what they needed to get back on track. Emory spotted the man chatting with his two furry companions as he shopped. He frowned. Perhaps Blue wasn't as stable as he'd hoped. He stepped closer to read his name badge: Peter Cary, MD. Cardiac Surgeon.

"Jackpot!" Emory shouted, almost giddy with excitement. A heart doctor for Blair. She would be beside herself, and he was fairly certain the irony wouldn't be lost on the audit committee. It was perfect.

Emory phased into the Earth realm and rushed back to find Blair just as a tall woman in four-inch Louis Vuitton boots strolled down the aisle toward her. The woman's cropped blazer and tailored black pencil skirt hugged her toned body. Tight voluminous curls framed her oval face, and her rich brown skin had a cool undertone. She bore only the slightest traces of makeup, allowing her natural radiance to shine through. She reached for a can of cat food near Blair, and a pink diamond ring sparkled in the bright fluorescent lighting.

"That's a gorgeous ring," Blair said, staring at the stranger.

"Thank you." The woman extended her hand, and Blair grasped her fingers, admiring the beautiful stone from different angles.

Emory sighed. The last thing they needed was yet another distraction, but he knew how much Blair enjoyed making new friends. He pulled out his phone and crossed into the Enarine realm, out of sight. His time would be better spent verifying the doctor's credentials.

The woman suddenly clasped both hands around Blair's. "Your hands are like ice, my dear."

The hair on the back of Emory's neck stood on end, and he took a closer look at the woman. She had no aura.

"I'm sorry." Blair released her grip. "My friend always says the same thing. I must have an iron deficiency."

"A deficiency of some sort." The woman searched Blair's eyes then gave her a reassuring smile. "No matter. Do you have a lot of pets to shop for?"

"No, I'm waiting for my friend to get off work." Blair picked up a long stick with purple feathers tied to the end. "What about you?"

Emory frantically dialed Petros's number. His supervisor answered on the third ring. "Shouldn't you be working, boy?"

"A security agent is interrogating my client," he said through clenched teeth.

"Interrogating?" Petros asked. "That's not really Hera's style."

"We have a new addition to our family," the woman said to Blair. "My husband and I just adopted a kitten for our twin girls."

Her face lit up. "I had a kitten when I was little too."

"Do you want to see a picture of them? The girls just adore him! They call him Charlie." She pulled out her cell phone and shared the screen with Blair, scrolling through photos.

Blair was so enthralled that Emory was half tempted to take a peek. "She's good," he murmured.

"We only send our top agents," Petros said.

"That's so cute," Blair said. "How old are your daughters?"

The woman gave a proud smile. "They just turned six." She placed her phone back into her designer purse. "Do you have any children?"

"No, no, no," Blair said with a slight chuckle. "As my friend often reminds me, I can't even keep my houseplants alive, despite my best efforts."

"Does your boyfriend want kids?"

Emory ran his fingers through his hair. "Now she's asking personal questions!"

"It's her job to gather information," Petros said calmly.

Blair laughed and twirled a feathered toy between her fingers. "I don't have a boyfriend. And I'm not sure if my friend wants kids. I never asked him."

"What would she do to me if I interrupted and pulled Blair away?" Emory asked.

Petros grunted. "Do you really want to anger a security agent when she's in the middle of an assignment?"

Emory couldn't afford to cause a scene. "I have to go," he grumbled and hung up.

"So you're unattached?" the woman said.

"Fortunately, yes."

The agent appeared troubled by Blair's comment. "Why do you say that?"

Blair looked about then lowered her voice. "Honestly, I have no interest in a relationship right now."

Emory paced the floor. He had no idea what sort of information the security agent was seeking, but Blair was pouring herself out like a fountain.

"Dating can be so disappointing," the woman said sympathetically. "Seemingly endless rendezvous with tedious, dreary people that lead nowhere."

"Exactly." Blair spun the feathers in the air a few times. "Except in my case, I'm the tedious one. My dates have all been with very interesting and attractive men."

The stranger's melodious laugh was infectious. "You're adorable!" She picked up two cans of organic kitten food. "Just remember, you'll know when you've found the right one. You'll feel it."

Blair smiled wearily. "Maybe."

They wrapped up their pleasantries, and Emory waited for the agent to depart before materializing beside Blair.

"Emory, I just met the nicest woman—" She pointed the feathered toy down the aisle, but the woman was nowhere in sight.

"Blair, I need you to stop talking to random strangers and focus." He snatched the toy from her hands and threw it onto a shelf. "I just found you a rich, handsome doctor who loves dogs."

She grabbed his arm before he could cross over. "But I'm not into dogs."

"Neither am I. They drool, they shed, they poop—but that's not the point."

"Fine," Blair said resignedly. "Where is he?"

"One aisle over."

Blair sighed and headed toward the grooming supplies. She turned the corner, and a large blue shopping cart slammed into her hip, knocking her to the hard tile floor. Emory shot the oblivious doctor in the heart.

"Very subtle," she muttered from the ground.

"I'm so sorry!" The doctor rushed to her side. "Are you hurt?"

"I'm okay." Blair got to her feet and peeked inside his shopping cart, where two small dogs were wagging their bushy white tails. "Are they all right?"

He scratched behind their ears, and they melted at his touch. "They'll be fine."

"Can I pet them?"

"Of course! They love the attention."

Blair reached into the cart. Both dogs lunged at her, and she snatched her hand away before they could clamp down on her fingers. They barked, less than pleased with her attempts to charm them. Emory backed away. His close proximity wasn't helping their situation.

"Bart, Baxter!" They fell silent at the doctor's firm command. "I-I'm so sorry. They never behave like that."

She smiled politely. "It's not your fault."

"I feel so bad. First I ram you with my cart, then you almost lose a limb."

Blair laughed, and the doctor's expression softened. "My name is Peter, and those two rascals are, of course, Bart and Baxter."

"I'm Blair."

"Well, Blair, I'd like to make up for the bad behavior of the Cary family. This really isn't like us at all."

"How do you propose to do that?" she asked with a slight grin.

"Dinner tomorrow night...?"

"Will Bart or Baxter be picking me up?"

"Neither," he said, pulling out a small pad and pen. "They recently lost their driving privileges."

Blair laughed, and he handed her the writing pad. Emory glanced behind to see if he had an audience to his successful match, but the security agent was nowhere in sight. Blair quickly scribbled down her number.

The doctor ripped out the thin piece of paper and placed it in the interior pocket of his suit jacket. "I'll call you."

"I look forward to it."

Blair wandered down the aisle while the good-natured doctor continued his pet shopping in the opposite direction. Emory placed his bow across his chest and walked beside her, taking a closer look at her downcast eyes. It was clear she wasn't actually looking forward to the date. She wasn't even faking a smile.

She stopped midstep, the soles of her leather boots squeaking against the tile floor. "Peter?" she called.

"Yes?" His wide grin faded when he saw the distress on her face.

"I'm sorry. I can't go out with you."

Emory rubbed his temples. There was no way for him to regain control of the situation.

The doctor nodded, mistaking her meaning. "Are you free next weekend?"

"No, you don't understand. I just came out of a series of strained relationships, and right now, I'm not in a position to form any sort of emotional attachment." She clasped her hands in front of her and squeezed so hard her knuckles cracked. "You seem like a genuinely nice person, and I don't want to waste your time."

"I see." He watched her, his brow furrowing. "Well, I wish you the best."

"You too," she said.

Blair hurried toward the exit, with Emory close behind in the Enarine realm. The frigid winter air hit him like a brick wall as he stepped out of the store. She approached his motorcycle and grabbed her helmet. Her fingers trembled as she attempted to unbuckle the clasp, and she fumbled with the cumbersome strap, unable to loosen it. Emory materialized beside her, pried the helmet out of her hands, and unbuckled it in one swift motion.

Suddenly, Blair turned and clung to the collar of his leather jacket, burying her face in his chest. "I couldn't do it."

"It's okay." He wrapped his arms around her frozen body. "I didn't like his stupid dogs."

"It's been six months. I should be able to feel something. *Anything*." Blair searched his eyes. "Shouldn't I?"

"We'll find someone you connect with," he soothed. "I promise."

"What if we don't?" Blair pulled away. "What if you get banished, and I end up here alone and—"

"Stop." Emory clenched his teeth. "I can't think about that right now."

Blair bit back another objection and leaned her head against his chest. He was as unnerved by her disquieting thoughts as she was. Despite her chill, he held her close without a word and purposely slowed the beating of his heart. He knew he couldn't completely ease her troubled mind, but at least the steady rhythm of his Vycrin heartbeat would have a calming effect on her. Her muscles began to relax.

Emory peered across the parking lot and caught sight of the security agent leaning against a black Mercedes as she talked on the phone. She gave Blair a friendly wave, her pink diamond ring glistening in the sunlight. Blair waved back.

"Who is that?" Emory asked casually.

"The woman I was telling you about. She was giving me dating tips."

"Taking relationship advice from strangers again?"

"It's not like it matters." Her voice was barely above a whisper. "It won't change anything."

His matchmaking methods weren't working. Usually, he could rely purely on his instincts to secure a partner for her. Now she wasn't even willing to go through with a first date. They were both tired and burned out. "We should take tomorrow night off."

"Are you being serious?" she said.

He rubbed her back to keep her warm. "Let's stay in and order Chinese food."

Blair had often teased him about being homeless because he spent so much time at her apartment. She glanced up at him and quipped, "Your place or mine?"

Emory didn't hesitate. "Mine."

CHAPTER 16

"What does yours say?" Emory had tossed his crumpled fortune aside on the quartz kitchen island. It had never crossed his mind to read it. "Those things are a total sham."

"What's the point of opening a fortune cookie without reading the fortune?" Blair asked, snatching up the discarded piece of paper. "Yours says, 'Excitement and intrigue follow you closely wherever you go.'" She opened her fortune cookie. "Mine says, 'Something you lost will soon turn up.'" She pondered the short phrase then frowned.

"See what I mean?"

"You might be right," she agreed, tossing it back with the other fortunes.

Eight containers of Chinese food were scattered across the island as they shared an assortment of entrees and appetizers from Blair's favorite restaurant. It was a completely new experience for Emory—he'd never before had a guest in his home. That morning, he'd spent a solid hour dusting and making sure everything was in its place. It was. It always was. He spent the remainder of the day pacing as he waited for Blair. When she arrived, she immediately made herself comfortable at the kitchen island and was so excited about his appliances that she didn't even care to see the rest of the house when he offered to give her a tour. It didn't take much to impress her.

Emory reached past Blair and picked up a large heap of lo mein with his chopsticks. "You and I are going to a wedding in May," he announced before taking a large bite.

Blair gasped. "Laith proposed?"

"Hardly." He spoke between chews. "Hana's a bridesmaid in her cousin's wedding, and she was given a plus-one."

Blair looked impressed. "They're getting serious."

"Darion bought a suit."

"Very serious." She bit into an egg roll. "Has he said it yet?"

"No." Emory picked over the shrimp fried rice. "I shot him three times at that concert last week, and the best he could choke out was that he was 'deeply attracted' to her."

Blair's forehead wrinkled. "What does that mean?"

"I have no idea. My guess is the rapid succession of arrows muddled his brain."

"Or he doesn't love her."

Emory's hands dropped to his lap. "What do you mean?" he asked, confused.

"Maybe he doesn't love her."

"That can't be. I shot him directly in the heart, and I wouldn't have done so if I wasn't sure of the match."

"Your arrows are potent," Blair said, taking another bite. "But you once told me you can't force someone to feel love if it's not in their heart. There must be something holding him back. Something you've overlooked."

Emory mulled over Darion and Hana's past encounters. "She is very private," he concluded, after a while. "He tells her everything, but she rarely brings up her past."

"Maybe he doesn't feel like she's been completely open with him."

Emory thought about how Blair wasn't always open with *him*, and he understood why Darion might not express his true feelings if he sensed something was missing from his relationship with Hana. He grabbed a bottle of red wine and picked up her empty wineglass. "Do you think he's still hung up on the fact that she doesn't really want kids?"

"It's possible." Blair leaned her elbow on the island and rested her chin in her hand. She watched him pour her a glass of wine. "Do *you* want kids?"

"I... I don't know." He slid the glass to her. "Do you?"

She took a sip. "I think so."

Emory poured the last of the wine into his glass. Most Vycrin were concerned about three things: finding their soul mates, helping *other* people find their soul mates, and procreating. Emory wasn't quite like others of his kind. "Starting a family isn't something I think about."

She tilted her head. "Why not?"

"Because..." He hesitated, swirling the wine in his glass and watching rivulets of the liquid creep down the sides. "I'm not open to the idea of marriage."

Blair sat up straighter. "How can you say that?" she asked, indignant. "Your entire existence revolves around love and getting couples to commit to each other."

"Exactly. Which is why I don't believe in true love."

"You don't believe in true love?" Her tone was skeptical.

"No," Emory said with little emotion. "I don't."

"Then why do you do any of this?"

"It's my job."

Blair shook her head in dismay. "Someone like you shouldn't have any authority over love."

"I agree," he said, unabashed.

"So how did you end up with such a terrible occupation?"

He slowly swirled the contents of his glass. "In our culture, Vycrin are taught that we spread love and desire throughout the universe to prevent civilized societies from dissolving into chaos and ruin. Without our involvement, entire worlds crumble."

"You don't believe that?"

"I don't know if I do or not." He drank a portion of the dry wine. "But my father was a true believer. He claimed love was the most powerful force in the universe." Emory tapped a finger rhythmically against the glass, and the deep-red liquid shuddered with the beating of his heart. "And he loved my mother deeply." His throat tightened. "After her death, he experienced a complete mental collapse. Grief consumed him. His emotional instability compromised his work, and over the course of several years, he made a series of unsuitable matches, resulting in one permanently broken heart. After his hearing, he was banished from the Earth realm, and I was summoned to take over for him when I turned eighteen."

Emory finished the last of the wine and placed his glass on the smooth island. "So to answer your question..." He stared into her dark eyes. "No, I don't believe in true love because I know what it can do to people when they lose it."

A single tear rolled down Blair's cheek. Emory reached up and cupped her face in his hand, wiping away her cold tear. "I didn't mean to make you cry."

She gently leaned against his hand. "Have you ever been in love?"

Emory backed away. "No. I never allow myself to get that close to anyone."

"That's why you don't understand your clients." Her voice was soft. "You have no idea what it feels like to expose your heart to someone else."

Emory fell silent. It was true that he kept everyone at a distance to avoid the emotional entanglements that had ruined his father. He'd never once considered his lack of personal experience with relationships to be a hindrance to his job.

Blair's attention fell upon the scattered mess of half-eaten Chinese food, and she began placing covers on some of the containers. "We ordered too much again."

Emory helped her pack up the leftovers. She stacked the containers, and he placed them in his stainless-steel refrigerator. He lingered in front of the open double doors, cool air blowing down on him. Blair wet a cloth under the sink faucet and wiped up the remaining crumbs from the countertops.

"We should play a game," he suggested.

She looked up at him, intrigued. "What kind of game?"

"Kottabos." He closed the refrigerator doors and pulled a bottle of wine from a lower cabinet. "It's a game my family likes to play."

"Teach me."

"Grab a corkscrew."

She found a silver corkscrew in a drawer and followed him to the living room. "I love games," Blair said with a giggle as she sat next to Emory on his long gray couch. "Especially ones that involve wine."

Emory smiled. He reached under the glass coffee table for two wide bowl-shaped drinking cups. The shallow terracotta vessels had symmetrical handles and were decorated with elaborate ancient banquet scenes.

"What are you doing?" she cried. "These are priceless antiques."

"It's okay. My grandparents would be proud I'm keeping the tradition going. These are called kylix." He uncorked the bottle of red wine, and the strong, sweet aroma filled the room.

Blair closed her eyes, inhaling deeply. "Where did you get the wine? It's heavenly."

"My uncle owns a vineyard in California, and I asked him to send me a couple of bottles."

Blair chuckled. "I didn't know Vycrin were in the wine industry."

"The vineyard exists solely in the Enarine realm." Emory scraped the corners of the expensive label with his thumbnail. "It's a love potion."

Blair's smile faded. "It's always about business with you, isn't it?"

Emory felt a prickle of guilt. "You're my client, first and fore-most."

"I know. You constantly remind me." Blair leaned closer and ex-amined the bottle with curious eyes. "It will make me fall in love with... you?"

"No, nothing like that," Emory said. "It will simply enhance what is already deep within your heart."

"How will I know if it works?"

"You'll feel whole again."

Blair's dark eyes met his. "And if I don't?"

"Then we'll have to try something else," he said soberly.

Blair smoothed out the creases of her blouse. "How do we play?"

Emory partially filled the drinking bowls and handed her the vessel with more wine in it. He positioned a throw pillow on her left side. "The objective is to get the last drops of your wine into the bowl on the coffee table, but the catch is you have to stay in a reclining po-sition."

Emory drank the strong wine. A warm sensation spread through his entire body. Wine made from the enchanted vineyards of the Enarine realm had the potential to cause inebriation in both humans *and* Vycrin. They certainly wouldn't be finishing the bottle. He took up half of the couch as he leaned on his side, close to Blair, and curled his finger around one of the handles of the kylix. With a flick of his wrist, he sent the last few drops from the cup flying into an empty silver bowl in the center of the table.

Blair clapped with excitement. "You make it look so easy."

"Try it."

Emory watched Blair as she swallowed the pinot noir. She rested on her left side and aimed the heavy pottery at the wide silver dish. Her position was awkward, and red wine catapulted across the coffee table and spattered across the thick white area rug. She gaped at Emory in horror.

He frowned. "Hmm… not even close. This isn't going to be much of a competition."

Emory refilled their drinking bowls, adding more than he had poured in the first round. The wine tasted sweeter than he remembered. All of the strain and tension in his body melted away. He took aim. The remnants of his cup glided into the silver container.

Blair sipped her wine and fixed her eyes on the target.

"Take your time," he instructed, "and focus."

She turned to him with a smile. "You're slurring."

He ignored her. His uncle's wine wasn't *that* strong. Crimson drops rained onto the glass coffee table, hitting every spot except the center basin.

Emory held back a chuckle as he poured more wine. "Imagine the shame of you losing a drinking game. It will be as if your college days were for nothing."

He swallowed the contents of his bowl in three gulps. The room was heating up. He leaned on his side and completed another flawless round.

Blair drank from her bowl. "I think the wine is messing up my aim."

Her third attempt flew backward and caught Emory in the eye. He let out a startled yelp and fell flat on his back, the strong liquid burning his pupil.

"I'm so sorry!" Blair cried. She placed the kylix on the coffee table and straddled his chest.

"How is that even possible?" he said, blinking hard.

"Can you see?" Blair spread his eyelids open with her cold fingers. She inspected him with worried eyes, her face inches away from his.

"Get off of me!" He grabbed her by the waist and tossed her to the opposite end of the couch. He crawled on top of her. "You're the last person who should be administering first aid."

Her giggling made him smile. Heat pulsed through his body, and he rested his forehead against hers to cool down. "Is it hot in here? I'm hot. Let's go to the balcony. Have I shown you the balcony?"

He jumped to his feet, and Blair sat up. "What's wrong with you tonight?" she asked with a delighted grin.

Emory drank from the bottle and handed it to her. She drank a large gulp and followed him to the balcony. He opened the glass doors, and a cool gust of wind rushed over them.

Emory breathed in the crisp night air. "Much better."

He slid out a metal chair from his round cast-iron table for Blair. She swayed slightly before settling next to him and placing the half-empty bottle between them. His three-bedroom penthouse over-looked the Potomac River and the bright twinkling lights of the cap-ital.

Blair pulled her feet onto the chair and wrapped her arms around her legs. "Thanks for inviting me over. Your place is beauti-ful."

"You really like it?"

"It's perfect. I wouldn't change a thing."

Emory smiled. "Liar."

"Maybe some colorful paint." She had a small sip and handed him the bottle. "Or cute throw pillows."

He grunted. "That's why I'd never let you decorate my home."

Blair stifled a giggle. "I couldn't spend a lot of time here anyway."

"Why not?" he asked, somewhat disappointed.

"No TV."

He let out a chuckle. A Vycrin owning a television would be madness. Though it wouldn't be difficult to keep secret. No Vycrin would dare enter another's home without permission—it was very bad form, and there was no telling *where* in the universe one might end up. The particular coordinates etched into Emory's doorframe opened a portal that sent unwanted guests directly to a seedy little joint in the Thiyden realm where he'd once gotten food poising so bad he thought he was going to die.

"I'll buy one," Emory stated.

"Just for me?" she teased.

"Only for you."

A soft breeze blew across the balcony, and they fell into a meditative silence. "Can I ask you a personal question?" Blair said after a while.

He swallowed a mouthful of wine and nodded.

"Out of everyone in this realm," she said, "why did you choose me as one of your clients?"

Emory gazed across the tranquil waters. "I thought if your soul was as beautiful as your outward appearance... you would make someone very happy one day."

"Really?" Her voice was soft.

Emory burst into laughter. He loved how gullible she was. "No. I saw you dancing at your sister's wedding and couldn't take my eyes off you." He leaned closer. "What kind of move was that, anyway? You landed *so* hard, I swore you broke your tailbone."

Blair tried to suppress a smile and confiscated the bottle. "Obviously, I was drunk, you fool."

Emory shook his head. "That's when I knew I had to have you." He settled back in his chair. "I didn't have a suitor to match you with at the time, so I took you as a solo client."

She gave him a stern look out of the corner of her eye. "That had better not be in your audit report."

"You know I omitted certain details from your file." He stifled a chuckle. "If Petros found out that was the only reason I secured you as a client, he'd put me on an automatic suspension and confiscate my arrows."

Blair sipped the wine. "Who's Petros?"

"My supervisor." Emory wrestled the bottle from her cold fingers and swallowed a generous portion. "I've known him all my life—he was close friends with my father. But he doesn't tolerate any 'tomfoolery,' as he would say."

She quietly pondered his words. "Do you really just keep me around for your own amusement?"

It took everything in his power to keep a straight face. "Absolutely."

She grabbed the bottle, grinning wickedly. "You're cut off."

"Blair!"

She scrambled to her feet as he tried to take what was left of the wine from her. She ran into the living room, and he followed in close pursuit, hurtling over a leather ottoman. Blair jumped onto the couch and stood on the firm cushions.

"You want it?" She twisted the bottle in his face.

Emory reached for the bottle as Blair hopped off the back of the sofa and ran into the kitchen. He cornered her behind the island. She smiled and guzzled down the remaining wine. Emory shoved the barstools out of his way and climbed onto the quartz countertop. Her eyes widened. She was unable to contain her laughter, and thin red drops sprayed from her lips. Emory lunged for her and fell off the island. He slammed onto the hardwood floor with a loud thud. Ignoring the shooting pain from his crushed limbs, he grabbed her ankle before she could dash away.

"Let go!" she shrieked.

Blair shook him off and charged down the hallway toward the bedrooms, empty bottle in hand. Her wild giggling spurred him on. Emory rushed to his feet and switched realms, slipping in front of her. He entered his master bedroom seconds before she slammed the door and locked it. Emory materialized into the Earth realm and tripped on a thick area rug. The thought occurred to him, as he fell to the ground, that his uncle's wine was a bit stronger than he remembered. Blair took a step back in the dark and stumbled on top of him, laughing. The bottle slipped out of her fingers and landed on the plush carpet. Emory caught her before her head could hit the floor. He liked how she fit into his arms.

"You cheated," she complained.

"I'm a god." He climbed over her. "I can do anything I want."

Blair, half-hidden in the dim light of the moonlit bedroom gave him a playful look. "You're only half god."

"The Vycrin side is dominant. It negates any inferior species."

She bit back a smile. "You think I'm inferior?"

Emory grinned and brushed curly strands of hair away from her face. "Which one of us is on top?"

Blair broke into an uncontrollable fit of laughter. The room tilted.

Emory searched her dark eyes. "How do you feel?"

"I feel goood..." She snickered.

Heat rushed through his body, and he felt a twinge of vertigo. Emory distracted himself from the unsettling sensation by focusing on her lips—her perfectly formed lips. He wondered why he'd never noticed how alluring they were until that moment. He was tempted to trace their edges with his tongue.

"Emory?" Blair whispered, closing her eyes. "Can you do something to make your room stop spinning?"

"I can try," he said in a soft voice.

Emory leaned closer, lingering over the scent of her flowery perfume. His pulse hastened. He gave her a light kiss on her cheek. When she didn't pull away, he brushed his lips against her icy neck, tenderly kissing her exposed skin. He closed his eyes and gave in to the overwhelming desire building inside of him. The biting chill emanating from her body failed to overtake him as he caressed her soft skin with his tongue. Emory slipped his hand up the back of her shirt, pulling her into him.

Blair let out a quiet snore.

Emory's eyes shot open. He sat motionless, waiting for her to move. Her second breath confirmed his fears—she was sound asleep. Emory's heart raced. He inched away, moving gently enough not to wake her. Then he knelt by her side and stared down at her in the dark room. The intense craving he'd felt when he touched her had been intoxicating. His heart ached, knowing she was unable to feel even the slightest connection between them despite his efforts.

A dizzy spell crept upon him. *Stupid wine.*

Emory scooped Blair into his arms and hauled her onto his bed. He collapsed beside her. His head pulsed. They were going to be wrecked in the morning. He made a mental note to speak with his uncle about the potency of his blends.

Blair let out a loud snore that reminded him of a lumberjack. Emory laughed hard, rolled off the edge of the bed, and passed out.

CHAPTER 17

A loud ringtone jolted Emory awake. He found himself face-down on the floor, drooling on the carpet. Brilliant-white sunlight poured into his master bedroom through the sheer drapes, and he cursed himself for not getting blackout curtains. The phone rang again. He had difficulty lifting the weight of his head.

"Emory..." Blair called out from the bed, her voice hoarse. "Your phone."

His bruised body felt like a furnace. "Answer it," he begged.

The high-pitched clanging was deafening. Blair covered her face with a feather pillow and moaned. "Make it stop!"

Emory dragged himself to his feet and climbed onto the bed. He reached across Blair and grabbed his cellphone from the nightstand.

"Hello?"

"Hi, this is Malena. I hope you don't mind, but my sister gave me your number." Her nervous words were muffled by two chattering voices in the background. "Blair didn't pick up when I tried calling her this morning, and I was wondering if she was with you."

"It's your sister," Emory whispered. He tried to hand Blair the phone, but she waved him away. "She just woke up. We overslept."

The voices in the background went silent, and there was a long pause.

"I was just wondering if she was joining us for brunch," Malena said.

"Yes!" Blair yelled through the pillow. "I need something to absorb all the alcohol."

Emory grabbed a small remote from the nightstand and put the ceiling fan on the highest setting. "Did you hear her?"

Malena contained a chuckle. "Do you want us to pick her up?"

"I can take a taxi," Blair said into the pillow.

"I'll bring her to the restaurant," Emory said.

Blair slid the pillow away from her face, her eyes narrow. "You should come too," she declared. She half shouted into the phone, "Emory's coming too!"

"Fabulous!" Malena said. "We'll see you both in twenty."

Emory hung up. "Do you think you can shake it off in the next ten minutes?"

"I'll get it together," Blair muttered. She rolled onto her stomach and stuffed her head between the pillows.

Emory leaned on his side and rubbed her frozen back with the tips of his fingers. He wished he had shown a bit more restraint with the wine so she didn't have to suffer the ill effects. The bottle they'd shared over dinner, compounded with the one they drank during the game, had pushed her well over her limit.

After a few minutes, he spoke up. "I'm sorry about last night."

"Why are you sorry? I had fun. Didn't you?"

He continued to massage her. Clearly, she didn't remember the kiss, and Emory didn't know whether or not to be relieved. Despite the chill, touching her made his heart race. "I did." Emory slowly drew figure eights on the small of her back.

"Stop." Blair curled onto her side and faced him. "That tickles."

Emory searched her eyes. "You don't like when I tickle you?"

She smiled. "I didn't say that."

Emory pulled her closer and squeezed her waist.

Blair laughed and squirmed out of his reach. "You're going to make us late." She crawled off the bed and scampered into the master bathroom. After a moment, he heard water running.

Emory stared up at the twirling fan blades, attempting to sort out his thoughts. He liked waking up with her. It felt natural.

He shook his head. *What am I thinking?* Their evening together had been a mistake—it had muddled his good judgment. Clients were clients. Not equal partners, and certainly not companions. He needed to regain control, and he was going to start by establishing clear boundaries in their relationship.

Emory got up and started getting ready. His eyes shifted to the open bathroom door. "You gave your sister my number?"

The water shut off. Blair peeked out of the bathroom, a yellow toothbrush dangling from her mouth. "Yeah, in case she ever needed to reach me when I was out with you." She continued brushing her teeth. "Is that okay?"

"It's fine. I wouldn't want her to be worried about you. I just think we should establish some—is that my toothbrush?"

"Yes." She pulled it out of her mouth. "Do you mind?"

A strange form of lunacy was overtaking his rational mind. "Not at all."

· · ❧ · ·

THIRTY MINUTES LATER, Emory and Blair entered a crowded restaurant. Hungry patrons lined the wood-panel walls of the front entrance, and those fortunate enough to find seats slumped down on narrow benches as they surveyed the menu. Blair didn't bother the frazzled hostess—she had no trouble spotting her friends at the far end of the restaurant. She waved and headed in their direction.

"Wait!" Emory grabbed her arm. "What do I say to them?"

Blair seemed puzzled. "You can say anything you want. They're my friends."

Emory shifted. "I've never—I don't usually have conversations with other humans, aside from you."

"Don't worry." She patted his arm. "You probably won't get a word in edgewise."

Blair led the way to a round table where Preya, Savannah, and Malena were waiting for them to arrive.

"Sorry we're late," Blair said.

A dark-haired woman with a sleek modern bob got to her feet. She was poised, her posture almost too perfect as she walked over to them. Her soft smile mirrored Blair's, and the two women had a similar russet-brown complexion. Malena stood five inches taller than her younger sister.

She wrapped her arm around Blair in what was more of a chokehold than a hug. "Rough night?" she said under her breath.

"I don't remember," Blair mumbled.

Emory stifled his disappointment. It was probably for the best.

Malena shook her head and playfully slapped her sister's backside before returning to her seat.

Blair turned to Emory. "That's my sister," she said, indicating Malena, "and this is Preya."

There wasn't a hint of amusement in Preya's eyes as she studied him. Her copper skin was without blemish. Layers of long burgundy hair framed her face but did little to soften her sharp features.

After a few moments, she gave a nod of approval. "We were beginning to think Blair made you up."

Blair smiled. "Wouldn't be the first time!"

They all laughed.

"And this is Savannah," Blair concluded, gesturing to the last woman at the table.

Savannah's pointy nose scrunched up when she smiled at Emory. Her blond pixie haircut complemented her heart-shaped face, and her warm beige skin had a golden overtone. She brushed renegade bangs away from her eyes to get a better look at him. She was petite and compact, like Blair.

"So you're Blair's new buddy, huh?" The pixie's voice was deep.

Emory nodded. He kept his hands tucked in the pockets of his leather jacket, his fingers clenching the interior fabric. Blair nudged him gently. Emory reached across the table and gave each of them a firm handshake, the physical connection sealing their memory of him forever.

"Nice to meet you." His voice was trembling. "Blair talks about you all the time."

Emory helped Blair take off her short jacket and pulled out a seat for her. He settled next to her without a word. He stared at the menu, unable to concentrate with all of the eyes bearing down on him. A waiter came by with drinks and placed a glass of water in front of him.

"We ordered your usual." Savannah downed her mimosa and started on another.

The waiter put a Bloody Mary in front of Blair, who gagged. Emory grabbed the strong drink, swallowed the whole thing down, and removed the empty glass from her sight. He bit into the celery garnish and handed her his tall glass of water. She had a sip and thanked him under her breath. Her friends exchanged surprised looks but said nothing.

"The rest of the orders are in," the waiter said. "What can I get you two?"

"I'll have pancakes, bacon, and home fries." Blair turned to Emory, who was struggling to make a decision. "He'll have a Greek omelet with extra olives."

Emory handed back the menu, grateful that she took the guesswork out of everything. He just needed to get through the hour without saying anything unusual.

"What do you do for work?" Preya asked.

He glanced at Blair.

"Emory's in HR." Blair sucked on a small ice cube as she spoke. "He's a real people person." She winked at him.

Emory gave them a weak smile. "I love humans."

The ladies burst into a fit of laughter.

"He's cute," Savannah said.

"How did the brochures turn out?" Blair asked Preya, changing the subject.

She rolled her eyes. "Don't get me started."

"They didn't like your design?" Savannah asked.

"Our art director decided she wants us to go in a different direction—creatively."

Malena seemed baffled. "What does she mean by that?"

"It means we have to start from scratch," Preya said scornfully.

"Again?" Savannah grimaced. "I'd quit on the spot!"

Emory could not keep his knee from bouncing. Blair slowly slipped her cold fingers between his and held his hand under the table. He stopped shaking. Her touch was soft, and he was suddenly able to focus on the fast-paced chatter that ensued—the drycleaners ruining outfits, their new workout routines, the best hair conditioners. *Coconut oil? Who in their right mind would put food in their hair?* Emory decided he would try it. The chatter moved on to babies, the idiots who held up traffic, and the futility of priority boarding. After twenty minutes, Emory even knew how to laugh at the appropriate times.

The waiter came by with their food, and the table fell silent for the first time that afternoon. Blair cut into her fluffy pancakes.

"They didn't give you enough syrup," Emory said.

Blair shrugged. "It's fine."

"Don't be ridiculous. I'll get you more." He got up and said to her friends, "Blair likes to drown her pancakes. I swear, she doesn't even like pancakes—she just likes syrup."

"Don't encourage her sweet tooth," Malena teased.

"Ignore her!" Blair said. "She's a health nut."

Emory grinned and left to search for their waiter. The champagne-fueled brunch was going better than expected, and he'd almost let his guard down. *Almost.*

"What happened last night?" Preya whispered urgently.

Overhearing this, Emory glanced over his shoulder. The three women were huddled together with their full attention on Blair. He quickly crossed into the Enarine realm and disappeared from view. He moved closer to the table to listen in on their conversation.

Blair pushed her plate aside and spoke in a low voice. "This time, I *really* wish I knew."

Savannah pounded her small fist against the table. "You always do this. Think harder."

"I'm serious," Blair said, a tinge of regret in her voice. "I have no idea."

Emory couldn't fathom why that bothered him so much. He had evaded a potentially embarrassing situation with his client. He should have been relieved. But he wasn't.

"What's the last thing you remember?" Malena asked.

Blair tapped her nails against the table. "He invited me over for dinner, and we ordered Chinese food." She snapped her fingers. "Then we played a drinking game—"

"Who won?" Preya interrupted.

"I'm not sure," Blair said. "It seemed like one of those games no one ever really finishes."

Savannah nodded. "Like Monopoly."

"Halfway through the game, Emory said he was hot, so we went outside. The next thing I know, he's chasing me off the balcony... then I woke up—fully clothed—in his bed this morning."

Savannah sat back and folded her arms. "What a lame night."

"In all seriousness," Malena said, "you're getting too old to be waking up in strangers' beds, so at least it was Emory's."

"It shows a level of maturity," Preya said in agreement. She took a sip of champagne. "Except the blacking-out part."

The women broke into laughter. Emory didn't know what to make of the conversation, and he certainly couldn't ask for clarification since he shouldn't have been eavesdropping in the first place. He decided it was best to focus on something that *was* in his control. He materialized in the Earth realm, secured a larger container of syrup, and returned to the table.

"And I have to find a cute dress for a wedding Emory's taking me to," Blair said as he settled beside her.

"You should go with something strapless," Malena suggested.

"But nothing too slinky," Preya warned.

"Who cares about a silly dress?" Savannah turned to Emory. "What happened after the balcony?"

He shifted slightly. Blair was snickering and trying not to choke on her pancakes. "Go ahead. Tell them."

Emory's heart raced. He wondered if the entire situation was some sort of elaborate setup to get him to expose his inner feelings. *Are all women capable of such manipulation? And why in a group setting?* Perhaps they were stronger in numbers. *Mind control.*

"Blair fell asleep," he said calmly, "so I put her to bed."

The women sat in silence for a long time. Blair licked her fork, a hint of a smile flickering at the edges of her mouth, and didn't make eye contact with any of her friends.

Preya raised her glass. "To maturity."

Their collective laughter echoed through the restaurant. Emory relaxed. There was no setup. They were just a harmless bunch of lushes.

Emory slid his plate next to Blair's. She cut a small portion of his omelet and ate it as he picked up a slice of bacon from her syrup-drenched plate.

Savannah's tiny mouth twisted to the side. "I thought you said he was selfish and didn't like to share his food with you."

Blair poured the last of the syrup over her home fries. "That was just when we first started hanging out."

Emory glanced at Blair. "Selfish?"

Savannah ticked off a list on her fingers. "And arrogant and bossy and critical—"

Malena kicked Savannah under the table.

"Don't worry, Emory." Blair had another bite of his omelet. "I've never said anything behind your back that I haven't told you to your face."

"Oh..."

Emory wasn't sure how he felt about her perception of him. He failed to hear the conversations that followed as he pondered her statement. He'd never given a second thought to what humans might think about him, but that was because no one ever remembered him. As it turned out, one person in his life who could form an opinion about him had only negative things to say. He ate the rest of his meal in silence and didn't realize he'd made it through the meal until a busboy removed his empty plate.

"You can split the check five ways," Malena said to the waiter.

Emory was shaken from his trance. "I'll take care of it." He handed the waiter his credit card before anyone could raise an objection.

"You should bring him along every time," Preya said to Blair.

"He's like your little pay pal." Savannah giggled and nudged Malena. "Get it?"

Blair shook her head as she rose to her feet. "He's not an ATM, ladies."

Emory jumped up. "Where are you going?"

"To the bathroom."

"Can't you hold it?" he whispered.

"Do you want me to pee on your bike?"

Emory stood and thought, weighing the pros and cons.

Blair rolled her eyes. "Two minutes. You'll be fine."

Emory lowered himself back to his seat as she left him alone with her friends.

A smile parted Savannah's lips. "We don't bite."

"Too hard," Preya added.

They laughed. The waiter returned with the receipt, and Emory took his time signing the bill. He felt Malena staring at him, and the sudden silence at the table was unnerving. *Two minutes.*

"Are you stringing Blair along?" Malena asked.

Emory met her serious gaze. "No. I want to be with her."

"Good." Malena sipped her champagne. "Because she deserves better than the losers and deadbeats who have somehow managed to weasel their way into her life."

A wave of guilt washed over him. "Blair is very special to me, and I care about her deeply." He clenched his jaw. He sounded like one of his swooning clients. *Why am I admitting my feelings to her friends?* It was the mind control. Even after the champagne and the cocktails, they were fully capable of drawing out his emotions. The drinking was just a ruse. *Women!*

Malena sat back and gestured to the other ladies. "Is there anything you'd like to ask us about Blair?"

Emory nervously twirled the pen between his fingers. "I don't know her favorite flower."

"Roses," Preya said. "Preferably red."

He forced himself to stop fidgeting. "What can I do to make her happy?" he asked softly.

Savannah spoke up. "Be nice."

"Obviously you care about her," Preya chimed in. "So treat her like she's important to you."

Emory wasn't sure if he wanted an answer to the one question that had plagued him all afternoon. "Has she ever said anything good about me?"

Malena finished the last of her champagne before responding. "She said you always watch out for her, and you would never abandon her."

A sliver of hope—Blair trusted him. He was someone she could rely on. Someone important in her life.

Blair approached the table, smiling, and grabbed Emory's shoulders. "What are you all talking about?"

He glanced up at her. "You."

Blair laughed. "Right!" She squeezed his shoulders. "Take me home. I need a nap."

Blair hugged her friends goodbye and wrapped up bits and pieces of their conversations as Emory lingered by her side. His head hurt. He didn't know how she kept track of it all. He followed her to the exit.

"Aren't they fabulous?" Blair said.

Emory glanced back at the table. Malena gave him a warm smile and winked.

"Fabulous," he replied in all honesty.

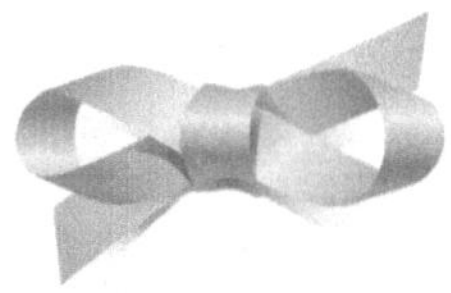

CHAPTER 18

"Is this legal?" Blair whispered as she and Emory entered the first floor of an abandoned factory building.

The entire level had been transformed into a makeshift art gallery showcasing independent work. It was clear the space was not regulated by the proper authorities, and Emory was certain they would have to make a hasty departure if law enforcement arrived. Blair accepted a glass of white wine from an individual who was far too young to be serving them.

"I highly doubt it's legal," Emory answered.

She took a sip and grimaced.

"What's wrong?" he asked, frowning.

"Sorry. I'm having a hard time going back to the cheap stuff after drinking your wine."

Emory didn't reply. They inspected a colorful canvas that, according to the placard to the left of it, was supposed to represent "the suffering and torment of the artist's soul." It looked like a five-year-old had painted it. Blair was far more interesting to gaze at. Her black sweater dress and high-heel boots made her fit in with the eclectic group of artists.

He cleared his throat. "You look pretty in that dress."

Blair smiled. "Thanks." She tugged at the short hem. "I couldn't believe it fit."

"Ah." He searched his mind for something nice to say. "You lost weight."

"Yes! You're the only person who noticed." She wrapped her arm around his. "I lost a pound and a half."

Emory relaxed. He enjoyed having her near him as they wandered through the exhibit together. He didn't understand human art, but Blair seemed to enjoy trying to make sense out of each of the pieces. He sighed when he caught sight of Darion and Hana. For a brief moment, he'd forgotten he was at work.

"Do you want me to..." Emory hesitated. "Do you want to meet someone?"

Blair sighed. "Can we skip it tonight?"

He fought the smile that was creeping into his face. It had been over a week, but she hadn't gone on a single date since the evening they'd spent together. "Sorry, I have to go."

"Don't worry about me." She nudged him playfully. "Free wine, appetizers, bizarre art—I think I'll be okay."

He gripped the strap of his backpack. "I'll find you as soon as I'm done."

Emory crossed over to the Enarine realm, leaving her alone in the unusual gallery. The air was still—too still. He shuddered. Abandoned buildings made him uneasy. Areas that contained high levels of decay opened portals to the Thiyden realm. The old factory was in fairly good condition, but Emory kept his guard up nonetheless. He didn't want to risk being dragged into that foreign realm accidentally. The last thing he wanted to do was spend hours searching for a portal back into the Earth realm when he could be with Blair. He wanted to be near her every waking hour of the day and was anxious whenever they were apart. With his feelings for Blair obscuring his focus, he found it increasingly difficult to concentrate on his clients.

He had to get a grip on his emotions. They were there for one reason alone—his meeting with the audit committee was less than a week away, and Darion had yet to express his feelings about Hana. Emory was determined to get a verbal declaration out of his client before turning in his report.

Hana clasped Darion's hand and led him through the exhibit. They stopped in front of four abstract portraits.

"You painted those?" Darion asked in amazement.

She nodded. "I wanted to show you what I've been working on in my classes."

"They're incredible." He kissed her forehead. "I'll commission one for my apartment. Wouldn't that look great over the couch?"

She let out a laugh. "I would do it for free."

Emory was impressed. He'd had no idea his client was so artistic.

"Hana?" a tall young woman with stringy blond hair said from behind them.

Hana turned, her face falling. "Valerie," she said flatly. "I didn't expect to see you here."

Emory grabbed a silver arrow from his quiver. He didn't know what to make of Hana's reaction.

"How are you?" A thin smile spread across Valerie's lips as she embraced Hana. "We heard rumors you were back, but I didn't believe it."

"Back?" Darion interjected. "Back from what?"

Hana gently pushed him in front of her, ignoring the question. "Valerie, this is my boyfriend, Darion."

Valerie gave him a limp handshake. "Nice to meet you." She regarded Hana with a feigned look of concern. "How are you really?"

"I'm fine. How are you?"

"Oh, you know me. Same old same old." She eyed Hana as though hoping to find some sort of imperfection. "Well, you look great. Really healthy."

Emory was confounded by the peculiar interaction. He had no idea what Valerie was implying.

"I am, thank you." Hana linked her arm around Darion's. "It was nice seeing you again."

Hana dragged Darion away before the woman could open her mouth to say another word. Emory trailed behind as Hana led Darion to the opposite end of the gallery, away from the small clusters of people studying the artwork.

"Who was she?" Darion asked.

Hana glanced about as though searching for any other familiar faces. "Just someone I went to art school with."

They came to a stop and stared at a white canvas with a single black dot in the right-hand corner, but Darion couldn't let it go. "She said she couldn't believe you were back. Back from what?"

"I dropped out of the program after my junior year," Hana replied coolly, avoiding his eyes. "I took a couple of years off. Now I'm back."

"Why did you take the time off?"

"Work," she answered quickly.

"At the coffee shop?" He could not disguise the suspicion in his tone.

Hana sighed. "Yes. At the coffee shop. Why are you suddenly so interested?"

Darion looked at her in disbelief. "Why are you being defensive?"

Emory loaded his bow. She was hiding something deep within her heart.

"I'm sorry." She forced back her irritation. "I just don't like people getting in my business. Valerie's nosy."

"Valerie isn't the one asking you questions." His eyes were fixed on her. "I am."

"Fine." Hana folded her arms. "What do you want to know?"

"You love art, and you're clearly talented. So why did you really leave school?"

Hana's teeth were clenched. She was like a vault—all of her secrets were locked inside, and Darion didn't have the code to unlock them. Emory shot her in the heart. Nothing would be accomplished if she didn't feel she could trust him completely.

"Because I had a breakdown," Hana whispered. "Mentally."

"From the stress?"

"No. I suffer from depression."

"You do?" Darion sounded as shocked as Emory felt. "How long have you—"

"Since I was a teenager."

Emory began pacing. He had nothing in his records about her history, as he had done no research before selecting her as a client. He stopped in his tracks as he recalled what he'd first written about her in his personal field notes: *Miserable-looking barista who probably needs a boyfriend.* He decided to burn his notes as soon as he returned home. They were rubbish—and they made him seem incompetent.

"So..." Darion took his time to choose the correct words. "You left school to get additional help?"

"Yes."

After a while, he asked, "How bad did you get?"

She hesitated. "Bad."

Darion shifted as though no position made him comfortable. "What did you do?"

"Too many pills." She spoke without any sort of emotion. "Eight-week hospital stay."

They moved on to the next painting. "And now you're okay?"

Hana remained silent. Emory raised his bow and shot another arrow at her. She was worse than Blair. Every time he thought he knew her, she would reveal a completely contradictory side of herself.

"I'll never be totally okay," Hana said at last. "It's something I'll have to deal with for the rest of my life. That's why I take my meds and go to therapy."

Darion gasped. "You go to therapy?"

Hana leaned closer and spoke under her breath. "Why do you think I'm always busy Wednesday nights?"

"I assumed you were working."

"I don't work on Wednesdays."

Darion ground his teeth. "Why did you wait this long to tell me?"

"You never asked," she replied innocently.

Emory threw his hands up. "You women are all the same!" he yelled, despite the fact that she couldn't hear him.

"If your friend hadn't just put you on the spot," Darion said, "you still wouldn't have told me."

Hana looked away. "Would it have made a difference if I did?"

"I-I don't know." He shook his head, looking disillusioned. "I just can't believe I'm finding out about this now after we've been together for six months."

"It's not something I go around telling strangers."

"I'm not a stranger." Darion's tone was firm. "I'm your boyfriend."

"That was a very dark time in my life." Hana turned back to the painting, her face pinched. "It's difficult for me to talk about."

He stared at her. "I still had a right to know what I was getting into."

"Point taken," Emory said. It was his fault for focusing too much attention on Darion's commitment issues when he should have been helping Hana feel comfortable enough to open up about her personal struggles.

"*Getting into*," Hana murmured. "Meaning you never would have asked me out if you had known about my issues."

"No," Darion replied. "I'm not saying that."

"What *are* you saying?"

"It's... it's a lot to process, Hana." Darion studied the canvas, but it was clear his mind was far from the painting. "I think I just need some time."

"I understand." Her expression lacked any sort of emotion. "You think we should break up."

"That's not what he's saying!" Emory shouted. "Listen to what he's saying!"

Darion's mouth was agape. "What?"

"You need time to figure out if you want to be with me."

Darion grasped her hand. "I need more time *with* you." He laced his fingers between hers. "I want to know who you are, Hana. Not who you pretend to be."

She wrapped both hands around his. "In that case, I have to tell you something else."

He leaned closer. "You can tell me anything."

"I... I hate ice cream."

Darion relaxed. "I knew it. That's why you always let me pick the flavors." He let out a heavy sigh, and a small smile crossed his lips. "We have a lot of catching up to do."

Emory twirled an arrow between his fingers as he watched Darion and Hana walk through the gallery hand in hand. Their pastel-orange auras did little to set his mind at ease, despite the fact that the two of them were committed. He had underestimated the seriousness of their relationship. They were not as volatile as his other clients, but he needed to rid himself of the misguided belief that their issues were inconsequential. Much more time and effort were needed to solidify their union. They would have to learn to get beyond the surface and work through their differences. It was imperative that he exercise better judgment to move the relationship forward, not covering over serious matters simply because *he* believed they were insignificant.

Emory's thoughts shifted to Blair, and he contemplated the intricacies of his evolving sentiments toward her. Before formally binding himself to Blair, he wanted to be certain her condition was improving. But while trying to mend her heart, he couldn't continue to prevent her from courting potential suitors and risk being in breach of contract. If that happened, his funds would be completely cut off. He found it difficult to reconcile his responsibilities as her matchmaker with his sudden desire for intimacy. Acting on personal impulses would compromise his professional standing, and dwelling on that fact kept his thoughts in check—for the most part.

He spotted Blair examining a sculpture made entirely of wire hangers. His eyes drifted down her curvy body, and his pulse hastened.

Frustrated, he raised his bow and shot an arrow at her heart. The heavy silver arrow glided through the air, emitting a high-pitched wail as it careened toward her chest. The arrow, unable to penetrate its target, bent in half and dropped to the floor.

Emory grabbed another arrow from his quiver. He crouched down and slammed it into the cement as hard as he could. "Selene!"

The force of the arrow cracked the concrete. Emory's heart rate slowed, and the world around him crept to a stop. Particles of dust were suspended in the air as the time frequency of the Enarine and Earth realms came into alignment. Each breath felt like an eternity. He fought through the lightheadedness. It would pass. Everything began to speed up. People in the Earth realm were suddenly moving faster than he was.

A dark vortex swirled into existence in front of him. The forceful winds almost knocked him backward, but there was no sound. There was never any sound. Brilliant flashes of blinding white light illuminated the Enarine realm, and a slender woman stumbled out of the maelstrom. The portal twisted violently behind her and imploded within itself. The time frequency stabilized, and Emory's silver arrow clanked against the floor.

Selene stood before him with a bow and custom quiver haphazardly slung over her shoulder. Her tawny light-brown skin had warm yellow undertones, and her thick raven hair was pulled into a single braid that ran down the length of her back. Emory scrambled to his feet. Standing, they were almost at eye level with one another.

Selene sucked on a pink lollipop. "What's the emergency?"

"I need—"

Selene tore open his leather jacket and patted him down. Her fingers poked and prodded his tense body. He bit back his aggravation. She grabbed hold of his chin and examined his face in her usual brusque manner. She peered at him through curious eyes.

"You're not even bleeding." There was a hint of disappointment in her voice.

Emory removed her hand from his face. "I need a favor. Off the record."

"You summoned me here for a favor?" she cried. "I was right in the middle of my stories!"

He nearly choked. "You have a television?"

"Of course not!"

Emory raised a single eyebrow.

Selene sighed heavily. "Okay, Talos owns one, and he got me into this one program." She brushed back stray hairs that had fallen out of place. "He records the new episodes so we can watch them together."

Emory cracked a smile.

"Shut up, Emory." Selene grabbed her bow and snatched a bronze arrow from her quiver. "Why did you drag me here?"

"I have a situation." He pointed across the art exhibit at Blair.

Selene squinted. "I can't make out her aura."

"That's because her heart is broken."

"What happened?" Selene shifted her lollipop to the corner of her mouth with her tongue. "Was her lover killed in a car accident or something?"

Emory cringed. Healers were notoriously callous—at least, that was how they came across. They had the unique ability to absorb the emotions of others, and since the majority of their assignments centered on death and loss, they maintained a level of distance from both humans and Vycrin in an effort to remain grounded.

"Blair hasn't been through anything that traumatic," Emory admitted.

"Then what do you expect me to do?" Selene demanded. "My arrows can only repair a heart that's suffered a traumatic loss. I can't fortify a heart that's broken any other way. You know that."

"I'm not asking you to fortify her heart." Emory lowered his voice. "I'm asking you to help me break the barrier surrounding it."

Selene's lollipop almost fell out of her mouth. "That method isn't sanctioned in this realm."

"But if it works—"

"It's too risky." She continued sucking her candy. "If we both strike her heart at the same time, she'll lose her ability to feel *all* of her emotions."

"Temporarily," Emory said. "But the barrier will be broken, or at the very least, it will be in a weakened state."

"Do you hear yourself? Even if the negative side effects only last for a few weeks, how could you possibly justify that on your audit report?"

"I'm facing banishment." Emory's gaze upon Selene was unyielding. "A suspension is worth the risk."

Selene put her arrow back into her quiver and started to walk away. "I'm not going to jeopardize my career over a human."

"Please..." Emory grabbed her hand and gently swept his thumb across her fingers.

Selene froze as he let down his guard, and they linked. He allowed her to sense the depth of his emotions. His frustration. His despair. His unrequited love.

Her eyes met his. "It's like that, huh?"

Emory nodded.

Selene quickly pulled her hand away. She stepped back and took a moment to gather herself. "We keep this between us."

"You were never here."

She nocked a bronze arrow in her bow, and Emory did the same. They both aimed at Blair's heart.

"On three," Emory said.

"Three."

They both released the bowstrings. The arrows tore through the air and nearly collided as they approached the target. Both arrows struck the invisible barrier guarding Blair's broken heart with a loud boom. Emory flinched. He'd never heard such a sound. He exchanged a worried glance with Selene. She snatched another arrow from her quiver, and Emory followed suit.

"Three," she said.

Boom... boom... boom. The steady sound of their arrows slamming into the barrier shook Emory to his core. There was no sign of it weakening. He watched in silence as arrow after arrow plummeted to the hard cement floor, bent and broken. His heart sank.

Selene lowered her bow. "What did you do to her?" she uttered in dismay.

Emory stared at Blair. "Tell Talos I'm sorry for ruining his date."

"It wasn't a date," she snapped.

He didn't feel like arguing with his healer. "Did you have enough time to grab your wallet?"

Selene shook her head. Emory reached into his pocket and handed her two hundred dollars to take a taxi home. She tucked the money into her quiver.

"Next time you summon me, I expect to see a flesh wound at the very least," she teased.

She was clearly trying to lighten his mood, but Emory could barely muster a reply. They stood side by side and watched Blair. Suddenly, Selene yanked the lollipop out of her mouth and wrapped her arms around his neck. He tried to back away, but she held him closer. Emory had no siblings, but his bond with Selene was as close as he would ever come to having a sister. He stopped resisting and gave in to her touch, allowing her to ease his pain. She brushed her warm cheek against his as they embraced, and for a brief moment, the aching in his heart subsided.

Selene slowly released her grasp, and Emory let out a shallow breath. "Thanks."

She bit into her lollipop, completely dispassionate. "I was serious about what I said."

"I know." Emory readjusted his leather jacket. "I'll make sure I'm gushing blood next time."

She smiled and flicked her half-eaten candy into his chest. "See you around, Em."

Selene crossed into the Earth realm and departed from his company. Emory weaved around the eccentric displays until he was in front of Blair. She looked through him, unable to perceive his presence between realms. He reached out and caressed her face with his hand, but she couldn't feel his touch. She walked past him at a lingering pace, her world out of sync with his.

Stifling his disappointment, he materialized behind her. "See anything interesting?"

Blair spun around. "I swear you're going to stop my heart one day," she said, pressing a hand to her chest. She noticed the look on his face and frowned. "How did it go?"

"You were right about Darion. He must have sensed Hana was keeping something from him."

"Did she finally open up?"

"Yes." He tightened his backpack strap around his shoulder. "After a great deal of encouragement on my part."

"In that case, you probably need this more than I do." Blair handed him her glass and went back to squinting studiously at an abstract portrait of an artist's cat. "How many arrows did you use?"

Emory drank the rest of her wine. "Too many."

CHAPTER 19

Emory didn't recall the white leather couch in the small waiting room of the Earth realm being so stiff. A young secretary tapped away on a computer keyboard and paid little attention to the anxious Vycrin. He kept replaying his first meeting with Themis and Petros. His knee bounced up and down, shaking the manila file folder that rested on his leg. The secretary stopped and glanced up at him.

"Sorry," Emory muttered, planting both feet on the ground.

The sound of light typing echoed throughout the space as the secretary continued writing. Emory wiped his sweaty palms against his black linen pants. This time, he was prepared. His documentation was submitted ahead of schedule. He was familiar with all of his clients. And he was wearing a suit. Yet he could not seem to slow the beating of his heart.

Themis entered the waiting room through double glass doors. She exuded elegance and grace. Her short silver hair glimmered in the light, not a single strand out of place. She kept her hands clasped behind her back. "Thank you for taking the time to meet with us, Emory."

He quickly got to his feet and buttoned his suit jacket. He nodded respectfully and followed Themis down the hall to a small conference room. Three other individuals sat at the opposite end of the table, waiting.

"Introductions will be brief," Themis stated. "Our field agent you know, of course."

Argus rose from his chair and adjusted his expensive silver-and-pink cufflinks. "Emory."

"Cousin." Emory kept his tone neutral. The committee didn't need to know how much they despised one another. Negative distractions would harm his case.

"Argus will be handling research and development," Themis continued. "Our security agent, Hera, is in charge of reconnaissance."

Hera approached with a friendly smile and extended her hand. "Wonderful to officially meet you."

Emory suppressed his deepest emotions and shook her hand. Vycrin could sense the condition of another's heart through physical contact, but security agents were chosen for their heightened ability to perceive thoughts and intentions. But Hera's touch was soft, her heart nurturing and warm. He could trust her. Emory briefly let down his guard and linked with her. She released her grip and stepped back.

Hera caught his eye. "I look forward to working with you."

"Likewise," Emory said honestly.

"Petros, our senior matchmaker, will be handling your personal assessment."

Petros gave him a hearty clap on the back. "How are you, my boy?"

Themis motioned for Emory to take a chair across from them. "Please have a seat."

The secretary appeared carrying a tray of crystal glasses and a pitcher of water with sliced cucumbers floating inside. Themis waited for everyone to be served. The young woman lingered at Argus's side as she filled his glass. He brushed her long flaxen hair aside and whispered into her ear. Argus would flirt with any single woman within a ten-foot radius. *Pathetic.*

The secretary let out a playful giggle.

"Thank you, Despina," Themis said sharply, raising her voice.

The young employee composed herself and returned to her administrative duties, closing the glass doors behind her.

"We received your documentation and appreciate your prompt attention to this matter," Themis began. "As everyone has had a chance to review your current clients, this meeting will be brief. I'd like to start with your recent match, Darion and Hana."

"Their relationship is progressing at an acceptable rate," Argus said.

"They're adorable," Hera chimed in. "However, I have some concerns."

Petros said, "As do I."

"I wasn't aware of any problems." Emory saw the astonishment on their faces, and he clenched his jaw shut. He opened his file and skimmed through his notes.

"The discussion regarding her health should have been addressed sooner in their relationship," Petros said. "It's disconcerting that he was so blinded by his feelings that he didn't take the time to delve into her past."

"Not that it's insurmountable," Hera reassured the group. "He has since shown increasing determination to get to know her on a much deeper level."

"He has also attended one of her group-therapy sessions," Emory added. "So he's taking it seriously, and he's supportive."

"What about her aversion to children?" Themis asked.

"I get the sense that she would be open to the idea," Petros answered, "but doesn't respond well to pressure."

"That's understandable." Hera looked at the board members with hopeful eyes. "But she might have a change of heart if she felt secure in the relationship."

"I have recently adjusted my strategy to assist her in that regard," Emory said.

"Darion is a planner," Argus said. "And he is not going to propose without being certain she wants to start a family."

"Propose?" Emory said. As soon as the question escaped his lips, he regretted it. After all, it was his job to know such things. He just didn't realize the couple was that serious.

Petros's voice was firm. "The point of making suitable matches is for the purpose of long-term commitments."

"That was your original intention when you sought them out, wasn't it?" Themis asked.

Emory drank half of his water. Forming long-term commitments wasn't exactly one of his strengths. He'd never sealed an engagement for any of his former clients. "I'm just cautious, since he hasn't communicated his feelings for her."

"He does have difficulty expressing himself," Hera said. "However, we believe he just needs the proper encouragement."

"I'm sure you can handle it," Argus said to Emory.

Themis drew a circle around a section of her notes. "We'd like you to apportion more of your time to their development and determine if they're truly a suitable match."

"Understood," Emory said. He believed they were compatible, and he was determined to prove it to the committee.

"Let's discuss Amir and Joey," Themis said.

"They're young, but I feel they are well matched," Hera said. "They support each other on an emotional level."

"However, the relationship is not helping Amir's coursework," Argus said. "His grades have plummeted since their union."

"Get the boy a tutor," Petros said in his gruff tone. "Problem solved."

"I'll ensure that he passes." Emory sipped more water in an attempt to mask his nerves. "Joey will be traveling soon, so there will be fewer distractions."

"See to it." Themis flipped through her notes. "Why hasn't he introduced her to his parents yet?"

Emory opened his mouth, but nothing came out. He had no idea why the young man was hiding his relationship from his parents. They seemed like a close, supportive family.

"I believe he's worried about their reaction," Hera said when no one offered an explanation.

"Is it justified?" Themis asked.

"Not from what I've observed," Argus answered.

Petros pushed their file aside. "I believe the boy's own insecurities are magnifying the situation."

"This is his first serious relationship," Hera said. "It may take him more time to come to terms with his feelings."

"Keep a close eye on them, Emory," Themis instructed. "Young love is easy to manipulate, but we want to ensure that their experience will result in emotional growth."

"Noted." Emory scribbled across his paper: *Cut distractions. Meet his parents. Keep them happy. Keep them ALL happy.*

Themis let out a heavy sigh. "Moving on to Laith and Karina."

"They r-recently got a puppy," Emory stammered. The committee members were not impressed. He buried himself back in his notes.

"No ring, no proposal, no wedding?" Petros yanked his brown suit jacket over his round belly and sat back. "I'm done with them."

"Let's be reasonable," Themis cautioned. "All relationships progress at different rates, and marriage doesn't guarantee a couple's success. My main concern with them is that there is little evidence that their union is built on a solid foundation."

"In the past six months, you've used ninety-eight arrows on Laith and only forty-six on Karina," Argus said. "It almost appears as though you're avoiding her. Why the discrepancy?"

Emory set his pen down to prevent himself from twirling it. The numbers exposed everything. "I noticed an abnormality in Karina's aura. There is a slight chance she may be falling out of love with Laith."

"So, you're afraid of her," Argus said.

Emory raised his voice. "I'm not afraid of anything."

"Perhaps what Argus means," Hera spoke calmly, "is that you're afraid of exacerbating her condition."

"Yes," Emory said, irritated that he'd let Argus get to him. "I'm focusing my attention on Laith to reinforce their bond until Karina's aura shows signs of improvement."

"For goodness' sake," Petros muttered. "No marriage proposal after nearly a decade? They're a lost cause."

Themis gazed at him over her glasses. "Need I remind you of Trevor and Madison?"

"They were like my own children," Petros protested.

"Yes," Themis replied. "And you coddled them for twelve years. They never married but remain a happy and healthy couple even after thirty years."

He turned to the other board members with a proud smile. "They just had their first grandson."

Hera held her hand to her heart. "Adorable."

"My point is," Themis continued, "Emory can close their case once their union has reached a point of self-sufficiency and his involvement is no longer mandatory."

I'll never be rid of them. Emory pushed the thought aside. He would just have to work harder. He was certain of their love. Their relationship was salvageable.

Hera folded her hands on the table. "What do you feel is their major issue?"

Emory spoke up. "Fundamentally, I think it's a breakdown of communication."

"Clearly," Argus scoffed.

Emory ignored his cousin. "I think they can rekindle the love they once shared with positive experiences."

Themis tapped the tip of her pen against the conference table. "How do you plan to accomplish that?"

He drank the rest of his water and searched his frantic mind for a strategy. He placed the crystal glass on the smooth table. "The beach," Emory said, surprising himself. "They both love the beach."

Hera's face lit up. "Very romantic."

"I plan to accompany them on vacation to help facilitate a constructive experience," Emory said. "It could prove effective to reinforce their love in a relaxed environment instead of through heated exchanges."

"That plan has potential," Themis said. "Be sure you do everything in your power to help them resolve their differences. They are a serious liability."

"I will handle it," Emory said.

Themis flipped through her notes. "Finally, we have the matter of your single client, Blair."

Emory's chest tightened.

"I'm concerned about her," Hera said. "Her heart is shattered to pieces."

"Usually, a broken heart begins to mend within a few weeks," Petros said. "I haven't seen a case this serious in years."

Emory knew Petros was referencing his father's mistake but was polite enough not to mention it directly.

Themis gave Emory a stern look. "You must resolve her case as quickly as possible. Find her a suitable match, one that she cannot deny."

It didn't need to be said that if he failed, he would be banished from the Earth realm for all time. He would never see Blair again.

"I will."

A moment of silence passed.

"You've been spending a great deal of time with her," Argus said.

Emory clenched his fist under the conference table. "In the matter of dealing with her broken heart, I've followed the protocol and enlisted her help. In the process, she has become a friend."

Petros sat up, curious. "A girlfriend?"

Emory coughed. He needed more water. "No."

"Is she trustworthy?" Themis asked Hera.

Emory's heart beat so hard that his entire body was shaking. He held his breath.

"I assessed her threat level and found no malice in her heart," Hera said. "It appears she has formed a genuine bond of friendship with Emory. There is no indication that she will spread knowledge about us, and I don't feel she is a threat to him or this organization."

Themis turned to Argus. "Do you agree?"

"She is very discreet, and I don't believe she poses a direct threat to Emory." He lowered his voice. "More of a distraction."

"Excellent!" Petros clapped his hands together. "As long as you both continue to use good judgment and don't draw any negative attention to yourselves in public, I see nothing wrong with the friendship."

"Back to the matter at hand," Themis continued. "What's being done to mend her broken heart?"

Emory shifted in his chair. "I've already eliminated dozens of unsuitable individuals, and I'm in the process of narrowing down potential matches."

"Long-term?" Themis asked.

"Yes." Emory ignored Argus's piercing stare. "My goal for Blair is a healthy and stable relationship leading to a long-term commitment in the very near future."

Themis pushed her pale-pink reading glasses up the bridge of her nose, scrutinizing the paperwork in front of her. "Your notes indicate that she is currently unaffected by both arrows and love potions..."

"Love potions?" Petros chuckled with delight. "Going old-school, my boy. I like it."

"How did you determine that?" Hera asked.

"I initiated a game of Kottabos using a bottle of pinot noir from my uncle."

"Susy's still in business?" Petros said.

Hera gasped. "From the vintage 1967?"

"That's correct," Emory said.

Hera gave an approving nod to the board members. "That was a very good year."

"It had no effect on my client beyond the normal effects of alcohol," Emory said.

"And how much of it did you drink?" Argus asked.

Emory glared at him. "I'm sure I don't know what you're insinuating."

"I'm surprised," Themis interjected. "That's a very potent blend. You're positive?"

"She had no reaction," Emory said with little inflection.

Petros eyed him as Themis wrote down her final notations.

"Well, I think that answers most of our questions." Themis piled her paperwork and rose to her feet. "Thank you for your time, Emory. We will continue to evaluate your ability to make decisions based on the well-being of your clients and assess your effectiveness as a matchmaker. We will reconvene on the first day of the autumn equinox and make a final decision regarding your compliance based on your overall performance. You're dismissed."

Emory made a hasty departure from the boardroom. His head reeled. Shuffling through the barrage of questions they had posed, he had difficulty remembering his responses. He waited for the elevator in anxious silence, his black suit drenched in sweat. The elevator doors opened, and Emory let out a sigh of relief as he entered. The doors crept closed.

A large hand slammed between the doors, forcing them open again. "Going down?"

Emory gestured for Petros to step inside. They rode down two levels in absolute silence. Suddenly, Petros whipped out his pink paisley handkerchief and used it to push all the remaining buttons.

"What are you—" Emory choked back a complaint.

The elevator came to a stop at the next floor. The doors opened to an empty hallway then crept closed again.

"Blair, huh?" Petros said.

I should have taken the stairs. "Yes."

"Good. You need a nice girl like that in your life." Petros stuffed the handkerchief back into his pocket. "She can knock some of that cynicism out of you."

The elevator slipped down another level. The glowing yellow buttons were a blur.

"What am I doing wrong with her?" Emory asked.

"Focusing too much attention on what you think she wants instead of what she needs."

"I've tried to give her what she needs," Emory said in dismay. "She rejects everyone. No one is ever good enough."

His thick eyebrows furrowed. "That's because you've failed to find a man who is willing to give of himself completely. She needs someone who isn't afraid to be vulnerable before she can let them in."

Emory cleared his throat. "How much time do you think I have before the damage becomes irreversible?"

"Every heart is different. It could be weeks or months."

The doors continued to open onto empty floors as they spoke. Petros let out a heavy sigh. "If it doesn't mend soon, they will have to send Argus."

Emory ground his teeth. "That's not fair. She's *my* client."

"She'll still be your client, but he's an expert matchmaker," Petros insisted. "He can help you find a suitable match for her before it's too late."

"I don't need his help. I know her better than anyone else."

They gazed down another empty corridor.

"Are you in love with her?" Petros asked.

Heat flashed up in Emory's face. "I... I don't know."

"It's a simple question."

Emory repeatedly tapped the button to close the doors. The elevator moved on. His dull reflection through the double doors was distorted.

"She doesn't feel anything for me," Emory muttered.

"I asked how *you* feel about *her*."

Emory shook his head, unable to choke out a response.

"Well, not to worry." Petros straightened his suit jacket. "Argus will have Blair engaged in under a year—"

"I don't want her to be with anyone else!"

The elevator shuddered. Petros stared at Emory, who remained silent, stunned by his own sudden loss of control. Petros was unusually calm. The doors opened onto the second floor, and Petros exited.

"Then I suggest you work quickly, Emory."

The doors slid closed.

CHAPTER 20

Joey gripped the tall microphone stand in her shaky fingers. She opened her mouth but had difficulty reciting the words written on her tattered piece of paper. In the Earth realm, Emory and Blair watched her from a small table in the back of the dimly lit restaurant. He considered boosting Joey's confidence with one of his arrows but decided against it. If the poetry reading went poorly, he didn't want her associating negative feelings with the relationship.

Joey spotted Amir, who gave her an encouraging nod from across the room. With his warm reassurance, she began. "This I know." She pushed her glasses up the bridge of her nose. "As a rose shrivels and dies, my love will survive. This I know. As doves fall from heaven, my love remains even. This I know. As the night grows dark, this is more than a playful lark. This I know. My love is true. This I know."

An unbearable silence enveloped the room. Amir's feverish clapping rang out from the back corner, and the entire room broke into a respectful applause.

"Thank you," Joey said, her soft voice echoing through the small restaurant. She dashed off stage and joined her adoring boyfriend at the table.

Emory turned around just in time to see the bewildered expression on Blair's face. "Your thoughts?" he asked.

"It was—" She searched for an appropriate response. "It was very... what's the word? Heartfelt."

"It was nonsensical drivel," Emory said in disgust. "Someone needs to teach her basic iambic pentameter before her next assault on the English language."

Blair sipped her martini, her mouth quirking in a half smile. "You're being a bit harsh."

"Her major is English. *English*."

She cringed. "Maybe you should stop distracting her so she can devote more time to her studies."

"Good point." Emory did a visual sweep of the room. "Have you found anyone yet?"

"Nope." Blair pulled the long toothpick out of her martini glass. She stared into Emory's eyes and licked all three olives. "You want it?"

He refused to look at her ruby lips. "No, thank you."

She twisted the toothpick between her fingers. "You know you do."

Emory leaned across the small round table and lowered his voice. "Pick one, please."

Blair scraped the olives off the toothpick with her teeth and took her time chewing. "Tonight we should switch it up. You should shoot yourself a pretty girl, and I'll watch you seduce her."

Stalling tactics. It was going to be a long night.

"That's not how this works," Emory said.

Blair flicked the toothpick onto the table. "You're probably out of practice."

"I'm Vycrin," Emory said with a smirk. "That's not something I need to practice."

"Cocky too," she muttered.

He gawked at her. "What did you call me?"

She spoke up in a louder voice, "I said you're cocky."

Emory grabbed her chair and slid her next to him, almost spilling her martini on her dark-blue jeans. "I didn't hear you."

Blair forced herself to keep a straight face. "Yes, you did."

He met her eyes. "Say it again."

"You... cocky."

Emory brushed her curly hair aside and whispered in her ear, "You like it."

She shook her head. "I like nice guys."

"You like me." Emory leaned closer and kissed her cheek. "You can't deny it..." His soft lips grazed her icy neck as he slid his hand down her leg. He gently squeezed the back of her knee and let out a desperate sigh. "I want you to come home with me."

Her jaw dropped. "Umm..." Her voice was shaky.

Emory sat up. He tilted his head. "Satisfied?"

Blair drank the rest of her martini in two large gulps. "You don't need any practice."

Emory pushed her chair away from him. "Can we get back to work now?"

She cleared her throat and pointed to a man at the bar. "I'll take that one."

The gentleman's thick black hair was dreadlocked and tied back to expose his defined cheekbones and flawless skin. He let out a pleasant laugh as he exchanged banter with one of the servers. The man had been one of the first poets to read that night, and much to Emory's disappointment, he'd had a decent command of the English language. Emory got to his feet.

Blair smiled into her empty glass. "That round goes to you." She glanced up to find her new suitor standing over her with two martinis in hand. She fluffed her hair. "Hello."

"May I sit with you?" he asked.

"Of course. My name's Blair."

He grinned and took Emory's seat. "Trent."

Emory stood in the Enarine realm, frustrated that he hadn't elicited anything more than "Umm" from her. He wanted a stronger reaction. He needed to know she felt something for him before he could tell her about his growing feelings for her.

Blair's muffled laughter echoed throughout the Enarine realm, and Emory glared at her new suitor. He found it difficult to focus on anything other than the whirlwind of emotions she stirred up in him. He experienced love, lust, and jealousy, all in the span of two minutes. No wonder humans were so irrational when they were in love. *Who can think under such circumstances?* He moved closer to Amir and Joey's table and resolved not to allow Blair to further distract him from work.

"How are your plans coming for spring break?" Amir asked Joey, diving into their plate of appetizers.

"We're almost done," Joey replied. "Kali and I already booked our flight, and I found some inexpensive hostels along the way. I just wish you were coming with us."

"Nah. You girls will have a fun time together."

She cut a pot sticker in half and took a bite. "What will you be up to while I'm gone?"

"Sitting alone in my dorm, waiting for my beautiful girlfriend to return from traveling the world."

She chuckled and brushed her curly red hair away from her face. "You're such a bad liar."

He laughed. "Actually," he said quickly, "my brother's driving down to visit."

Her countenance fell. "Oh."

He shoved two miniburgers into his mouth. "It was a very last-minute trip."

"Are your parents coming too?" Joey asked.

He chewed and gestured to his mouth, unable to give a reply.

She frowned. "Yes or no?"

Amir stared into her yearning eyes. He nodded.

Her eyes narrowed. "You haven't told them, have you?"

Emory rubbed his temples. She wasn't going to like his answer.

"I haven't had the chance yet," Amir said quickly.

Joey huffed. "We've been dating for almost seven months."

"I was going to—I am going to," he stammered. "I just have to find the right time."

"You stayed with my family through the *entire* winter break," she said bitterly. "Where did your parents think you were?"

A waitress filled up Amir's water glass, and he swallowed three hearty gulps. "I told them I was staying on campus to complete some extra-credit assignments."

"Extra credit?" She glared at him. "*I'm* your extra credit?"

"Babe, can't we talk about this later?"

"Talk about what? How you're waiting for me to leave the country so you can go visit your family and pretend I don't exist?"

"That's not it at all!"

Emory aimed his bow at Amir. He couldn't afford to let the situation escalate.

"Explain it to me, then," Joey demanded.

"It's not as easy as you make it sound," Amir said, a hint of desperation in his voice. "I come from a very strict background. I have to ease my parents into the idea that I might be interested in someone who doesn't share my culture."

"You're embarrassed by me. Just admit it."

Emory shot the young man in the heart. Amir needed to reassure Joey of his devotion.

"Joey, I'm not embarrassed by you." Amir leaned across the table and whispered, "I love you."

Emory shot Joey in the heart.

Joey smiled and blushed. "I love you too." She pushed her plate aside. "If you need more time, I understand." She tapped his foot under the table. "I think we should get the check so we can go back and... *study.*"

Emory ground his teeth as Amir scrambled to his feet and rushed to pay their bill. Amir's hormones were going to destroy his GPA. He couldn't afford to fail another test. Emory decided he would start leaving subliminal messages around the young man's dorm to encourage him to seek tutoring. He was also going to reduce the number of arrows he used on the couple. Their burnt-orange auras meant he wouldn't have to expend too much energy to keep their relationship strong. They were devoted to each other.

Emory scanned the restaurant for Blair. He found her handsome suitor alone at the bar, scrolling through his phone. He frowned. A new poet appeared on stage and began to read, drawing the attention of the crowd. After searching the dining room, Emory knew there was only one other place Blair would be.

"Blair?" he called out, entering the ladies' room. Emory heard feet shuffling. "Are you in here?"

A heavy sigh emanated from the far end of the room. He peeked under the stall and recognized her leopard-print heels. "Are you decent?"

"Yes."

Emory squinted through the stall and found Blair sitting fully clothed on the toilet. Her arms were folded across her stomach.

"Why are you sitting on that filthy toilet?"

She stared down at the dark, grimy tiles. "I don't want to do this anymore."

"I agree," he said, forcing his voice to sound upbeat. "The bathroom is no place to loiter, so clean yourself up, and get back to the bar. Trent is waiting."

"You're not listening." She shifted. "I don't want to go back out to Trent."

"Just give him a chance." Emory almost choked on his words of encouragement, but he reminded himself of his obligation as her matchmaker. "He seems like a nice guy."

"They're all nice guys. That doesn't change the fact that I don't feel anything for them."

He leaned his forehead against the cold metal door and closed his eyes. "What do you want me to do?" he whispered.

"I don't know anymore. I didn't think it would be like this. I feel so empty. Like part of me is missing." Blair stood, her hopeful eyes searching his through the narrow crack. "There has to be some other way."

He shook his head. "There is no other way."

"Are you sure?"

"I'm positive."

"But this isn't working," she said. "It doesn't matter how many men I meet—"

"You have to keep trying."

"I can't..."

"You have to," he said more firmly.

"Why do I—"

"Because I don't know how else to fix you!" Emory shouted.

Blair shrank back and wrapped her arms around her body.

Emory lowered his voice. "I desperately want to mend your broken heart," he said, unable to hide his heartfelt regret. "But I can't change what I've done to you."

"So..." She leaned her head back and blinked rapidly, tears welling in her eyes. "This is it."

Emory hesitated. "This is it."

Blair unlatched the door and went to the sink without a word. She examined her reflection in the mirror and smoothed the wrinkles from her white blouse. "How do I look?"

He couldn't take his eyes from her. "Beautiful."

She exited the bathroom, unable to force a smile.

A miserable silence enveloped the room. The remainder of the evening would play out like so many of their encounters. Blair would charm her way through the initial meeting, he would shoot the gentleman near the end of the date, and they would arrange a second meeting. Then a third. Then a fourth. Then Emory would watch the unsuspecting suitor fall in love with the woman *he* wanted to be closer to.

Emory yanked a large stack of paper towels from the dispenser and shoved them into his backpack. He charged out of the bathroom and approached Amir and Joey's empty table. Their plates of half-eaten food still littered the surface, and the waitress hadn't been by to pick up her tip. Emory piled the leftover sliders, french fries, and pot stickers onto one plate. He ignored the bewildered looks he received from other diners as he grabbed a bottle of ketchup and squeezed hard, covering the food in the sweet red sauce.

Back at the bar, Blair let out a soft laugh, and Trent playfully nudged her. Emory rushed toward the oblivious pair as they engaged in idle chatter. He stumbled forward with clumsy steps and tripped in front of Blair, splattering the plate of food into her chest. She gasped and jumped to her feet, ketchup dripping from her silk top.

"*Je suis désolé!*" Emory stammered, crouching to his knees. "*Je ne peux pas supporter de te voir avec lui.*"

Blair's mouth dropped open. The words were true, even if Blair had no idea what he was saying—Emory couldn't bear seeing her with that guy. Actually, he couldn't bear to see her with *anyone*, let alone Trent.

"What an idiot!" Trent muttered as he scrambled to find extra napkins.

Speaking to her in a language she didn't understand was so much easier than baring his soul in English. He didn't have to hold back. "*Je voudrais te serrer dans mes bras et effacer toute la peine que je t'ai causé,*" Emory said to Blair as he stood. If only his touch really could mend her broken heart. *Wishful thinking.*

Trent returned with the napkins, and Emory snatched them away and tried to sop up some of the ketchup from Blair's shirt.

"It's okay," Blair said, backing away, clearly overwhelmed. "I just need to go home."

"I understand." Trent glared daggers at Emory.

She picked up her purse and made her way through the crowded bar, carefully keeping her ketchup-smeared clothes from touching the other people. Emory grabbed hold of her thin fingers. He gazed into her eyes and kissed the back of her cold hand.

"*Je t'aime.*"

Trent looked at him, perplexed. "What did he say?"

Stunned, Blair turned to Trent. "I think he said, 'Sorry for the mess.'"

Blair hurried out of the small restaurant, drawing sympathetic comments from other diners. Emory flipped open his wallet and took out sixty dollars in cash, enough to cover Blair's drink and compensate for the ruined evening.

He tossed it to Trent. "*Elle est à moi,*" he said fiercely. At least, he wanted her to be his, and his alone.

Before Trent could respond, Emory exited the establishment through the back doors. He found Blair in the secluded parking lot behind the dumpsters, her hands covered in sauce and bits of french fries.

"The ketchup was a nice touch," she said as he approached.

He smiled. "I thought so too."

Blair tore off her ruined blouse and threw it in the dumpster. "I never liked that shirt, anyway."

Emory opened his backpack and handed her the stack of paper towels. Blair shivered in the cool spring air as she wiped ketchup from her neck and chest. He looked away, trying not to stare at her black push-up bra. He ripped off his leather jacket and wrapped it around her shoulders. The large jacket overwhelmed her small frame. They walked toward his motorcycle, and Blair slipped her arms into the overcoat, zipping it closed.

"Thank you for getting me out of there," she said in a soft voice.

"It wasn't a good match." Emory put on his helmet and climbed onto the motorcycle, starting the engine.

Blair positioned herself behind him. She strapped on her helmet and wrapped her arms around his waist. The dark streets were empty as he drove through the city. Cool air rushed past them, and he peered up at the night sky, admiring the beauty of the moon and stars. For that moment, it was as though they were the only two people in the entire realm.

A traffic light ahead of them turned red, and they rolled to a stop. Emory released the left handlebar and took her hand. He intertwined her delicate fingers between his.

Blair leaned closer and tightened her arms around his waist. "What did you really say in the restaurant after you kissed my hand?"

"I said..." Emory clung to her frozen fingers. "Sorry for the mess."

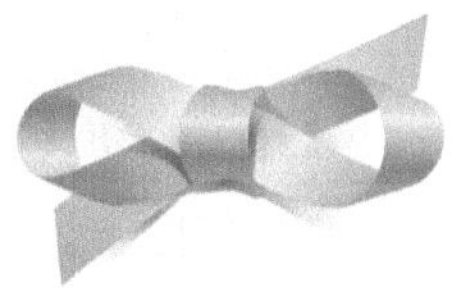

CHAPTER 21

Emory stood at the door of Blair's apartment, hiding a single red rose behind his back. It had been more than a week since the poetry reading, and they hadn't been together since then. He was anxious to see her again. When he called her and suggested they take the weekend off, she was so elated she insisted on making him dinner Saturday night. He was never one to refuse an invitation.

Emory knocked and waited. The door swung open. Blair smiled at him and wiped her hands on a black-and-white polka-dotted apron.

"You're early," she said.

Emory handed her the flower, and she gasped.

She brushed the soft petals across her nose and inhaled. "Who told you?"

He leaned against the doorframe. "Preya."

"You really were talking about me," Blair said, mildly amused.

Emory entered her home, and the fresh aroma of rosemary filled his lungs. She locked the door, and he dropped his backpack at the entrance.

"What are you burning?" he teased.

"Your dinner."

Emory was glad to see her in better spirits. He was determined to make sure their evening together was perfect. Her small square table was already set with two place settings, lit candles, and a bottle of wine. Blair returned to her narrow galley kitchen, with Emory in tow. He checked on the plant next to the sink to ensure that the soil was moist. The dark-green leaves were thriving.

"How was brunch?" Emory asked.

"Fun, as always." Blair slid three olives onto a fork and handed it to him. "Preya got the promotion, so we had a couple bottles of champagne on her."

He ate one of the olives. "At ten in the morning?"

"It was closer to eleven." Blair tossed romaine lettuce into a glass salad bowl. "And Malena just found out she's pregnant with baby number three—"

Emory laughed. "Did your brother-in-law go into convulsions?"

Blair raised her eyes to the ceiling and grinned. "It's like the man has no idea where babies come from." She sliced a cherry tomato in half and ate it. "He's shocked every time she gets pregnant."

"How's the one with the crazy knitting fetish?"

"Savannah's doing well. She joined a book group."

"Good for her." Emory ate the rest of the olives and tossed the fork in the sink. "She needed a new hobby."

"Where did you end up today?"

"Karina dragged Laith to a cooking class."

"Sorry I missed it," Blair said, giggling. "Was it a disaster?"

"As always." Emory sighed. "They're not nearly as entertaining as they used to be." He had been leaving Laith and Karina subtle hints and subliminal messages to get them to plan a beach trip over the summer, but he wasn't looking forward to it. Their constant bickering was starting to get on his nerves, and he couldn't understand why. They'd once been his favorite clients. *Second favorite.*

Emory leaned on the counter behind Blair and watched her chop vegetables. Her hands were so small and delicate. He imagined how it would feel to have her slender fingers caressing his body.

"What did you learn to cook?" she asked, tearing him from his fantasy.

He cleared his throat. "Lobster bisque."

"That sounds delicious." She scooped diced tomatoes into the bowl. "When are you going to make it for me?"

"Next weekend." Emory grabbed the strings of her apron and pulled her next to him. "When did you get this?"

"I've had it for a while."

He twisted her around to inspect the dainty ruffled pockets. "Liar! It's brand-new."

She rolled her eyes. "Okay, I bought it this morning."

"If you're trying to impress me, it's not working." He gave the strings a rough tug. "I like stripes, not polka dots."

She elbowed him playfully in the stomach, and he let go. "Not everything is about you." Blair returned to the opposite counter and chopped cucumbers for their salad.

He leaned over and peered at her through curious eyes. "You did your makeup?" He glanced around the apartment. "Are we expecting guests?"

Blair winked at him. "I always look this beautiful."

Emory stepped closer. "Most times I come over, it looks like you're reenacting *The Walking Dead*." He brushed her dark hair aside and nipped her neck. "I want to suck your blood!"

"That's a vampire, you fool!" She gave a barely suppressed laugh as he gnawed on her neck. "Get your genres straight!"

Her skin was ice-cold, but he still enjoyed flirting with her. "Vampires, zombies—whatever." Emory pushed her against the counter and squeezed her waist. "What else did you do for me today?"

"Stop!" Blair giggled and squirmed out of his reach. "I need to finish dinner."

Emory watched her in silence. "You look beautiful tonight," he said softly.

Blair smiled but didn't turn around. "Make yourself useful and slice the bread."

A baguette lay across a cutting board behind her. Emory removed a long knife from the wooden block on the counter. He sliced two thin pieces then turned back to Blair. She was still smiling. She'd gone to so much trouble for him. If she was trying to let him in, it meant the barrier was weakening. He had to move fast. He crossed into the Enarine realm and rushed to the front door to retrieve his quiver. He pulled out a single arrow and returned to the kitchen.

Emory stood behind Blair, clenched the silver arrow in both hands, and raised it over his head. He bore down and stabbed her in the back as hard as he could. The arrow slammed into the invisible barrier and shuddered violently in his strong grip. The screeching and wailing emanating from her was horrific—as though her broken heart was being tortured by the sharp arrow. He gritted his teeth and pushed against the powerful force with all of his strength. A brilliant crystal aura surrounded her, and he turned away, unable to bear the radiant light. The light rippled, and the arrow ricocheted off her body. The sharp silver tip flew backward, slicing the palm of his hand. The intense light dimmed, and the screaming faded into oblivion.

All that could be heard was the trickling of Emory's blood hitting the tile floor. Sharp bursts of pain pulsed through his open wound. He materialized back in the Earth realm and squeezed his hand shut to stop the bleeding. He knocked the bread knife off the counter, startling Blair.

She spun around and gasped. "Are you okay?"

He crouched to the ground. "I just—I cut myself."

Blair caught his bloodied hand in her apron and guided him to the bathroom. He rinsed his hand under cold water while she rummaged under the vanity for the first-aid kit he'd recently bought her. She hopped onto the sink and placed the red plastic case on her lap.

"How did that happen?" she asked, pulling out bandages and a roll of gauze.

"It was an accident."

Blair patted his hand dry with a clean cloth. "Vycrin shouldn't play with sharp objects."

"Or dangerous women," he mumbled.

She tilted her head to the side. "What's that supposed to mean?"

"Nothing," he said quickly.

Blair applied pressure to his hand and waited for the bleeding to stop. The cut was deep. She wrapped gauze around his hand, her cold fingers sending chills through his body as she tended to his wound. He shuddered.

She looked at him with concern. "Does it hurt?"

"No. It's fine."

Blair finished wrapping his hand and snapped the large kit closed. She slid off the edge of the sink, and Emory grabbed her arm. He stared at her bloodstained apron. He'd ruined it. He ruined everything.

"I'm so sorry," Emory said.

"It's okay." She gave him a reassuring pat on the shoulder. "I'll clean everything up, then we can have dinner."

They returned to the kitchen. Blair wet a paper towel and cleaned his blood from the tile floor. Emory could barely watch. He felt sick. She picked up the knife he dropped, turning it over in her hand. There were no traces of blood on the blade. She glanced over at Emory, and their eyes met.

The loud buzz of her kitchen timer rang throughout the apartment, startling them both. Blair jumped to her feet, washed her hands, and grabbed a pair of faded oven mitts. The rack of lamb hissed and sputtered as she lifted the broiler pan out of the oven and placed it on the counter to rest.

Emory sat at the table in a pensive silence while she plated their food. Wax rolled down the edges of the tall candles as they burned. His hand stung. He clenched his fist, refusing to give in to the pain and the overwhelming disappointment in his heart.

Blair placed their plates on the table and put a small bowl of olives next to Emory. She settled next to him and poured them each a glass of wine. He doused his food with olive juice, and she slowly cut into a roasted potato. The clanking of their silverware was deafening. She watched him out of the corner of her eye, but he wouldn't look at her.

Blair chewed a tiny piece of lamb. "How many arrows did you break?"

Emory glanced up at her. "Tonight?"

She nodded.

"Just the one," he said.

Her knife scraped against the plate. "How many in total?"

The garlic potatoes felt as though they were lodged in his tightening throat. "I stopped counting."

She dropped the knife and stabbed at her food with a fork. "I hate when you do this."

"Do what?" he said, feeling defensive. "It's my job."

"It's not your job to constantly check the status of my heart," she said between chews. "You don't do that with any of your other clients."

"Actually, I do. But you're the only client with a broken heart, so of course I'm going to monitor you more closely." The lamb was cooked to perfection, but he could no longer taste it. "You're a liability."

Blair tossed her fork onto the plate. "Sometimes I feel like we've moved beyond our client-matchmaker relationship, and then you say something like that."

His heart sank. "Blair, if there's even the slightest chance that I can reverse your condition, I'm going to do it."

"You need to learn boundaries." She picked up her wineglass. "You slip in and out of realms, inserting yourself in people's private affairs without their knowing it, but you can't do that with me—not anymore."

"I know," Emory muttered. "It's infuriating."

"You shouldn't *want* to." Blair slammed her glass on the table. "We're supposed to be friends."

They sat without exchanging another word, but neither of them touched the remainder of their food.

"Why don't you just ask me how I feel?" Blair said.

Emory bit into an olive. "About what?"

She drank her entire glass of wine and poured another. "Anything you want."

"Fine." He pushed the bowl aside. "How do you feel about Vycrin?"

"I've only met one."

Emory twirled his fork between his fingers. "How do you feel about the one you've met?"

"Well, at first I thought you were arrogant and insensitive. But now that I've gotten to know you, I think you're very kind and thoughtful. You care about people even when you pretend not to."

Emory placed the fork back on his plate. "How do you feel knowing my arrows still don't work on you?"

She paused. "Conflicted."

"How do you feel when I tell you... I'm tired of watching you go out with other men?"

Blair leaned closer. "Seriously?"

Emory nodded.

"Thrilled."

He felt a glimmer of hope.

She relaxed and took a sip. "Are you saying you're not going to match me with anyone else?"

He hesitated. "Yes."

Blair was quiet for a while. "Good."

Emory watched a thin swirl of white smoke rise from the flickering candle. "How do you feel when you're with me?"

"Tonight?"

"Tonight."

"Angry, annoyed, frustrated." She set her glass on the table. "Sad that my broken heart caused you pain."

He looked away from her, unsure of her meaning. "What pain?"

She gestured to his bandaged hand. "That looked like a deep cut."

Emory stared into her eyes. "When you're with me on the days I don't try to assault you, how do you feel?"

Blair folded her napkin until it was a small triangle. The silence was agonizing. "Happy," she said finally.

"Just happy?" Emory felt burning desire whenever he was near her. Every stolen glance, every smile, every touch made him want her more.

"Just happy." She drank the rest of her wine. "Can you live with that?"

He couldn't. "I'll try."

Blair's eyes pleaded with his. "Can you promise not to shoot me again?"

Emory spoke softly. "I promise."

"And the next time you want to know if my heart is still broken..."

Emory reached across the table and brushed his fingers across the back of her icy hand. "You'll tell me."

CHAPTER 22

"You may kiss the bride."

Blair screamed and grabbed Emory by his suit jacket. They stood on a raised white platform alongside the large wedding party, their presence concealed within the Enarine realm. She jumped up and down, cheering for a couple she had never met. Emory tried to hold back a smile. Her reaction was more enjoyable than the actual nuptials. He would have to bring her to more weddings.

The lavish outdoor ceremony overlooked a picturesque botanical garden, filling the air with the fragrance of lavender. Lush orchids cascaded down the awning, and white mesh fabric swayed in the soft breeze. Elegant vases overflowed with elaborate floral arrangements throughout the grounds of the large estate.

Three hundred guests joined in applause as the bride and groom kissed for the first time as a married couple. They turned and faced their guests, unable to conceal their ecstatic grins. Light music played in the background as they walked hand in hand down the aisle. Six bridesmaids and groomsmen followed close behind their newly married friends. The procession moved at a slow, fluid pace, out of sync with the Enarine realm.

Hana wrapped her hand around her escort's arm, her eyes scanning the large crowd. Emory grabbed an arrow from his quiver. Hana caught Darion's eye and smiled. Emory shot Darion in the heart then reloaded. Darion smiled back at his girlfriend as though spellbound by her beauty. Emory's second silver arrow sped through the air and slammed into Hana's back, striking her heart. Reinforcing their love would help to solidify their memories of the wedding and create a positive bonding experience.

"Nice shot," Blair said.

"Thank you." Emory slipped his bow over his head and positioned it across his chest.

Guests rose to their feet and mingled with one another as the bridal party gathered for their photo session. The warm spring air was a welcome change after weeks of harsh winter weather. Blair's strapless navy blue cocktail dress complemented her red Louboutin shoes.

She sighed. "That was a beautiful wedding."

Emory gave a slight nod.

"You don't seem very impressed," Blair commented.

"It was simple enough."

"Simple?" Blair appeared stunned. "That wedding must have cost a small fortune."

He shrugged. "I'm used to Vycrin weddings."

"What are they like?"

"Our weddings are four-day events. We have the pre-wedding festivities, the commitment ceremony, the wedding itself—"

"Commitment ceremony?"

Emory maneuvered around a nervous cocktail waiter. "A couple's union is only recognized under Vycrin law after the commitment ceremony, when two souls are bound together."

Blair's eyes widened. "What does that entail?"

"It's a private Vycrin ritual," he said quickly. Emory thought back to the hundreds of celebrations he'd attended over the years. "And as for the actual wedding, we usually have around seven hundred guests."

She nearly choked. "Seven hundred?"

"When you factor in family, friends, and coworkers, the numbers add up." They strolled between the wedding party and a photographer as she snapped photos. "There are a lot of us."

"You have to invite every Vycrin on the planet?"

"No, that would be ridiculous." He chuckled to himself. "But I would have to invite the ones I know, even the ones I'm not particularly fond of."

"W-What?" she stammered. "Why?"

He looked at her, puzzled. "Excluding a Vycrin from a wedding is insulting."

They passed Darion as he socialized with Hana's family. His outgoing personality made it easy for him to mingle with strangers, and he seemed eager to make a good impression.

The back of Emory's hand grazed Blair's. "What kind of wedding do you want?"

"I don't know. I never really thought about it."

"Liar."

Blair smiled. "I haven't thought about it *lately*." She peered across the enchanting garden. "I think I want an outdoor wedding."

"At a vineyard?"

Her face lit up. "That's a good idea."

"And we'd have to make sure you had a truckload of roses."

"Nothing extravagant," she corrected. "I want a small, intimate wedding."

He nodded.

Blair glanced up at him. "Unless my future husband has an insanely large family like yours."

"I doubt half of my family would show up," he scoffed.

She frowned. "Why not?"

"They'd probably think it was a hoax."

"That's why you shouldn't go around telling people you don't believe in love or marriage," Blair said. "You'll look like a fool when your invitations go out."

He smiled, and they wandered on through the gardens.

Blair stopped. "Are you really against marriage, Emory?"

The wind swept her hair upward so that it blocked her face. He reached up and brushed the soft strands away from her deep-brown eyes. She would make a beautiful bride.

"Yes."

Blair didn't break her gaze. "Liar."

She walked on. Emory felt the guarding walls around his heart crumbling, and he trailed behind. They approached an eight-foot hedge of green foliage and realized it was the entrance to a maze.

Blair gasped. "I've never done an outdoor maze before."

He drew up next to her. "Should we go inside?"

"I don't know. It might take us a while."

"It won't take more than fifteen minutes." Emory took her by the hand and pulled her into the maze. "Trust me. I have an excellent sense of direction."

* * ❧ * *

ONE HOUR AND FIFTEEN minutes later, Emory and Blair walked into another dead end.

"How did we get here?" Emory asked, completely turned around. He had no idea humans were capable of designing such elaborate labyrinths.

Blair shook her head. "I stopped keeping track after we reached the fountain."

"The fountain..."

Emory was in his own world. They'd run into four pitiable souls by the fountain, but he had decided against asking them for directions. Emerging from the Enarine realm would have given them a fright. Also, they appeared to be just as lost as Blair and Emory.

Blair followed close behind as he backtracked three maneuvers. She sighed. "We should just pick a direction and plow through the bushes until we get out."

"Absolutely not. That will mess up your hair, and I spent five hours at that stupid salon, waiting for you." Emory continued down a winding path. "The washing, the blow-drying, the conditioning—"

"Stop complaining," Blair said with a laugh. "My girl wasn't even booked that day, and I warned you it would take the afternoon."

"I thought you were exaggerating."

They rounded a corner and unexpectedly tumbled out of the maze.

"Finally!" Blair cried. They caught sight of the stately mansion in the distance, where the reception was already in progress. "I didn't think we'd get out before sunset."

"Me, either," Emory said, lingering behind. He needed to push her back into the Earth realm when she least expected it. It was safer that way—less shock to the body. They hiked through the sprawling estate and watched the sunlight slip away.

"Next time we should get a map before—" She spun around to find Emory charging toward her. "Don't you dare!" She ran backward, away from him.

"You said you wanted to dance all night." Emory slowed to a stop. "How are you going to do that in this realm?"

Blair removed her heels and clutched them to her chest. "Stay back!" she shrieked.

Without warning, she broke into a sprint and ran toward the mansion. Emory followed in close pursuit, and her hysterical laughter echoed throughout the Enarine realm. Blair ran up the steps to the mansion, and Emory grabbed her by the waist.

"Wait!" she yelled.

Emory scooped her into his arms and carried her into the manor. Guests sauntered past, unable to see them.

"Put me down!" Blair struggled to break free, and he held her tighter.

"Promise you won't run away from me?" he demanded.

Blair's face was serious. "I promise."

Emory lowered her to the ground. Blair looked up at him and giggled. She darted off in the opposite direction, running up a flight of stairs. Emory smiled and chased after her.

Blair ran through the halls, unable to control her wild laughter. Emory grabbed her arm, but she squirmed out of his reach. She ran down a long hallway and turned a corner. Emory quickly followed and ran past a large window. The thick curtain moved. He pivoted, crouched in the opposite corridor, and waited. He peered around the corner in time to see Blair slowly emerging from behind the drapes. He crept up behind her as she slipped into one of the bedroom suites.

An ornate king-sized bed occupied a large portion of the space, and a tufted sofa was positioned on the opposite side of the room. Blair headed to the seating area, winded. She wiggled her shoes back onto her feet. Emory ran up from behind and slammed his palms into her back.

Blair gasped at the sudden blow and flew onto the bed, landing in the Earth realm. Their combined merriment minimized the unsettling effect of the jolt. She rolled onto her back, laughing and struggling to catch her breath.

He crawled on top of her. "You're getting sloppy."

Blair snickered. "Maybe I wanted you to catch me that time."

Emory's gaze shifted from her dark eyes to her full red lips. She smelled like jasmine with a hint of citrus. He wanted to taste her. His heart beat hard against his chest as he leaned closer. He brushed his cheek against hers. Her frozen skin stung his face.

"Am I keeping you from work?" Blair whispered into his ear.

He pulled back. "Yes."

She bit her lower lip. "Then come find me when you're done."

Emory climbed off the bed and hurried out of the room, leaving Blair alone in the large suite. He crossed into the Enarine realm, and his arrows rattled in his quiver as he made his way down the stairs. Blair confounded him, but he needed to focus on his job.

In the banquet hall, Hana and the other duty-bound bridesmaids were going from table to table, greeting guests. She reached Darion's table and kissed him on the cheek. "Are you having fun?"

"I just spent forty minutes talking to your father about fishing. I think I'm finally on his good side."

Hana laughed. "So you're having a blast."

"I am." He drank the rest of his champagne. "Do you have a few minutes, or does the bride need you?"

Hana glanced at her cousin, who was preoccupied, and signaled for Darion to follow her to the French doors leading to the expansive balcony. They slipped out of the banquet hall, undetected by everyone except Emory. Ornate white blooms and hydrangeas filled the veranda, and tall candelabras lined the edges of the stone building, but Emory's mind was not on the décor. He had no idea what Blair really wanted. She seemed perfectly content with their current arrangement—whatever that was. He didn't even know the rules or boundaries.

His clients drifted over to the wide railing overlooking the moonlit grounds.

"You are so beautiful," Darion whispered.

Hana smiled, and Darion leaned against the stone barrier. Emory noticed that Darion's hands were shaking. He and the young man were both suffering from the same affliction: self-doubt.

"I realized something today," Darion continued.

She stepped closer. "What?"

Emory drew an arrow from his quiver. At least he could help Darion overcome some of his insecurities. He had no such remedy for himself.

"I realized how fortunate I am to have you in my life."

Her voice was soft. "You've said that before."

"I know. It's just that today I felt—I feel like I'm really glad I'm with you."

"I'm really glad I'm with you too." Hana patted him on the back. "You didn't have to bring me out here to tell me that."

"I also wanted to tell you..."

When he paused, Emory fired the silver arrow into his chest.

Darion took a deep breath. "You're very special to me."

Emory let out a frustrated sigh.

Hana held her hand to her heart teasingly. "You're so sweet."

"I'm not kidding."

"I didn't think you were," she said in a mild tone. "Thank you for telling me that."

Soft music floated out of the banquet hall and onto the balcony.

"We should go back inside," Hana said after a long silence. She slowly moved toward the double doors.

Emory tried again. He fired a second arrow into Darion's heart.

Darion's solid-orange aura deepened to crimson—reflecting the feeling he'd had when he first fell in love with her. He ran up and grabbed Hana's hand, turning her around to face him. "I'm trying to tell you... *Saranghae*."

Hana remained still. "You do?"

He pulled her closer. "Yes."

A smile crept across her lips. "Then... say it again."

Darion held her soft face in his hands and kissed her. "I love you, Hana."

She wrapped her arms around his neck. "I love you too."

Emory twirled an arrow between his fingers, watching his clients embrace. He felt a profound sense of satisfaction for his work, something he'd never experienced until that moment. It was the healthiest match he'd ever established. He was able to bring his clients closer together and reinforce their bond of love. Their relationship was stronger because of him, not in spite of him.

Hana and Darion reentered the wedding reception, holding hands and whispering to each other. Emory grinned and followed behind, eager to spend the rest of his night with Blair. He wasn't going to overthink every move—he was going to allow their relationship to evolve naturally. His smile faded when he spotted her on the dance floor in the arms of another man. Heat crawled up Emory's neck, and he clenched his bow so hard his fingers almost bled. He moved in and circled around the pair, hidden behind the veil of the Enarine realm.

Argus grasped Blair's hand and swayed to a slow tempo. "Are you here for the bride or the groom?"

"Technically, the bride," Blair said. "You?"

"Neither." He clasped her hand tighter. "I just came to dance with you."

She smirked. "Right."

"You're very pretty." Argus twirled her around.

"Thank you. You're very handsome."

He swept her toward him. "I know."

Blair laughed and rolled her eyes. Emory wanted to strangle his cousin for stealing Blair's attention, but he couldn't cause a scene—especially not at a wedding. It was a sacred occasion.

"Your boyfriend left you here alone?" Argus asked.

"I don't really have a boyfriend."

"No?"

"Well, I came with a very good friend." Blair hesitated. "But I wouldn't call him my *boyfriend*."

Emory chafed. She could have said that to anyone else. Not to his cousin.

Argus quirked an eyebrow. "Your friend has commitment issues?"

"No, it's not him." Blair smiled. "He's perfect."

"Perfect?" Argus echoed. "You must like him a lot."

Blair wouldn't meet his eyes. "Do you have a girlfriend?" she asked, clearly wanting to change the subject.

Argus slid his hand up her back, pulling her closer, making Emory want to break his wrist. "Several."

"I don't doubt that," she said with a laugh.

"None that would describe me as *perfect*, though."

She looked mock startled. "You must be doing something wrong."

A wicked grin spread across his lips. "Oh, I *like* you."

The song faded. Argus released her hand but continued to hold her close. Blair seemed unable to pry her eyes from his. Thirty seconds. Emory was going to give his cousin thirty seconds. Then there would be a scene.

"Thank you for the dance," Blair said.

"It was a pleasure meeting you." Argus brushed her hair behind her ear and whispered, "I bet I could find you someone better."

Argus lingered and kissed her on the cheek. Her mouth opened, but he departed the dance floor before she could make a reply. Rage welled in Emory's throat. He resisted the urge to charge after Argus and pummel him in the face. If he did that, he would be written up for misconduct, which was exactly what Argus wanted—for Emory to lose control and prove he was unfit for his assignments.

Suddenly, a drunken bridesmaid bumped into Blair. "Hey! That hot guy promised me a second dance." The whirly bridesmaid grabbed Blair's shoulder. "Where'd he go?"

Blair scanned the crowd dazedly. "I have no idea."

Emory had little trouble keeping track of his cousin as he crossed into the Enarine realm and moved away from the crowds. Despite the rising temperature under his collar, Emory calmly walked up to Argus and stood by his side. They watched Blair dance with her new friend from the bridal party.

Argus spoke up first. "She's a little too short for my taste."

Emory couldn't contain his venom. "Touch her again, and I'll kill you."

"Relax, cousin." Argus raised his hands. "I'm unarmed. This is strictly a social visit, off the record."

Emory maintained a calm façade. "Why are you really here?"

"I noticed you've been keeping her to yourself lately," Argus remarked. "You haven't matched her with anyone in eighteen days."

Nineteen. "I was going to tonight."

"You've always been a terrible liar, Emory." Argus unwrapped a stick of gum and began chewing loudly. "She's certainly a step up from the delinquents you used to mess with in Thiyden."

Emory cracked his knuckles. "That was a long time ago."

"It was indeed. And I don't blame you for pursuing a human. I love being able to capture their complete, undivided attention."

"I don't make it a practice to entrance my clients," Emory said through his teeth.

Argus narrowed his eyes. "After all the time you've spent with her, you've never—"

"Just once," Emory said. "When we first met."

"Ahh..." Argus popped his gum. "You want to know that her attraction to you is genuine."

Emory loosened his tie.

"Who would have guessed you were a purist?" Argus said, sneering. "How is that working for you?"

Emory inhaled sharply and slung his longbow over his shoulder.

"My fingers are still numb." Argus rubbed his hands together, attempting to regain feeling after his prolonged exposure to Blair. "Is that why you didn't kiss her?"

Emory ground his teeth.

Argus smiled. "If it was me, I would have ravished her by now."

"She's not like the senseless women you fool around with."

"Always so touchy, Emory." Argus gave him a sly look. "I'm just saying, I don't think she'd object if you were a bit more… forward."

Emory stared at Blair through the dim ballroom lighting. "It's not that simple."

Argus raised a single eyebrow. "You *are* Vycrin, aren't you?"

"Meaning?"

"Love should be second nature," he said. "Especially making love—"

"Shut up, Argus."

Argus laughed and straightened his cufflinks. "I just hope you're able to thaw your little ice queen before the damage becomes irreversible—for your sake and hers." Argus clapped him on his shoulder. "We're family. I'll give you a month before I go to the board with my findings."

Emory nodded. Argus was insufferable, but he never broke his word.

"Enjoy the rest of your evening." Argus saluted Emory and sauntered out of the ballroom.

Emory's mind raced. He had one month to formally commit to Blair or risk having his accounts suspended for being in breach of contract. One month. And she couldn't see him as anything other than a friend.

Emory caught sight of Blair and the inebriated bridesmaid stumbling out of the reception hall, and he tried to regain his composure.

Switching realms, he called out, "Blair!"

She turned and caught his eye. "Where have you been?" She looked relieved.

"Working."

"Well, you sent me the most arrogant and self-absorbed man I've ever met." Blair steadied the bridesmaid in her arms. "He was a great dancer, though, and he smelled amazing. I should buy you that cologne."

Emory clenched his fists as Blair helped the young woman down the broad hallway, away from the festivities. "Where are you going?"

"I didn't want her to embarrass the bride." Blair shook her head. "Weddings can be rough when you're single. You should have seen me at Malena's wed—oh, that's right. You were there."

Emory pushed open the door to the ladies' room, and Blair propped up her new friend.

The bridesmaid poked Emory in the chest. "I love your girl-friend."

Blair dragged her into the bathroom, and the door slammed shut behind them.

Emory sighed. "So do I."

CHAPTER 23

"You're sure she can't see us?" Blair muttered.

Laith and Karina's dog growled and barked at Emory and Blair as they sat on the couple's large deck. The humid summer air was stifling to breathe.

Emory remained motionless. "Positive."

Dogs—"man's best friend"—loved humans and despised Vycrin. Emory wasn't entirely fond of them either. The large puppy charged in his direction.

"Shelby!" Karina shouted. "Get back here!"

"Don't yell at her," Laith said. "Maybe she saw something."

Karina rolled her eyes. "There's nothing out here. The dumb dog barks at everything."

Laith whistled and snapped Shelby out of her frenzy. "Inside," he commanded.

Shelby ran into the house through the back door.

Karina sighed. "There's something wrong with her."

"You just have to be patient with her," Laith muttered, adjusting the gas on their chrome outdoor grill.

Karina stepped up behind him, holding a plate of raw meat. "Well, she can't stay here when my sister comes next week. My brother-in-law is allergic to dogs."

"Or your sister and her husband can stay somewhere else," Laith countered.

Karina handed him the plate. "They're staying here," she said firmly.

"I don't force you to hang out with my family."

She glowered at him. "You barely *speak* to your family."

"Exactly."

"I haven't seen them in a year," Karina said. "They're only staying for a week. Not even a week—six days."

"I thought we had a pretty clear understanding about our living arrangement," he said stiffly. " We agreed that neither of us should have friends or family crash at our place. It's too disruptive."

"That was fine when we were in the apartment. Now we have plenty of space for guests. I don't think having them stay with us for a few days is really a burden."

"It is for me," he said, placing the burgers on the grill. "Your sister annoys me."

"Well, you annoy me sometimes." She snatched the empty plate from him. "So we're even."

As the unhappy couple argued, Blair covered her face and turned away.

"Your nosy sister and her husband can get a hotel," Laith said.

Karina scowled at him. *"Te voy a dar una palmada en la cara."*

"You know I don't speak Spanish," Laith said.

Emory leaned over to Blair. "Karina threatened to slap him."

"Not again." Blair folded her arms. "That never ends well."

"Forget it," Karina said. "I don't need my sister seeing what a tool you are and reporting back to my mother."

"Like that matters. Your mother can't stay sober long enough to remember she *has* two daughters."

"Oh, Laith," Blair said under her breath.

Emory loaded his bow and took aim. "Bad form."

Karina slammed the plate onto the ground. The loud crash muffled the expletives spewing from her mouth. Broken pieces of porcelain flew off the wooden patio and littered the soft green grass.

Emory shot Laith in the heart.

A look of horror crossed Laith's face. "I-I'm sorry. I didn't mean that!" he stammered.

Emory reloaded.

"Karina, I'm sorry!"

She pushed him away and screamed at him in Spanish when he tried to touch her.

"Your sister can stay with us," he said over her shouting.

Emory shot Karina in the heart. Her pale-orange aura changed to solid black.

"Forget it!" she said. "They can get a hotel and find their own way around the city!"

Blair lurched forward in her seat. "Why didn't that work?"

Emory fumbled with another silver arrow. He couldn't allow her heart to turn against Laith. They had already built a life together.

"Karina, I'm serious." Laith put his hand on her shoulder. "They can stay with us as long as they like."

She refused to acknowledge him. Laith wrapped his arms around her shoulders and held her close. Smoke billowed up from the grill. Karina's aura alternated from black to red to black—her heart was conflicted. Emory waited. Her aura morphed into a deep-burgundy hue. Emory seized the brief opening and shot her a second time, quelling her apathy.

Karina spoke into Laith's shoulder. "You really don't mind?"

"It's fine," he soothed.

"I'll keep them occupied. You won't have to see them very much."

Laith stroked her hair. "I'll be working all week, so you can have time alone with them. And I'll just plan to go camping with the guys on the weekend."

"That's fine." She leaned her head on his shoulder. "Thank you for compromising."

"Anything for you."

Karina nestled in his arms for a moment more, then they both turned their attention back to their burning food and the shattered debris.

Emory squinted. The faint orange aura surrounding their bodies was difficult to make out.

Blair sighed heavily. "What were you thinking, pairing them together?"

"It was a long time ago." Emory ran his fingers over the arrows left in his quiver. "When I first started working, I paired couples based on looks. I figured if I was forced to watch them all day, they should at least be attractive."

She scowled at him. "That is so shallow."

"I said it was a long time ago."

"No wonder they're a train wreck."

Emory rubbed his eyes. "I don't know what to do about them."

Blair shrugged. "Don't do anything. Let them break up."

"How can you say that?"

"Their relationship is toxic," Blair said. "Are they compatible on any level?"

He plucked a silver arrow from his quiver. "They both love dogs."

"You're wrong." Blair crossed her legs and straightened her miniskirt. "Karina was testing him by asking for something she knew he didn't want, and he called her bluff."

Emory twirled the heavy arrow between his fingers. "They have history."

Blair watched the couple clean the shattered porcelain off the lawn. "No amount of history can fix a couple who fundamentally shouldn't be together."

"So far, it's worked," he offered weakly.

Blair faced him. "What if they get married?"

"Then their case will be closed."

"No, what will happen to them *after* they're married? Will you still be around to intervene?"

He stared at the spinning arrow. He'd never once thought about the couple's future. He couldn't even imagine them growing old together.

"The best-case scenario is they get married, you're off the hook, and they're divorced within a year." Blair grabbed his arm to stop him from twirling the arrow. "Why would you put them through that?"

Emory looked into her eyes. "They're a liability. They could ruin my career."

"I don't believe you would put your career above a client's well-being." Her gaze was unwavering. "That's not the kind of man you are."

Emory sat in silence. He found it difficult to watch Laith and Karina's interactions. He knew they loved each other, but dragging that love to the surface every time they had an explosive argument masked the true depth of their incompatibility. A proposal was unrealistic and ill advised, but he feared a serious breakup before his follow-up conference with the audit committee.

Shelby barked from the window, angry with the unseen intruders. Emory slid the arrow into his quiver and slung it over his back. "Let's get out of here before they let Shelby out again."

They walked out of the wearisome couple's backyard and toured their affluent neighborhood. The suburb was located just outside the city, providing them with a pleasant change of scenery. They watched the sun set in the distance.

"That's a pretty house," Blair said, pointing to an expansive two-story home.

"It could use more plants on the porch."

"And rocking chairs," she added.

"Or a porch swing."

"Good one!" They stopped in front of the brick home. "Should we knock and tell them how they can add more curb appeal?"

Emory peered through the windows. "They don't appear to be home. But it looks like they have a pool."

Her eyes widened. "Can we check it out?"

Emory grasped her hand, and they trespassed onto the property. A tall wrought-iron fence enclosed the entire backyard, and a luxurious cabana overlooked the far end of the pool. Blair ran toward it and collapsed on the plush outdoor mattress. Sheer white linens draped the canopy and swayed in the warm summer night's breeze. Emory approached and tossed his bow and quiver onto the grass. He climbed in next to her and lay across an oversized throw pillow. They gazed up at the starlit sky through the thin fabric.

"Smart," Blair said. "They spent their money on a tropical oasis instead of rocking chairs."

"Do you like this house?"

"It's absolutely beautiful." She stretched across the mattress. "I love everything about it."

Emory did too. It would be a perfect place to settle down. "Do you want a house like this?"

Blair burst into laughter. "No!"

He frowned at her, confused. "But you just said you liked it."

"It already takes me three hours to clean my apartment. I don't want to clean a house this big."

"I'd help you clean it," he offered.

Blair curled onto her side and faced him. "We don't have enough furniture."

He shrugged. "I guess we'd have to fill it with other things."

"Like what?"

Emory thought for a moment. "Little people."

Blair's dark eyes turned serious. "And who's going to watch the little people while I'm at my spin classes?"

He grabbed her by the waist and pulled her closer. "Does it count as a class if you fall off the bike within the first ten minutes?"

She chuckled and pushed him away. Emory was certain she would be a fun mom—like his was. Blair slid off the bed and strolled the length of the pool, bright underwater lights illuminating her path. Her noisy flip-flops slapped against the soles of her small feet.

"For your information, that instructor was *trying* to kill us."

Emory crept up behind her. She spun around. He froze midstep.

"Were you about to knock me into the bushes?" she asked.

"Of course not. You said you were tired of landing on hard surfaces, so I was going to shove you into the pool."

She gave him a stern look.

"What?" He flashed her an innocent smile. "Your hair's already curly."

"Fine," she said, turning her back to him. "You'd just better be glad I like you so much. No one else would be able to get away with something like this." She took a few calming breaths.

He ran toward her.

"Wait!"

Emory stumbled to a stop seconds before reaching the paved tile surrounding the pool. "What's wrong?"

Blair slipped out of her flip-flops. "Let's try it facing each other. We've never done that before."

"No. You have to be completely relaxed, or your body will go into shock." He backed up again. "If you see me coming, you'll tense up."

"What if I close my eyes?" Blair unbuttoned her denim miniskirt.

"No."

Her skirt dropped around her ankles, and she kicked it off. "Please?"

His resolve was weakening. "Absolutely not."

"Just this once?" Her tank top landed on the pile of clothes, and she tightened the straps of her bra.

Emory's eyes shifted everywhere but in the direction of her half-naked body. He needed to maintain his good sense. "I don't think so."

She adjusted her purple ruffled boy shorts. "I promise I won't tense up."

The pleading look on her face was too much. "This is a terrible idea," he muttered as he stripped down to his boxers.

Blair let out a gleeful giggle and stood on the tips of her toes at the edge of the pool.

Emory lined up in her path across the yard and dulled his senses. "Close your eyes."

She shut her eyes. Her slow, controlled breaths were barely audible, and her limbs dangled by her sides. The only sound he could hear was that of his heavy footsteps bearing down on the thick grass. Emory crouched down and dove toward her. Blair gasped. He slammed into her waist, shoulder first, and wrapped his arms around her as they careened into the pool and switched into the Earth realm. He felt no connection to her.

The clear, tepid water engulfed them, and they sank to the bottom of the ten-foot-deep pool. Emory released his grip and swam to the surface. He blew out a breath, wiping water from his eyes.

"I don't think that was any better," he said. No response. Emory scanned the edge of the pool but found that Blair had not emerged from the water. "Blair?"

He spotted her at the bottom of the deep end, where she lay motionless. He dove under the water. His heart raced with each frantic stroke as he approached her limp body. He grabbed hold of her and pulled her back to the surface, gasping for air as he hauled her body over the side of the pool. He scrambled out of the water and onto the rough ground, dragging her across the grass.

"Blair?" He shook her shoulders. "Can you hear me?"

She was unresponsive. He checked for her pulse and leaned closer to see if she was breathing. Nothing. He'd never witnessed a crossing that went wrong.

Terrified, Emory started doing chest compressions on her.

"Wake up, wake up!" he muttered anxiously between compressions. Water dripped from his hair onto her limp body. "Please wake up."

He tilted her head back and pinched her nostrils. He covered her mouth with his and blew into her lungs. His second breath lasted less than a second, but he felt a biting chill from her skin. There was no sign of movement.

"You can't just leave me." He began another round of compressions, pressing into her chest at a constant steady rate. Emory's arms began to weaken with each desperate motion. His eyes stung as tears clouded his vision.

"I love you." He breathed into her mouth, pulled back, and stared down at her stiff, frozen body. Drops of water rolled off her cheeks, and he realized they were his tears. "Did you hear me?" he pleaded, his voice rising. "I love you!"

He kissed her. A soft wind blew across the grass, and he crumpled over her lifeless body, sobbing, overcome by crushing helplessness. He clenched his shaking hands.

"You can't do this to me!" he screamed and slammed both fists against her chest as hard as he could.

Blair's eyes shot open, and she catapulted into a seated position, letting out a horrifying screech. Her entire body shook from the sudden blow, and tears poured from her eyes. She clasped his arms and wouldn't let go. Her loud sobbing replaced his, and Emory blinked his tears away before she could see them. He wrapped his arms around her and clung to her quivering body.

"That w-was much worse." She could barely choke out the words. "It was better from behind."

"I told you it was a horrible idea!" He couldn't keep his voice from trembling. "You never listen to me."

She buried her face in his shoulder, sobbing. "You shouldn't let me get my way all the time."

"You're ridiculous, Blair." Emory squeezed her closer. "I swear... you make me so angry."

The feeling of her beating heart against his chest made him feel excited, anxious, and agitated, all at the same time. She already had power over his desires. Now that small pulse inside her controlled his fears, insecurities, weaknesses, and doubts. And there was nothing he could do about it.

CHAPTER 24

Emory watched Hana wrap her hand around Darion's as they strolled through the large county fair. Their ruby-red auras shimmered brightly—they were completely in love. Darion kissed her on the cheek. A small child burst between them, and Hana stumbled backward.

"Yuck!" the child shouted. "Uncle Darion, that's gross."

Hana rolled her eyes and folded her arms across her chest. Darion wrapped his arm around her.

"Tyrone, she's my girlfriend."

"Really?" Hana teased Darion. "You're trying to reason with a five-year-old?"

"I'm six!" Tyrone protested. "I told you that, like, a hundred times."

"Nobody cares how old you are," his brother, Dominic, said, his mouth stuffed with the last of his popcorn. "I have to go to the bathroom."

"Again?" Hana said. "You just went."

"Babe," Darion said calmly, "I'll take him. You stay here with Tyrone."

Hana gave him a quick peck on the lips. "Hurry back, please."

Darion ushered his nephew to the portable restrooms while Hana scrolled through her phone. Emory had tried to keep Blair in his sight line, but it was impossible while he was working. He debated leaving the couple early. He was only there to help Hana feel more comfortable around Darion's nephews, but Darion was already doing a successful job of setting her mind at ease. Their relationship was strong.

"Can I hold my tickets?" Tyrone asked Hana.

She handed him a string of red tickets and went back to texting.

"Can I get cotton candy?" Tyrone asked.

"In a bit," she said without glancing up from her phone.

"Please? Please? Please?" The child was going to wear her down.

Hana huffed and handed him five dollars. "Just be quick."

Tyrone snatched up the money and took off running. Emory scanned the area for Blair. His constant concern for her well-being was all-consuming. Two weeks had passed since the episode at the pool, but that evening was the first time she'd felt well enough to go out. The shock to her body had been greater than even he imagined. He should have known better. Crossing over was not something to be taken lightly, especially not with her broken-hearted condition. When they arrived at the carnival, she hadn't asked to join him on his assignment with Darion and Hana—and he hadn't offered.

Darion was playfully roughhousing with Dominic as they returned from the lavatory. Hana slipped her phone into her purse.

"Where's Tyrone?" Darion asked.

"He went to get cotton candy," Hana replied.

Darion's eyes were wide. "By himself?"

Emory jumped to attention. He'd completely forgotten about the child.

"He was begging for sweets," Hana stammered. "I gave him money to get what he wanted."

Darion pushed past her and rushed into the crowds. "Tyrone!" he shouted.

Emory's heart was racing. It had all happened so fast.

Hana ran to Darion's side. "I-I'm sorry, I didn't know!"

"You gave a six-year-old money and sent him off alone!" Darion shouted. "Are you completely insane?"

Hana's back stiffened.

Darion looked horrified. "Oh, Hana. I didn't mean it like that."

Emory slung his bow over his shoulder. Finding Tyrone was the priority. He'd deal with his clients later. Hana maneuvered around clusters of people and called out for Darion's nephew. Darion grabbed Dominic's hand and quickly followed after her.

"Hana, I'm sorry," Darion said. "I didn't mean—"

"I don't care!" Hana yelled. "We need to split up and find him."

Darion sprinted in the opposite direction with Dominic by his side.

Emory stayed with Hana as she frantically searched the grounds.

"Come on, Tyrone," she muttered. "Where did you go?"

Hana passed a wide mobile snow-cone trailer, and Emory suddenly heard snickering. He peeked around the colorful cart and found Tyrone crouched down, hiding. As soon as Hana was out of sight, Tyrone dashed to the fun house. Emory ground his teeth. The young man needed a firm talking-to for getting everyone's emotions in a frenzy. Emory followed him into the maze of mirrors. Blinding white lights shone down from overhead, and Tyrone stared at rows and rows of his own reflection in awe. Emory materialized behind him.

"I've had just about enough of your antics, boy!" Emory shouted. He cringed, suddenly understanding how Petros felt.

Tyrone gasped and spun around. Emory dilated his pupils and captured the boy's full attention. The boy's expression went blank. It was difficult to hold young children entranced for very long. They were too unstable. Their minds were not fully developed, and they had a tendency to question everything.

Emory knelt down to Tyrone's level and lowered his voice. "Your uncle and Hana are very worried about you." Emory spoke in a calm tone so as not to ignite any negative emotions. "When you leave this building, go straight to a bench and sit down. Don't move a muscle until they find you." Emory rose and towered over the child. "And be nicer to Hana."

Emory blinked hard and disappeared into the Enarine realm. Tyrone staggered through the rest of the maze in a dazed stupor. They emerged from the mind-bending attraction, and Tyrone immediately found a picnic bench and sat down. Emory stood behind him to ensure that no one went anywhere near the child while they waited.

Hana was the first to spot him. "Tyrone! Are you all right? Where did you go? We were so worried!" She fumbled with her phone and flipped her long, tousled hair over her shoulder. "Yes. I found him. He's here with me, by the fun house."

Hana collapsed next to Tyrone and let out a heavy sigh of relief as she hung up.

"I'm sorry, Hana," Tyrone said sincerely.

"Don't be sorry, sweetie," she said, patting his knee. "I shouldn't have left you alone."

Moments later, Darion and Dominic rushed over to them. "Is everyone okay?" Darion knelt in the grass and gave his nephew a hug. "You scared us for a second there."

"I think I got lost," Tyrone said.

"I told you," Dominic said in an authoritative big-brother tone. "He's always getting turned around."

Darion squeezed Hana's hand. "Thank you for finding him."

She pretended to be preoccupied with her phone. "Yep."

Darion closed his eyes and cracked his neck. "Do you guys want to go on some rides?"

"Let's go on the Tilt-A-Whirl!" Dominic said, clearly unaffected by the ordeal.

Tyrone perked up as the lingering effects of the entrancement wore off. "Then the teacups!"

The young boys led the way through the fairgrounds with Hana and Darion following close behind. Emory walked beside them and twirled a silver arrow. The tension between his clients was unbearable, but if he shot either of them before they resolved their feelings, their bond would be weakened.

The boys eagerly boarded the Tilt-A-Whirl while Hana and Darion waited for them by the metal gates. The children settled into the spinning car and locked a long safety bar over their laps.

Darion spoke up. "That comment I made earlier—"

"I don't want to talk about it," Hana said.

The cars began to move in a slow circular motion. Within a matter of moments, the cars whipped excited riders around at increasing speeds. Darion rubbed his eyes. "Well, what do you want to talk about?"

"With you? Nothing right now."

"I didn't mean anything by that." Darion let out a frustrated sigh. "It's not like you're so perfect you've never slipped up."

Emory loaded his bow, not exactly sure where the conversation was heading.

Hana's jaw dropped. "What are you talking about?"

"I heard you with my sister."

Hana pressed her lips together and glanced up at the sky. "That was a joke."

"I didn't find it funny."

"Darion—"

"Do you know how long it took me to grow this goatee?"

Hana spoke in a serious voice. "Five years."

"Five years, Hana! That's commitment. That's dedication. That's nothing to scoff at."

"You're right." Hana stepped closer to him. "I shouldn't have been making light of it. I'm sorry."

Emory shot Hana in the heart. Reinforcing her love for Darion when she empathized with him would help her overlook small transgressions.

"And I know you didn't mean to hurt my feelings earlier," she said.

Darion's nephews laughed hysterically as the cars whirled to a stop.

"Can we not fight anymore, please?" Darion said.

Hana nudged him. "Hurry up, before the kids see us."

Darion smiled. He pulled her closer and kissed her.

Emory returned an unused arrow to his quiver, content with the couple's progress. It was all just a big misunderstanding. Easy fix. And he could finally focus on Blair. He scoured the carnival and found her waiting for a food order at one of the vendors. He placed his bow across his chest and phased back into the Earth realm. The distinct smell of hamburgers and fried foods filled the air.

He approached her from behind and wrapped his arm around her shoulders. "How are you feeling?" he asked gently.

Blair held on to him with her cold fingers. "I'm still sore."

They hadn't spoken about the incident at the pool or about the intense bond it had created between them. They hadn't spent more than twenty-four hours apart since it happened.

"I'll send you to the spa tomorrow for a massage," Emory said.

"Or," Blair countered, leaning her back against his chest, "you could save your money and do it yourself."

He pondered the idea. "I'd rather watch you get naked and have someone else do all the work."

"Lazy pervert..." she muttered, grinning.

He smiled. "What did you order?"

"A hot dog, french fries, chicken tenders, and fried Oreo cookies."

Emory cleared his throat. "I see your appetite has returned with a vengeance."

"I didn't forget about you. I got the fries for us to share."

He gently leaned his chin on her head. "So generous."

"I know." She squeezed his arm. "How did it go with the kid-dos?"

"They're warming up to her." Emory sensed her cheerful mood but slipped regretfully out of her reach, unable to bear her icy touch against his skin any longer. She readjusted her V-neck top as he rubbed his hands together.

"It's eighty degrees," Blair said, dumbfounded. "How can you be cold?"

He shrugged. "I felt a chill."

Emory found it increasingly difficult to keep secrets from her, but similar to Vycrin, humans had the ability to conceal their true feelings from others. If she knew he could sense her deepest emotions through touch, she would instinctively shut him out. All humans did. It was their defense mechanism. It was the same reason that humans without auras were considered untrustworthy—most of the time, it meant they were hiding something.

They picked up their tray of food and found seats at a rickety old picnic table away from the crowds. Emory ate some of Blair's french fries. "Do you know what these could use?"

She took a bite out of her hot dog. "Olive juice," she answered between chews.

"Do you think they have any?"

"I doubt the county fair stocks olive juice just for Vycrin." Blair shoved the remainder of her hot dog in Emory's face, taunting him. "You want it?"

Emory grinned, grabbed her cold hand, and stuffed the entire hot dog into his mouth, leaving only a small piece of white bread between her fingers.

"Emory!" Blair cried. "That was mine!"

"You shouldn't put your food in other people's faces," he said through a mouthful of food.

Blair smiled and ate a chicken tender. "You never took the bait before."

"How will you be able to go on any rides after gorging yourself on this much food?"

She bit into a fried Oreo. "We'll have to start slow."

• • ❧ • •

THEY RODE THE CAROUSEL four times. Blair sat on a stationary horse and rested her forehead against the long gold pole, moaning. Emory stood beside her on the platform, shaking his head. It was just like the fiasco with the food truck, only this time he knew what to do. Emory rummaged through his backpack, tore open two shrink-wrapped tablets, and handed them to her.

"Thanks." Blair chewed the chalky tablets, her face pinching in a grimace.

Emory gently rubbed her back. "That's what I'm here for."

Thirty minutes later, they advanced to the bumper cars. By the time they exited the Musik Express, Blair was almost back to normal. They strolled through the fairgrounds as darkness fell. Hundreds of colorful bulbs lit up the rides and vendors. The smell of popcorn permeated the air as they passed noisy booths full of clamoring fairgoers attempting to win prizes.

Emory and Blair crept through a line for a ride called Zero Gravity. Terrified riders on rollercoasters screamed in the distance. She reached into the back pocket of her shorts and pulled out their tickets. Out of the corner of his eye, Emory noticed the attendant ogling Blair's cleavage. *Punk.*

Emory put his hands on her hips and pulled her next to him. "Do you meet the height requirement?" he whispered.

Blair giggled. The young man looked in the opposite direction. Emory kept her close as she handed him their tickets.

They found two empty spots and buckled the loose straps around their waists. The ride started, and the world became a dizzying blur of bright colors as they spun out of control. Emory had never understood the human fascination with disorienting one's senses, but Blair's high-pitched screams made him laugh.

They exited the metal platform, debating their next move. In the distance, Emory spotted a ride called the Super Shot. "That looks like the tallest ride here."

"That's wild." Blair peered up at the brightly lit ride. "I bet you can see the entire fair from the top."

"The sights must be amazing," he mused.

"Should we check it out?"

Emory stared up. "We could."

It didn't take them long to cross the dusty fairgrounds. They snaked through a short line and reached the front, where the towering ride came into full view.

Blair seemed unable to pry her eyes from the top. "That's really high."

Emory handed an attendant their tickets. They found two empty seats and settled next to each other. Blair's hands trembled as she tightened the seatbelt across her lap. Emory pulled down the harness and locked it in place. The attendant walked around to ensure that all of the passengers were safely strapped in and secure. Blair leaned her head against the back of the seat and remained motionless.

"Blair," Emory said after some time.

Her voice was barely above a whisper. "Yes?"

"I have to tell you something I've never told you before." Sweat beaded up on his forehead.

She clenched the seat. "What?"

"I..." He swallowed hard. "I'm terrified of heights."

Blair's head snapped around. "I'm terrified of heights too."

He met her eyes. "Then what are we doing here?"

They sat in an unbearable silence for a moment.

"Let us off!" Emory yelled to the attendant.

"We changed our minds!" Blair fumbled with the safety harness, but it didn't budge. "We want to get off!"

The impassive attendant ignored their pleas. He flipped the switch and started the ride.

"We're going to die." Emory leaned his head back and closed his eyes. "We're going to die."

"We'll be all right," Blair assured him shakily as she clutched the harness. "I saw some children board the ride. If children are around, nothing bad can happen."

"I'll be honest," he said. "Logic isn't your strong suit."

The ride began its slow ascent.

"Why didn't you tell me you were afraid of heights?" she demanded.

"I think what we have here is a classic example of miscommunication." Emory focused intently on the dark sky as the ride crept upward. "I recently noticed this happening to my clients when one person fails to voice their opinion due to uncertainty over their partner's reaction—"

"Thank you, Emory," Blair interrupted. "I'd love to hear the rest of your insights on human relationships after we're safely back on the ground."

"Sorry." He closed his eyes.

Blair began to hyperventilate. "Is there anything else you've been keeping from me due to uncertainty over my reaction?"

The ride climbed to the top and stopped. Emory slowly opened his eyes and stared out at the expansive fairgrounds. The sight was beautiful and terrifying at the same time.

"Yes," he answered.

The ride dropped.

Blair let out a horrific shriek. Emory's stomach drifted into his chest, creating a sinking feeling. He gritted his teeth as they plummeted to the ground at unfathomable speeds. Other passengers cheered during the agonizing free fall. *Crazy humans.*

Seconds later, the ride slowed to a stop. Emory gasped. Happy fairgoers unbuckled their harnesses and climbed out of their seats. Emory's heart raced, and he had trouble breathing. Drops of sweat rolled down the side of his face. The attendant approached Blair and Emory, who were frozen in their seats.

"Guys, you have to get off now."

Emory ripped his moist palms from the handlebars, and Blair pushed the black cushioned harness over her head. Emory's body trembled when his feet hit the ground. Teenagers ran past them, laughing with delight. Blair's legs wobbled as she shuffled across the makeshift platform.

Emory clasped a flimsy metal railing with one hand and offered Blair the other. He led her down the shaky, uneven stairs to solid ground. "I guess we'll have to work on our communication skills."

"Do you want to start now? What were you going to say before we dropped?"

Emory clung to her cold fingers. He knew he wanted the one thing she couldn't give him, but keeping his love for her a secret was slowly destroying his soul. "I-I was afraid to tell you..." Blair looked up at him with wide eyes. "What is it?"

His heart was pounding so hard he could barely think straight. "I—"

Someone's gum popped. Emory blinked. Argus was standing behind Blair, six feet away. Emory clenched his jaw shut, and his cousin disappeared into the Enarine realm.

Blair squeezed his hand. "Emory?"

Emory blinked rapidly. He didn't want it to happen that way. He didn't want to pour out his heart to the only woman he ever truly loved with his cousin listening to every word. What they had between them was special and private—not something to be shared with anyone else. And if she didn't feel the same away... if she rejected him...

"I was afraid to tell you at the wedding," Emory said. "That narcissist you were dancing with was my cousin."

Blair gasped. "You're kidding. The one you're always talking about?"

"Yes." Emory glared over her shoulder. "That pompous windbag was Argus."

Blair gave him a sly grin. "Good thing I didn't go home with him. That would have been embarrassing for everyone involved."

"You have better judgment than that."

"I don't know." Blair linked her arm around his, and they headed down the dirt pathway. "He was very charismatic, and I didn't want to say it then, but he kind of looked like you."

"We don't look anything alike!" Emory cried.

Blair held back a chuckle. "I'm just excited that I finally met someone in your family."

"Not anyone of consequence," he muttered.

Blair stopped in her tracks. "Because I'm of no consequence?" she said over the chaotic carnival music. "Because I'm just a client?"

Emory's eyebrows shot up. "That's not what I said."

She didn't break her gaze. "That's what you implied."

"Blair..." Emory spoke only loud enough for her to hear. "I think we're having one of those miscommunications."

She slipped her hands into the back pockets of her shorts. "What should we do about it?"

Emory shrugged. "Ice cream?"

She surveyed the swarms of people surrounding them. "Here or at your place?"

"You pick."

"Your place," she said after a while. "I'm tired of rides."

"Me too." Emory wrapped his arm around her icy shoulders and led her away from the blaring attractions. They'd had enough rides for one day.

CHAPTER 25

Blair clasped a filigree cuff bracelet around her wrist and held her arm out to Emory. Hundreds of white booths lined the streets of the annual Arts and Crafts Festival. The summer sun beat down on eager patrons and craftspeople alike.

"It looks nice on you." Emory took a sip from their bottle of water. The cool liquid was a welcome contrast to the blazing heat. "Do you want it?"

She twisted the ornate silver piece to view it from another angle. "You don't have to buy me anything."

"I asked if you wanted it."

She smiled and nodded.

Emory tossed her his wallet. "Don't do too much damage while I'm gone."

Blair grabbed his arm before he could slip away. "I was also thinking about getting something for your coffee table. It's so bare."

"Nothing pink," he warned.

She feigned shock at the very notion. "What do you take me for?"

"I know you, Blair."

She held back a grin. "Fine."

Emory crossed into the Enarine realm and left Blair to her shopping spree. He had to get to work. Amir and Joey's relationship had begun to stagnate. They were committed, but Joey no longer mentioned meeting his family. Emory wasn't sure what had changed in her, but it wasn't a positive sign. A few booths over, Joey handed Amir half of the gluten-free vegan pastry she had purchased.

She watched Amir with playful eyes as he ate it. "What do you think?"

He chewed slowly and flashed a fake smile.

She let out a short laugh. "We can go back to the guy selling gyros for lunch."

Joey finished the rest of the small pastry and followed Amir into a booth selling organic soap. She held one of the bars to her nose and breathed in the fragrant scent. "I applied for a new scholarship," she said without turning around.

"That's great!" Amir replied enthusiastically. "I know you were stressing about the fall semester."

Her eyes were hopeful. "Do you think I'll get it?"

"Of course you will." He lost interest in the scented merchandise and set it back on the table. "They'd be crazy not to award it to you."

She grabbed his hand, her face serious. "It's a study-abroad scholarship."

"What?" Emory shouted. "When did this happen?" He froze. After Joey's trip, she had repeatedly mentioned how eager she was to return to Europe. He'd assumed she was just going through a phase.

Amir's cheerful expression shifted. "What?"

Joey hesitated. "I was thinking of spending my junior year in Europe."

Amir looked bewildered. "Are you serious?"

"It would only be for nine months, for the fall and spring semesters."

Amir yanked his hand away. "You're planning to leave for a *year*, and you're just now telling me?"

Emory paced back and forth outside of the booth. His client list would be reduced to that of a novice.

"I've thought all of this through," Joey said calmly. "If we alternate visiting each other during the breaks, we'll never be apart for more than three months at a time."

"That's typical." Amir stormed out of the booth. "You plan your entire life first, then you squeeze me in as an afterthought."

"I thought you'd be happy for me!" She followed after him as he pushed through the crowds. "This is a great opportunity."

"For you. It's always about you."

"What do you expect me to do? Put my life on hold?"

He blew out an angry breath. "I didn't say that. I just wish I was actually an important factor in your life."

"You are!" She increased her pace to keep up with him. "Nothing is official yet. I may not even be selected. I just wanted to let you know so you wouldn't be shocked if I did get into the program!"

Amir kept walking. "How nice of you to let me know two months before our classes start."

"Amir!" Joey grabbed his arm, and he stopped. "Please don't do this. Can we just talk about it?"

The misery and distress on her face seemed to stifle his aggravation. The couple found an empty bench, and Amir slumped down next to her. Joey sighed and brushed her wavy hair away from her face.

"Lots of people have long-distance relationships," she said soothingly.

"Have you ever been in one?"

She folded her hands in her lap. "No."

Amir shook his head in disbelief.

The experience would result in emotional growth for Joey because it would force her to become more independent, and Amir's coursework would no doubt improve, but the situation wasn't ideal—for Emory's career. Emory's college students were his most dependable clients, the proof he needed to show the board he could handle young love.

"We'll both be so busy with school I'm sure the time will go by quickly," Joey said. "Plus you have the guys here."

Amir scoffed. "Somehow, I don't think they're going to fill the gap of my girlfriend being a million miles away."

"I'm sorry." Joey lowered her voice. "I didn't think you would take it this hard."

"Really? You thought I'd be excited to see you leave me?"

"I'm not leaving you." Her voice quavered.

He glanced over at her just as her eyes began watering. "Don't do that."

She sniffed.

"I'm the only one who should be upset, Joey." Amir refused to look at her. "You've had time to think and plan this whole thing out."

Joey let out a soft whimper and covered her face. A silver arrow struck Amir's heart. Amir needed to feel secure in the relationship in order to comfort Joey. It was going to be a difficult transition for both of them.

The young man suddenly wrapped his arms around his girlfriend and pulled her closer. "Don't cry," he whispered. "We can make it work."

Joey rested her head on his chest. "I don't care how much distance is between us. I still want to be with you."

He held her tighter. "I want to be with you too."

Emory lowered his bow. The delicate state of Joey and Amir's current bond made him weary. Distance created unique obstacles for most relationships, but such difficulties were often magnified in young couples.

Emory wandered through the Enarine realm, contemplating his next move with Amir and Joey. His follow-up audit meeting was scheduled for the autumn equinox, just weeks after the start of their junior year. It would be difficult to keep their relationship strong if his efforts were focused solely on Amir.

The people in the Earth realm walked at a listless pace around him, and a vendor selling exotic tropical plants caught his attention.

He placed his bow across his chest and entered the booth. Delicate orchids in full bloom greeted him, and he debated whether or not to buy one for Blair. They would have to keep it at his house to ensure that it was properly watered, but since she'd been spending most of her time at his place anyway, she could still enjoy the blossoming plant. He leaned closer.

"Shopping for someone special?"

Emory stepped back to find Hera smiling at him. A white sleeveless maxi dress hugged her athletic frame, and a colorful silk head scarf accentuated her thick curls. Her casual attire did little to set his mind at ease.

"I-I wasn't expecting you today," Emory stuttered.

"I know. But I need to talk to you."

He shifted. "If I had known, I would have prepared a brief update on my clients—"

"I only came to talk to you about one." Hera leaned against the long table and studied his face. "You've discontinued your efforts to find Blair a suitable match. You're aware that you're in breach of contract."

It was more of a statement than a question. Exactly one month had passed since Argus confronted him about Blair. His cousin had kept his word, but his adherence to rules and regulations was maddening. Emory nodded.

"Petros begged me not to freeze your accounts. He assures me you have the situation under control." Her dark piercing eyes searched his. "Have you told her?"

Emory swallowed. "Not yet."

"Why are you holding back?"

Emory's throat tightened. "Because she doesn't feel the same way about me."

"You knew Blair was incapable of returning your affection," she chastised gently, "yet you still chose to form a close attachment to her. You've made yourself vulnerable, yet you refuse to expose your vulnerability to her."

"I didn't purposely fall in love with her. It just happened."

"We don't have an issue with a romantic relationship between you and Blair," Hera assured him. "I believe she's had a very good influence on you. You've been much more engaged at work and compassionate with your clients. But you know the rules."

"Can't they make an exception? Or amend my contract?"

"When you pierced her heart and took her on as a client, you entered a binding agreement," Hera said firmly. "It's your responsibility to provide her with a suitable romantic partner or assume that role yourself. Preventing Blair from courting potential suitors while at the same time refusing to commit to her yourself constitutes an abuse of power."

"Hera..." Emory took hold of her wrist and brushed the tips of his fingers against the palm of her hand. "Read my heart. There is no cruelty or malice."

Hera gently clasped her hands around his, reinforcing their link. "I know your feelings for her are sincere." She stroked the back of his hand with her thumb as she spoke. "But Blair is either your client or your companion. She can't be both."

"We've been together for almost a year, and it hasn't caused any serious issues—"

"Under normal circumstances, we would not interfere with the natural progression of a Vycrin's romantic relationship." She released his hands. "However, we are well aware of how serious her situation has become."

Humans floated around them in the Earth realm, unaware of their presence.

"I just need a little more time," Emory said.

Hera reached into her quiver. She threw the shattered remnants of her gold arrow onto the table. The mangled pieces clanked as they landed on the white tablecloth. Heat rose into Emory's face. He had trouble hearing anything over the heavy beating of his heart.

"How much more time do you really think you have?" Hera whispered. "The barrier has shown no signs of weakening."

Emory stared down at the broken arrow. "How can I commit to someone who doesn't love me?"

"Do you truly want to be with her?"

He peered into Hera's eyes. "With all my heart."

"Then you *know* the answer to that question."

Emory wasn't sure he did know the answer.

"Before I go—Petros wanted me to bring you a gift." Hera reached into her quiver and handed him a bottle of wine. "From the vintage 1978. It was a very good year."

Emory slid the love potion into his quiver. Every little bit helped.

"You should drink some as well." She smiled. "To calm your nerves."

Emory let out a weary chuckle. "Thank you, Hera."

Hera and Emory crossed into the Earth realm and parted company. The summer heat suddenly felt oppressive. He wiped his sweaty brow with the back of his hand. He needed to regain control of his relationship with Blair then deal with his other clients.

Emory found Blair buying homemade candles and went to stand beside her. She shoved his wallet into the back pocket of his jeans and playfully smacked him on the butt.

"I kept it under a thousand," Blair said with a giggle. She glanced up at him, and her smile faded. "I'm kidding. It was thirty—"

"It's not that."

They moved on to the next booth, and she peeked into the bag at the candles. "We can put them in the master bathroom if you think they're too girlie for the coffee table."

"No, we can put them on the coffee table," he said quickly.

Blair gently rubbed his arm with her frozen hand. "Are you feeling all right?"

He took a moment to gather himself. "What do you think about getting away for a few days… with me?"

Blair's eyes widened. "Just us?"

The words rushed out of his mouth. "No, on my business trip."

"I thought you wanted me to house-sit while you were away. You didn't even tell me where you were going."

Emory hadn't been looking forward to the trip, or to being away from Blair, but he'd intended to focus solely on his problematic clients. "Laith and Karina are going to a beachfront resort in South Carolina, and I booked a suite in the same building."

Blair tore open her purse and retrieved her cell phone. "Keep talking, I'm listening."

He swallowed nervously. "I need to reaffirm their love during positive interactions, and their vacation may be the best opportunity."

"Hmm…" Blair tapped her phone with swift strokes. "They need all the help they can get."

"It's important that my superiors see advancement in their relationship."

"Mm-hmm?"

He cleared his throat. "I'll get a car and take care of the travel arrangements."

"Hmm."

"You won't have to worry about any of the expenses."

Blair gave a distant nod without glancing up.

Emory ground his teeth. She wasn't even paying attention. "Forget I said anything. I probably shouldn't have asked."

Blair made one final tap on the small screen. "I just bought a bikini." She turned the phone around for him to see her new purchase. "How sexy am I going to look in that?"

Emory gaped at the screen.
She grinned. "What day do we leave?"

CHAPTER 26

" *That's* the car you got?"

Emory wasn't sure if the stunned expression on Blair's face was quite the reaction he had been hoping for. "You don't like it?"

Blair dropped her bags on the sidewalk and circled the black 1965 Mustang convertible. She ran her fingers along the smooth lines of the classic vehicle. "You rented this for the beach?"

"No." Emory was perplexed. "I bought it."

She laughed. "Of *course* you did."

"If you don't like it—"

Blair silenced him with a single glance. "It's perfect."

Emory smiled and loaded her bags into the back seat. He opened the heavy door. "Do you want to drive?"

Her mouth dropped opened. "Seriously?"

"Of course. You're the reason I bought the car."

The cream leather hugged Blair's petite frame as she settled into the driver's seat. Emory shut the door and crouched next to the car as she adjusted the mirrors. He enjoyed watching her.

"How do I look?" she asked, slipping on her dark sunglasses.

He couldn't tear his eyes from her. "The car suits you."

He climbed into the car as she pressed down on the clutch and turned the key. The throaty roar of the engine effectively did what it was supposed to do—excite Blair. She practically melted. She stroked the thin steering wheel and stared at Emory through her sunglasses.

"I love you," Blair said.

Emory's heart pounded, and his mouth suddenly went dry. "I love you too."

Blair let out a high-pitched squeal and bounced up and down in her seat. "And I love the beach! And I love this car! And I love that we're going to the beach in *this* car!" She threw her arms around his neck and gave him a tight hug. "You're such an awesome friend."

Friend. A vintage car and four nights at a beachfront resort, and he was still just a friend. His approach was all wrong. Subtlety wasn't working.

Blair hit the gas and pulled into the street. "I'm basically taking 95 South the whole way, right?"

"Yes." He swiped his phone to verify the driving directions. "The GPS estimates we'll be there in six hours and forty-three minutes."

She shifted into second gear, a wicked grin coming over her face. "I'll do it in five."

. . ❧ . .

FIVE HOURS AND FORTY-three minutes later, the black convertible rolled into a parking space in front of a towering condo building. Waves crashed in the distance, and salty sea air permeated the clear sky.

Blair cut the engine. "All I'm saying is—"

"Stop. I don't want to hear it," Emory said. Every hair on his body was standing on end. He unlatched the seatbelt and climbed out of the car. "The earth is not your personal racetrack!"

"I'll pay for the ticket, Emory! What are you so mad about?"

He grabbed their bags from the narrow back seat. "I'm mad because we're not supposed to be drawing negative attention to ourselves, *and* I had to use two arrows just to get the sheriff to reduce your fines!"

"He was such a nice man," she mused.

Blair slid out of the car and followed Emory to the elevators. The doors opened, and he punched the button for the eleventh floor. Blair stood near him as the elevator climbed to their level. Emory took a step to the side, away from her. Without a word, she stepped next to him once more. He smirked and whacked her hard with her leopard-print bag. She stumbled and almost fell to the floor. Blair glared at him, yanked the bags out of his hands, and pounced on him.

"Get off of me!" he yelped.

She wrapped her legs around his waist and squeezed. "You think you can get rid of me that easily?"

Emory spun around in an attempt to shake her off, but she buried her face in his neck and clung tighter. Her frozen body sent a chill through him. He slammed her back against the elevator wall.

She laughed. "Don't fight it!"

He pinched her waist. She twisted and turned as he tickled her without mercy.

"Say it!" he said.

"No!" Her wild giggling echoed throughout the small space. "You can't make me!"

"Say it!"

Blair struggled to catch her breath, but he wouldn't let up. She wheezed. "You're the sexiest love god on the planet!"

Emory smiled and pushed her against the wall again. The rapid beating of her heart against his chest heightened his senses, and his eyes began to dilate. He contracted his pupils. If Blair held any sort of romantic love for him in her heart, he could enhance her pleasure and desire. But her heart was cold—she would be entranced by him instead.

He looked away. "You're ridiculous, Blair."

The doors opened. She slipped out of his arms and readjusted her clothes, trying to compose herself. He picked up their bags and led the way down the open hallway. A warm breeze blew over them. They entered the rental unit, and Blair gasped.

Floor-to-ceiling windows framed the living room, giving them a full view of the deep blue ocean beyond. Teal and coral throw pillows lined the modern couches, and crystal pendant lights hovered over a glass table in the dining area. Emory locked the door and dropped their bags.

Blair shook her head. "You might have overdone it."

"I'll give you a tour." He held her hand and led her through the kitchen overlooking the living and dining rooms. Her fingers brushed the light granite countertops.

"This is where you'll be spending your evenings," Emory declared. "Making me dinner."

She opened the stainless-steel refrigerator and frowned. "I can't. No olives."

He peeked inside. It was empty. "I forgot to tell you. You also need to go grocery shopping while I'm working."

She folded her arms. "Can I do your laundry while I'm here too?"

Emory opened a small closet in the corner to reveal a stackable washer and dryer.

She laughed. "Is that the only reason you brought me along?"

Emory lifted her onto the countertop so that her feet dangled over the white cabinets. "Actually, I already made all the dinner reservations. Tonight, you'll have to dress up."

She smiled. "What's the occasion?"

He leaned his forehead against hers. "You'll see."

"Why do you always make me wait?" Blair ruffled his thick hair with her fingers. "Your hair is so soft! What have you been using?"

He shrugged. "I started a new regimen."

Emory went back to the front door and scooped up her bags. She followed him down a narrow hallway to the master bedroom. Blair ran in and leapt onto the king-sized bed. A comfortable reading area had been arranged near sliding glass doors, maximizing the views. Blair peered into the adjoining bathroom. A long double sink, Jacuzzi tub, and luxurious walk-in shower with a ceiling-mounted rain showerhead completed the lavatory.

"The bathroom is bigger than my apartment," she said, stretching across the white down comforter.

Emory placed her bags on a pale-blue chaise lounge by the sliding glass doors. "This one's your room."

She pushed herself up. "Why'd you get two rooms?"

"Because I want to be able to get some sleep on this trip."

Blair curled up with a pillow, scowling. "What's that supposed to mean?"

"You know *exactly* what that means."

She hurled the pillow at Emory. "For the last time, I don't snore that loudly!"

"You can't deny it," he said, sidestepping the soft missile. "I have the recordings." He opened the sliding doors leading onto the balcony. "It's like spooning with a chainsaw."

"You secretly like it." Cool sea air rushed into the room and parted the layers of thin curtains. "Why else do you let me sleep over all the time?"

Emory smiled and pretended to be preoccupied with corralling the unruly drapes. They would eventually end up in his bed. He'd made sure he picked the room with the bigger television. Blair jumped up and pranced out onto the balcony barefoot. She peered down at the multiple pools surrounding the resort. Children shrieked with excitement and splashed water out of the swimming pools while their adults lounged in hot tubs on the opposite end of the property, soaking in the silence.

"Honey!" Blair cried. "They even have a lazy river!"

Emory started. "Did you just call me 'honey'?"

She didn't turn around. "No."

He stepped onto the balcony and stood behind her, grinning. "Yes, you did. I heard you."

Blair leaned against the railing and stared out into the ocean. Emory curled his finger around the belt loop of her shorts and tugged slightly. "Why are you embarrassed?"

"I'm not." Blair clung to the railing. "I just... I don't call anyone that unless I have feelings for them."

"You don't have feelings for me?" he asked in a lighthearted tone.

"Don't tease me about that, Emory," she whispered bitterly.

His heart twisted. He pulled her next to him and forced her to look at him. "I'm sorry. I shouldn't have said that." Her eyes were distant. "You don't have to be embarrassed. It didn't mean anything to me." He almost convinced himself that it was true. "I have to go to work, so get your bathing suit on." He gave her a peck on the cheek. "Sweetheart."

Blair held back a smile.

CHAPTER 27

From the Enarine realm, Emory watched as Laith dug a large beach umbrella deep into the sand. Thick navy-blue fabric flapped in the wind as he pried it open. Blair was a few yards away, setting up their space. Her wide-brimmed hat blew off, and she chased it along the seashore. Emory stifled a chuckle and tried to remember that he was not *really* on vacation. Karina laid out their towels and settled onto the warm ground. She grabbed a book from her colorful tote, and Laith crawled next to her.

"Reading anything good?" he asked.

"Nothing that would interest you," she replied, flipping to a frayed, earmarked page.

He stared out at the vast ocean without a word. Emory drew his bow and shot a silver arrow into Laith's chest.

Laith turned back to Karina. "Do you want to go for a swim?"

"No, thanks." Her mirrored sunglasses made it impossible to read her expression.

"Are you sure?" Laith hooked his finger around the strings of her bikini bottoms. "It'll be fun."

The corners of her mouth began to soften, but she shook her head. His fingers danced up the side of her body, tickling her. She let out an involuntary chuckle and squirmed out of his reach. Things were going better than Emory had expected. His clients rarely had playful interactions like he had with Blair.

"I'm serious," Karina said. "I just want to read my book."

"You can read any time." He closed her book and tossed it in the sand.

"Laith—"

He swept her into his arms and slung her over his shoulder. Her laughter drew the attention of other beachgoers as he charged toward the water.

"Stop!" she shrieked. "Put me down!"

"Speak up! I can't hear you!" He stopped as soon as he was knee deep in the ocean water. "You want me to let you go?"

She dangled upside down, her long hair swaying from side to side in the wind.

"Put me down!" she cried. Water splashed into her face, and she laughed.

"Okay," Laith conceded. He slid her off his shoulder and held her in his arms. Laith slowly leaned in and kissed Karina's lips. Her aura blazed crimson red. Emory had never seen her so in love. He quickly reloaded, seizing the opportunity to enhance her affection for Laith. His arrow struck Karina from behind. She wrapped her arms around Laith's neck as his desperate hands explored her body.

A heavy wave collapsed over them. The startled couple was tossed under the water and carried along the sea floor away from the shoreline. Laith jumped up first and grabbed Karina's hand. She emerged from the water tattered and disoriented. Laith coughed violently, and Karina gasped for air. Her bikini was twisted out of place, and his expensive sunglasses hung askew on his face. They gaped at each other, stunned. Karina chuckled, and Laith smiled. Suddenly, they both broke into hysterical fits of laughter.

Emory walked barefoot through the hot sand and materialized in front of Blair.

She gave an enthusiastic round of applause from her lounge chair. "Well done!"

"Thank you. I think they've made some real progress today." He dropped his bag and settled in next to her, adjusting his chair up a notch. Then he rested his bare back against the warm mesh fabric and flipped open *Les Misérables* while she continued reading a thick book with a dragon on the cover.

"Did you know there's a beautiful love story in this book?" he asked after a while.

"How many times have you read that?" Blair said into the pages of her novel.

"Over a dozen," he said in bewilderment.

Blair peered at him through her dark glasses. "And you just realized that?"

He creased the page to one of his new favorite passages. "I knew there was a love story, but I never realized how deep and tragic it was."

"You never cared about the characters, huh?"

She went back to reading about mythical fire-breathing creatures. Emory put on his sunglasses. In truth, the only reason he had purchased the book was for its title. At that time in his life, he looked down on humans for getting caught up in their emotions and firmly believed they deserved whatever pain and misery they heaped upon themselves. He'd had no appreciation for the true depth and complexity of human relationships. He'd come to see that their powerful bonds of love strengthened the very fabric of society. He felt foolish for not realizing that earlier in his career... though if he had, he would not be sitting beside the woman he so desperately wanted to make his companion.

Blair stretched across the long chair. "Do you want to take a dip in the ocean with me?"

He didn't glance up from his book. "You know the answer to that question."

Blair curled onto her side and watched him read. "Then why are you wearing swimming trunks?"

"Because that's what humans wear to the beach," he said sarcastically.

She let out a heavy sigh. "But I don't want to swim by myself."

"And I don't feel like floating in filth." He turned another page.

She tossed her book aside. "Fine."

Out of the corner of his eye, he watched her peel off her thin white cover-up. Her black-and-white-striped bikini hugged the curves of her body, accentuating a few of his favorite features.

A bottle of sunscreen landed hard in his lap, jolting him upright.

"Make yourself useful," she ordered, plopping down next to him.

Emory stared at the bottle. The biting chill emanating from her bare skin caused his muscles to tense up. But it was worth the pain. He poured a generous portion of sunscreen into his hands and rubbed the thin cream across the cool surface of her shoulders, savoring the feeling of her silky skin beneath his fingers. She closed her eyes. He massaged the lotion down her back then slipped his hands around her body and across her bare stomach. His fingers went numb. He couldn't handle it.

Irritated, Emory pushed her forward, away from him. "There," he said gruffly. "You're all set to play in the muck and mire."

Blair grabbed the sunscreen. "Well, I can't have you roasting out here while I'm gone." She squeezed the bottle and squirted a thick zigzag pattern down his chest. "There you go."

Emory smirked and grabbed her arm before she was able to scurry away. "You're not even going to offer to help me?"

She gave an innocent shrug. "You don't want to play with me, so I don't want to play with you."

He pulled her closer. "Bribery?"

Blair swiped a dab of sunscreen from his chest and tapped him on the nose. "Compromise."

Emory gazed at her through his dark glasses. "I suppose that's what people do when they're in a relationship."

"It is," Blair said firmly. "And you need the practice for when you get a girlfriend."

"I don't need the practice," Emory said in a serious tone. "I already have you."

Blair burst into laughter. "I mean a *real* girlfriend!" She splattered the sunscreen across his chest with her icy palms, rubbed him down, and jumped to her feet. "Let's go. I've been waiting all afternoon for you."

She took off running toward the ocean, leaving Emory in a disillusioned silence.

Subtlety. Was. Not. Working.

CHAPTER 28

Emory anxiously approached Blair's bedroom. She had spent the last hour and a half getting ready for dinner, and he couldn't imagine what was taking her so long. He reached for the doorknob and paused. It was probably best not to rush her—he wanted the evening to be perfect. He suppressed his nervousness and knocked. The door swung open, and Blair stood within, wearing a sleeveless black crochet dress. She held a makeup brush in one hand and a container of foundation in the other.

Blair bowed and made a grand gesture, ushering him into the room. "You may come in." She chuckled as he stepped inside. "You don't normally knock."

"I didn't want to be rude." His eyes fell upon the dresser. An empty glass was next to the open bottle of pinot noir from Hera.

Blair caught his gaze. "I left the rest of the fancy potion-wine for you so you wouldn't accuse me of killing the bottle again."

Emory inspected the remains. More than two-thirds of the love potion was gone. "Very generous."

She smiled. "I was thirsty." Blair returned to the bathroom to finish applying her makeup.

Emory didn't mind. Love potions were only effective when the individual was in a positive emotional state. He just needed to keep her happy. He surveyed her room. Her wet bikini dangled from the doorknob, beach towels littered the floor, and the rest of her clothes were strewn across the bed.

"I think your suitcase vomited," he said gravely.

She popped her head out of the bathroom and winked at him. "Just making myself at home."

Emory piled her clothes together and started folding them. He enjoyed the light scent of perfume on her garments.

"We have to stop by the grocery store after dinner so we can stock up on ice cream for the weekend." Blair stood on her toes and applied mascara. "I practically starved myself for the last three weeks just so I could fit into that bikini."

"I know. You've been intolerable." He switched into a high-pitched voice. "'I'm hungry! Don't let me eat that! Give me a bite! Hide it! I want chocolate—get me chocolate!'"

She laughed. "I don't sound like that."

He smiled. "You're right... your voice is a little higher."

Emory wondered why she had packed so many shoes for a four-day trip. He lined her flip-flops, sandals, sneakers, pumps, and stilettos along the wall according to height.

"I lost ten pounds, so it was worth it." Blair dusted her face with powder. "Your jeans even zipped."

Emory didn't bother asking why she was trying on his clothes again. The intricacies of the female brain boggled his mind. He hung her sundresses in the closet. "You didn't need to lose any weight. You looked beautiful the way you were."

"That's so sweet of you to—whoa!" Blair stepped into the room and examined the neat stacks of clothes. "You're amazing! I didn't even know thongs *could* be folded."

He cleared his throat. "Ready?"

Blair darted to the opposite end of the room to gather her belongings. He tried not to stare at her legs, though he was fairly certain being ogled had been her intent when she'd bought the short dress. Stackable gold bracelets jingled as she grabbed her high-heeled sandals.

Emory buttoned his blazer over his light-blue dress shirt. "Blair, there's something I want to discuss with you over dinner."

She steadied herself on the dresser as she clasped her shoes. "What?"

His chest tightened. "I don't want to talk about it here."

She picked up her small clutch. "Is everything okay?"

He tried to speak in a casual tone. "There are some details about my contract with you that I think you should be aware of, for future reference."

"A business meeting, huh?"

He stuffed the cork back into the bottle of wine. "Something like that."

Emory led her out of the condo, and the sound of crashing waves echoed in the distance. They boarded the elevator, and he pressed the button for the ground floor. If Hera's wine was going to have any effect on her, it would be soon. Once that happened, he might not feel so foolish about moving forward. But a rejection from her would still destroy him. He couldn't even think about it.

Blair glanced up at Emory with a carefree grin. "Tomorrow, we should watch the sun rise on the be—"

The doors slid open on the tenth floor, and Laith stood in front of them with a large suitcase in his hand.

"Move, Karina!" he shouted down the hall.

A door slammed.

Emory grabbed Blair by the waist and pulled her to the back of the elevator. She leaned against his chest and avoided making eye contact with the couple. It was always awkward to be in the close proximity of his clients after secretly watching them from the Enarine realm. Laith stepped inside as Karina appeared with their puppy. Shelby growled and barked when she caught sight of Emory. Blair jumped back slightly.

"Shut up!" Karina screamed.

Laith yanked the leash away from her and silenced the dog. The couple kept their backs to Emory and Blair as the elevator continued to the ground level.

"Your problem is you never listen." Karina's tone was sharp.

"You said you wanted to go home," Laith fired back. "We're going home."

She wrung her damp hair over her shoulder. "Why don't you just admit—"

"I meant what I said!" Laith's voice bellowed throughout the small space. "I'm not going to apologize for your hurt feelings."

Blair's body tensed up, and Emory wrapped his arm around her shoulders.

"Screw you," Karina muttered.

The doors opened onto the parking lot, and Laith charged out of the elevator with Shelby following close behind. Karina lumbered toward his vehicle.

"Get in the car, you—"

The elevator doors closed, cutting Laith off. Emory didn't move.

Blair sighed and pushed the button for their level. "I'll go pack."

"Quickly, please."

They reached the eleventh floor and ran down the corridor, plowing through the front door of the condo. Emory rushed into his room to retrieve his backpack and the duffle bag he hadn't gotten around to unpacking. He entered Blair's bedroom and swooped up her clothes, piling everything into her luggage. Blair dashed into the bathroom and gathered her cosmetics.

Emory's hands shook. He'd planned to tell Blair at dinner that he had developed feelings for her, that his entire existence revolved around her happiness—and that he liked it that way. He'd planned to declare his love for her and ask her to become his companion.

But there would be no dinner.

Emory grabbed the wine from the dresser and drank directly from the bottle, gulping down the rest of its contents. The strong concoction burned his throat, but the rage and anger pouring out of his heart negated the effects of the potion.

Blair returned to the bedroom with her arms full of makeup. She looked at him with alarm. "Are you all right?"

Emory hurled the empty bottle into the bathroom. It shattered against the tile wall, sending shards of glass dancing across the floor. Blair stood, stunned. Emory stalked over to the nightstand, scribbled a note to the housekeeper, and left a two-hundred-dollar tip.

"I'm fine," he lied.

He gathered their bags and locked up the rental unit. They entered the elevator and rode down to the ground level in silence. Emory stared at the chrome doors, his mind blank. Blair's cold touch jolted him back into reality. He sighed. The potion had had no effect. Her condition showed no signs of improvement.

Blair wrapped her fingers around his. "I'm sorry things didn't work out," she said in a soft voice.

Emory squeezed her icy hand. "Me too."

• • ❧ • •

RAIN SPLATTERED AGAINST the cloth hood of the convertible as Emory and Blair sat in the parking lot of a gas station. It had been the longest two hours of his life. He watched his clients through the chrome driver's-side mirror.

Laith jumped out of his car and into the rain. He left the door open as he pumped gas, loud music blaring from the speakers. Karina's yelling was barely audible over the noise.

"Shut up and walk your dog!" he shouted into the car. He slammed the door and stormed into the convenience store.

Emory clutched the bottom of the steering wheel. Blair curled her legs up in the passenger seat and ate a bag of chips as she peered out the side window. She had lined the dashboard with an assortment of snacks, and her loud chomping took the place of their usual conversation.

"Can you stop crunching, please?" Emory said through clenched teeth. "It's annoying."

"Sorry." Blair remained still for a long time. She reluctantly put a kettle-cooked chip in her mouth. It snapped between her teeth. Emory closed his eyes. She started chewing faster and swallowed. "I'm sorry." She twisted the chrome knob on the radio. "Maybe music will help."

A country song blasted over the speakers and overpowered the sound of her munching. Emory switched it off. He sat back. Blair's eyes bore down on him, but he refused to look at her. She opened a package of peanut M&M's, placed two chocolates in her mouth, and paused. She turned away and bit down.

"I don't want you to be my client anymore," Emory blurted.

"What?" She faced him, horrified, and swallowed the candy. "Why not?"

"Because—"

"Is it the chewing? Because I can finish my snacks on that bench over there. I promise you won't even hear me."

"It's not that."

"Is it—am I too difficult to work with?" she asked.

"You're not too difficult to work with."

"Then why would you say something like that?"

He drew in a deep breath. "I've been doing a lot of thinking."

"Is that why you've been so distant lately? Because you don't want me around anymore?"

"No, it's not like that."

"Then why can't I still be your cl—"

Emory slammed his fist against the steering wheel. "Stop talking, and listen to what I'm trying to say!"

The steady splashing of rain filled their agonizing silence.

"What are you trying to say?" Blair whispered after some time.

Emory's heart pounded in his chest. "I'm saying I want... I need—"

Shelby's heavy tail slammed into the back of the Mustang. They both jumped. Her frazzled owner chased after her, trying to grab the leash as it dragged across the wet concrete.

Emory lowered his head and cursed under his breath.

Blair grabbed his arm. "Emory, we can't let anything happen to their puppy. It's all they have."

He retrieved his love token from his locket and handed it to Blair. "You go right, I'll go left."

He darted out of the car and charged through the Enarine realm in pursuit of the canine. He removed his bow from across his chest and heard the clicking of Blair's heels as she crossed over and darted in the opposite direction.

They had little trouble overtaking the puppy and Karina, both of whom were moving in slow motion in relation to Emory and Blair. The two of them planted themselves in front of the dog and stretched out their arms. Shelby froze. She growled at their familiar presence but didn't move. Karina snatched the muddy leash from the ground, and the puppy barked in a wild frenzy.

"Stop it!" Karina screamed.

Laith came out of the convenient store. "What's going on?"

"She's going nuts, and I can't control her!" Karina clenched the thick leash. Shelby's loud barking echoed through the parking lot.

Laith grabbed the leash from Karina. "Sit!"

Shelby sat, still appearing uneasy with the unseen creatures in front of her. Laith tugged the leash and guided her back to the car, leaving Karina in the rain. She gazed up at the dark sky with tears streaming down her face.

Emory grabbed an arrow from his quiver and aimed his bow at her heart. The taut string pressed against his cheek, pricking his skin. Everything was so much harder than it needed to be. Karina covered her mouth to smother the sound of her crying. Emory felt her pain. Blair stared down at the murky puddles surrounding them as though unable to watch.

Karina sobbed uncontrollably. Dark makeup ran down her face as she struggled to regain control of her emotions. Laith sat in the front seat of his car, unwilling to comfort his distraught partner. He never compromised—and neither did she. Emory lowered his bow. He returned the silver arrow to his quiver and stepped back. The cold rain splattered his face. After a few minutes, Karina composed herself and returned to Laith for their long ride home.

Blair stood silently by Emory's side. She opened her mouth to say something but appeared to be at a loss for words.

"Their love isn't strong enough to withstand their differences," he said. "It was wrong for me to keep them together."

She wrapped her arms around her wet body and shivered. "What are you going to do?"

"What I should have done from the beginning. Let them go... and deal with the consequences of my actions."

Blair took her time to reply. "You know I'll support whatever decision you make."

"I know."

The rain poured down over them, and they watched the unhappy couple drive out of the rest stop.

Emory finally spoke up. "There's no easy way to do this."

She handed him the copper coin. "There never is."

His eyes darted across the desolate parking lot. "We can do it on the hood of the car."

"No," Blair said firmly. "I don't want to dent the Mustang."

Emory snapped his locket closed and slid it under his dress shirt as Blair headed toward the picnic benches. The image of her lifeless body flashed into his mind. His heart beat faster.

"I can't do this." Emory backed away. "I can't do this."

"Hey..." Blair stepped closer and gently cupped his face in her cold hands. Her dark gaze was somber. "Let's both agree this is the last time. I won't cross over with you again until—"

Emory rested his forehead against hers. "Not until your heart is mended."

Blair's voice was little more than a whisper. "Right..."

He swallowed his apprehension. Blair's slow breaths were steady as she walked toward a patch of grassy earth behind the convenience store. She tilted her head back and closed her eyes. Emory slammed into her back. Their pain was sharp and deep. Blair skidded across the uneven turf and landed in a muddy puddle. Her fingers sank into the thick sludge as she pushed her body off the ground.

Emory rushed to her side and knelt down. "I'm so sorry."

"It's okay," she said softly. "I have a change of clothes."

"No." He gently held her face and brushed specks of mud from her cheek with his thumb. "I'm sorry about the trip." He grasped her cold hand and helped her back to her feet.

"It's not your fault." She attempted to wipe mud from her dress, but it smeared through the crocheted fabric and stained the silk. Hand in hand, they walked back to the car.

Emory handed Blair a dry beach towel, and she crawled into the cramped back seat of the convertible. He started the engine and drove out of the gas station as Blair shuffled through her bags.

It *was* his fault. All of it. Every excursion they'd been on together, every outing, revolved around his other clients. Not once had he ever made it about her. Not once. After all the time they'd spent together, he had never taken her out on a date.

Blair slipped out of her muddy dress, and Emory caught a glimpse of her shapely figure in the rearview mirror. He stared back at the road.

"I guess we'll have to get you a new dress."

CHAPTER 29

Emory ran up seven flights of stairs to Blair's office. From the Enarine realm, he overtook a small group of women carrying on a private conversation in the stairwell. He hoped he wasn't too late.

The last time he'd seen Blair was the night he dropped her off at home after the beach trip. He'd made no attempts to contact her in more than a week and hadn't returned any of her calls. His days and nights had been filled with Darion and Hana. Reinforcing their bond was essential to his audit, but in the process, he had neglected Blair. He was finding it difficult to maintain a work-life balance, but he was determined to make it up to her.

Emory reached Blair's cubicle and plopped down in the chair beside her desk to catch his breath. Blair's fingers danced across her keyboard as she worked, completely oblivious to his presence. The phone rang in the cubicle next to her, and she glanced at hers.

Blair suddenly peeked over her shoulder. Her coworkers were preoccupied. She reached for her cell phone and settled back in her office chair. Unable to contain his curiosity, Emory stepped behind her to see what she was looking at. She swiped through photos of them. The bizarre art exhibits. Secluded motorcycle rides. Bowling. Swimming in the ocean. The Super Shot. Emory asleep on her couch. The wedding.

A smile spread across her lips, but it quickly faded. It took everything in his power not to cross over and talk to her. He didn't want to ruin the surprise.

"Excuse me, are you Blair?"

Startled, she shoved the phone into the top drawer of her desk. A deliveryman hovered over her, holding a bouquet of two dozen red roses. "Yes?"

"These are for you."

She stared at the beautiful arrangement as he placed the vase on her desk.

"Sign here, please." He handed her a cluttered clipboard.

Dazed, she scrawled her name across a tattered piece of paper.

"Have a nice day," he said cheerfully.

"You too."

The pleasant aroma of the flowers filled the air. Blair picked up a tiny envelope from the center of the bouquet and opened the card with shaking fingers.

It read: *A car will pick you up tomorrow at 7:30 p.m.*

"Blair?"

She turned to face another courier with a large box. Right on time. Emory could finally relax.

"This is addressed to you," he said. "Please sign here."

Blair signed his electronic tablet with unsteady hands, and the messenger was on his way before she could thank him. She pried opened the long box. A red embroidered gown lay folded inside. She stroked the delicate fabric between her fingers. The look of astonishment on her face was worth the three hours it had taken him to find the dress she liked at the mall.

A coworker stopped midstep and gasped. "Wow! What's the occasion?"

Blair stared at the elegant chiffon dress. "I think I have a date."

Emory smiled.

• • ❧ • •

EMORY STOOD AT THE entrance of a luxury hotel, waiting. He straightened his bowtie and buttoned his tuxedo jacket. He caught himself pacing and shook the tension out of his hands. A dark limo rolled to a stop in front of him. He froze.

The driver exited and opened the passenger-side door. Taking his hand, Blair stepped onto the empty sidewalk. The high neck of her sleeveless gown created a dramatic silhouette. Her thick curls were swept to the side, accentuating the plunging cowl back of her evening gown. The skirt skimmed the ground as she walked toward him. Emory's pulse raced at the sight of her, and he found himself speechless.

"You clean up nice," she said in a playful tone.

Emory stared at her. "You're beautiful."

She smiled nervously and looked away. "What's the occasion?"

He gestured to the entrance. "A fundraiser ball."

"Is Laith—"

"He's on a camping trip."

Blair studied him, inquisitively. "The college kids?"

"Penniless."

"Darion and Hana?"

"Out of town."

"So who's here?" she asked.

Emory extended his arm. "You and I."

Blair eagerly accepted his polite gesture and allowed him to escort her into the hotel. As they made their way to the banquet hall, Emory savored the feeling of her hand on his arm, despite the chill. Some of the most influential people in the city were attending the black-tie affair, but Emory's only focus was Blair. The guests mingled and socialized as appetizers were passed around. A waiter offered Blair a glass of champagne. She stuck close to Emory and sipped the bubbly wine.

A live band played in the background, and Blair and Emory observed couples making their way to the dance floor. Emory caught

Blair's eye and motioned toward a pair to their right. "What do you think?"

The man's arms were wrapped around his partner, and she clasped her fingers behind his neck as they swayed to the music.

"Recently married," Blair said decisively.

"Oh yeah?"

"Look how close he's holding her." Blair had another sip of champagne. "And she keeps admiring her ring when he's not looking."

Emory nodded. "What about them?"

Blair watched a silver-haired couple dance cheek to cheek. "High school sweethearts. They'll be together forever." She scanned the ballroom and spotted a nervous couple dancing with a respectable amount of distance between them. "What about those two?"

"New love," he said.

"Why do you say that?"

"They're out of sync. He keeps stepping on her toes."

They both laughed.

"She doesn't seem to mind," Blair said. "She hasn't taken her eyes off of him."

"Then it must be true love."

They examined the crowd in comfortable silence. Tiny flashes of light twinkled across the floor from the crystal chandeliers overhead.

"We've spent a lot of our time together watching other people," he said after a while.

She swirled her drink. "Bad habits."

Emory turned to her. "Will you dance with me?"

Blair nodded, drank the rest of her champagne, and quickly deposited the empty glass on a passing waiter's tray as though worried Emory might change his mind. She took his hand, and he led her to an empty space on the dance floor. Emory laced his fingers between hers and placed his other hand around her waist. They moved effortlessly to the slow tempo.

"Where have you been?" Blair asked. "Why did you disappear on me like that?"

"I realized something after our trip. I need to separate my work life from my personal life."

"That's your excuse? You were working?"

Emory twirled her around. "Darion's been looking at rings."

Her eyes widened. "An engagement?"

"My first, *if* I can secure it." They swayed to the steady beat. "I need to prove to the audit committee that I can close my cases."

Blair squeezed his hand a little too tightly. "Your fingers don't appear to be broken."

"I'm sorry I didn't call you." Emory tenderly kissed the back of her hand. "This is my way of apologizing."

"You think you can just buy me off with expensive gifts and fancy galas?"

He cocked his head. "Did it work?"

"Of course it did, you fool."

They both chuckled and accidentally bumped into another couple. Emory apologized profusely and quickly regained his composure.

"Roses are my favorite," Blair said in a soft voice.

He stared into her eyes. "I know."

"You didn't have to do that."

"I wanted to."

She kept her eyes fixed solely on him. "What are we *really* doing here, Emory?"

His heart raced. "I think I found the perfect man for you."

She didn't break her gaze. "What does he look like?"

"He's tall... and I think you'll find him handsome."

Her mouth quirked. "Does he have a job?"

"He has a very good job," Emory said. "And he owns a sports car."

"Why is he still single?"

Emory slid his arm around her lower back and held her closer. "Because he didn't think he could ever find true love."

She tightened her slender fingers around his hand. "Do you think he'll like me?"

Emory wanted to feel her heart beating with his. "I'm *certain* he will."

"How do you know?"

"Because..." Emory whispered in her ear. "You have a beautiful soul."

Blair held her breath. "Where is he?"

"He's... I'm..." Emory slid his hand up her bare back, desperate to feel her warmth.

His fingers pressed into her icy skin.

Emory's heart sank. The gifts, the countless hours together, the intimate conversations, his displays of affection, his unconditional love... and she didn't possess even the slightest inkling of love for him in her heart.

He released his firm grasp and pulled away. She didn't have a chance to stop him before he withdrew into the crowd, leaving her alone in the center of the ballroom. The people around him moved at a languid pace as he retreated into the Enarine realm.

Suddenly, he sensed a familiar, unsettling presence. Argus stood at the opposite end of the room, his bow raised, an arrow pointed in Blair's direction.

"No," he pleaded. The sound came out in a whisper.

Argus released the single arrow. Emory rushed back over to Blair. He was too late.

A tall gentleman tapped Blair on the shoulder. "Are you here alone?"

She turned, startled. "Umm... I think so."

"I hate coming to these events alone," he said. "But it's for a good cause."

She searched the room. "Yes. A very good cause."

"My name is Kenneth, by the way."

She blinked. "Blair."

"What a beautiful name."

She peered at him with narrowed eyes. "You'll have to excuse me. I wasn't expecting... you."

He let out a hearty laugh. "I'm going to take that as a compliment."

Her smile was emotionless.

"Do you want to dance?" he asked.

Before she could respond, he took her into his gentle arms and swept her across the dance floor. She didn't look him in the eye as they slow danced together. Emory ran his fingers through his hair and paced up and down the dance floor. He'd been warned that the board would send Argus to intervene. Kenneth was now Argus's client. If Emory interfered with the match publicly, they would strip him of his duties.

"I know we just met," Kenneth said, "but do you want to get out of here and grab something to eat?" He smiled at her. "Maybe some real food instead of these baby portions?"

Blair laughed nervously. "Okay. I think so."

Kenneth released her hand. "Perfect."

"Just let me get my things."

"I'll have the valet to bring up my car and meet you outside. It's the red Porsche."

She smoothed the thin creases of her gown. "I'll meet you outside, Kenneth."

He departed, and Blair rushed out of the ballroom. Emory followed her from the Enarine realm. The scurried tapping of her heels caught the attention of the hotel staff lingering in the hallways, ready to serve their guests. Her reflection was almost a blur in the mirrored corridors as she dashed to the restroom. The dimly lit room was empty. She made her way to the sink and steadied her shaking hands on the long double-basin countertop.

Blair stared into the mirror. Deep sadness crept into her eyes. A single tear rolled down her cheek, and she let out a muffled cry. It tore Emory to pieces. Blair covered her mouth with quivering hands as her teardrops splashed onto the marble countertop. Her sobs echoed hollowly off the tile walls. She folded her arms across her trembling body as she wept bitterly.

Emory materialized behind her, and his solemn reflection appeared next to hers in the long mirror. She gasped and spun around. Emory stepped closer. He reached up and held her soft face in his hands, brushing away her icy tears with his fingers.

"I'm sorry," she whispered. "You probably think I'm the most ungrateful woman in this realm."

His heart ached. "No."

"You sent me that man—Kenneth—so my case could be closed." There was no sparkle left in her eyes. "I guess you were serious when you said you didn't want me to be your client anymore."

"Blair…" Emory leaned closer to kiss her lips.

She turned aside and pushed him away. "No, it's okay." Blair slipped out of his grasp. "I'll be okay." She straightened the formfitting gown. "How do I look?"

Emory was gutted. He wanted more than she could possibly give him. "Perfect."

She forced a smile. "I promise I won't mess this one up."

Blair hastily exited the restroom and hurried to the entrance of the hotel. Emory staggered after her, watching miserably as Kenneth helped her into his car. Out of the corner of his eye, he saw someone else watching her leave. Argus caught Emory's gaze and gave him his usual condescending salute. Emory blinked, and his cousin vanished.

Enraged, he charged into the Enarine realm. "Argus!"

Argus faced Emory with his bow in hand. His expression was in-different. "What is it, cousin?"

Emory punched him in the jaw. The explosive force sent a sharp pain shooting up Emory's arm. Argus stumbled back and dropped his bow. Blood spurted from his mouth and onto the light tile floor. He glared up at Emory. In one swift motion, Argus grabbed him by the neck and slammed him against the wall of mirrors. He pinned him with a single hand and tightened his grip around Emory's throat.

"You think this is some sort of game?" Argus said between clenched teeth.

Emory choked. "You knew how I felt about her!"

"But she didn't!" Argus shot back. "You left her alone on the dance floor because you were too cowardly to tell her how you feel. You put too much emphasis on your own pride!"

Emory drove his knee into Argus's stomach. The blow forced Argus to release his grip. Emory slammed his fist into his cousin's face, knocking him backward. Argus charged forward and wrestled Emory to the ground, slamming him onto his back. Pain shot through Emory's spine, fueling his anger. Argus whaled into Emory's face with heavy blows. Emory reached for Argus's stray bow and smashed it across his face. Argus crumpled to the ground, and Emory rolled to his side, out of reach. He scrambled behind his cousin and wrapped his arm around his neck, strangling the air from his lungs. Argus gasped violently, unable to breathe.

The light tapping of stiletto heels echoed throughout the Enar-ine realm. Hera drew a gold arrow from her quiver and raised her bow. She shot Emory in the shoulder, throwing him backward into the wall. She raised her bow again, and shot Argus in the arm. He flew in the opposite direction and landed hard.

Emory wrapped his trembling hand around the arrow protrud-ing from his shoulder. He knew what was coming—gold arrows sent painful bursts of electricity throughout the body, limiting a Vycrin's ability to move. He tore the arrow out of his shoulder and wailed in agony. Blood soaked into his suit jacket and trickled down the tips of his fingers. Sharp pain pulsed through his body, making it difficult for him to focus. He gasped and crawled across the floor, trying to find relief on the cool tile. Argus braced himself and ripped the arrow from his arm. He smothered a painful cry and collapsed onto the ground.

"You two are worse than my children." Hera strode between the cousins, who lay prostrate on the floor, bleeding and struggling to catch their breath. "Get up!"

Emory and Argus crawled to their feet, away from her. It was never a good idea to anger a female Vycrin.

"Hera, I—"

She raised her hand, silencing Argus. "Leave us."

Argus glared at Emory and staggered down the hall away from them. Emory held his throbbing shoulder as she turned her attention to him.

"Have you completely lost your senses?"

"Argus—"

"Argus was working under orders," Hera said. "I'd like to know why the woman you claim to love just left with another man!"

"I tried to—"

"I don't want to hear excuses." Hera's eyes blazed. "Why did you hesitate?"

Emory trembled with pain and misery, reluctant to speak. "She's so cold. I thought by now that she would feel something for me. *Anything.*" He looked away. "But she doesn't—she can't love me."

Hera took hold of his hand. "You can't see what's right in front of your eyes. Argus was right. Your pride got the best of you." She swept her fingers across his palm, reading his innermost emotions. She slowly inhaled and released her grip. "You are not to contact Blair in the Earth realm again. Go about your official duties, and work with Argus to make sure she and Kenneth establish a commitment."

Blood pulsed from the wound in Emory's shoulder. "She shouldn't be with him."

"The matter has already been settled. You settled it when you left her alone on that dance floor."

"But—"

"It's settled!" Her words echoed throughout the Enarine realm. Emory fell silent.

Hera lowered her voice. "If you approach the board in breach of contract, preventing the *one woman* whose heart you've broken from finding love and happiness, Petros and I will not be able to protect you."

"I want to be with her," Emory declared.

"I know how much you care about Blair." Hera stared into his eyes. "But you've lost sight of the fact that, as your client, her emotional well-being takes precedence over your wants and desires. If that means she needs to be with someone else, someone who can commit to her without reservation, then so be it."

"But I..." He couldn't choke out a complete sentence. "I love her."

Hera's dark eyes were unyielding. "So will he."

Emory's heart shattered. He fought to blink away the tears in his eyes as his cousin approached again. Hera glanced at Argus, who was clutching his arm and trying to get the bleeding to stop.

"Argus did his job," Hera said to Emory. "Now, go do yours."

An overwhelming sadness enveloped Emory. He walked away without uttering another word. There was only one woman who could help him.

CHAPTER 30

Emory stepped out of the private elevator to his penthouse and crossed into the Enarine realm. The gold numbers on his front door were a blur. His mind was fixated on Blair. It was difficult to focus on anything other than the yearning in his heart. He barely noticed the sharp bursts of pain emanating from his open wound as he dropped his bow and quiver. Arrows clattered against the marble floor and scattered across the foyer.

Emory knelt down, picked up a silver arrow, and slammed it into the ground. "Selene!" he cried out.

The tile cracked. Time slowed down. His heavy eyelids closed as his beating heart stopped. It would all be over soon. She could take away his pain. A burst of air whipped his hair back, and lightning flashed around him. He opened his eyes to find Selene standing over him. The time frequency stabilized, and a dark portal closed behind her.

"There'd better be blood," Selene sang out.

Emory didn't move. Selene dropped to her knees, tossing her bow and quiver aside. She gently stroked his bruised cheek. The throbbing pain stopped instantly, and the swelling in his face diminished.

"Who hurt you?" she asked softly.

Emory wouldn't meet her eyes. "Will you come in, please?"

Selene dusted off her multicolored leggings as they crossed into the Earth realm, and she followed him to the door. Her faded hoodie partially covered a tank top riddled with tiny holes, and her thick black hair was barely contained in a bun.

"Sorry for dragging you out of bed." Emory unlocked the front door and switched on the lights.

Selene lingered behind. "Emory," she called out, "I'm not human."

He stopped in his tracks. "Sorry. I'm used to—her."

Emory stepped behind Selene and gently grasped her hand, pressing it against the doorframe. He matched his breathing with hers. The rough markings carved into the wood could only be seen in the Enarine realm, but as their hearts beat in unison the elaborate writing pulsed bright yellow.

"You are welcome in my home," he declared formally.

Emory let go of her hand and led the way down his long hallway to the kitchen. He twisted in an awkward position as he struggled to peel off his cumbersome suit jacket. Selene sucked her teeth and yanked it off in one swift motion. Emory cried out in pain.

"Don't be a baby," she said, tossing his jacket aside. "Take off your shirt."

Emory unbuttoned his bloody dress shirt and Selene carefully examined his shoulder. She took a deep breath and gently placed her hand over his open wound. Warmth spread through his shoulder, and the stinging dissipated. Muscles slowly regenerated. His skin stretched and tightened, closing the wound. In that moment, even his longing for Blair waned. Selene pulled her hand away, and he was once again flooded with overwhelming sadness.

Selene stepped back. "What happened to Blair?"

Emory shook his head. "Argus."

"She's not even his type." Selene washed her bloody hands and had a seat on one of the barstools. "He likes those flighty girls that don't challenge him."

Emory's eyes met hers.

"Oh, this is bad." Selene reached into the pocket of her hoodie for a lollipop. She fumbled with the wrapper and tossed it onto the kitchen island. "You know he's an expert matchmaker, right?"

"Yes, I'm constantly reminded of that."

"He has an impeccable record. If he's been watching Blair for any length of time, he'll know exactly what type of man she'll fall for—"

Emory slammed his fist against the countertop. "He doesn't know her."

Selene sucked on her candy. "What are you going to do?"

"There's nothing I can do. I'm not allowed to contact her."

Selene's eyes narrowed. "When was the last time you followed the rules?"

Emory inhaled sharply. "I'm in the middle of an audit, and I have one couple uncertain about embarking on a long-distance relationship, and another couple on the brink of terminating their relationship."

She crunched on her candy. "So, you summoned me to your home in the middle of the night to whine and complain about Argus?"

Emory held out his hand. "I don't even know why I brought you here."

Selene dropped the remnants of her lollipop into his palm, and he scooped up her candy wrapper.

"I knew your house would be immaculate." Selene brushed off her hands. "You could teach Talos a thing or two. I swear I spend half of my time cleaning up after him."

Emory threw away her trash. "That bad, huh?"

"Oh, it's terrible. Sometimes I'm at his house for hours, tidying up and putting everything back in its place."

"Clever guy," Emory said under his breath.

"What?"

"Nothing," Emory said quickly. "I didn't know partners spent time together outside of work."

Selene shrugged. "It's convenient. We keep the same hours, and he even carved my name into the threshold so it wouldn't be such a hassle to enter his home." She leaned closer with a mischievous smile. "Where do your coordinates send unwelcome guests?"

"Do you remember that dump in Thiyden where I ate that fish that wasn't really fish?"

Selene gagged and covered her mouth. "Please don't remind me. I was nauseous for a month after healing you."

"Where do yours go?"

"My favorite cemetery in Massachusetts," Selene said brightly. She kicked off her sneakers and strolled into the living room. "This is a cute little place you've got." She picked up a candle from the coffee table. "It's cozy. I expected something bigger."

Emory took the candle from her and placed it back where it belonged. "It's big enough."

Selene gasped and spun around. "You have a television!"

"It's not mine," Emory insisted. "It's hers."

Selene folded her arms across her chest. "I don't believe that one bit."

"It's the truth."

She ran her fingers across the colorful throw pillows along the couch. "I'm guessing these are hers as well?"

Emory bit back his irritation. "We bought them together."

Selene gave him a sly grin. "I wonder where else she left her mark."

"Don't you dare."

He blinked, and Selene disappeared into the Enarine realm. He grunted and charged down the hall to his master bedroom. The door to his walk-in closet was wide open.

"Don't touch anything!" Emory shouted.

A frilly sundress whapped him in the face. He yanked the garment off his head, and a pointy stiletto hit him in his bare chest.

"How many shoes does the girl have?" Selene dug though the closet and tossed Blair's personal effects over her shoulder.

Emory caught Blair's clothes in midair. A light familiar fragrance lingered on her garments, and he pushed aside his misery. "I let her keep a few outfits here so she didn't have to keep going back home to get her clothes."

"You're going to need a moving van just to return all of her junk."

"It's not junk!"

Selene held up a blue wig and twisted it around. "Kinky."

"It's not like that!" Emory snatched the wig away from her. "I never—we never—"

Selene raised a single eyebrow. "Are you going to finish that thought?"

He ground his teeth. Selene always knew which nerves to pluck.

Selene jumped up and maneuvered around him. "I can't imagine what I'll find in the drawers."

Emory dropped Blair's clothes to the floor. "This is exactly why I've never invited you over."

Selene stopped in her tracks, her mouth agape. "Is that...?"

Emory sighed heavily. "Yes."

"You have *two* television sets?"

He closed his eyes and nodded.

Selene gaped at the forty-inch screen mounted on the wall above the dresser. "You really love her."

Emory's heart was heavy in his chest. "I let her go tonight."

Selene slid Blair's scattered perfume bottles into a neat line along the dresser. "Humans can't cross into the Thiyden realm," she said softly. "If you get her back, and you still fail your audit... you'll never see her again."

Emory turned away. "I can't work with her dominating my every thought."

"That's the real reason you brought me here tonight."

He swallowed hard. The only other time he'd burdened Selene with such a weighty request was the night he found out his father could never return to the Earth realm. "Will you do it?"

"All you had to do was ask, Em."

Selene slowly lowered herself to the plush carpet and slipped her rings off of her fingers. Emory knelt in front of her and removed his watch and the silver chain with his locket. She took off her earrings, and he helped her unlatch an ornate ruby locket from around her neck. They pushed their jewelry and precious metals into a small pile away from them.

"Don't think," Selene said. "Just let it flow."

Emory drew in a breath, and Selene gently cupped his face in her hands. A rush of emotions poured out of him all at once. He blinked rapidly but couldn't stop himself from crying. He hated the sound of his choked sobs, but he was unable to suppress the aching in his heart. Tears began to stream down Selene's face. She leaned her forehead against his and wept uncontrollably as she absorbed his deepest emotions. He had lost everything. His family. His friend. His future. Loneliness consumed every ounce of his being. He desperately clung to Selene, the only source of comfort he'd ever known before Blair. Selene gasped. Emory's heart suddenly went numb. The room was silent. Selene backed away and stared into his eyes. Her expression was void of all emotion.

"You're stabilized," she said mechanically. "Try not to touch anyone."

Selene grabbed her jewelry from the pile and stood up. The deep-red ruby from her locket appeared black. Emory glanced around the room, unable to perceive colors. The entire world had become nothing more than muted tones of gray. Selene wiped the tears from her eyes and unwrapped another lollipop.

Emory felt nothing. "Thank you."

"Whatever." Selene sucked on her candy and sauntered out of his bedroom. "Don't get banished."

CHAPTER 31

"Uncle Darion is here!"

Darion scooped his three-year-old niece into his arms as he entered his sister's home. The girl's thick curly hair bounced against his face as he gave her a peck on the cheek. From the Enarine realm, Emory leaned on the front door behind his clients, devoid of all emotion. His vision was cloaked in gray, making it impossible to detect even the slightest traces of their auras—another side effect of being in stasis. It had been a week since the fundraiser, and he found himself feeling detached from all of his clients.

Darion spun his niece around, and she giggled.

"Did you miss me?" he asked.

Her head bobbed up and down. "Did you bring me toys?"

He laughed. "You'll have to wait and see."

She let out a high-pitched squeal and wrapped her small arms around his neck.

"Did you say hi to Hana?" he asked.

The small girl waved at Hana from over his shoulder.

Hana grinned and waved back. "Hello, Jayla."

Emory's bow felt heavy against his back, but he refused to give in to the lethargy. He had a job to do.

Darion lowered Jayla to the floor. "Where's Mommy?"

Jayla grabbed his pant leg and led the way to Darion's older sister, Kendra, who hovered over the kitchen sink, chopping carrots into bite-sized pieces while their mother stirred egg salad. The faint aroma of herbs filled the kitchen.

Emory had no appetite. After three days of forgetting to eat and drink regularly, he decided it was best to set an alarm. His dinner reminder hadn't gone off yet.

"You put Kendra in charge of the cooking?" Darion asked his mother warily. "Will it be edible?"

"You'll eat it, and you'll like it," Kendra declared, laying the knife on a cutting board and giving her brother a warm embrace. "You have no choice. Just like my kids."

Hana lingered behind in the doorway. Darion's petite grandmother came around a corner and poked Hana in the side, startling her.

"You're losing too much weight," the elder woman teased. "There won't be anything left for my grandson to hold on to."

"Leave her alone, Gram." Darion's mother beamed at Hana. "You look beautiful as always."

Hana smiled and twisted her long hair over her shoulder. "Can I help with anything?"

Kendra motioned toward an empty serving platter on their round breakfast table. "You can take that tray out to Wade." She handed Jayla a slice of carrot as she spoke. "He's almost done grilling."

Hana joined Darion's brother-in-law on the patio and closed the sliding glass door behind her. Emory stayed with Darion. He'd spent six solid days with his client, and his persistence and determination had finally paid off.

Kendra spun around. "Did you get it?"

Darion reached into his pocket, and all three women huddled around him. He opened the small velvet box, and they shrieked in unison. Jayla shoved her way into the huddle on her tiptoes, trying to see what everyone was so excited about.

"Shh!" Darion said, putting a finger to his lips.

"It's beautiful," his mother said.

Kendra pulled his hand closer, examining the ring. "When are you going to ask?"

Darion grinned. "I'm planning to ask on our one-year anniversary in September."

"Ask what?" Jayla asked.

"I'm sending her on a six-hour treasure hunt, starting at the coffee shop," he replied eagerly. "I've designed a detailed map of all the pivotal moments in our relationship, and I'm going to drop clues at each location that will eventually lead her to me." Darion slipped the black box back into his pocket. "When she gets to the last destination, she will find me on bended knee in front of the hot-dog stand where we had our first unofficial date."

His mother blinked. "Well. That's very... elaborate."

Emory had no opinion regarding Darion's proposal, but one thing was certain—he was going to be there every step of the way. Securing their engagement meant securing his position. That was all that mattered.

Kendra hesitated. "You're going to send her all over the city just so she can end up a block from her starting point?"

"It's ingenious, isn't it?" Darion said. "She'll never expect it."

His grandmother shook her head. "Just don't wait too long to ask her. She might lose interest."

Darion laughed and kissed her on the forehead. "It will be soon."

The sliding door flew open, and they all turned around, their faces relaxing when they caught sight of Kendra's husband, Wade.

"Dinner's ready," he announced.

Kendra clapped her hands together. "I'll set the table."

Hana returned to the kitchen and did a double take when she saw Darion. "What's going on?"

"Nothing," he said.

His family scattered. "What were you all talking about?"

"Gram's apple pie recipe," Kendra said a little too quickly.

Hana appeared skeptical. "Is that right?" she asked Darion. "Did you write it down?"

"No need." He tapped the side of his head. "I took mental notes."

"Good. Now you can make it for me. You know how much I love pie."

Darion smiled, wrapped his arm around her shoulder, and led her to the backyard. Kendra busied herself arranging place settings at the patio table while her mother poured everyone drinks. Emory's phone chimed. It was too early for his dinner alarm.

He scrolled through a text message from Argus: *Your girl has her third date tonight. You'd better show up this time.*

Emory shut off his phone. He had no intention of being distracted. Darion and Hana were his priority. He removed his bow from across his chest and stepped out onto the deck. The air was stagnant. His eyes darted across the fenced-in yard. The ground shuddered violently, and a heavy force swept him off his feet. He gasped.

"Boys," Kendra called, "if I have to tell you one more time…"

Emory crashed into the railing and fell to the floor with a hard thud. He couldn't feel the blow. His mind raced as he desperately tried to crawl away from the magnetic force. The crushing weight it exerted against his body took the air from his lungs. He gulped in a breath. Emory was dragged off the deck. His bow flew into the air and landed in a flowerbed. He dug his fingers into the soil and moist grass in a futile attempt to claw his way back to safety.

Darion's nephews jumped off their swing set and ran toward the patio as Emory skidded past them in the opposite direction. He slammed into the six-foot fence. The wood cracked and whined from the pressure. His back was contorted around his quiver as his body was pinned against the barrier. Emory's heart should have been pulsing frantically. It wasn't.

He turned his head, and his cheek was sucked against the wooden planks. He squinted through a narrow crack. Weeds and patches of tall grass littered the adjoining yard. Off in the distance, he spotted an abandoned home. The windows were boarded up, but the back door was wide open. There was no light—only darkness. Voices whispered in Emory's ear, echoes from the Thiyden realm. He closed his eyes.

There was a reason Vycrin avoided areas with heavy concentrations of rot and decay. Decomposing matter created small rifts between realms, and Thiyden was a world that absorbed the energy of advanced life-forms. The rift was expanding, feeding off of Emory's unguarded heart and opening a portal into the Thiyden realm. Under any other circumstance, he would have been able to fight it. His negative energy—be it fear, anger, sadness, hatred—would have been strong enough to repel the invisible force. But he was without emotion. He was dead inside.

· · ❧ · ·

THE FAMILY EXCHANGE lively banter as they enjoyed their cookout, completely unaware that Emory was plastered to their fence. He had spent the last twenty minutes trying to conjure memories that would incite enough of an emotional reaction to free him from the portal's energy. Seeing Blair at the bottom of the pool. The fundraiser. Blair crying. Losing her to another man. He was like a stone. There was nothing but emptiness in his heart.

Dominic tapped his father on the shoulder. "Can we play video games now?"

"After you finish your vegetables," Wade replied.

Dominic pouted, but Tyrone was already shoveling broccoli into his mouth.

"Done!" Tyrone announced.

"That's not fair!" Dominic whined.

Wade shrugged. "He beat you to it."

Dominic chewed the last of his food and swallowed it down. He turned to his father. Wade dismissed them with a nod of approval, and they darted into the house.

"I'm first!" Tyrone shouted.

"No, I am! I'm older!"

"I finished first!"

Kendra sighed and said to Hana, "See what you have to look forward to?"

Hana laughed. "Fortunately, that's not something I have to worry about."

Darion looked at her, puzzled. "Why not?"

She met his eyes. "Because I don't plan on having kids."

Emory barely heard a word of their conversation as he struggled to lift his arm.

Darion's voice got a little deeper. "I love kids. I want a few."

She raised her eyebrows. "Kids are probably not in my future."

Gram gave her daughter a sweeping glance. Darion's mother frowned at him.

"Well... not right now, of course," Darion said.

"And I have no idea if I'll ever be ready to have kids," Hana said.

Emory's hand was sucked over his head. His fingers dangled just above his arrows.

"Well, sure. We won't have them right away." Darion wiped his face with a napkin. "But we'd have to start planning within a year or two."

She moved potatoes salad around on her plate. "I don't understand why we need to have every detail planned out at this point," she muttered.

"It's not *every* detail," he replied calmly. "I just like to know our lives are on track."

They both fell silent. Arrows rattled wildly in Emory's quiver as he attempted to grab one.

"Are you saying you don't like kids?" Darion asked.

"Of course not." Hana sighed. "I just don't know how I feel about being a mother right now."

Darion waved off her objection. "Sure, you say that, but—"

"Really?" Hana gave him a sharp look. "We're having this conversation *right now*?"

"When else are we going to have it?"

"*Uheegaupnae...*" Hana muttered. She suddenly glanced around the table. It was clear she was embarrassed at having this exchange in front of his family. "Please excuse me."

Hana shuffled to her feet and hurried back into the house. Darion sat in silence. His sister cleared her throat and scowled at him. He threw his napkin down and left the table.

Emory's fingers curled around a single arrow, and he clenched it in his hand. Selene was going to kill him. Emory jerked his arm off of the fence with the last of his strength and stabbed himself in his newly mended shoulder.

A sharp burst of pain tore through his arm. Emory howled in anguish. His heart pounded in his chest, and sweat poured down his face. Vibrant colors filled his field of vision, replacing the monotone black and white, and the magnetic force released him. He dropped the bloodstained arrow and fell to the ground, landing on bruised knees. The pain began to fade. Emory scrambled across the yard and charged toward the house. He snatched his bow from the crushed flowerbed and ran up the stairs of the deck. A shroud of gray enveloped the world around him. He stumbled backward a few paces as the portal pulled at his heart. Emory clung to his fear. He rushed forward, yanked the sliding glass door open, and slammed it shut. Without the heavy force weighing him down, he felt like he was floating.

His body trembled as he staggered into the living room to find Hana crying on the couch. Darion was kneeling beside her, speaking in a low tone.

"I just want to go home," Hana whispered.

"Fine." Darion got up. "I'll tell them you're not feeling well."

He left the room, and Hana dissolved into a fit of tears. Emory settled beside her. Blood trickled down his arm, but he couldn't feel it. Physical pain wasn't enough to pull him out of stasis. Once again, he was numb. Deep down, he wanted to console Hana and tell her everything was going to be all right, but he couldn't. They were two worlds apart.

And he was late.

CHAPTER 32

From the Enarine realm, Emory watched Blair knock a neon-yellow golf ball into the air. She squinted through the bright-white lamps of the nighttime driving range as Kenneth cheered her on. Emory wasn't the only one watching the couple. He quietly approached his cousin from behind.

Argus spun around. "Good of you to come to work today."

Emory grunted, finding it difficult to muster up the energy to speak.

"That was a nice shot!" Kenneth said. "You're a natural."

Blair frowned. "I still think something is a little off."

"Do you mind if I give you some pointers?" Kenneth asked, setting up another ball for her.

"Sure."

"Your swing is very consistent, but your grip could be better." Kenneth stepped behind her. He slid his hands down her arms and repositioned her hands on the golf club. "Does that feel better?"

Kenneth's strong cologne permeated the air. Blair breathed deeply and nodded.

"Try it now," he said.

Blair swung. The small white ball sliced through the air and landed meters beyond her previous attempts.

Her eyes widened. "That actually worked!"

"I told you." Kenneth gave her shoulder a reassuring squeeze then set up another ball for her. "You're a natural."

"What exactly am I doing here?" Emory asked Argus.

"Didn't you hear Hera's instructions?" he asked, exasperated. "We're supposed to work together to ensure that they establish a bond."

"So," Blair began, "what do you do when you're not helping people perfect their golf swings?"

"I founded a nonprofit organization that provides healthcare to children in third-world countries."

She positioned herself next to the ball. "So you like kids?"

"I love kids. I can't wait to have my own."

Blair smashed the ball into the air, and he placed another one in front of her. Emory looked Kenneth up and down. He would no doubt charm Blair's nieces. He seemed like the doting type.

"You said you didn't have any children, right?" Kenneth asked.

"No kids. I have a houseplant, though." Her swing was lopsided, and the ball only went six feet away. "Actually, it's wilting, so I don't even have that anymore."

He laughed. "Maybe I should come by and try to resuscitate it."

Blair squeezed the golf club tightly. "Maybe." The ball flew through the air in a straight line. "Do you know CPR?"

"In my early twenties, I worked as an EMT and a firefighter. But that was just to pay for college."

She ground her teeth. "Did you model on the side too?"

He cocked his head to the side. "How did you know?"

Blair swung and missed. She mumbled something and kicked the white golf ball off the platform. "Do you mind hitting a few? I think I need a break."

Kenneth jumped to his feet and offered her a small stool to sit on. "Do you want me to get you some water?"

"No, I just want to watch you."

Kenneth pulled a club from his golf bag and set up a ball. He lined up several perfect shots in a row.

Argus eyed Blair carefully. "Why is she upset?"

Emory cracked his neck. "Because there's nothing for her to dislike about him."

"That doesn't make any sense."

He sighed. "That's because you don't know her."

"Kirk or Picard?" Blair asked after a long silence.

"Picard." The ball sliced through the air, and Kenneth turned to her. "But I'm partial to *The Next Generation*."

She frowned. "Me too."

"See what I mean?" Emory said. "She's trying to find a reason to blow him off."

"Even if she tried, I'd make sure my client put forth an effort to work things out with her."

If Emory had the ability to express his emotions, he would have smirked. Instead he stared blankly across the driving range.

"Do you want to try again?" Kenneth asked. "I don't want to monopolize the game."

Blair picked up her golf club. "Do you want to grab some Chinese food after this?"

His face lit up. "That's my favorite."

"I'll bet," she said testily.

Emory nudged Argus. "Five more minutes, and she'll be done with him."

Argus drew a silver arrow from his quiver. "Not on my watch."

"I should make you my famous chow mein sometime," Kenneth said. "I love to cook."

Blair set up a golf ball and smashed it hard. "Of course you do."

Argus shot Kenneth in the heart and reloaded before Emory had time to register what was happening.

Kenneth placed a gentle hand on her shoulder. "Am I upsetting you?"

She swallowed hard. "Why would you say that?"

"I sense that you're unhappy." He examined her with concerned eyes. "Or am I misreading you?"

"I'm sorry." She cleared her throat. "I wasn't trying to be sarcastic."

"Did I say something wrong?"

Blair shook her head, frustrated. "No, you're... perfect in every way."

"Not in every way," Kenneth corrected. "I have my vices."

Blair perked up. "Like what? Drugs? Gambling? Masochism?"

"Chocolate," he said in a very serious voice. "I can't get enough of the stuff."

She laughed and looked away.

"He's too perfect," Emory heard himself say. "She's not going to give him a chance."

"We'll see," Argus said smugly.

"I can't compete with you," Blair said.

"I'd never ask you to." Kenneth's gentle voice was soothing.

She sighed. "You're everything I've been searching for."

He stepped closer. "Is that a bad thing?"

Blair gazed into his dark eyes. "I'm not sure."

Emory took a step forward, but Argus moved in front of him. "Don't you dare."

"Are you afraid to fall for me?" Kenneth whispered.

Blair was holding her breath. "Yes."

Argus took aim and shot Kenneth in the heart a second time. His aura burned crimson. He pulled Blair close and kissed her. The golf club slipped out of her fingers, and she closed her eyes, allowing herself to be taken in by his embrace.

Emory stood frozen. Kenneth was a good man, and she liked him. Logically, it made sense. *Logically.*

"I'm sorry." Kenneth gazed into her eyes. "I couldn't let another second go by without kissing you."

"Don't apologize." Blair lifted herself onto her toes and kissed him back. When their lips parted, she murmured, "I like a man who's decisive."

He smiled. "I'm glad."

Argus lowered his bow, and Kenneth slid his hands down Blair's hips as he kissed her. Emory wanted to be furious and fly off in a blaze of anger, but he was unable to stir up any sort of emotion.

"Well, it looks like you have everything under control," Emory said with no inflection. "Your client appears to be enthralled with my client. What more needs to be done?"

Argus slung his bow over his shoulder and pulled out two sticks of gum. Emory couldn't even feign irritation. Normally, Argus's loud chewing would have sent him into a mild rage.

"You're not even going to try?" Argus demanded. "What if her heart is open to him?"

"Why don't *you* give it a shot?" Emory said.

Argus clenched his fist. He outranked Emory, but status was inconsequential. Once a silver arrow pierced the heart of a human, the contract between matchmaker and client was sealed. Only Emory's arrows could ignite love in Blair's heart.

Argus spit his gum out at Emory's feet. "Do you know what pisses me off about you, Emory?"

He gave an indifferent shrug. "What?"

"You never finish anything. It's just like when we were kids. You start losing a game, and you quit. You have a crush on a girl who doesn't notice you, and you date her best friend. Your assignments get difficult, and you drop out."

Emory stood, without moving. His dinner alarm should have gone off already. He glanced at Argus. "I'm sorry. Were you done?"

Argus peered at Emory through narrow eyes. "How's Selene?"

"What—"

Argus grabbed hold of Emory's wrist, almost cutting off his circulation. Emory's heart contracted violently in his chest as he was flooded with his cousin's unfiltered emotions—rage, spite, animosity. Emory gasped, and they linked. His suppressed feelings for Blair came rushing back at once, and Argus quickly let go. Emory staggered backward away from his cousin. He blinked hard and tried to shake off the burning sensation that was creeping into his eyes as he struggled to regain control of his emotions.

"Blair's a kindhearted woman." Argus glowered at him. "Don't drag her down with you."

Argus crossed back into the Earth realm, leaving Emory shattered and weak. He watched Blair wrap her arms around her new suitor. She was so affectionate. He'd never been able to get that close to her.

As much as he wanted to, Emory couldn't look away from the couple. His heart pounded so hard he was afraid it would beat right out of his chest. His longing for Blair was suffocating. He wanted to be rid of the pain. He *could* be rid of it—rid of her. Emory snatched a silver arrow from his quiver, nocked it in his bow, and took aim at her heart. She was so happy with Kenneth.

Emory's vision blurred.

He desperately wanted to be free of her control, but he couldn't bear the thought of his arrow hitting its mark... of losing his best friend forever. So instead, he tore himself away and withdrew.

CHAPTER 33

"I don't normally write haikus," Joey said. "But since I'll be leaving for Madrid soon, I'm going to keep it short and sweet for you guys."

Emory anxiously watched Joey from the far end of the restaurant. Dark sunglasses hid his dilated pupils. He was unable to control his powers and had remained in his home for three days to prevent himself from accidentally entrancing unsuspecting humans. He'd thought venturing out at night would be easier. It wasn't.

Joey adjusted the tall microphone to her height and looked out into the crowd. "Soaring above clouds. Flying. Falling. Failing." She paused for dramatic effect. "As with the phoenix."

Amir stared into his drink. She caught a glimpse of the perplexed faces in the room, and her cheeks turned red. Amir gave some half-hearted applause, and scattered clapping filled the room.

She sighed into the microphone. "Thank you."

Joey left the stage and joined Amir at their table. Emory blew out a nervous breath and entered the Enarine realm. Blinding yellow light burned his retinas as a rotund gentleman crossed his path. Emory blinked rapidly, trying to adjust to the intensity of the colorful auras surrounding him. He squeezed his eyes shut and staggered over to an isolated corner of the restaurant. He grabbed an arrow and slammed it into the ground.

"Selene!"

The arrow heated up in his hand, and he quickly let go. It clanked to the floor. Emory lowered his head. It was too soon. Selene wasn't stable enough to be summoned.

Emory whipped out his phone and frantically dialed her number.

"Good evening," Talos's deep Southern drawl greeted him. "You've reached Selene's phone."

"Talos, it's Emory. I need Selene. It's an emergency."

"I'm sorry, but Lenny's not feeling well at the moment." Talos lowered his voice. "She's on her cycle. And you don't want no part of this, bro."

"Is she really bad?" Emory asked.

"Give me my phone!" Selene screamed in the background.

"And we're back to rage," Talos said cheerfully. "I made you some coffee, darlin'. It's on the counter."

Selene sighed heavily. "You're too good to me. I don't deserve you."

"Guilt," Talos muttered into the phone.

Emory rubbed his sore eyes. It took time for healers to reach equilibrium after absorbing the pain and suffering of others. Selene had to cycle through various emotions multiple times before being able to ground herself again. Emory regretted putting her through the ordeal.

"When will she cycle back to normal?" Emory asked.

"Right after the tears," Talos replied. "You'll have about two minutes, if you don't trigger her."

"It's cold!" Selene began sobbing uncontrollably. "My coffee is cold!"

"I'll make you a fresh batch," Talos said calmly. "Why don't you talk to Emory in the meantime?"

"Okay..." Selene sniffed. "Emory?"

"Hey, Selene." He tried to keep his voice steady so as not to alarm his healer. "How are you feeling?"

"I feel fine, thanks for asking." Selene's voice was back to normal. "What's the emergency?"

"Something's wrong with me." Emory glanced over to his clients. Their brilliant-orange auras burned his eyes. "I can't see."

There was a long pause. "I told you not to touch anyone."

"It wasn't on purpose," he said. "I assure you."

Brief physical contact with another person would have allowed him to come out of stasis gradually. His plan was to *accidentally* bump into a stranger on the Metro or in a crowd—but that wasn't possible. His vindictive cousin had made sure of that.

"Was the person who pulled you out of stasis in an elevated emotional state?" Selene asked.

Emory could still see the ferocity in Argus's eyes. "Highly elevated." Emory tilted his head back to prevent tears from spilling out. "I don't know what to do. I've never had this happen before. If I can't work—"

"Calm down. Your senses are heightened from the sudden spike of emotions. Try to concentrate on a single object. The rest of the world will fade into the background."

Emory picked up his silver arrow and stared intently at the sharp tip. It was a blur. He squinted, but his eyes refused to focus.

"It's not working." He shifted from foot to foot. "It's not working, and I can't lose another account. Blair's with this new guy, and I think she's falling for him, and I can't reach out to her without them knowing—"

"Get a grip, Emory!" Selene shouted. "You have people who are depending on you!"

Emory snapped to attention. He took in a shallow breath and concentrated on the arrowhead. He had a responsibility to his clients, no matter what personal struggles he was experiencing. The silver tip came into focus, and the light around him dimmed.

"Thank you." Emory returned the unused arrow to his quiver. "I needed that."

"I know. You're a mess without her."

He slid his sunglasses to his forehead. "I'm sorry I put you through a cycle again."

"Stop being so sentimental," Selene said. "It's my job to take care of my people. Now, make sure you take care of yours."

"I'll let you know how it goes," Emory said. "Tell Talos I said goodbye."

"Talos is here?" she asked, paranoia creeping into her voice. "How did he get into my house?"

"You're at my house, darlin'," Talos said from a distance.

"How did I get here?" Selene demanded. "Is that coffee? I said I wanted espresso!"

Emory hung up. It was best to leave her in the care of her partner. He was much better equipped to handle such situations. Emory grabbed his bow and approached his clients. He just needed to maintain a calm state of mind.

"You never said what you thought of my poem." Joey twirled her curly hair between her fingers. "I was trying to symbolize the journey I'm about to embark on."

"It was good," Amir said with little inflection.

Her mouth curved down. "Just good?"

His eyes shifted. "Pretty good."

Joey leaned back in her chair. "You're still mad."

He shrugged. "I'm happy for you."

"For us."

"No," he said. "For you."

Emory loaded his bow. They had a higher probability of maintaining a long-distance relationship if they could work through their issues before she left to study abroad.

She sighed. "I wish you were coming with me."

Emory released the silver arrow into the young man's chest.

"I hate flying," Amir said.

Emory blinked. He wasn't anticipating a negative reaction. His client's heart had grown colder in a matter of days.

"You never told me that," Joey said surprised.

"Why would I?" Amir asked bitterly.

Joey slid her small plate aside. "Because I tell you everything."

"I know." Amir drank the last of his soda. "Like how wonderful your classes are and how good your grades are—"

"Do you expect me to feel sorry for you because you picked the wrong major and now you're failing your classes?"

"I didn't pick my major."

"That's right," she said. "You let your parents dictate every aspect of your life. What you study, who you love… and then you complain that you have no choice in the matter."

He slammed his glass on the table. "I wasn't complaining."

Emory fumbled with another arrow. He tried to control his breathing, but his mind started racing. *If I can't keep them together, I have no chance with Blair. She'll forget all about me. She'll move on with her perfect man, and they'll start a perfect life together…*

The room was getting brighter.

"When are you going to stand up for yourself?" Joey said.

Amir wiped the condensation from his glass. "You don't understand because you were raised to pursue whatever *dream* popped into your head, no matter how ill conceived."

Amir was detached. Emory would have to focus his efforts on Joey. Timing was critical.

Joey's face fell. "I thought I could at least count on you to be supportive of my aspirations."

"How can you say I'm not supportive? I've attended every agonizing poetry reading since the moment we started dating."

She pushed her wavy hair aside. "You say that because you don't appreciate the craft."

"Just the opposite. I actually love poetry. I've been writing since I was in middle school."

"Then why didn't you like my poem?" There was hurt in her voice.

Amir laughed. "You missed an entire syllable in the second line of your haiku!" He shook his head. "That's basic syntax."

Tears filled her eyes. "If you're so much better at this than me, why did you come to my readings?"

"Why do you think? Because I love you!"

Emory aimed in Joey's direction. Her aura blazed like the sun. He closed his eyes and let go of the bowstring. The arrow whistled through the air as it soared across the room. It struck Joey's left arm with a loud thump. Emory gasped in horror. The arrow turned white and disappeared in a puff of smoke. Another amateurish blunder added to his tainted record.

Tears fell into Joey's lap.

"I would have done anything to be with you." Amir's brow wrinkled in a scowl, and he looked away. "Not that any of it matters now."

Joey grabbed a napkin and wiped her face.

Amir continued, "And since we're finally being honest, I am mad that you're spending a year away from me."

"It's only nine months," she whispered. "I promise."

"And I'm mad that you're going to be four thousand miles away."

She sniffed. "You might get used to flying."

"Or..." His voice was barely above a whisper. "I might not try."

Joey froze and stared at him in shock. "Is that what you want?"

Amir remained silent for a long time. "For right now," he said at last, "I think it's best for both of us."

Joey let out a quiet sob, and he turned away as though unable to bear her sadness compounded with his own. Joey dashed to the ladies' room, crying.

Emory's mind went completely blank. He slid his sunglasses down over his eyes and crossed back into the Earth realm. He was getting used to the darkness.

CHAPTER 34

Emory hunched over stacks of paperwork piled on his kitchen island. He wrote a long note in Darion and Hana's file, circled it, and then crossed it out. Simply purchasing an engagement ring would mean nothing to the board. He rubbed his sore eyes and tried to concentrate. The negative side effects from being jolted out of stasis had finally worn off, but Emory was still incredibly irritable. He grabbed Blair's folder and paused. He hadn't worked on her file since the night Argus had paired her with Kenneth.

A loud knock startled him out of his trance. He jumped to his feet and went to the front door. Blair stood outside, smiling.

"Emory."

His chest tightened at the sight of her. "What are you doing here?"

Her smile cracked. "The concierge recognized me and let me up." Blair shifted. "If this is a bad time—"

"No." Despite Hera's warning not to interact with Blair in the Earth realm, he opened the door wider. He was soon to be unemployed anyway. *What difference does it make?* "You can come in."

Blair entered his home and made her way to her favorite spot at the kitchen island. She placed her bag on the empty stool where Emory usually sat. She glanced at him then did a double take. "You look like you haven't slept in days."

Emory shrugged. He was having a hard time getting his bloodshot eyes to focus. He filled a chrome teakettle with water, and they waited in silence for it to boil. He pretended to be preoccupied with the French press to avoid looking at her.

Blair crossed her legs. After a few minutes, she got to her feet, readjusted her jeans, and sat again. "So... how have you been?"

"Fine." Emory lost count of how many tablespoons of coffee he'd put in the bottom of the press. "You?"

"Good. Great, actually."

Emory didn't turn around but caught her reflection in the teakettle as he poured hot water into the glass pot. He stirred the coffee.

"I've had a lot of time alone to really think," she continued.

"About what?"

Blair fidgeted with her cuff bracelet, the same one he'd bought for her at the art fair. "About my... feelings."

He stared at the plunger for a while before responding. "Regarding your new suitor?"

"Yes," she said, sitting up straight. "I wanted to thank you for that."

Emory popped the lid off a glass container of sugar. "Please don't thank me."

"But you helped me to put things in perspective," she insisted. "I never knew what it felt like to be in a good relationship until now."

The plunger reached the bottom of the pot, compressing the dark-roasted grounds. He wished his chest would stop hurting so he could breathe. He poured the coffee into a mug and stirred in four heaping teaspoons of sugar. He handed her the steaming cup of coffee, and her fingers brushed against his. Emory grabbed her hand.

"Your hands are still cold," he said in amazement.

Blair pulled away. "What are you talking about?" She reached for her bag, and her eyes landed on a folder with her name on it. Emory shifted the file to the bottom of the stack.

"What's that?" she asked.

"Work."

She smiled. "I'm really in your files?"

"Of course," he replied stiffly.

Blair settled back and blew into the small mug. "I hope you wrote all good things about me."

"I haven't finished your report yet." Emory had no desire to formally acknowledge Kenneth as Blair's love interest.

She sipped her coffee. "How did the others turn out?"

Emory leaned against the island. "Amir broke up with Joey."

"What?" Blair gasped. She lowered her cup. "Why?"

"She got the scholarship."

Her features crumpled in a sympathetic frown. "I'm so sorry."

He shrugged.

"At least Darion and Hana—"

"Decided they needed a break to reevaluate their future together."

Blair glanced at the documents, suddenly suspicious. "They were all unaffected by your arrows?"

He slid the container of sugar to the back of the counter. "I wasn't able to intervene in time."

"Why not?"

"Does it matter?" he said flatly. "I don't want to do this anymore."

Blair placed her cup on the island. "It's your job."

"It won't be after my final meeting with the committee."

She eyed him carefully. "You're not going to restore any of your matches?"

Emory remained motionless. He wanted to say there was nothing he could do, but she was too stubborn to accept that as an answer, so he kept silent.

"You can't leave *everyone* unhappy," she said.

"Not everyone is unhappy." He gathered the documents together into one neat pile, suddenly angry. "I saw you with that moron, Kenneth—"

"Don't call him that."

Emory bit back another rude remark.

"You've been watching me?" she asked.

"Of course I've been watching you. It's still my job until your case is closed."

"Why didn't you cross over and talk to me? I haven't seen you in two weeks."

"I couldn't seem to find a moment when your tongue wasn't down his throat," Emory said. "You almost appeared to enjoy it."

She glared at him. "I *did* enjoy it." Blair slowly took a sip without taking her eyes from Emory. "Not that it's any of your business what I do when I'm with him."

"Anything that involves you is my business," he said snidely. "You should know that by now."

"I'm not your property, Emory." She clenched the handle of the mug. "Don't treat me like you own me."

He shook his head. "You don't appreciate anything I do for you."

Blair slammed the mug on the island. She raised her voice. "You deserted me at the fundraiser, forced another man on me with your arrows, then disappeared for weeks without a word." She stared at him with fury in her eyes. "What exactly do you expect me to be appreciative for? Enlighten me."

He laughed mirthlessly. "If you knew how one-sided our relationship was, you wouldn't be sitting there with that smug look on your face."

"Don't you dare speak to me like you're an authority on relationships when you treat your job with disdain. You're disrespectful to your clients and unsympathetic to their plight."

"What would you know? You've been in a stable relationship for all of two weeks."

Blair folded her arms across her chest. He hated the way she sized him up.

"I don't even know why I'm arguing with you," she said. "I'm finally with a man who cares about me. A man who isn't afraid to be open with me—"

"Exactly!" he shouted. "And you don't feel anything for him!"

"I *do* feel something for him!" she screamed. "Kenneth is everything I asked for! He's perfect!"

Emory clenched his jaw. "You can pretend, like you always do. But I know you're not in love with anyone."

"How would you know?" Blair looked at him with sharp eyes. "You promised not to shoot me again."

"I don't have to break another hundred arrows to know you're not in love."

Emory reached across the island and grabbed her wrists. "Your skin is ice-cold, Blair."

She tried to slip out of his grasp, but he strengthened his grip.

"What does that mean?" she demanded.

"It means Vycrin can feel the condition of a person's heart by touching their skin." He let go of her. "And your heart is still broken."

Blair gaped at him. "You never told me..."

"Why do you think I can't get close to you?" Emory said. "You think I don't want to?"

"Why did you keep that a secret from me?" Blair's voice was trembling. "After all this time?"

"Because I don't tell you everything."

"But I thought..." She held back her tears. "I thought we were friends."

"We are not friends. We never really were, Blair." Emory's gaze was cold. "You are nothing more than a client."

Blair opened her mouth but didn't utter a sound. Her hands were shaking. She reached into her bag and pulled out a small box wrapped with glossy black paper and a white bow. She hurled the gift at Emory as hard as she could. He ducked. The box smashed into the

French press, shattering glass across the countertop. Coffee dripped down the dark cabinets.

"You're a lousy matchmaker." Her eyes blazed with indignation. "And a pitiful excuse for a man."

Blair grabbed her purse and stormed down the long hallway. Emory didn't move. The front door slammed so hard his teeth rattled.

CHAPTER 35

Emory stared down at the small box. The one person he couldn't bear parting with was gone because of the harsh and insensitive words that masked his true feelings.

He knelt down and unwrapped the gift. Inside lay a stylish pale-pink tie. He removed the rolled silk fabric from the box, and a tiny white envelope fell to the ground. Emory tore it open and read the short note.

I miss you.

Emory's heart ached. The note blurred as tears formed in his eyes. He would never be able to take back his thoughtless, bitter words. The hurt he'd seen in Blair's eyes tore at his very soul. Nothing could stem the guilt that threatened to drown his heart. He was unable to restrain his emotions, and his intense sadness morphed into violent rage.

Emory rose and charged through the door of his office. He did one sweep of the room and found what he was looking for. He clenched his arrows in shaking palms.

He knew exactly who his *victim* would be.

· · ❧ · ·

LAITH TIED A BLACK blindfold across Karina's eyes. "No peeking!"

She let out a giggle of excitement. "What's this about?"

"Shh!" Laith led her out of their home. "It's a surprise."

From the Enarine realm, Emory followed behind his clients with his bow in hand. He wasn't the least bit surprised that they hadn't broken up after the beach trip. Bitter arguments and emotional flare-ups were a normal part of their relationship.

Laith guided Karina down the front steps, and she clung onto his hands. When they reached the sidewalk, he stopped.

"Surprise!" Laith cried as he tore off the blindfold.

Karina's mouth was agape. A brand-new yellow Corvette was parked in their driveway. He looked from her stunned face to the car.

"What do you think?" he asked eagerly. "It's the color you wanted."

She was silent for a long time. "You bought yourself a sports car?"

"No," he said. "I bought it for us."

Karina slowly circled the new vehicle. "Where did you get the money?"

He buffed out an invisible scratch from the door with his sleeve. "I've been putting some aside for almost a year."

"A year?" she intoned.

"Just about. I was almost able to pay for the whole thing in cash." Laith opened the passenger door. "Hop in! I'll take you for a ride."

Karina stared at him. "All this time... you were saving for a car?"

Laith raised his eyebrows. "What did you think I was saving for?"

Karina's onyx-black aura was terrifying to behold. She slammed the door shut. "Unbelievable."

Laith stepped back, shocked.

"Nine years, I've waited for you," Karina said. "But now I see it's never going to happen."

"What are you talking about? I thought you would be happy."

"About what? A stupid car?"

He ground his teeth. "What more can I give you?"

"I want the only thing I've ever asked for!" she cried. "I want commitment!"

"You have my commitment!" Laith shouted. "Our relationship has lasted longer than some marriages!"

She lowered her head. "You don't get it."

A long, terrible silence fell between them. Laith would never understand. He couldn't see the value of what he had right in front of him.

"Fine." Laith locked the car. "I'll get rid of it."

"That's not what I said."

He stormed up the driveway. "If it's going to cause arguments, it's not worth keeping."

"This isn't about the car." Karina grabbed his hand, her eyes pleading with his. "Why won't you marry me?"

"I..." Laith hesitated.

Her expression grew cold. "That's what I thought." Karina headed back up the steps.

Emory had let Blair walk out of his life without even fighting for her, and he wasn't going to let his client make the same mistake. His hands trembled as he raised his bow. The first shot struck Laith directly in the heart.

"Karina, I..."

Emory fired again. His life was meaningless without Blair. *What is the point of breathing if I can't be with her?*

"Please don't go," Laith begged.

Karina turned around. "There isn't anything left between us."

"But I don't want you to leave."

Emory shook with anger. He had broken the trust of a woman he didn't deserve to be with in the first place. "Just ask her," he muttered bitterly.

Two consecutive arrows flew from his bow and lodged in Laith's chest. They pulsed red and disappeared.

"We can work this out," Laith insisted.

Emory would never love another woman the way he loved Blair. He raised his bow and fired again. "Ask her, you coward."

"Please just wait..." Laith's voice faded.

Why couldn't I tell Blair I loved her? The high-pitched whistle of another arrow filled the air. "Ask her!"

Laith stood where he was, unmoving.

Why couldn't I say it? Emory dropped his bow and snatched an arrow from his quiver. He charged at Laith and let out a guttural roar. "Ask her to marry you!"

Emory slammed the sharp silver arrow into Laith's chest and twisted it over and over, digging it into his heart. Then he backed away. The arrow pulsed red and disappeared.

Laith stumbled backward. He gazed up at Karina's retreating back. His body was engulfed in an aura the color of blood.

"Marry me."

A roll of thunder sounded off in the distance. A single drop of rain fell on Emory's face.

Karina froze. "What?"

Laith climbed the brick steps, his stride steady. "Marry me."

She peered through him. "You're not serious."

"I've never been more serious in my life."

Karina looked dumbfounded. "What? When?"

"Thursday afternoon," he said firmly. "We'll both take off from work early and go to the courthouse."

Karina shook her head. "That's in four days."

"Please." Laith grabbed her hand. "Marry me."

Her black aura shifted to maroon. There were still traces of love in her heart. A small smile spread across her astonished face. "Okay."

He leaned closer and kissed her.

Emory stared into the heavens as heavy rain began to fall on him, saturating his clothing. The emotional crash Laith was going to experience when his arrows wore off was going to be devastating. It would take weeks to recover from the depression. Forcing Laith to propose had done nothing to ease the intense anguish of Emory's broken heart. In that moment, he realized nothing would alleviate his longing for Blair. Lightning flashed around him, illuminating the sky in purple bursts. He closed his eyes. A strong gust of air blew from behind, but he didn't turn around.

"Hand over the artillery, boy."

Emory glanced over his shoulder to find Petros and Hera standing under an oversized umbrella, the black polyester fabric flapping in the wind. He removed his quiver from across his chest and snatched his bow from the wet ground.

"I told you from the beginning," Emory muttered. "I never wanted this job."

Petros inhaled sharply and confiscated his bow and arrows. "Your father left you in this realm because he wanted the best possible life for you, and you've squandered it."

"I've frozen your credit cards and suspended your pay," Hera said.

"She came to me!" Emory shouted.

"I'm done with your excuses, Emory," Hera said with no emotion. "Finalize your official field notes, and be prepared to meet with the board one week from today."

Emory shot a glance at Petros. "You moved up the date?"

"No, *you* moved up the date. By being reckless and irresponsible." Petros's eyes hardened, and he lowered his voice. "He's going to be very disappointed."

A chill went through Emory's body. Rain poured down as he turned on his heel and walked away. At least he wouldn't be drinking alone that night.

CHAPTER 36

Darion sat alone at the far end of a rowdy sports bar. His eyes were fixed on a set of large televisions overhead, but his expression was blank. Emory plopped down two seats away. He was drenched. Drops of water flew from his fingers as he signaled the bartender.

"I need a shot of tequila and a Corona with lime." Emory was determined to spend every last dime that he had left. Money was worthless in the Thiyden realm.

Darion glanced over his shoulder as Emory shook the water off his wet clothes. The man behind the bar wasted little time completing the simple order and returning to his other customers. Emory downed the shot and pointed to a stack of napkins next to Darion. "Are you using those?"

Darion pushed them closer to Emory. "Knock yourself out."

Emory ran his fingers through his matted hair and used the napkins to dry his face. Matchmakers ideally did *not* interact with their clients because they did not want to run the risk of being recognized and raising suspicion unnecessarily. A Vycrin's goal, when it came to matchmaking, was to remain invisible. Emory had no goals.

"Rough night?" Darion asked.

"Rough month." Emory shoved the lime into his bottle with his thumb and swallowed down half of the beer. "I'm about to get fired."

Darion grimaced. "Sorry, man."

"It's okay. I hate my job."

"What do you do?" Darion asked.

"Human resources. What about you?"

"I work in IT."

"Staring at computers all day, huh?" Emory said. "You must need a lot of coffee."

"Yeah, I do." Darion stared into his glass and spun it around a few times. "Actually, I met my girlfriend at a coffee shop."

Emory grunted. "That's random."

"Right?" Darion said in amazement. "It was weird how we instantly hit it off. It's like we were made for each other. I've never met another woman like her."

Emory gulped down the rest of his Corona. "She sounds perfect."

"She is." Darion drank what was left of his beer then pushed the glass away. "We're kind of on a break right now, though."

"Sorry to hear that."

Darion shrugged. "We have some issues to work out."

Emory nodded. "Then it's probably for the best."

"I mean, it's not like we have *major* issues," Darion continued. "She's on the fence about having kids because she has some... health issues."

"I see."

"But she would make a great mom." He chuckled. "You should see her with my niece and nephews."

"Maybe she just needs some time," Emory suggested. He'd been wanting to say that to his client for months. Hana didn't like feeling pressured.

Darion sighed. "She said she's open to the idea but not anytime soon."

He consolidated all of his used napkins into a single pile. "What's the rush?"

Darion looked as though he was pondering his words. "I guess... there is no rush." He sounded surprised.

Emory signaled the bartender and ordered two more beers. "The next round is on me." He moved to the seat next to Darion and extended his hand. "I'm Emory, by the way."

"Darion." They shook hands. "I'm just used to having a set plan, you know? I like to know my life is on track."

The bartender slid their drinks to them.

"Women throw everything off track," Emory said. "Take my situation. I run around with this woman for a year—I mean, sometimes I was *literally* running around with her." He nudged Darion in the chest. "She's one of those girls who likes being chased."

Darion chuckled. "Is that a thing?"

"She swears it is, but I have no idea." Emory swallowed the bitter liquid. "Anyway, after a year together, she drops me out of nowhere and starts dating someone else."

Darion winced. "Ouch."

"I admit it was partly my fault," Emory said ruefully. "I was never completely honest with her."

Darion clapped him on the back. "I'm sorry, man."

"What makes it worse is that her new boyfriend is a complete moron."

"Oh yeah?" Darion sounded intrigued.

"Rich, thoughtful, funny, easygoing." Emory slammed down his bottle. "It makes me want to punch him in the face."

"If Hana was ever with anyone else…" Darion said. "I couldn't handle that."

Emory took his time before responding. His client was in a delicate emotional state. "I'm sure you would move on eventually."

"No, I'm serious." Darion reached into his pocket and pulled out a small velvet box. He flipped it open, revealing a three-stone engagement ring.

Emory gawked at the stunning diamond ring as though seeing it for the first time. "Wow."

The ring shimmered in the dim light, and Darion seemed to be lost in thought. "Poor planning on my part."

Emory shook his head. "Love never works out the way we plan."

"True." Darion sighed as he put the ring back in his pocket. "I'm not even sure it's worth it anymore."

Emory tried to remember what his life was like before the night he touched Blair and sealed himself in her memory. Before she ever got under his skin. Before he wanted to share his soul with her.

"When you find the true love of your life," Emory began, "she's the only person in the world who can make you feel pure, unbridled happiness when you're together... and drive you to utter despair when you're apart." Emory swirled the beer around in the tall bottle. "That's when you know it's worth it."

Darion raised his eyebrows. "You think so?"

"Trust me." Emory downed the last of the beer. "I'm an expert."

CHAPTER 37

Emory wrapped his new pink tie around the collar of a white dress shirt. There was a time when he actually thought he despised pink, but now he realized that what he had really despised was what it represented: pure love. A love he would never have. He stared into the mirror. His motions were mechanical, his eyes devoid of emotion. The last wedding he would ever attend in the Earth realm was going to be at a courthouse. On a Thursday. It was a fitting conclusion to his miserable career. He knew he needed some caffeine to prevent his nerves from becoming rattled.

Emory entered the kitchen and flipped open a container of coffee grounds. He glanced at the space on the counter his French press had once occupied.

He sighed. It was going to be a long day.

· · ✦ · ·

EMORY TRIED TO STIFLE his irritation as the hefty gentleman in front of him in line debated whether to order regular cream or skim milk for his coffee. Like it mattered—like any of it mattered. He scanned the small café in the hopes of catching even a glimpse of Blair. His heart sank when he realized she wasn't going to make an appearance.

"May I help the next customer?"

Emory looked up and found himself face to face with Hana.

"I need a medium coffee with two shots of espresso." He handed her his debit card.

"No problem," Hana replied in a cheerful voice.

Hana tapped the digital register and swiped his card. As she handed it back, Emory spied a shimmer of light out of the corner of his eye. His mouth fell open.

"That's a beautiful ring."

"Thank you." Hana smiled and gazed down at her diamond ring. "We got engaged last night."

"L-Last night?" Emory stammered.

She nodded, pouring his coffee with a happy grin.

Emory gaped. "May I ask how he proposed?"

Hana leaned closer. "Well, we had taken time away from each other to sort some things out—it was the worst week of my life." She waved her hand as if dispelling the bad memories. "Anyway, he came to my apartment last night, saying I was the true love of his life. He said I was the only person in the world who made him feel unbridled happiness and that being apart drove him to utter despair." She sighed and held her hand to her heart. "I'd never heard him talk like that."

"Really?"

"Then he got down on one knee and proposed."

"Well..." Emory was stunned. "Congratulations."

"Thanks!" Hana handed him the tall cup of coffee. "Where are you headed all dressed up this morning?"

Emory stared at her with newfound determination. He had established a real, lasting connection between Darion and Hana. When two people were truly meant to be together, they would find a way. He knew this. He believed this—and it was time he set matters straight.

He buttoned his dark suit jacket. "I have a plane to catch."

• • ❧ • •

EMORY CHARGED THROUGH the doors of the campus library. He scanned the large study hall, searching through the students deliberating over their textbooks. He caught sight of a distracted individual in the far corner of the room. All of his books were closed, and he scribbled illegible notes across a legal pad.

"Amir?"

The preoccupied student jumped up, startled. He quickly flipped the pad over. "You must be Dale."

Emory frowned. "Dale?"

Amir seemed puzzled. "I'm supposed to meet my new tutor here."

"That's right." He snapped his fingers. "No, my name's Emory." He gave Amir a firm handshake. "I'll be replacing Dale."

"Oh, okay." Amir sat back down, looking a bit confused.

Emory settled across from him and scanned the stack of textbooks. "From my understanding, you're enrolled in a civil engineering course?"

"Yes, the class starts next week," Amir said. "I figured I might as well get a head start on studying the material again."

"Again?" Emory picked up one of the books from the pile and skimmed through it.

Amir rubbed the back of his neck. "I failed it last semester."

Emory nodded sympathetically. "What do you think was your biggest issue?"

"My girlfriend." He laughed, but Emory saw the hurt behind his eyes. "Ex-girlfriend."

Emory straightened his suit jacket. "So, no distractions this time?"

"None."

"Let's see where you are with your notes." Emory reached for his notepad.

Amir clutched it. "That's not school related."

Emory pretended to be surprised. "My mistake."

Amir shrugged. "It was just some things I wrote for Joey."

Emory raised a single eyebrow. "Your ex?"

"Yes," he muttered. "But I ended it with her because she's studying abroad this year."

"I see. Well, at least you had closure so you can move on with your studies."

Amir frowned. "Actually, I wanted to say goodbye to her, but I didn't get the chance."

"Then go to her dorm and say goodbye so we can get to work."

"I can't. It's too late." Amir lowered his head. "She's at the airport. She leaves for Madrid in less than three hours."

Emory slammed the textbook closed. "Get your passport."

. . ⌘ . .

"SHE'S STILL NOT PICKING up." Amir paced the smooth floor of the airport terminal with his cell phone pressed to his ear. "Do you see it?"

Emory scanned the monitors. "Her flight departs in fifty minutes from Gate E42. We just have to get to Concourse E."

"How?" he asked miserably. "They'll never let us through security without tickets."

"I'll take care of it."

Emory grabbed him by the arm and ushered him into the shortest line for international flights. A polite front-desk clerk representing AeroMexico waved them forward.

"I need two one-way tickets to Guadalajara," Emory said. "Departing as soon as possible."

She eyed them carefully. "Just the two of you?"

Emory was unfazed as he placed their passports on the counter. "Yes."

She clicked away at the keyboard and computed the total. "That will be $768.36."

Emory handed her his debit card and held his breath. He rarely kept more than a thousand dollars in his checking account. There was never any reason to hoard money. He suddenly understood why Blair was so frugal. He would never tease her about it again. The clerk processed the charge and handed back the card. He let out a sigh of relief. Amir's jaw dropped.

"Trust fund," Emory said.

Amir seemed too stunned to reply.

"Please proceed to Gate E40." She handed them their tickets and IDs. "Have a wonderful flight."

They wove through the crowds to the security checkpoint. It took them thirty minutes to shuffled through the line of irritated travelers. An officer scribbled on their tickets and waved them toward the scanners. Amir removed his shoes and put his personal items in a gray plastic bin. His hands were shaking.

"Don't be nervous," Emory said in a reassuring tone. "You can do this."

They quickly put their backpacks on the long conveyer belt and cleared the scanners without incident. Emory found the closest empty bench, and they sat to retie their shoes.

"What should I say?" Amir asked.

"It's just like we went over in the car." Emory adjusted his dress shoes. "Stick to your plan."

He shifted. "Do you think it will work?"

"All you can do is try." Emory glanced at his watch and jumped up. "We have to move."

They sprinted down the broad hallway past vendors selling over-priced merchandise and restaurant bars that were filled with weary travelers.

"What does she look like?" Emory asked.

"She's really short and has red hair. She usually wears glasses, but sometimes she'll wear her contacts—and she's got, like, these cute little freckles that she hates, but I think they're hot…"

Emory nodded and allowed the young man to continue rambling. They came to an abrupt halt in front of Joey's gate. Emory searched the rows and rows of passengers with frantic eyes.

"I don't see her," Amir said, turning away. "Maybe she went to buy a magazine."

Emory caught sight of Joey wedged between a loud businessman talking on a cell phone and a frazzled couple trying to soothe their crying toddler. He grabbed Amir's arm, refocusing his attention.

"Is that her?" he said, pointing to the downcast young woman wearing a hoodie.

Amir gaped. "Yeah, how did you—"

"Hurry. You don't have much time."

Amir clapped him on the shoulder. "Thanks, Emory." He rushed over to her.

Emory crossed into the Enarine realm and followed behind his client, unseen.

"Joey!" Amir called out.

She yanked out her earphones and jumped to her feet. Her eyes were puffy and red. "What are you doing here?" she asked breathlessly.

"I couldn't let you leave without saying goodbye."

She wiped her face. "How did you find me?"

"That's not important. There's something I have to do before you leave." With trembling hands, Amir pressed the FaceTime app on his phone and dialed home.

"Hello, Amir!" his cheerful mother greeted him on the screen.

"Mom, is Dad there?" Amir's voice was tense. "I need to talk to you both."

"I'll get him." His mother walked through the house. "Amir needs to speak to both of us," she said under her breath. "I don't know, he didn't say."

Joey stood across from him, shifting in an uncomfortable silence. Both of his parents suddenly appeared on the screen.

"Hello, son." His father did not look amused. "What's this all about?"

"Mom, Dad... I want you to meet Joey." Amir pulled her next to him so they could see her in the screen.

Joey, in shock, gave a nervous wave.

Amir took a deep breath. "She's my girlfriend."

His mother let out an excited cry and covered her mouth.

"It's about time," his father muttered.

"So nice to finally meet you," his mother crowed. "We've heard so much about you."

"What?" Amir stared at them, confused. "How did you—"

"Your brother told us about her months ago," his father said gruffly. "We were waiting for you to get the nerve to tell us yourself."

She nudged her husband. "Don't be so hard on him. You know how sensitive he is."

Amir shifted uncomfortably, and Joey blushed as she tried to hold back a grin. Emory soaked in their conversation.

"I'm just saying," Amir's father continued, "at the rate he's going, we might not get another call from him until he's leaving for the honeymoon."

"Dad!" Amir cried.

"Don't listen to him." His mother focused her attention back on Joey. "By the way, we loved the pictures of you two hiking in the mountains this summer."

Amir and Joey exchanged shocked glances.

"We're glad you're getting him off the couch," his father said. "When he lived at home, he spent all of his time in front of those mindless video games."

His mother squinted at the screen. "She's very pretty, son."

Amir smiled at Joey, who smiled back. "I know."

"Where are you headed, Joey?" his father asked.

She spoke up. "I'm leaving for Madrid."

"You've got yourself a world traveler!" Amir's mother gave a nod of approval. "Very nice."

"Have a wonderful trip," his father said kindly.

"Um..." Amir was momentarily at a loss for words. "Her flight's about to leave, so I'm going to say goodbye."

"In that case, we'll let you two go." Amir's father leaned closer to the camera. "And Amir, if you ever wait that long to call us again, your mother and I will hunt you down and—"

Amir's mother jabbed him in the chest. "We'll talk to you soon." She blew them a kiss, and the screen cut out.

A smile crept across Joey's lips. "You came here to introduce me to your parents?"

"Yes."

Joey jumped into his arms and enveloped him.

"I couldn't let you leave without telling you that I love you." He held her close. "And I'll wait for you."

"I love you too," she whispered. "I'll come back every three months, I promise."

They held on to each other, ignoring the crowds around them. Emory wished Blair were with him to share the moment.

Emory phased back into the Earth realm. "How did it go?"

Amir started. He lowered Joey to her feet. "I stuck to my plan," he stated confidently.

"It looks like it worked," Emory said, impressed.

Joey glanced up at Amir. "Who's that?"

"He's my new tutor," Amir replied. "He drove me here to say goodbye to you so I could focus on my studies."

"Thank you so much." Joey flashed Emory an appreciative smile. "You have no idea what that means to me."

Emory reached out and shook her hand. He wanted her to remember him. "Not a problem."

Amir kissed Joey's forehead, and she closed her eyes, wrapping her arms around his waist.

"Well, I have to get going," Emory said, pulling a hundred-dollar bill out of his wallet.

"What's this for?" Amir asked as he pressed the bill into his hand.

"An airport shuttle back to the campus."

"Wow, thanks." Looking a little confused, Amir tucked the money into his back pocket.

"Don't mention it." Emory tightened his backpack over his shoulder. "Read chapters one and two before Monday."

"I will," Amir said. "Thanks again. For everything."

Emory turned on his heel to leave.

"Where are you off to now?" Joey asked.

Emory readjusted his pink tie. "I have a wedding to stop."

CHAPTER 38

Emory weaved through traffic, trailing Laith's Corvette. His heart was racing. A large SUV cut him off, and he laid on the horn. The female driver made a wildly inappropriate gesture and screamed out the window as Emory sped up and swerved around her. He ignored her obscene ranting. Road rage was the least of his concerns. He caught up with the Stingray and glanced around his car, calculating ways to minimize the impending damage. His seatbelt was secure, but he gave it a firm tug, tightening it across his waist. He let his foot off the gas, leaving a few car lengths between him and the Corvette.

The traffic light ahead turned red, and he held his breath. The Corvette rolled to a stop. Emory downshifted into second gear and jammed the gas pedal. He clenched the steering wheel with a powerful grip and squeezed his eyes shut, bracing for the inevitable impact.

The horrific sound of shattering glass and splintering metal shredded his eardrums. The impact threw Emory's entire body forward, and his forehead smashed into the steering wheel. He slammed his foot on the brake pedal, but the new car had already done the work of forcing the convertible to a stop. Pieces of the Corvette were crumpled on the hood of his car.

He reached for the door handle with trembling hands. The vehicles behind them came to a screeching halt. He stumbled out of the car and landed on his knees on the hard pavement. Gravel shredded his dark suit as he crawled around the car to the sidewalk, and people in the surrounding lanes slowed down to stare at the spectacle.

Emory struggled to stand on his battered knees and leaned against the ruined Corvette. He pounded on the passenger window. "Is everyone all right?" he shouted.

Karina raised her head from the deployed airbag. Emory met her eyes for the first time. The driver's side door swung open, and Laith jumped out. Emory breathed a sigh of relief. The car was destroyed, but his clients were safe.

"It was a red light!" Laith screamed. "How did you miss that?"

Emory's vision blurred, and he shook off the throbbing pain between his temples. "I'm so sorry."

Laith spewed profanities at him, but Emory couldn't hear anything over the ringing in his ears. Emory opened the passenger door and offered Karina his hand. She grabbed hold of him. A small bouquet of store-bought flowers fell from her lap and landed on the rough granular sidewalk as he helped her out of the car. She trampled across them in a dazed stupor, and the battered petals were crushed under her high heels.

"Are you all right?" Emory steadied her shaking body in his arms. Blood ran down her nose, staining her short lace wedding dress. She clung to Emory. Fortunately, she didn't appear to be badly hurt—just in shock.

"You idiot!" Laith shouted. "I just bought this car!"

Emory held Karina until she stopped trembling. "I'm so sorry about your dress," he said softly. "It was very pretty."

She glanced at Laith, who was still screaming.

"No... no it wasn't," Karina said. "I hated everything about it."

The smell of gasoline and oil filled the air. Karina's eyes shifted from the plumes of smoke rising from the metal remains of the cars to the shards of glass scattered across the pavement.

"This is all wrong..." Karina uttered.

"My insurance will cover the damage," Emory said. Nothing could repair their special day. He'd made certain of that. Any positive memories of their wedding day would be marred by the accident.

"No, not that." Karina raised her voice. "Laith!"

Laith stopped, noticing the deplorable state of his fiancée for the first time.

Karina spoke up. "I don't want to marry you."

His mouth fell open. "What?"

"I couldn't admit it to myself." She looked to the shattered cars. "But this is all wrong."

He shuffled forward. His voice was husky. "What are you saying?"

"I'm saying I love you." She stepped closer, regaining her balance. "But I don't want to marry you."

Laith stared at her, speechless.

"You knew. That's why you could never bring yourself to ask me." Karina wiped the blood from her face and dried her hand on her wedding dress. It was forever ruined. "We shouldn't be together."

Laith didn't move. His eyes shifted downward.

"I'm going home now," Karina said softly. "And then I'm leaving."

Emory backed away. He had done more than enough damage. He stepped into the street and signaled a taxi. The large sedan came to a stop next to him, and he opened the door for Karina. She took a deep breath and approached the vehicle.

"Wait!" Laith ran up to her. He cupped her face tenderly in his hands. "I always loved you."

"I know," she whispered. "I loved you too."

Laith kissed her lips, and a single tear slipped down his cheek. He wrapped his arms around her and closed his eyes, holding her tight. His voice cracked. "We'll both be okay, right?"

She buried her face in his shoulder. "We'll be okay." They held each other as sirens began to echo in the distance. "Take good care of Shelby," she said in a soft voice.

He nodded but seemed unable to speak.

"Don't forget the good times," Karina whispered. Her tears soaked into his dress shirt.

Laith stroked her hair. "Never."

"And I'm sorry for all the times in between."

He held her close. "I'm sorry too."

She kissed him one last time, and they let each other go. Laith staggered toward his mangled car while the police stepped onto the street and began interviewing witnesses. Karina climbed into the taxi, and Emory shut the door.

"I'm truly sorry for the pain I caused you both," Emory said. He meant it from the depths of his heart.

Karina grabbed his arm through the window, her eyes somber. "We were about to make a serious mistake."

Emory gave her hand a reassuring touch then handed the driver three hundred dollars. "Please take her anywhere she needs to go."

Karina glanced back at Laith, and they exchanged heartbroken gazes. He looked away, and she closed her eyes, tears streaming down her face. The taxi pulled away.

An emergency worker approached Emory. "Sir, do you want us to take a look at that gash on your forehead?"

"No. I'm perfectly fine." Emory stumbled slightly. His battered knees were of no help.

"Sir, where are you going?"

Emory walked away from the wreckage. "I have a dinner reservation."

The man spun around and signaled another paramedic. Before he'd turned back, Emory crossed into the Enarine realm and disappeared.

CHAPTER 39

Emory clung to a metal railing and limped up the stairs to an exclusive rooftop lounge. His left knee was shattered. He spotted Blair and Kenneth sitting on a narrow couch, and his heart practically leapt in his chest as he made his way over to them. Golden light shimmered down the tall buildings surrounding them as the sun set over the city.

Argus materialized in front of him, blocking his path. "Where do you think you're going?"

Emory shook off his burry vision. "I need to talk to Blair."

Argus grabbed his arm and dragged him into the Enarine realm. "She's on a date with *my* client."

A soft breeze swept Blair's hair into her face, and she brushed her dark curls behind her ear. "Do you want to split a few appetizers?"

Kenneth smirked. "A few?"

Blair smiled and leaned back against his chest as they shared a single menu. "I want a little bite of everything."

"Please," Emory said. "I have to apologize to her."

Argus's dark eyes flickered with amusement. "You had your chance with her, and you blew it. Like you always do."

"You're so tense," Kenneth remarked.

Blair sat up. "I'm sorry."

"Why are you apologizing?" Kenneth asked. "Obviously, I'm not doing my job as your boyfriend."

Blair shifted. "It's not you. I had a fight with a close friend, and I spent all last night rage cleaning my apartment to get rid of anything that reminded me of him, and as I was hauling out two trash bags full of clothes and jewelry I suddenly realized the other half of my stuff was still at his house, and I had to drag everything back up to my apartment—"

Kenneth broke into laughter. "It's okay. You don't have to explain anything." He gently kissed her cheek. "I don't mind trying harder."

Argus flashed Emory a wry smile. "I think it would be better for everyone if you left."

Blair settled back against Kenneth. "You're sweet. I probably just need a vacation."

"I should take you to my condo in Miami sometime. Do you like the beach?"

Her expression turned serious. "Yes. I love the beach."

"Maybe when the weather gets colder, we can plan a little getaway."

"I-I'm sorry." Blair slowly slipped out of his arms. "I'm having a hard time with this."

Kenneth's forehead wrinkled. "There's no pressure. I just thought you might like a relaxing vacation."

Blair folded the menu and placed it on the coffee table. "And then what?"

"I don't know," he said carefully. "We would have to see where things go from there."

She squinted at the sun's reflection in the buildings. "I don't want to get married."

Kenneth chuckled. "I think we're a little far from that point, considering we met less than a month ago."

Blair squared her shoulders. "I don't want kids."

Kenneth tilted his head. "Okay... well, that's also not really anything we need to be thinking about right now."

Argus drew a silver arrow from his quiver, but Emory grabbed his arm. "I have nothing left to lose."

"I like my apartment," Blair continued, "and I don't want to move in with you."

Kenneth took his time sipping his lemon water before responding. "I'm not exactly sure where this is going."

Argus shook Emory off, stepped forward, and raised his loaded bow in Kenneth's direction. Emory lunged at Argus and wrestled him to the ground. The arrow went askew, emitting a high-pitched whistle as it failed to reach a target. They landed with a hard thud, Argus's bow skidding across the hardwood floor.

"You idiot!" Argus shouted.

"If you think we're moving too fast..." Kenneth shook his head. "What exactly are you saying?"

Emory scrambled across the floor on bruised knees and clutched Argus's bow with trembling fingers. Argus grabbed him by his suit jacket, dragged him backward, and strangled him from behind.

"Give it to me!" Argus shouted.

"I'm saying," Blair whispered. "I want to be alone."

Emory gasped for air. He lifted the longbow over his head and smashed it against the floor with the last of his strength. The bow cracked and splintered. Argus froze in stunned silence.

Kenneth tried to take Blair's hand, but she pulled away.

"I don't understand." Kenneth swallowed hard. "What can I do to make things right between us?"

Blair stared out at the fading sunset. "Nothing."

Emory dragged himself to his feet and staggered toward the balcony with Argus's mangled bow in hand.

"As I said..." Emory flung his cousin's bow over the edge. "I have nothing left to lose."

A waitress placed two glasses of white wine on the low coffee table in front of Blair and Kenneth. "Can I get you two anything, or do you need a minute?"

"We need a minute," Kenneth replied with no emotion. The waitress went on her way, and he turned back to Blair. "So, I guess that's it."

She nodded. "Our time is up."

Argus stood on the opposite side of the couple, watching them say their final goodbyes. He glared across at Emory. "They're going to bury you for this."

"Let them." Emory matched his gaze. "I only care about one person in this realm."

Kenneth gathered his belongings and parted ways with Blair, leaving her alone in the elegant lounge.

"I'll see you in three days, *cousin*." Argus spit out the last word with such venom it might have stung if Emory had a shred of nerves left in his body. He didn't.

Argus spun on his heel and followed Kenneth down the stairs to the lower level of the restaurant. Emory could only imagine what his cousin was going to divulge in his final report. It didn't matter. None of it mattered. Only she mattered.

He hobbled toward Blair as she dialed a number on her cell phone.

"Hey, Malena, my dinner thing fell through, so I was thinking about stopping by to see what you're cook—"

Emory materialized in front of her. "Hi."

Blair's eyes narrowed. "I'll call you right back." She hung up the phone and shoved it in her purse. "What are you doing here?"

Emory shifted slightly. He knew he deserved her icy reception. "I need to talk to you. May I sit with you?"

Blair gave an indifferent wave of the hand. He could almost feel the tension in her body as he sat beside her. She crossed her legs and yanked her striped pencil skirt down over her knee. Her tone was harsh. "If you think you can just—"

"I miss you too."

Blair fell silent. He massaged his sore knees. He was a disheveled mess. His suit fell on his body in a wrinkled heap, unable to maintain its original form. The expensive garment was torn in random spots, and his white dress shirt was speckled with blood and dirt. His tie—the pink tie she had given him—appeared to be the only article of clothing left unscathed.

Her expression softened. "You're bleeding." The cold tips of her fingers brushed against the cut on his forehead.

He flinched.

She curled her hand into a fist. "I... I forgot."

"Blair." Emory held her hand. "I'm sorry for the hurtful things I said to you."

She avoided his gaze. "I shouldn't have assumed I was anything other than your client."

"You're more than that to me." Emory gently rubbed her frozen fingers between his. "I said those things because I didn't want you to know my true feelings."

Her eyes met his. "Why would you hide your feelings from me?"

"Because I knew you didn't—*couldn't* feel the same way about me."

Blair pulled her hand away. "I've always considered you a friend. And despite what you said, I know you think of me that way too."

"No, it's more than that." Emory took her hand once more and held it to his heart. "I didn't want you to know I had fallen in love with you."

Blair shook her head and slipped out of his grasp. "No. You can't just say that to me."

"I tried to show you," he spoke softly. "But nothing I did would mend your heart."

"You're a liar," she said through her teeth.

His stomach dropped. "I'm telling you the truth."

"It's always about your job, Emory." Her eyes were cold. "Is this your last-ditch effort to save your career because I broke up with Kenneth?"

Emory's eyebrows shot up. "This has nothing to do with him."

She folded her arms. "Right..."

"I didn't choose him for you. They sent another matchmaker in my place because I was too afraid to admit my true feelings, knowing you felt nothing for me in return." Emory placed a gentle hand on her shoulder. "It was selfish to put my feelings above yours, and I'm sorry."

She rose to her feet and walked toward the glass railing overlooking the city. The sun painted the sky orange as it dipped below the horizon. A sharp pain tore through Emory's leg as he followed after her.

Blair's eyes welled with tears. "You have brought me nothing but heartbreak and misery since the moment you dragged me into your world." The hurt in her voice cut at his soul.

"I know I don't deserve a second chance—"

"What do you really want from me? You can't even touch me!"

"I don't care!" Emory's tie swayed in the wind as he moved closer to her. "I just want to be with you."

She wrapped her arms around her body and stared off into the distance.

Emory took Blair by the arm and turned her around to face him. "I have nothing in this world but you."

Blair opened her mouth but choked up, tears pouring down her cheeks. "What if I can't... if I never..."

"It doesn't matter." Emory reached down and gently wiped her tears away. "You have my heart. I belong to you."

Emory leaned closer and brushed his lips against hers. He drew her into his strong arms and felt her icy tongue against his. The light flowery fragrance on her skin fueled his passion as he inhaled her familiar scent. He tightened his grip around her waist, feeling her heart beat with his. He slid his hand up her back and cradled her head as he kissed her. Emory pulled away and looked into her deep-brown eyes.

"I love you, Blair." He spoke the words that had been begging to escape for so long, suddenly not caring if he had to fight the chill and the feeling of unrequited love for the rest of his existence. Simply being near her was worth any pain and heartache.

Blair closed her eyes and exhaled. Her body shuddered. She wrapped her arms around him and buried her face in his neck. He held her close, and the chill began to fade slowly but steadily. From her tender embrace, he could tell that she sensed it too. In that moment, he forgot about the accident and his injuries... and the potential backlash. There was only Blair. She clung to him more tightly, and suddenly, Emory found himself enveloped in her long-lost warmth.

"I love you too," she said softly.

He slid his hands down her body, unable to let go, feeling his heart fill with light again. "Sorry I messed up your dinner plans with your sister."

"It's okay." Blair stood on her toes and rubbed her nose against his. "You can get me Chinese food tonight."

Emory smiled. "Absolutely."

She ran her fingers through his disheveled hair. "What happened to you today?"

He drew her toward him. "I had to make sure all of my people were taken care of."

Blair leaned in for a kiss then hesitated. "Is *all* of this going in your report?"

"No. My personal life is private." Emory kissed her soft cheeks one after the other. "Whatever happens between us stays between us."

Blair let out a faint sigh as he smothered her with affection.

"Come home with me," Emory whispered.

She clung to his arms. "Where did you park?"

Emory rested his forehead against hers. "Blair, I have to tell you something you're not going to like."

She stared up at him. "What?"

He swallowed hard. "I totaled our Mustang."

A grin crept across her face. "It wasn't very practical, was it?"

"I didn't mind." Emory kissed her warm lips. "As long as you were happy."

Blair smiled and slipped her arms inside his suit jacket. "I couldn't be happier."

CHAPTER 40

Emory's heavy footsteps echoed off the marble floors as he crossed the lobby of his office building. He stopped in front of the elevators and took a moment to gather himself. He wished Blair were by his side. He needed her desperately.

Emory reached for the button, but Argus came up behind him and punched it first. Emory stepped back slightly. They hadn't spoken since the incident on the roof.

"Morning," Emory said after an awkward silence.

Argus spit his gum into a wrapper and tossed it in a wastebasket. "You're early."

"The buses were on time today."

Argus glanced at him. "Bike's in the shop?"

"Ran out of gas," Emory stated. "And money for gas."

Argus straightened his pink cufflinks. "Pity."

Emory tried not to let the silence get to him. He needed to maintain his mental calm. "I hired a master craftsman to repair your bow."

"A pointless gesture," Argus spat. "I'm an expert matchmaker. I have twelve other bows at home."

"Did you receive it?"

"They delivered it last night." Argus hit the button again as if to speed up the elevator. "It could use some scuffing up. It's too perfect now."

The doors chimed, and they stepped inside. Emory pressed the button for the twelfth floor, and they started their agonizing ascent.

"How's your client?" Emory asked.

"Excellent," Argus replied. "He's taking his new girlfriend to meet his mother next weekend."

Emory expected nothing less. "Good to hear."

"How's yours?"

"Blair's had better nights." That was true for both of them. After Emory had explained the situation with the audit, he promised her that they would spend whatever time they had left together. He held her through the night and tried to ease her troubled mind, but she didn't stop crying until exhaustion finally overtook her and she drifted off to sleep. He'd remained awake the entire night.

"And how are you?" Argus asked.

Emory couldn't lie. "Petrified."

"You should be."

Emory stared at his reflection in the metal doors. "Before we go in there, I just wanted to say I'm sorry for the fight at the fundraiser."

Argus didn't move a muscle. "Trying to save your skin?"

"No," Emory said. "I was in the wrong, and I'm genuinely sorry for the way I behaved."

"Whatever," Argus muttered. "My sister punches harder than you."

"Your sister's vicious. She could take both of us, hands down."

Argus cracked a smile and they both chuckled. The doors opened, and Themis stood before them with a stern look on her face. Argus's expression went blank.

"Join the others in the conference room," Themis said to Argus.

Argus followed her orders without hesitation and was out of sight a minute later. There was an iciness to Themis that Emory had never felt before in her presence.

"Please refrain from crossing realms until the proceedings have concluded," Themis said. "This is your official warning, on the record."

Emory had no intention of running. They could find him any-where, anytime. He would only be delaying the inevitable. "Under-stood."

Emory followed Themis down the hall to the conference room. No one greeted him when he entered. He sat across the table from his superiors in a nervous silence. Emory adjusted his favorite pink tie and braced himself.

Themis began. "Let's start by reviewing your recent appropri-ation of funds." She skimmed his expense report. "I see there is a charge of $768.36 for two one-way tickets to Guadalajara."

"Guadalajara?" Petros echoed. "What in tarnation were you do-ing in Mexico?"

"I didn't actually use the tickets," Emory explained. "But it was a necessary expenditure to take my clients' relationship to the next lev-el."

Themis kept reading. "And one hundred dollars for an airport shuttle?"

Emory spoke up. "To return my client to his campus."

Themis crossed off a line. "Two hours later there is another ex-pense for three hundred dollars." Her brow wrinkled. "This time to a taxi driver?"

Emory cleared his throat. "My client's home was in the suburbs, outside of the city. I would like the record to reflect that the funds came from my personal account, not the company credit card."

"Duly noted," Hera said.

Themis straightened her silk scarf. "I see there is a health insur-ance claim of three thousand, five hundred dollars for physical ther-apy due to... whiplash?"

"Yes," Emory replied. "I was in a minor fender bender with two of my clients."

"And there is also an auto insurance claim of fifty-five thousand dollars for a totaled Corvette?"

Emory nodded.

Petros tugged at his tight suit jacket. "Busy month?"

"Busy *day*," Argus corrected.

"Well, that covers your most recent expenses." Themis composed herself. "I'm more concerned about two memos here under Misconduct. One is regarding the assault of a superior officer?"

Emory shifted uncomfortably.

"You can disregard that claim," Argus cut in. "We settled our differences."

Themis made a note. "Moving on, then." She adjusted her reading glasses. "The second complaint is regarding artillery. It says here—am I reading this correctly?" She leaned over to Petros to verify the documentation.

"Yes, ma'am," Petros replied. "Seven arrows on a single target within a three minute period."

Themis removed her glasses. "To cite the use of excessive force would be an understatement," she said sternly. "Explain yourself."

"I apologize," Emory said. "I fully admit I was emotionally compromised at the time of that incident. It will not happen again."

"Your apology is noted." Themis folded her hands. "Nevertheless, there *will* be consequences for this grave misconduct." She paused, allowing her words to sink in. "First, we would like to go over your client list. We have your field notes but request that you personally inform us of their current status."

Emory shuffled through his folders. "Darion and Hana have set a date for their wedding."

"And when is that?" Petros asked.

"The second Saturday in May."

"This will be your *first* wedding in the twelve years you've been a matchmaker," Argus said. "Is that correct?"

Emory didn't budge. "That's correct."

Themis wrote a brief annotation. "Go on."

"Amir has a new tutor and is now passing all of his coursework. Joey is enjoying her classes in Madrid, and their long-distance relationship has remained healthy and strong. Amir has made plans for Joey to meet his parents in person when she returns home for the winter break."

Themis's expression hardened. "Karina and Laith? What of them?"

"As you probably deduced from the accident report, Karina and Laith have terminated their relationship. But I feel it was for the best. They weren't meant to be together. I know it's my role, my duty, to establish long-term commitment, but I couldn't keep watching them suffer."

The board members spoke amongst themselves for a few minutes. Emory remained silent and tried not to twirl the pen in his hand. They settled back in their seats.

"Please continue," Themis said. "What is their individual status?"

"Karina moved in with her sister," Emory said. "But she was able to apply for a job transfer within her company and is looking for an apartment."

"And Laith?" Themis inquired.

"He got the house," Emory said. "And the puppy."

There was a collective nod. The boardroom fell silent for a moment. Emory controlled his breathing, but it did little to slow his racing heart.

"That leaves Blair," Petros said.

"I would hardly call her status report *complete*," Argus stated.

"Not by any stretch of the imagination," Hera added.

There was only one word in Blair's updated file: *Closed*.

"Do you care to elaborate?" Themis asked.

Emory placed his pen on top of his folders. "Blair and I are secretly engaged. We felt it was best to hold off from telling our friends and family due to the precarious nature of my... *situation*."

"A wise decision," Themis said.

"Blair doesn't know this, but I've legally transferred everything I own to her. The condo, the motorcycle—all of my Earthly possessions." Emory's voice cracked. "If things don't work out for us, she can sell everything, and at least I'll know she'll be cared for financially."

Themis pushed Blair's folder aside. "Do you regret being her matchmaker, Emory?"

"I don't regret choosing her as a client." Emory's gaze was unyielding. "I don't regret the time I've had with her, and I don't regret falling in love with her."

Themis removed her glasses. "So you wouldn't have done anything differently—with any of your clients?"

"I've clearly made mistakes. But I stand behind every decision I've made regarding my clients recently. I firmly believe some relationships are worth fighting for, but there are times when you have to be prepared to let love go."

Themis glanced at Petros, who gave her a slight nod.

"Part of being a matchmaker, Emory," Themis said, "is knowing when you've made an unsuitable match. We've been waiting for you to realize this for quite some time now. Had you *not* interfered with Laith and Karina's wedding, the outcome of this meeting would not be the least bit favorable. You made the right decision regarding their union."

Emory was stunned. His ears were ringing. He could barely make out the conversation the board members were having amongst themselves.

"Close your mouth, boy," Petros said.

Emory clenched his jaw shut.

Themis adjusted her paperwork. "As you know, safeguarding the emotional well-being of humans is our first priority. I'm pleased you were able to mend Blair's broken heart before it became irreparable—even if your methods were somewhat unconventional. However, in light of the seven shots to Laith's heart, it's the board's recommendation to place you under a three-week suspension. Effective immediately."

Emory nodded. "I understand."

He peered across the conference-room table, but Hera was no longer there—she had crossed into the Enarine realm. A familiar tingling sensation crept through his body. He couldn't see Hera, but he felt her hand over his heart. He took a deep breath and waited for the uncomfortable feeling of pins and needles to pass. His body suddenly felt heavy as he became anchored to the Earth realm, barred from crossing back. Emory blinked, and Hera reappeared in her seat.

"Your accounts will remain frozen for the duration of your suspension," Themis continued. "When your restriction is lifted, you will resume your normal duties, and we would like you to increase your caseload to ten." She turned to Petros. "Agreed?"

"Agreed."

Emory's mouth was open again. Eight new clients. He would have to start researching potential candidates immediately.

Themis closed all of her folders. "Off the record, there is one small detail you omitted from Blair's file that I believe is of interest to everyone in this room."

"Not that we would ever pry into the private affairs of a fellow Vycrin," Hera added.

"I don't mind prying," Argus said with a sly grin.

Petros pounded his fist on the table. "Spill it, boy."

"Early Saturday morning, I took Blair out on a motorcycle ride to Swallow Falls," Emory said. "We got there ahead of the crowds and hiked a small trail through the woods to this beautiful waterfall. Blair was beside herself—she loves to be near water..." He cleared his throat. "Anyway, when we reached the waterfall, I got down on one knee and asked for her hand in marriage."

The board members broke into excited chatter, paying him little attention.

"Then I took her out for pancakes," Emory added.

Hera held her hand to her heart. "And the ring?"

"A flawless solitaire diamond in a fourteen-karat-gold setting. It was my mother's."

"That's the way to do it," Petros said proudly.

"I honestly didn't think he had it in him," Argus said.

Themis straightened her posture. "This meeting is adjourned." She rose from her seat, poised and collected. "I had my doubts about you, Emory. But you've proven yourself to be a capable matchmaker. Continue on this course."

"I will," Emory said. "I promise."

Themis extended her hand to him for the first time. She had a firm handshake, and he sensed the sincerity in her heart. Then Emory stacked his documents into a single pile and looked around the boardroom. "Invitations will be forthcoming once we set a date."

Petros gave him a broad smile. "I wouldn't miss it, my boy."

"We're looking forward to it," Themis said.

Hera's eyes sparkled. "I can't wait to buy the twins their dresses."

Emory turned to Argus.

"I feel like I should be allowed to bring two dates," Argus said.

Emory grinned. "I'll let Blair know." He picked up his manila folders and headed for the door.

"And, Emory..."

He stopped and faced his cousin.

"Congratulations," Argus said. "She's perfect for you."

CHAPTER 41

Emory clutched his backpack and took the stairs two at a time as he rushed up to Blair's apartment. He was late. Very late. Petros had insisted on meeting with him privately after the proceedings, and in Emory's haste to leave, he'd forgotten to call Blair from the office. His cell phone had been cut off for payments being past due, and he had no way of contacting her to let her know he was running behind. It didn't help that his bus was caught in traffic and he had to race down five blocks to get to her house.

Emory's heart pounded in his chest as he knocked on Blair's door. The television was on in the background. He cursed himself for not asking for a key. He'd never needed one in the Enarine realm. The door flew open. Blair burst into tears at the sight of him.

"It's okay." Emory dropped his backpack and swept her into his arms. "We're okay."

He held her close but could barely understand the words she was saying between sobs.

"I thought—when you didn't come back—"

"I'm sorry." Emory kissed away the tears on her cheeks. "I got held up."

Blair buried her face in his chest and clung to him. He leaned back against the door and let out a heavy sigh of relief. He didn't want to let her go.

"I'm paying off your stupid phone bill," she muttered. "I don't care what you say."

Emory chuckled slightly. "For the next three weeks, it'll be a little easier for you to keep track of me. I've been suspended."

Blair's eyebrows furrowed. "What does that mean?"

"It means I can't leave the Earth realm for the next twenty-one days."

She glanced at his leather bag. "But they gave your arrows back?"

"Well, I can't cross over until the restriction is lifted, but Petros returned my equipment with a little surprise." Emory opened his backpack and handed her a bottle of white wine. "He wanted to be the first to bestow a wedding gift."

"That was sweet of him." Blair examined the shimmering gold label and headed to the kitchen. "I'll get a corkscrew."

"No, no, no!" Emory grabbed the bottle from her and placed it in the cabinet on the top shelf. "That's not for now. It's for later—when we're ready to have little people."

"Oh..." Blair bit back a smile.

Emory lifted her onto the counter. "There are a lot of little things I'm going to have to teach you about Vycrin."

Her eyes met his. "Like what?"

"Like our traditions and customs." He stroked her cheek and held her delicate face. "And love rituals."

Blair gently leaned against his hand. "What kind of rituals?"

"Some that I can explain..." Emory brushed his thumb across her full lips. "And some that I can only show you."

She closed her eyes and gave in to his soft touch. "Well, you have some free time on your hands."

"It's going to take a little longer than twenty-one days," he whispered.

"I don't mind." Blair wrapped her slender fingers around his silk tie and pulled him closer. She kissed him. Emory closed his eyes and savored the warmth of her soft lips. She tasted sweet. Emory lifted her off the counter in one swift motion, and Blair wrapped her legs around his waist as he carried her into the living room. He held her tight and kicked off his dress shoes.

"Don't even think about it," Blair whispered playfully.

Emory spun around and tossed her across the couch. Her wild giggling filled the room as she landed on the fluffy cushions. He tore off his suit jacket and climbed on top of her.

"What are we watching?" Emory asked as he trailed kisses down her neck.

Blair let out a soft sigh. "*Battlestar Galactica.*" He wanted to devour her.

"Did they destroy the Cylon Basestar yet?"

"Not yet." Blair threw his pink tie to the floor. She slowly unbuttoned his dress shirt, her engagement ring glistening in the soft light. She glanced at the round solitaire diamond. "Does this mean we can tell people now?"

Emory slid his hand down her body and squeezed her thigh. "And set a date."

"When were you thinking?"

Emory brushed his nose against hers. "My uncle's vineyard is beautiful in the summer."

"How many people can it hold?"

Emory kissed her lips. "About six hundred."

Blair grinned. "Is that all?"

"It's not bad," he said. "For a Vycrin wedding."

. . ❧ . .

THE END

Acknowledgements

To the Red Adept Team: Thank you for turning my words into a book. It's still a little surreal.

To Lynn: Thank you for taking a chance on a new author who had a bit of trouble keeping her POV's straight. It was exciting to work with you, and I'm eternally grateful.

To my line editor, Sarah: Thank you for helping me whip my manuscript into shape. The beating was worth it.

To my content editor, Alyssa: Thank you for challenging me on every level. I tried to get a few things by you just for fun...I was unsuccessful.

To my mentor, Erica: Thank you for sharing your experience and guiding me through every step of this process. It would have been maddening without you. I owe you chocolate.

To my beta readers: Thank you for smiting my ego. Repeatedly. I'm a better writer because of it.

To my critique partner: Thank you for reading all 19 drafts, and having the decency to feign excitement each and every time. Without you, I'd still be hung up on "the pockets".

To my siblings: Thank you for supporting me through the rough times. No matter what I'm going through, I can always laugh with you guys because you truly get me.

To my mom and dad: Thank you for always believing in me. You've always encouraged my wild imagination, and you're the reason I finally buckled down and got serious about my writing.

To my husband: You are my perfect man. Thank you for showing me what true love is supposed to feel like. I couldn't have done any of this without you. (Seriously, baby doll. If it had been left to me, we would have STARVED these last 2 years while I played with my imaginary friends.) Domestic responsibilities will resume after book 2.

About the Author

Rashida T. Williams has been crafting stories for as long as she can remember. Over the years she developed a passion for writing, in part, because it allowed her to combine her two favorite genres: romance and fantasy. When Rashida is not writing she can be found playing video games, binge watching romantic movies, and looking for any excuse to cosplay. She lives in Florida with her loving husband who encourages all of her shenanigans.

Read more at www.rashidatwilliams.com.

About the Publisher

Dear Reader,

We hope you enjoyed this book. Please consider leaving a review on your favorite book site.

Visit https://RedAdeptPublishing.com to see our entire catalogue.

Don't forget to subscribe to our monthly newsletter to be notified of future releases and special sales.